Younger
Than
Springtime

Younger Than Springtime

GREG WILLIAMS

DONALD I. FINE BOOKS
New York

DONALD I. FINE
Published by the Penguin Group
Penguin Books USA Inc., 375 Hudson Street,
New York, New York 10014, U.S.A.
Penguin Books Ltd, 27 Wrights Lane,
London W8 5TZ, England
Penguin Books Australia Ltd, Ringwood,
Victoria, Australia
Penguin Books Canada Ltd, 10 Alcorn Avenue,
Toronto, Ontario, Canada M4V 3B2
Penguin Books (N.Z.) Ltd, 182–190 Wairau Road,
Auckland 10, New Zealand

Penguin Books Ltd, Registered Offices:
Harmondsworth, Middlesex, England

First published by Donald I. Fine Books,
an imprint of Penguin Books USA Inc.

First Printing, April, 1997
10 9 8 7 6 5 4 3 2 1

 REGISTERED TRADEMARK—MARCA REGISTRADA

LIBRARY OF CONGRESS CATALOGING-IN-PUBLICATION DATA:
Williams, Greg.
Younger than springtime / Greg Williams.
p.   cm.
ISBN 1-55611-511-3
I. Title.
PS3573.I449257Y6   1997
813'.54—dc20   96-38224
                      CIP

Printed in the United States of America
Set in Palatino
Designed by Irving Perkins Associates

PUBLISHER'S NOTE

For Diane

And with thanks to Herb and Nancy Katz,
Don Fine, and Tom Burke

CHAPTER 1

THE REWARD FOR success was this nightly commute back to Groveton. All around John Ashe his contemporaries were losing consciousness. Their graying heads bobbed in unison with the lurching of the train.

Back when he was twenty-five and just out of law school, John Ashe would have been working on his third margarita by this hour of the day in a bar full of the bright and beautiful, the young yet-to-make-its. By his calculation a hundred twenty-five-year-olds had five thousand years to live, and the more the longer, and the drunker the longer, and dinner was chips and salsa, but you got fried eggs and hash browns at two a.m., if you hadn't gone home with a girl. A fifty-year-old man had twenty-five years left, maybe, and the drunker the shorter, and dinner was low-fat, and eggs a rare treat your wife doled out like biscuits to a neutered house dog. She used to be young and beautiful, your wife, even sexy, but now had become a sort of matron whom the butcher and the baker fearfully called "ma'am," though her name of course was Elizabeth. These were the indications of success. This was what you wanted, wasn't it? What you signed up for.

Somehow Elizabeth always managed to be swinging through the foyer when he opened the front door in the evenings. "Look at this." She held up a news article, neatly scissored from the paper as if for possible framing. "William Newton was picked up in a prostitution sting. They're publishing the names of all the johns. Fortunately, you're not on the list."

"Hell, no, I told them I was William Newton."

1

"Oh, you."

He asked how it had gone at Groveton Country Day School, where she chaired the Department of English. Through the drone of her answer he considered William Newton while simultaneously gravitating toward the kitchen. Newty going to a prostitute. Not that Anne was the most desirable woman in the world, she hadn't exactly held up very well, but had Newty himself deteriorated to the point where now he had to *buy* it? The couples had once been close back when Anne had also taught at GCDS and the Newtons lived across town restoring that old Victorian. They had always smelled faintly of turpentine, to the point where it was suspenseful to watch Newty light a cigarette. You kept waiting for the poof of ignition, the translucent cloud of flame. Maybe in a sense it had finally happened. Thinking back, John calculated that it had been four years since he had seen either one of them. "But once we get through all these private school narratives," Elizabeth was saying, "then we can finally get to something that will actually broaden the kids instead of merely affirming their own experiences. What did I just say?"

"Broaden the kids, I was listening." He opened the fridge and scanned its contents. Something fattening, perhaps. Another layer of paint for those artery walls.

Elizabeth read the shelves over his shoulder. "Don't forget we're eating soon. You wouldn't want to stuff yourself."

"Yeah, I guess not." From across the room he coveted the contents of the liquor cabinet and waited for her dependable objection. She had arrived prematurely at that stage of life where a pleasurable indulgence is always considered along with its eventually fatal side effect—and now he felt her hand at the small of his back, steering him toward the living room.

"Why don't you go prop your feet up?" she said. "I'll bring you a lemon mineral water."

"On the rocks," she added a moment later, as if to pretend the drink were alcoholic.

He sat down in front of *Headline News* just at the end of the half-hour rotation when they always ran the dog stories and the building implosions. Tonight's fluff was a sentimental retrospective of the upcoming New York Marathon. Watching it, John felt a pang of regret that he had never run the thing. He had always thought there would be time later, failing to foresee that his Achilles' tendons would become as delicate as a couple of old rubber bands, dry and cracked with age. And if he even mentioned it—*honey, I might enter the New York Marathon.* The lectures, the harangues. Worst of all, she would be right.

Handing him the lemon mineral water, she rattled the ice cubes for a cocktail sound effect. "I suggested the Wharf House because they have a special heart-healthy section on their menu and several Jell-O-based desserts that just look spectacular."

"What are you talking about?"

She felt his forehead. "Are you okay? Our son turns twenty-five tomorrow, but we don't get him then because his MTV friends are throwing a party for him in the city. So we get him tonight. We discussed all this in detail just last week."

He took a sip of lemon mineral water. "Lee Thomas had a heart attack."

Elizabeth stood still for a moment, then began to sway just slightly. She reached back for the sofa arm and lowered herself onto the cushions. "What day is today?" she finally asked. "It's Thursday, isn't it? The Silver Milers were out jogging."

"It wasn't necessarily the jog."

"Did it happen during the jog?"

"Technically."

"It could just as easily have been you. Running around in the heat of the day in Central Park, fifty years old, it's irresponsible."

Careful to avoid sounding defensive, John tried to explain. "Lee only ran on Thursdays. I run three or four times a week. I'm in better shape, my body can handle it."

She waited for more information. He wouldn't volunteer it.

"How is he?" she asked.

"Well, Barradale called the ambulance right away, he had his cell phone."

"Oh, good, so Lee's all right?"

John shook his head.

"Oh, no." She raised a hand to her face. "His poor wife. What's her name again?"

John muttered something.

Elizabeth leaned forward. "What?"

"Lee socked away a few million. Poor Linda's rich."

* * *

SATURDAY MORNING JOHN poured himself a bowl of what he called
Colon Bran and unrolled the *New York Times.* He scanned the
front page and then, as usual, skipped to the obituaries. A grin
crept over his face—Lee had made it. A small article, sure, sort of
crushed from the top by the tribute to a young dancer who had
died of AIDS, and squeezed in on either side by notices for a
former undersecretary of state and a fifties movie actress. But
there it was:

Lee Thomas, 52, Lawyer

For years John had been a devotee of the *New York Times* obituary page. He would rate himself against those whose passing was
noted by the paper of record, wondering if he himself would
merit such attention when the time came. Of course, there were
factors you couldn't control. If you happened to die on the same
day as a former president, for example, your obit would look
ridiculously small next to his if it even appeared at all. Perhaps
even worse would be to die simultaneously with a more accom-
plished member of the same field, because then readers could
make direct comparisons instead of relative ones. *Lee Thomas, lawyer* would seem positively inconsequential next to *Lee Bailey, lawyer.* God, the mere thought of Bailey's future obituary left John
frustrated with a sense of inadequacy. It would be just his luck to
go down in a plane with Lee Bailey beside him in first class, the
older man probably not even spilling his drink as he took the
opportunity to ask one last insightful question establishing
whose fault was the imminent crash. One hundred and fifty others were also killed, the paper would say.
    Elizabeth padded into the kitchen in her chin-to-toe nightie.
    "Lee got an obit," he said.
    "Really? He was just a lawyer."
    "I'm just a lawyer."
    "Who cares what they write about you once you're dead, any-
way? That is such a man thing."
    As far as he could tell, she was right. It *was* a man thing. He
and his male contemporaries read the obituaries as carefully as

they tracked the value of stocks they owned. How convenient, and what a coincidence—or was it?—that the stocks and obits were usually in the same tidy section of the paper, Business.

BRENNA FRYERSON WAS surprised that he was even going to interview any of the other candidates to replace her. She had made clear her opinion that he should simply hire Maxine Estep, whose timely availability helped soothe Brenna's conscience about her own departure. Like many secretaries, assistants, and paralegals, she was convinced, and could provide supporting anecdotal evidence, that her employer would be lost without her. It was not necessarily a coincidence that Lee Thomas' longtime paralegal had quit just a few weeks before the poor man's heart attack, was it? The stress built up, Lee went for a jog, it didn't take a genius to make the connection. The least she could do was steer John in the right direction as far as replacing her.

"This Magnate girl's only twenty-two, if that," she said, holding the résumé by its upper right corner and wrinkling her nose. "Maxine Estep is the woman with the necessary experience. Running this office is very complicated. I'm surprised you think some hoity-toity Magnate girl could handle it." She rattled the preposterous résumé. "Just twenty-two years old, a child!"

"But, Brenna, I know you're not suggesting I discriminate on the basis of age."

She was a thick, middle-aged woman from one of the boroughs, John honestly could never remember which. Only rarely was she late for work, and only a few times in five years had she called in sick. Her work was way above average, sometimes rising to excellence, and John was surprised he wasn't sorrier to see her go. It would be nice to get someone new, a fresh voice for the intercom.

He took the résumé from Brenna and scanned it quickly. "This girl is the daughter of a guy I knew in law school. He called me about her a couple of days ago. So if it's okay with you, I want to do him the favor of interviewing her before I do the inevitable and hire Maxine."

"Fine. Go ahead and waste her time. I'm just saying."

It was Thursday. He would have interviewed Conifer's daughter and hired Maxine by now if not for the various contingencies that had arisen from Lee's sudden death. He had spent the better part of Monday resisting the sentimental notion that he should take on Lee's relatively new paralegal himself. He would no more have hired her than worn the dead man's sports watch, the band of which was whitened by the salt of his death sweat. Eventually she had been shunted off to one of the associates. The rest of the week he had spent going through Lee's office to collect his various personal belongings for the widow and review and reassign his case work as appropriate.

He had never been so depressed in his life, getting on that damn train every night and riding back to Groveton. As he slammed back glass after glass of lemon mineral water, on the rocks, and snuck an occasional non-breakfast bowl of Colon Bran, he wondered if all this life-prolonging moderation was worth it. Elizabeth had been jabbering all week about how for exercise he should not run but walk, preferably on a treadmill so it would be easier to monitor his heart rate and she would hear the thump if he collapsed to the floor.

Nathan Barradale showed up at lunchtime, and the two surviving members of the Silver Milers walked through parts of their Central Park route, remembering that Lee was as likely to drool over the ice cream carts as over the many young women whose beauty would sometimes inspire him to pick up the pace. And they remembered his joyfully undignified open-mouthed smile. In group photos he often looked retarded.

"I guess we grew into our originally facetious name," Barradale said. "The Silver Milers."

"Maybe we should call ourselves the Spry Sprinters or something."

"Or course, it's not true what they say about how we all deteriorate with age."

"Or the Virile Striders, I could grow into that."

"Look at Lee, he didn't deteriorate. Even in the beginning he was fat and slow."

Back at the firm, they stopped in the Hallway of Death, lined with portraits of the deceased partners of Masterson, Grandissime, and Barradale all the way back to Nathan's grandfather. In this heaven of John's predecessors all wrinkles had been omitted so that the men looked like wise old teenagers. The artist the firm had been using recently had adorned the four most recent decedents with the same red tie and gold clip, a detail which had struck John not all at once, for he never cared to scrutinize the paintings, but over time as he hurried through the Hallway with a guilty glance or two at his former partners, whose smug grins said that soon enough he would join them in committing the ultimate, final error.

Lee Thomas wore the same red tie and gold clip. The artist had also bestowed upon him a thoughtful, sedate, close-lipped smile—it's not so bad, John, up here on the wall.

HER GENETIC HERITAGE did not bode well for Elena Conifer's physical appearance, and neither did a 3.9 from Magnate University. John half expected to see her father's round, pocked face on a body by Dominoes.

Ordinarily Brenna would have just buzzed him and announced the interviewee's arrival, but on this occasion she stepped into his office without knocking and closed the door behind her. "So you've never seen this girl before?" Eyebrows raised, she looked mildly amused, as if in advance knowledge of some clever prank.

"What's wrong with her?"

She let go of the doorknob and crossed the room. "You know, John, I don't have much longer to work for you. What are you gonna do if I get a little uppity, fire me?" She sat down in his guest chair. "I'm not saying you can't hire her. You're probably going to want to, you're a man. All I'm saying is, you can't hire her."

Curious, he put down the brief he was reading. "I take it you think she's attractive?"

Brenna shifted her weight in the chair. "Are you sure your friends aren't playing a joke on you? Maybe they hired a girl to quote interview for the job end quote?" She searched his face. "For all I know, you're playing a joke on me."

He shook his head. "That wouldn't be very professional of me, would it? But then, neither would this." He opened his desk drawer. "I was going to give you this later, but now seems as good a time as any."

He handed her an envelope thick with what was obviously cash. Mouth open, she pulled back the flap. She was quitting so that she could spend more time with her grandchildren, and maybe it was John's regret that Lee Thomas would never have such a pleasure that had made him wax sentimental at the bank. "Twenty fifties," he said. Strangely, he could not look her in the eye. "With all the Lee stuff going on, I didn't have time to buy you a proper gift, I'm sorry."

She fanned the bills into a bouquet and sniffed them, rolling her eyes back as if in sexual ecstasy. "Oh, thank you, John."

He smiled. "Now can I interview my colleague's daughter?"

It was unlikely that John's own tastes in women would correspond to the norms of beauty in whatever borough had produced Brenna, and her reaction to the applicant raised his curiosity more than his expectations. If Elena Conifer was attractive, then Bill must have married up in the gene pool the way lawyers sometimes could. Still, it was hard to imagine. Bill had been hopelessly single throughout law school, to the point where some began to bandy about the notion that he was a homosexual. In any case, John was sure that he had never met the man's wife.

Then Brenna escorted Elena Conifer into the room, and he stood up awkwardly, she was so beautiful. "Elena?"

"Mr. Ashe?"

"John. Call me John."

Brenna raised her eyebrows at him as she withdrew, closing the door. Elena gave his hand a firm shake. He found the purposeful gesture endearing. She had probably practiced it with a girlfriend or maybe even with old Bill himself. "I'm Elena Conifer."

John made himself let go of her hand. "Have a seat."

She sat very straight on the lip of the guest chair, her hands resting on an open notepad in her lap. "I really need this job, Mr. Ashe. I don't know if my father explained things—"

"John. Call me John, please."

"Okay. John. I want to be completely open with you. I really need this job. Dad's been paying my share of the rent, I live with two other girls from Magnate, and he's starting to say things like I should go home to Connecticut and move back into my old room. I'm afraid not. Mr. Ashe—John—I won't do that. Lights out by ten-thirty, all that high school stuff. They'd probably revert to being high school parents, right? If you really thought it would help you decide, you could go through all the regular interview questions. Where would I like to be in five years? Out of law school and practicing with a firm of my own. What are my weaknesses? Well, I don't have any paralegal experience per se, but that's because I was too busy getting a three-nine at Magnate and an A-plus on my senior thesis, which was three hundred pages long. I'm smart, I can write—and if experience is the sole measure, then I'm technically unqualified for any job—and what it comes down to is I'm asking you to give me a chance because I deserve one, and I need your help."

He almost hired her on the spot. Maxine Estep was not going to appeal to his sense of charity. Indeed, there would be the unspoken implication that she was doing him a favor by consenting to the pointless formality of an interview.

In his own fairly handsome son, John had already noticed the beginnings of jowls and a slightly receding hairline, but Elena's poreless face bore no similar flaws into which time might drive a wedge. The skin at the corners of her eyes was as smooth as that covering her Hollywood cheekbones, and it would never wrinkle. Her lips would always be this thick, her nose this small and straight, her eyes this large and blue, her hair this thick and blond.

If a girl looking like Elena, desperate as she obviously was, started knocking on doors throughout the city . . . it gave John the shivers. There was no telling what might happen. It was not really a sexual attraction that he felt toward her, for he was clearly too old. Thoughts of kissing those lips, touching those breasts . . . ridiculous, harmless momentary fantasy. But he did feel an avuncular responsibility to hire her away from unscrupulous employers who might try to do those things and more. At the same time he would be doing old Bill Conifer a favor.

Yet he couldn't. He had to hire Maxine Estep, by far the more qualified applicant.

Coached to look him in the eye when she spoke, Elena nevertheless forgot not to pick at her cuticles. She pulled them back one by one until he glanced down at her hands and she stopped. Some of the color drained from her face as she considered her error. Immediately he felt guilty, to the point that he nearly told her to pick at her cuticles all she wanted.

"Where else have you applied?"

"Everywhere. Other law firms, sure, because that's my interest. But I'm not above waiting tables if it's that or move back home. I even thought about answering an ad for dancers."

"What kind of dancing?"

"It was just a passing thought, I would never do it. But I've been nude in public before, when I was visiting a friend at Princeton. Their sophomore year, at the first snow everyone takes off all their clothes and runs all over town. Guys and girls together. It's called the Nude Olympics. Dad had to help get me out of jail."

"Really?"

She nodded. "It's sort of embarrassing, I guess, but I can't really say I regret it. It was so cold, you wouldn't believe, doing push-ups and sit-ups. We had to take turns holding each other's feet down. But about the job, I don't care if I have to work late or skip lunches or whatever. I need the work, I'd be good at it, and I like you. Dad says you'd be a good boss."

Evidently she felt this last had been too forward, for she slumped slightly in her chair and devoted full attention to her cuticles.

"Thank you," John said. "Initial chemistry is important."

He answered her questions about law schools. She wanted to practice in Manhattan like her father. "I have a piece of advice for you," he said. "Don't live in Connecticut or Jersey like he and I do. You'll grow old on a commuter train. I often dream about the train like I used to dream about fields and tree houses and, I don't know, women." Dreams of women, just great. He needed to get a handle on himself. Should he apologize or would that only acknowledge the unprofessional nature of the slip, mark it in Elena's mind?

But she was smiling. "Don't you still dream about women?"

"I've been married twenty-five years."

"You must've been really young."

He assessed her face for any sign of irony or practiced flattery, and to his surprise saw none. "Well, I run. That probably helps. But I'm fifty."

"I wouldn't have guessed it."

"Hell, I knew your dad in law school, after all." Still warm from her compliments, he asked about her A-plus senior thesis.

"It's about discrimination against beautiful people. For every handsome person like yourself who does well in life, there are many more who aren't taken seriously. Of course, this is more of a problem for women. Reverse lookism is the technical term, but it's the idea that just because a person happens to be beautiful or handsome"—she indicated John with her hand—"he or she must therefore be stupid or incompetent. It's a problem we're just beginning to understand."

John nodded. He'd heard worse. He found himself having to suppress an obvious compliment about how she must have had personal experience in the matter. Maybe he would have said it had he been a much younger, much more careless man. Maybe if he were nineteen, with a good beer buzz. These days you had to watch yourself. The firm was especially vulnerable after Jordy Hamilton had brought on a lawsuit by complimenting a temp's high heels in conjunction with some comment about how he liked "shrimping"—sucking on people's toes. It was hard to put that word in a legal document.

So John said, "Reverse lookism. And I presume this is a possible direction for your future legal career."

"Well, somebody has to lay the groundwork. On the other hand, I can already feel myself being tempted toward the established fields. The money's better, the respect is there."

Smart girl and so young.

ON THE OTHER side of the door, Brenna Fryerson was bent over the bottom desk drawer, picking various makeup items from among the extra pens, paper clips, and other office essentials. In the far back corner of the drawer, a dullish glint of gold. Could it be? She reached, and retrieved an heirloom earring that she had given up for lost three years earlier, its mate useless in her jewelry box since that time. She was so happy and distracted that when someone said, "Excuse me," she was startled into bumping her head on the edge of the desk.

"Now look what you've done," said the voice. "I'd better go get some ice."

"I'm okay." Holding the sore spot, Brenna stared at the stiff older woman who seemed so irritated by her carelessness.

"I'm Maxine Estep."

"Oh! Oh, how are you?" She stood and shook Maxine's hand. "I just found my earring. John's very eager to meet you. He's only interviewing one other candidate, and she has virtually no experience whatsoever." She realized that her embarrassment was making her talk too much. It was hardly appropriate to discuss the other applicant's qualifications or lack thereof, but since John had virtually committed himself to hiring Maxine, was there really anything to worry about?

"I'm glad to hear that I'm the front runner."

"Experience counts," said Brenna. "It really does."

Maxine Estep was in her early sixties by now, of stern expression and fastidious personal appearance. Her uninterrupted career as a *legal secretary,* she still called herself, had begun sometime during the Eisenhower years. Within the mostly anonymous mush of the New York legal community she was almost as well known as some of the legendary attorneys she had served, all now dead or retired. Just last year the New York Bar Association had established the Estep Award, to be given annually to an outstanding paralegal chosen from among nominees from all major firms. And Maxine herself was something of a trophy. John could no more pass on the opportunity to hire her than an aging actor could refuse the Lifetime Achievement Award at the Oscars.

Her purse was so small that it wouldn't have held the loose change which made up the ocean floor of Brenna's huge shoulder bag. Her nails were short and unpainted, perhaps even professionally manicured, though Maxine didn't look the type.

Brenna felt herself wanting to fill the silence with words, any words. "I was so excited when I heard you were applying because John, brilliant attorney though he is, sometimes I think he'd lose his head if it wasn't attached. He's only concerned with one thing at a time, great concentration. There's no room left in his brain for something so ho-hum as remembering appointments. I sometimes sort of think of myself as an external hard drive to his multi-gigabyte brain, though I must say he gave an extremely generous departure gift. Well, it's too early for you to start thinking about that yet. But you know how Einstein couldn't understand the grocery bill? Same type of thing with John sometimes. How rude of me, won't you have a seat?"

"I prefer to stand." Indeed, Maxine was walking around the office, scrutinizing the edge of the carpet, where there was a thin gray line of lint. She took a swatch of the curtain between her fingers and raised it for a perfunctory sniff. A moment later she sneezed.

"Bless you," Brenna said. "I'm sure he'd let you make whatever improvements you want."

Eyes still watery, fingers still dusty, Maxine scanned Brenna's papered desktop. Brenna uncovered a box of tissues and held it out, an offering. Wiping the curtain dust from her fingers, Maxine stared disapprovingly at the overflowing waste basket. She wadded the tissue and managed to puzzle it into a small crevice. "How often do the cleaning people come?"

"Every other night, but they've been getting sloppy."

"They're not very good."

After a brief discussion of available cleaning services, Brenna remembered one more thing John's new paralegal would have to know. "I'm sure Elizabeth, his wife, will tell you about this, but it's his Achilles' tendons. They're so sore and inflamed sometimes that he really shouldn't even try to run, but tell him that, he doesn't listen. It's just a matter of time before one of them snaps. I'm so glad I'm not going to be the one who has to call Elizabeth and tell her her husband's laid up in the hospital after one of his Thursday jogs with . . . I guess just Nathan now. Lee Thomas, God rest, used to run with them, too. That is until last Thursday. You might have seen his portrait in the hallway. Heart attack."

Maxine checked her watch and sat on the lip of the couch. "He should be with me soon."

"Yes."

In fact, Brenna was surprised that he was spending so much time with the Magnate girl. Perhaps he had decided to tell her up front that he couldn't hire her, and now was busy muttering a mixture of consolation and advice. Brenna strained to hear, and yes, there it was—the young girl crying.

Or was that laughter?

"Sounds like the first interview is going well," Maxine said.

"Well, she just got out of Magnate and has no legal experience whatsoever. He's only even interviewing her because he knew her father in law school."

Satisfied, Maxine nodded. Then the door opened, she glimpsed her competition, and her lips seemed to get a bit thinner.

John stepped out behind the applicant, hands in his pockets and back slightly hunched, a posture Brenna had seen him use only around close friends like Barradale and, God rest, Lee Thomas. Nor did Elena seem appropriately nervous. In one hand she clutched the hardback notebook on which Brenna could see she had taken copious notes. She raked the fingers of her other hand through her thick blond hair—*brazenly*, was the word that came to Brenna's mind. Neither of the pair seemed to notice Maxine on the couch. For that matter, Brenna felt as though she herself had disappeared.

"I enjoyed meeting you," John said. "You've got a lot going for you, and you'll definitely be hearing from me one way or the other."

Code words for *we're hiring someone else.* Her shoulders sagged just a bit. "And one way or the other, John, I'm not moving back into my parents' house."

"Well, don't count yourself out here. I'm only interviewing one other lady, although she's been around forever. She's kind of an—"

"John!" Brenna nearly yelled. "Have you met Maxine Estep yet?"

Old dinosaur, is what he had been about to say. His heart racing with the magnitude of the near error, he turned to face Maxine. Her hair was the steel gray color of an old kitchen knife. She stood and extended her well-worn hand. It felt dry and crinkly in his. "Good to see you again, Maxine."

"Likewise, Mr. Ashe."

"I'll be with you in a minute."

To Brenna's surprise, he walked out of the office with the Magnate girl.

Maxine's formidable presence conveyed her historic competence and experience, and John was annoyed. She had undermined the sense of optimism he had tried to instill in Elena. "I really appreciate the interview," the girl said, walking briskly down the hallway. "It was good practice. Daddy told me there might be an inside candidate." She stopped at the elevators.

He touched her elbow and she turned to face him. "Elena—" Two words, *you're hired,* would have made her happy. But he couldn't hire her. "You did really well, okay?" Even the skin of her elbow was supple and warm.

"I enjoyed meeting you, John. Thanks."

She stepped into the elevator and reached out to shake his hand. He retracted his arm just before the doors closed, glad finally to stop sucking in his gut.

"Who was *that?*" Nathan Barradale was on his way back from a multi-martini lunch.

"Job applicant."

Nathan sniffed the air where she had stood. "Mmmm. I'll hire her. What did her hand feel like?"

"You should've felt her elbow." John looked down at his fingers. "It felt like, it felt like . . . youth."

"SHOULD I DO a welcome letter for Maxine?" In fact, Brenna had already drafted one on the computer. It was four o'clock in the afternoon, the Maxine interview had been concluded for over two hours now, and she was anxious to get her candidate hired. "I mean why wait? You know she's the best."

"Because." John was lying on the couch in front of her desk like a mental patient. "I haven't made up my mind yet. She's young, sure, but she's really, really bright."

"She's young and beautiful, all right."

"That's not what I said."

"Yes, it is. She looks like a goddess, John."

They stared at each other for a moment. "Have you ever heard of reverse lookism?" he asked. "It's the legal term that applies to the practice of discriminating against someone because she's incredibly beautiful. See, our natural assumption is that these people have it easier in life, that they don't have to work as hard as the rest of us, that they really aren't as smart. We make their good looks into some sort of disadvantage, almost like a physical handicap. It's a trap that's easy to fall into, and one I'd like to avoid."

Brenna rolled her eyes. "There's a trap you need to avoid here, I'm just not sure that's it."

"I'm going to think about it over the weekend." He stood before her desk, puffed out his chest a bit, sucked in his gut. "How old do you think I look?"

"Fifty."

He deflated like a balloon. He walked back into his office, which was no longer his office but the place where he had first met Elena, forever a more youthful place despite Maxine's visit in the interim. He picked up a long blond hair from the carpet and held it up to the light.

THE TRAIN RIDE back to Groveton. Elizabeth greeting him at the door. The continuing loop video of his late middle age.

When they had bought the house several years ago, John had not envisioned the structure itself but rather the Pawley's Island hammock he would string up in the backyard. He saw himself falling asleep with a book open on his chest, one arm dangling toward a half-empty beer bottle standing up in the grass with honeybees alighting on its rim. Never got around to putting up that hammock, though. The weekends were always taken up by some home-improvement project or social obligation or sometimes just simple rest and recovery after a hard stretch at the office.

Usually he consulted with Elizabeth about his hiring decisions, but today for some reason he didn't feel like mentioning the interviews he had conducted just a few hours earlier. He told himself there was no particular reason for this, just didn't want to bore her with his office news. She asked how his day had been. He said, "Fine." During a light dinner she passed along the most recent gossip about William Newton, which was that his prostitute had been a sixteen-year-old illegal immigrant from Mexico.

John said, "Well, this is the land of opportunity."

"Don't be crass."

Then there was the usual banter about GCDS, after which they spent the evening in a typical manner, he in front of the television with a lemon mineral water on the rocks, she in the kitchen grading her weekly essays from GCDS. This week's batch was on John Knowles' *A Separate Peace*. Occasionally she would sigh in exasperation at some grammatical error. "All the ones who can't write were in Myrna's section last year. I'm going to have to have an observer sit in on her classes."

He tried to imagine what Elena Conifer was doing this evening, how many heads she was turning in how many bars, how many young men were asking for her phone number, how jealous were her friends, necessarily imperfect by juxtaposition. He kept thinking about the smooth, warm skin of her elbow. He kept thinking about holding her feet down in the snow while she did nude sit-ups. Told himself to forget it but the image kept coming back, her ankles in his fists. He wondered if he would be unfaithful with her if he ever—silly hypothetical question—got the chance. No, the structure of his marriage was too sound, he told himself, sipping lemon mineral water and watching a building implosion on CNN.

```
┌─────────────────────────────┐
│                             │
│   C H A P T E R    2        │
│                             │
└─────────────────────────────┘
```

SATURDAY MORNING HE opened his eyes and walked painlessly toward the bathroom. Halfway there he realized that something was different, something had improved. His heels. For years now he had been plagued by bursitis of both Achilles' tendons, always worse in the mornings. On occasion he had to limp downstairs one step at a time like an old arthritic man and shuffle to the kitchen, where he would eat one of the several bran cereals Elizabeth would buy, all of which he called Colon Bran. As the milk dribbled down his chin he would admit to himself that today perhaps he should take a break from running so that his heels might recover. But the pain would subside just enough that by afternoon or evening he could trot three or four miles and ensure tomorrow's limp.

But this morning there was no pain. He flexed his feet one by one as Elizabeth's ursine snores rose up from the bed behind him. He continued on to the bathroom.

Something else was different. He did not have that familiar conviction that time had passed him by, that after the heaven of his youth the present was merely a purgatorial opportunity to get things paid for and horde some money before that hellish period of increasing physical decrepitude and mental decline known as retirement, down in Florida, followed by a lengthy hospitalization, tubes, machines, the bill a hundred grand, and finally a huge tombstone on filled-in swampland, and back in New York a portrait in the Hallway of Death. Red tie, gold clip, close-lipped smile.

He took a good morning whiz, his urine stream driving deep

and hard into the water. For a moment the sound drowned out Elizabeth's snoring. He reached into the shower for the jock strap and running shorts that he customarily hung over the hot water handle, lately for almost purely decorative reasons. Three days since their last use, they were dry and stiff with inadequately rinsed sweat and splashed-on soap and shampoo. The pouch of the jock strap felt like most people's elbow skin. As he pulled it on he could not even remember the last time he had gone for a run in the morning.

Down in the kitchen he drank a glass of water. The sun through the window spotlighted his legs, which were alabaster white and bald in patches from the perpetual friction of his suit pants. Why did he feel so young just now? He did not know, tried to guess. Was it having the house to himself at this hour on such a fine morning? The fact that his bursitis lay surprisingly dormant? Or was it the thought of Elena Conifer?

He had thought of her constantly since her interview yesterday, even as he nodded his head and smiled through Maxine Estep's flawlessly professional responses. Absurd rescue fantasies such as he had not allowed himself since college had begun playing themselves out in his mind on the train. While other graying heads bobbed in semiconsciousness, John Ashe was bursting into some place of abusive employment, turning over tables like Jesus in the temple, dragging a tearfully grateful Elena out by the wrist and then helping her find a more suitable job, thus winning forever her admiration and gratitude. Or saving her from a would-be rapist—rounding a corner just in time to see her being dragged into an alley at knife point. He imagined himself rushing into the alley, where he would find a board with a nail in it, or better yet a bat-sized length of pipe with which to smite the deserving offender. Again he would win her undying gratitude.

Yet in these and other fantasies the reward for his good deeds was never sex. Sex with Elena seemed so much more unlikely than, for example, saving her from a suicidal maniac who had taken her hostage on the Tappan Zee bridge that it really wasn't worth thinking about. He wouldn't really want to, anyway, she was so young. Instead he would become like an uncle to her, someone she would enjoy spending time with, someone to whom she would write while on vacations, or visit for personal advice, and whom she would give in return warm hugs of thanks.

He sat on the top porch step of his Groveton home and put on his running shoes. It was going to be an unusually warm day for November, but now there was still enough of a nip in the air to trigger a memory of autumn in Charlottesville, seven a.m., running down Rugby Road in his Virginia Law sweatshirt, his shoes crunching the fallen leaves. That was back before he even knew he had heels, or indeed any sort of perishable body part. Now when he stood his knees crackled.

Walking across the dry, brown grass, he set the timer on his wristwatch. Beeped it on just as he hit the street trotting.

It seemed particularly easy that morning. He thought about Elena's age estimate: early forties. Not fifty but early forties. His hair was on the grayish side and he had the beginnings of an accomplished belly, but he still looked youthful compared to most of his contemporaries. This he credited to running, to the sacrifice of his heels, but also to a certain willful resistance to getting older.

The first part of his route was fairly flat. Dr. Dowling the podiatrist had said that starting out on a hill would increase the likelihood of snapping one of the tendons as Al Gore had during that pickup basketball game with a bunch of congressmen. Usually even on the flat stretches every landing stung his heels, but for some reason not this morning. Suspicious of his good luck, he maintained a sensibly moderate pace, though his lungs and legs told him he could go faster.

It was a funny thing, watching someone you've worked with for so long being lowered into the ground. The reflective shine of the polished mahogany coffin had looked so familiar in tone that John made it a point, the following day, to check that they hadn't built it from the panels of Lee's desk. The desk was still there and intact, only now it encased Kelly Epstein, suffering that guilt peculiar to all inheritors whose thrill at the windfall outweighs their sorrow for the departed. In a fit of overcompensation she crossed the room, grabbed John's forearms, and gazed sympathetically into his eyes. "I want you to know how sorry I am. I know he was a good friend of yours."

"Thank you."

At thirty-four she had just made partner. It was reproduce now or never, and as far as anyone knew there was in her life no potential inseminator. Her lingering, unused fertility made her the sex symbol of the firm despite her ample beam and rather ordinary features. "I bet it's been a while since anyone touched her deeply," Lee Thomas had said once during a Silver Milers jog. "She's probably desperate, can you imagine? Too bad I'm married."

"Yeah," Barradale said, his voice curling with irony. "Otherwise she'd be all over you."

John had left her sitting behind the desk which she didn't even know yet was but a coffin for the living.

In the sunny chill of the November Saturday morning he found that he could pick up the pace a bit, still without pain but not yet without thinking about Lee. The guy had died harboring unresolved regrets. Not about things he had done—who regretted Phi Beta Kappa at Stanford, first in your class at Yale Law, and then a straight shot to partner in a major New York firm? No, Lee had died regretting things he had not done yet, the experiences he had forgone in doing exactly what he was supposed to do. Maybe his kids were spoiled and ungrateful, and his wife a stranger, but God bless him, they were sure as hell provided for. Widow Linda had the luxury of stylish mourning.

Elizabeth was no stranger; if anything she was too familiar. She had become a protector of routine whereas once, in their youth, she had been a source of spontaneity. He supposed that he shared some of the blame. But when he was always at the office or going to or coming from it, doing what he was supposed to do, earning several hundred thousand a year, how much energy was he expected to reserve for spontaneity? As for his son, the kid wasn't spoiled or ungrateful. Like many young people, Andy seemed to find the success of his parents unattainable, and so had fabricated philosophical reasons not to attempt it himself. John read judgment in the kid's decision to take a low-paying job in some peonic capacity at MTV. Holding cue cards, probably. Sooner or later, when the kid realized that he was not destined for fame, he would do the sensible thing and apply to law school. In the meantime at least he still kept in touch. He was coming over later that day, in fact, bringing a new girlfriend. If the summery forecast held, John would fire up the grill.

He began to accept that he was running pain-free. But approaching his first major hill he slowed deliberately, not wanting to push his luck just yet. Next thing he knew, he was halfway up it. Only at the very top did his legs begin to rebel, which was okay because now he could reward them with a nice stretch of flatness. He had gone two miles when the neighborhood began to awaken, and he saw gray-haired and bald men wearing bathrobes and cloth slippers opening their front doors to get the newspaper. No doubt they would all read the obituary page carefully. Some waved at John, and he returned the gesture, peer to peer.

"Good morning for it!"

"Sure is!"

He had driven this running route in his Sensible American Sedan, and so knew that the fifth-mile marker was the corner of the Maffazolis' driveway. On most days, if he was really pushing it, he would get this far in forty-one or forty-two minutes, but then would have to limp through a quarter-mile shortcut home. Now he looked for the Maffazolis' driveway, but something was wrong. The house was not up ahead, where according to his wristwatch it should have been.

It was behind him, he had already passed it.

He turned around and trotted backward for a moment. The Maffazolis' big colonial was at least a hundred yards in his past. Yet according to his watch he had been on the road now for only forty minutes. Unless the battery was dying, he had just run this route faster than on any occasion since he was forty-four or maybe even younger.

He kept going, allowing himself the indulgence of what for him was a reckless speed. The ten-K marker was the stop sign at Brandywine and Mapleton, and though he could not see it yet, *he could see it*, around the next corner and straight ahead for another hundred yards. He had not run his ten-K route in three or four years.

Among the distinguished residents of John's neighborhood were the Kurt Vermiels, he having won the Nobel prize in physics some years previous. Legend was that he got most of his ideas playing croquet, which was what he was doing now in his front yard, shuffling toward a wooden ball, using the mallet like a cane. Not bad for an old guy. He looked up at the runner.

John saw approval in the eyes of the old genius. Vermiel was ninety-five if a day, yet here he was out in the yard playing croquet. Not like Lee Thomas, who, when he had imagined his retirement, saw himself sitting on a beach somewhere drinking beer against doctor's orders. Maybe that had been part of Lee's problem. With his family provided for his work was finished. Perhaps he had died from lack of purpose.

Neighborhood legend Kurt Vermiel, whom John had never met but only read about, winner of the Nobel prize in physics, was waving and smiling. John waved back. The legendary Kurt Vermiel opened his mouth to speak—what would he say?

In a German accent: "Good day for it!"

"Sure is!"

John could see the ten-K stop sign up ahead now. He resisted the temptation to look at his watch. Just concentrate on the run, he told himself, run the race. His knees rose higher than at any time in recent memory, and the stop sign was approaching at almost bicycle speed. As his foot hit the pavement parallel to the signpost he pressed the stop button on his watch, barely hearing the beep over his heavy breathing. He crossed the street with his hands on his hips, his face turned skyward, eyes closed, lungs heaving. The morning chill had burned off, and his face was warm and sweaty in the sun.

He checked the watch.

ELIZABETH SQUINTED DOWN the street beneath the brim of her floppy gardening hat. When she woke up and found that his jock strap and running shorts were not hanging in the shower, she accepted that this would be the morning he finally crippled himself. So she had put on her gardening clothes, which would be comfortable enough for the emergency room, and now squatted on her hams before the azaleas. This recent unseasonable warmth had brought the dern weeds out again. Wearing John's oversize work gloves, she reached in to uproot them, checking over her shoulder every minute or so for her limping, perhaps crawling husband. Every time she heard a car coming over the hill she turned to look, thinking that perhaps this would be the good Samaritan in whose yard he had fallen moaning and clutching his snapped Achilles.

Finally there he was, walking, apparently without pain. He kept cocking his elbows parallel to the asphalt and pulling them back to stretch his chest. No doubt he was doing his best to conceal from her the harm he had done to himself. She shook the gloves from her hands and marched out to the edge of the yard to meet him.

"Are you okay?"

"Yeah, why wouldn't I be? You wouldn't believe what a good run I just had."

"What about your heels?"

"They're fine. That's just it. They didn't bother me at all."

"It's Lee, isn't it? That's what's making you do this to yourself. I can understand that but, John, I really do not want to spend all day in the emergency room."

"I'm not questioning what just happened to me. I just ran really well, better than I have in years." He told the story about Kurt Vermiel waving and smiling, actually *speaking* to him.

"Really?" She had always been impressed by the proximity of her house to Vermiel's, and equally disappointed that she had yet to meet the laureate. The guy was old, too, he might die soon. That John had managed to strike up a speaking relationship with Vermiel went a long way toward assuaging her irritation at his foolish morning run. "Well, anyway, your heels are all right?"

"Yeah, they're great."

"I just don't think you should push it."

She squatted on her hams again and reached for another clump of weeds. "Don't forget about Andy coming over."

"Yeah, who's he bringing?"

"He says it's a surprise."

Great. The last *surprise* had worn black lipstick and a dress that exposed the safety pin in her linty navel.

SHE DID NOT wear black lipstick, but she was a surprise. Kristen Newton, William and Anne's daughter. Andy and she had known each other as toddlers, drifted apart through adolescence and college, and found each other again in the city. Cute when she was a little second-grader, now she was a horsy-looking young woman whose poise and politeness bespoke the affluence of her parents and the quality of her GCDS education. Elizabeth had been her English instructor senior year.

John caught up with Andy in the kitchen. "Isn't she a couple of years older than you?" Through the window they could see Elizabeth and Kristen sitting out on the patio furniture.

"Yeah." The kid opened a Sam Adams. "Want one?"

John feigned equivocation.

"Come on, Dad, be a man. You can down it before Mom sees."

"Twist my arm." He took the bottle and turned its bottom to the ceiling for about four seconds, chugging.

"Damn, come up for air. Has it gotten that bad?"

John wiped the beer shine from his lips and slid the empty bottle across the counter. "She starts complaining if I have more than two on any given day."

"I guess that's her role. You're not getting any younger. Can't say I relish the thought of what happened to Mr. Thomas." A good sport, though, Andy opened another beer for his father. "There you go. 'Course, I'm sorry to be bringing up Mr. Thomas. I just expect you to be around for another thirty or forty years, even if it kills you." The light from the window accentuated his cheekbones; a lock of his dark hair arched spectacularly to the bridge of his nose.

"How's it going at MTV, son?"

"Still a slave, but we'll see. Next week I could be famous." Through the window he watched Kristen touch his mother's shoulder, laughing. "Funny, isn't it, how we're going out after all these years. You know her mom caught us playing doctor once. Kicked me out of the house. Not a very enlightened move, now that I think about it."

"Didn't thwart you in the long run, apparently."

"Certainly not. You and the Newtons are still friends, aren't you?"

"Well, I guess. We haven't seen them in a while." He considered passing along the prostitution news, but a mischievous discretion prevailed. "I don't recommend that you tell any hooker jokes at their dinner table."

"Oh, like I'd do that anyway." A moment later the kid said, "Prostitution should be legalized, of course."

John took another gulp of beer. "I'm sure Kristen's father would agree with you."

"Oh, we do agree on most political issues, it's great."

"Well, Kristen's a good solid girl."

Andy sighed. "Meaning . . . ?"

"Nothing. Isn't there a cute little recent Ivy League graduate out there, young so you wouldn't have to have kids right away?"

"You got someone in mind?"

"No."

"It's not like we're getting married, anyway."

Outside at the grill John performed his cavemanly duties with fire and meat. Flipped those steaks and waved the smoke away with his spatula. All day he had been waiting for his Achilles' tendons to seize up rigid as a couple of funicular cables, but they remained supple as surgical cord and completely pain-free. At the patio table he saw Elizabeth pour Kristen and herself each another glass of wine. Andy crossed the yard holding his fourth or fifth Sam Adams. "Mom tells me you went running this morning."

"Yeah, it was great."

"But I thought the doctor told you never to go running in the morning."

"No. He told me never to go running, period. I'm supposed to walk briskly, I believe is what he said."

Andy didn't say anything for a moment, trying to withhold his concern, some piece of advice. Elizabeth had obviously exaggerated things and worried the kid into her camp on this issue.

For the past twenty-five years John had bitten his own tongue, most of the time, knowing the kid had to learn for himself. Now he resented this little role reversal, this mini-coup the kid was staging. He flashed his son a don't-do-it look, but a shift in the breeze suddenly enshrouded him in beef smoke.

"Dad, I hope you'll be careful. I mean, with your heels and all that. Do you carry any identification with you when you run? What if you ever got hit by a car somewhere and you weren't in a condition to give your home address, Mom's name, that sort of thing? I just don't want a bunch of doctors standing around your stretcher saying, 'Think he's got insurance? Should we treat him?' "

"Don't worry about your old man so much, son. What do you expect me to do, lie in a hammock all day?"

"No, I just think you shouldn't let what happened to Mr. Thomas make you start exercising too strenuously. I'm right, aren't I, it's had an effect. I think you should just concentrate on being . . . active, I guess, and fit."

"Active, fit." John took a moment to flip the steaks. "I believe I know what that means. A stroll around the block and a spoonful of Metamucil." He flipped the steaks one last time. "Mine's done. I like mine still sort of bleeding. I'm trying to maintain my immunity to *E. coli* bacteria."

The conversation had depressed him somewhat, and now his Achilles' tendons were starting to harden. It was critical that he not show any discomfort. God forbid a limp—that would just send everyone into hysterics. They would accidently-on-purpose lose his running shoes as he himself had removed the shotgun from the bedroom closet of his mentally declining grandfather many years before. Everyone wanted you out of the way, it seemed, and the sooner the better. It struck him that Elizabeth and Andy seemed to expect him to die young—or maybe *young* was the wrong word, it was already too late for that. Die soon, rather. And the expectation was so strong that it bordered on desire. Except of course that they kept warning him not to do things that might kill him. That way they wouldn't feel so guilty when it finally happened. They could enjoy with clear consciences the insurance payoff and the small fortune he had amassed over the years. Because they loved him so, and because of what they expected of him, they were dangerous people.

Damn this Achilles. He flexed his foot and felt the pain shoot up through his calf.

A few minutes later, they were eating at the patio table, Andy with a fresh Sam Adams, the women with another bottle of wine, and John sipping lemon mineral water on the rocks.

Elizabeth looked under the table. "Is the ice lasting?" For John was quite literally cooling his heels in a tub of ice water, his pants rolled up to expose his pale white calves.

"It's fine, okay?" He tried to compensate for his terseness with a cheerful question to Kristen. "How do you like living in the city?"

"Oh, it's great, it's so exciting. I'm living with a bunch of my friends from college."

"I met a girl yesterday who's doing just that."

"Dad, everyone does that unless they're filthy rich. We should have a more equitable distribution of wealth."

"I agree, I deserve more."

Elizabeth was amused by his comment about meeting a girl. "Are you out trying to pick up chicks, dear?"

"Right. That's me. Actually, it was someone interviewing for my paralegal's spot. You remember Bill Conifer? His daughter."

Kristen Newton tossed back the rest of her wine and leaned forward with such significance that all eyes turned her way. "Not *Elena* Conifer."

"Yes, as a matter of fact. She a friend of yours?"

"I just know her." She sat back in casual refutation of her previous urgency.

"Bill Conifer's daughter," Elizabeth said. "Now *that* makes me feel ancient. You know, I think we have a picture of her when she was a baby."

"Do we?"

She stood up, put her napkin in her chair. "I think I know exactly where it is."

"Don't bother," John said. "You don't have to."

But a moment later she was back with a photograph album opened to a two-page spread documenting the Conifers' visit to the Ashes' Upper East Side apartment more than two decades earlier. Shag carpet. Elizabeth in knee-high boots. John Ashe with sideburns. And in nearly every photo he was cooing at baby Elena Conifer. One photo showed him holding her in his arms and grinning at her, his eyes full of instant true love. Bill Conifer stood by proudly, a short, roundish man, already bald. "I remember you absolutely adored her," Elizabeth was saying. "You didn't want to let her go."

"She has that effect on men, apparently," Kristen said.

Looking over John's shoulder, Andy said, "I can see why—that bald pate, so smooth, that drool, so clear."

John closed the photo album and held it across his lap, a tombstone.

"Well, what did you think of her at the interview?" Elizabeth asked.

He felt Kristen staring at him over the rim of her wineglass, which she kept raising to her lips despite its emptiness. "She seemed nice," he said. "She seemed very young."

"Well, I hope you can help her out, Bill Conifer's daughter and all."

"Ever heard of Maxine Estep? She applied, too."

"Oh." Elizabeth understood the significance immediately. "Well, that old warhorse can always get another job. Whereas Bill Conifer's daughter, you might be her best connection."

"So you think I should hire her?"

"I don't know." Elizabeth winked at Kristen. "Should I be worried? Just how pretty is she?"

"What did you think, Mr. Ashe?"

"I didn't really think about it. I guess she was presentable enough. During the interview I was mainly just scanning her résumé."

"She's gorgeous," Kristen said. "So gorgeous it's totally ridiculous. There should be a more equitable distribution of looks, I deserve better."

"You'll have to be sure and look more carefully next time, dear," Elizabeth said. "I'm surprised you didn't notice."

"I'll be sure not to make that mistake again."

Kristen said, "She looks like Grace Kelly with a nineties body."

"John, maybe you need glasses."

Later he limped out to the two trees between which he had always meant to string a hammock. He had done a little covert raid on the liquor cabinet, and now his lemon mineral water was actually a Bombay martini, very dry, two olives. It was three o'clock and the clouds had blown in, and he couldn't stop thinking about Elena. Grace Kelly with a nineties body, and he had held her when she was a baby. He was ancient, his heels turning to stone. Impossible that he could ever be more to Elena than a benevolent employer, a kind old man whom she would remember, after his heart attack or stroke, by the leathery smell of his office, his frail, doddering gait, and the coffin polish of his mahogany walls. The photographs had left him feeling like a child molester.

What he felt toward Elena now was akin to what he had felt at the age of thirteen when he had stared at, well, Grace Kelly, and was overcome with an inexplicable, unspecific longing. She had something he wanted badly; he just didn't really know what it was or what the hell would happen if he ever did manage to get it. He wanted something from Elena, something more than was reasonably possible, even something more than sex. From there his imagination failed him.

"Most people don't put olives in their mineral water." Kristen stood beside him, a Diet Coke in her hand.

"Most people don't put gin in it, either."

"Thanks a lot for having me over. It was neat to see you after all this time. I don't know if I would have recognized you on the street."

"Yeah, well, you're not the second-grader I remember, either."

She laughed. "You probably held me when I was a baby, too."

"Oh, don't bring that up, that's depressing. Hey, I'm going to talk to her on Monday, I'll say hello."

"Elena?" She balked. "Oh, don't worry about it."

"I'm not worried about it, it's no trouble."

"Might as well not, though. I see her every now and then at parties anyway." She sighed. "With all the men gathered around."

"Does she have a boyfriend?"

Kristen's eyes narrowed. He had the sensation that she could read his thoughts, which he imagined were printed on his forehead in simple, declarative sentences. "You'll have to ask her that," she said.

"Why don't you like her?"

She looked down. "I don't want to speak ill of her."

"You might be doing me a favor, save me from hiring a bad egg."

"Well, she just thinks she's so good-looking. And she really is, there's no question. It's just too easy for people like that, it promotes a certain laxness. They sort of breeze through life. It makes for shallow character. She's never really done anything to me personally, it's just the way she is."

Reverse lookism. John stared up at the sky. The conversation had been revealing enough of Kristen, but had only made Elena seem more interesting. "Well, I thank you for the insight," he said. Taking the hint, she changed the subject to the imminent rain.

THAT NIGHT, WEARING only his boxer shorts, he sat with his back against the headboard, waiting for Elizabeth. He could hear her in the bathroom, gargling. When she finally came out, he was annoyed to see that she was still fully dressed, as if the cookout had just ended. Without glancing over at him she went straight to her closet, took her chin-to-toe nightie from its hanger, and turned to go back into her bathroom. "Wait a minute," he said. "Why don't you undress in front of me? It's been a while."

She looked at him doubtfully, looked down at his boxers.

"You're my wife," he said. "Do you realize how long it's been since I've seen my own wife naked?" The answer came to him silently. It had been three or four years since that morning when he had barged into her bathroom looking for a safety pin. He had thought she was downstairs reading the paper, but there she stood, posing in front of the mirror with a coquettish look on her face, her cheeks sucked in, as if she thought herself a centerfold. He was horrified. So was she. Screaming, she turned to cover herself as if he were a stranger. For several days after that she was cold to him, stalking around the house, muttering about privacy, and he stopped complaining about her chin-to-toe nightgown, that sudden policy reversal endorsing her humiliation.

But now he wanted to see her naked.

She sighed. "How about if I put on my nightgown in the bathroom, you turn out the lights, and I come in and we can heave-ho under the covers?"

"What a novel suggestion." For years now that had been the only way she would do it. Straight missionary position, too. "Let me just ask you something, Elizabeth, so it's clear in my mind. Does this mean that for the rest of my life I will not see a naked woman except at the goddamn movies? Am I going to have to make love in the dark under the covers from now on? Why don't you start wearing men's pajamas? Since they have that fly in the crotch, you know. You wouldn't even have to lift up your night-gown."

She slammed the bathroom door. He got up, hobbled down-stairs one step at a time, and turned on *Saturday Night Live.*

SUNDAY MORNING HIS heels felt a little better. He took the Sensible American Sedan out for a spin just to get away from the house. Ten miles away, on a road he often used, he was surprised to see a Porsche dealership. Of course he had driven past it many times before, knew it was there, had seen ads for it in the paper, and could have given a stranger directions to it easily. But he had never really *seen* it before as a place he might go, not being into flash cars himself, considering them slightly crude demonstra-tions of wealth, the white man's equivalent to a rapper's King Tut gold.

The sight of a middle-aged white man getting out of a Sensible American Sedan sent the sales crew sprinting from the show-room, the winner of the race hanging onto the prize customer's elbow as if guiding a blind man through a mine field. But John could see well enough the silver convertible Porsche 911 which gleamed before him, a sleek manifestation of sexy financial wherewithal. The salesman kept looking back at the Sensible American Sedan. "That car you drove in here, that's like a wheel-chair compared to this. I'm not saying it's a bad car, hey, it's what my father drives. But he's sixty-five. You're what, just about forty?"

He spread his arms out toward the Porsche. "This is a unique statement of who you are, where you are, what you have accom-plished. It says that you've made a lot of money, but you're still a lot of fun. Get it? Almost no one can afford to drive this car."

"It just looks like fun."

He sank into the leather seat and turned the keys in the igni-tion. The car seemed to rise in the air a few inches and await his command. He merely thought about backing from the parking place, wheeling right so that he would face the street, and it was so. The street was a hundred yards away. He thought about go-ing forward, and suddenly the tires chirped against the asphalt and he had to brake to keep from nosing into the inferior traffic.

Backward, he commanded the car, bringing it to a stop beside the worried salesman.

"You didn't even take it out," the guy protested. "You didn't get the full effect, is something wrong?"

John climbed out, leaving a shoe print on the door. "Yeah, my name's not on the title yet. How fast can you fix that?"

AFTER DRIVING AROUND for a couple of hours, he spent the rest of the day in his study, going over his finances and trying to figure out a way to justify the impulsive purchase. The Porsche was parked in the driveway with the dealer sticker still on and the temporary license plate taped in the rear window. Elizabeth had barely said two words to him since his complaints of the night before. The Porsche at least gave her the chance to change the subject of the dispute from sex to finances. She stuck her head into his study; he looked up from his computer.

"I know you make most of the money," she said. "But a marriage implies a certain equality of decision-making when it comes to spending what is after all the income of a single entity, the married couple. I understand you regret getting older. You resent it. Lee's death has affected you more than you care to admit. But I hope that if you get anything out of this purchase, it is the knowledge that nothing helps. You are not going to be more agile, more attractive, or a better lover because you spent so much on an automobile. In fact, I think it's rather sad, but that's just me." She looked at him as if expecting an apology. "And it's so ostentatious, it's embarrassing. I wish you'd put it in the garage."

"Thank you for your opinion."

She slammed the door so hard that a crack appeared in the paint around the frame, and across the room a pen fell from one of the bookshelves.

```
┌─────────────────────────────┐
│                             │
│   C H A P T E R   3         │
│                             │
└─────────────────────────────┘
```

BRENNA NOTICED HIS slight limp. "You went running."

"Good morning to you, too."

"What did Elizabeth say?"

"She complained, of course."

"Nathan brought these down." She placed her hand on a stack of file folders, stuffed. "He needs you to look at them by this afternoon, he said it's real important. And Emile Grovay called again just absolutely demanding to speak to you, says he found a typo in the brief we submitted on his behalf, and as far as he's concerned it constitutes evidence of casual disregard, especially if he loses."

John was looking around at all the Post-it notes stuck to everything. He read the one on the fax. *Maxine, I've been after him for years to junk this for a newer model.*

"Well, I don't want her to think it's my fault," she said. "Or that I left a disorganized office."

"You won't have to worry about that."

"Thank you. So when can I call her?"

John paused at the door to his office. "Call her now if you want. Just tell her you're sorry, she's not right for the position." He had meant to barrel on into his office, but he couldn't resist looking back to see her reaction. She was sitting straight-backed in her chair, shoulders squared with a sense of purpose: to save him from this dreadful mistake.

"That girl? You're hiring that Magnate girl?"

John opened his office door and stood in the frame, facing Brenna. "I thought about it a lot over the weekend. Elena needs a break, she'll appreciate it. Maxine expects me to hire her, thinks it's inevitable. Don't think I don't know how it would turn out. Having Maxine working for me would be like working for Maxine."

"It's not my place to say, but you're not being very smart."

"No one thinks I'm being very smart lately. Would you call Maxine and give her the news, please? I'll call Elena."

He went into his office, leaving Brenna with the unpleasant task. She stared at the phone, could not bring herself to make the call just yet.

ELENA CONIFER PICKED up on the fifth ring, slightly breathless. She apologized, she'd just run straight from the shower. Her teeth chattered and her voice shook in the chill of her living room. "Our heat's so weak, oh, I'm freezing. What's up?" With a nipped squeal of gratitude she accepted the job and said she would be right down. John allowed himself to visualize her nude, wet race through a cluttered, cold apartment. He could see the goose bumps and beads of water on her skin. When Brenna stuck her head into his office, he was running a comb through his hair before a hand-held mirror that he kept in his desk drawer, until now secretly. He scrambled to put it back, that haste confirming his embarrassment.

"Bad hair day?" she asked. "Don't forget about the stack of Barradale stuff. You want me to bring it in?"

"I'll get to it, thanks."

He swiveled around in his high-backed leather chair and put the heels of his wing tips on the windowsill.

Elena arrived within the hour. He met her halfway across the office and shook her hand. The roots of her hair were still wet, and she was so excited that she almost gave John a hug, but managed to convert the gesture to a simultaneous patting of both his shoulders. Finally she composed herself enough to shake his hand again. "Thank you so much, you don't know how much I needed this. You won't regret it."

"I already don't."

She finally let go. "Well, what now?"

"Brenna's going to go over a few things with you. Then we'll go to lunch."

He escorted her back out to the reception area just as Maxine Estep entered from the hallway. "Hi, how are you?"

"Well, what a surprise," he said, looking at Brenna.

"Her phone was busy, okay? I tried."

Maxine said, "I was just in the area and thought I'd drop by. How's your search going?" She smiled very brightly at Elena.

He patted his new paralegal between the shoulder blades. "Great, it's over. She's starting right now."

"Oh?"

"Yeah, wanted to get a little fresh blood in."

"I see." Far from seeming disappointed, Maxine looked downright pleased. But she said, "I'm very disappointed that you apparently didn't consider my superior qualifications. You'll be hearing from me. Good day." She turned and walked out.

He said to Brenna, "See? You think I want someone like that working with me?"

"Okay, okay." She smiled up at Elena. "You and I have business to attend to, don't we?"

Back in his office, John looked down at his feet, flexed them both. He walked around in circles on the carpet, finally breaking into a jog. His Achilles' tendons, which just a few minutes before had been as sore as ever, now did not hurt at all.

IN BRENNA FRYERSON'S voice Elena detected a slight condescension, perhaps a little reverse lookism there, but in general the older woman was being helpful and friendly. The one thing Elena didn't understand was why all the Post-it notes were originally written for someone else. "Maxine" had been crossed out and "Elena" written in. She could only conclude that John had intended to hire someone else, who had declined the offer. She herself had therefore been his second choice, which only meant she would have to work even harder to prove herself an asset. "Inasmuch as you'll sort of control John's schedule and access to John, you're in sort of a powerful position. Everyone who needs to see him thinks it's absolutely urgent. Well, not to John it isn't, not usually. So occasionally you have to tell them no. Sometimes it gets unpleasant." She ticked a fingernail against the intercom. "Some days he's so busy he won't leave his office. I just pretend he's a personality trapped in this box."

"But I'll be doing research and stuff, too, right?"

"He'll have to get to know you before he trusts you with that. Could take years."

"He said he'd start me on it right away, actually."

"Oh."

Elena absorbed information with an ease that left her tutor skeptical. "Now, you're sure you understand this?" Brenna would ask, only to have the information repeated back to her in a more articulate manner.

"What's it like working for John?"

Brenna swiveled from the computer screen. "I'll tell you the truth, he's great. People all the time say to me, 'You work for lawyers? That's horrible, they're such A-holes!' And a lot of them are, I admit. Even John is when he has to be. But I respect him because he's always treated me well, and because he's taken such good care of his family over the years. His skin rarely sees sunlight, he works so hard. In the winter it's still dark when he gets here and dark when he leaves. I couldn't do it. He insists I take an hour lunch and go somewhere. I think he's worth every penny of his salary, which is huge. People say lawyers don't deserve all that money and I'm like, 'Oh, and you do? For what? For sitting on your ass all day and never finishing school?'" Brenna laughed. "Sorry, I just like the man. The truth is, he has no life. He gave it up for his family. Me, I couldn't have worked while my kids were growing up, wouldn't have wanted to."

"Men don't have to, either."

"That generation did, honey." She paused for a moment. "And he doesn't cheat on his wife like I suspect most of his partners cheat on theirs. He's a pretty good-looking guy, too, it's not like he hasn't had the opportunity."

"I wouldn't expect him to," Elena said. "My father speaks very highly of him."

Suddenly John's door opened and there he stood, hair freshly combed. "What's my schedule look like this afternoon?"

"It's completely full. And you've still got that Barradale stuff to go through."

"I'm thinking of taking a run."

"What about your heels?"

"Elena," he said, "something you should know. Whenever I say I'm going running, you should say, 'What about your heels?' Okay? And tell me to stretch, and tell me you don't want to have to be the one to call Elizabeth to tell her I'm in the hospital unable to walk."

Brenna explained. "His Achilles' tendons have been inflamed for years now; he won't follow doctor's orders, which are to stop running. Elizabeth and I have been after him for quite some time. He's not getting any younger."

"One more thing, Elena. I'm going to start driving to work. I'm sick of the cattle train. I'll need someplace to park my new Porsche."

"Your Porsche?" Brenna said. "John . . ."

"Nine-eleven. Convertible and everything." Flashing one more smile at Elena, he withdrew into his office. Brenna shook her head. "A Porsche," she said.

"He has good taste in cars."

"He needs a Porsche like you need Weight Watchers, dear."

The phone rang. Elena answered it. "I'm sorry, Mr. Grovay, he's in a meeting." She glanced over at Brenna, who gave her two thumbs-up and mouthed *perfect*.

JOHN USHERED THE old and the new into the Barrister Bistro. Brenna said, "I can tell he likes you. When I first started, he sprung for Chinese take-out, which we ate in the office while he explained how he wanted things done. He kept coming up with ideas, and I'd have to put down my fork and jot them down. I called it my chop suey list, it had so many stains on it."

Elena ate a lobster salad sandwich, licking mayonnaise from the sides of her fingers. She told stories about college, mentioned the hopeless immaturity of boys her age, and said again how fortunate she felt to be employed in some capacity that wasn't completely irrelevant to her future career.

"I was telling her it'll be a while before she does any research," Brenna said.

"Why would that be?" he asked. "She got an A-plus on her senior thesis. She can research, she can write."

Elena laughed at John's jokes and went out of her way to keep Brenna involved in what was in danger of becoming a two-way conversation. Finally she excused herself to go to the bathroom.

Brenna said, "Now, John."

"Uh-oh."

"I hope you're not going to do anything stupid like fall in love with your secretary. That would be so mundane. You don't want to throw away everything you've got."

"No, no." He took a sip of water. "But what is it exactly that I do have? It's a question I've been asking myself more and more since Lee's death. You know, that guy died never having been to Europe. He didn't even go the summer after college when everybody goes, when even I went. You know the first thing his wife did after the funeral? Flew to Paris. I'm not kidding, the Concorde and everything." This piece of information he had learned from Barradale, whose wife had called Linda Thomas just to check on things during the week after the funeral, when the real grief usually began, only to find that Linda didn't have time to talk. She was packing. John had been mulling it over ever since. "The things in my life, are they mine or am I theirs?"

Aware that on the walk from the office some passersby had taken Brenna for his wife and Elena for their daughter, he gave old dependable the rest of the day off and a five-minute head start from the restaurant. Walking up Fifth Avenue with Elena, he said, "I've been meaning to get some Godiva chocolates to keep around the office. You can pick them out."

"Oh, tempt me."

She carried the gold box in one hand, and with the other brought a truffle to her mouth and bit it in half, the caramel stringing from her teeth. Without looking at her, almost as if talking to himself, John said, "You know, I've always hated the man I am at this moment."

"What do you mean?"

"I'm an old guy walking down the street with a young woman." *Beautiful woman*, he kept himself from saying. "I'm so old I might have held you when you were a baby, you realize that?"

"You're not so old. You don't look it."

Young men were staring at him, a look in their eyes only slightly more charitable than hatred. He was practically strutting, he felt so alive and full of potential. He felt so young.

She said, "I was a bit flustered this morning when I first showed up. If I sounded more thrilled than grateful, I'm sorry. Now I can really say I really, really appreciate what you've done for me. It's a great help."

And he floated still higher on her gratitude and approval.

JOHN WOULD OFTEN find his descent to the locker room interrupted by the elevator's chime. From one of the lesser floors of Masterson, Grandissime, and Barradale a harried associate would step on, maintaining his hallway face, denied the precious sigh-length moment of privacy sometimes afforded by enclosed vertical travel.

"Keeping busy?" John would ask.

"You bet . . ." The younger man would pause somewhere between the inappropriate familiarity of *John* and the anachronistic formality of *Mr. Ashe*, finally opening his manilla folder rather importantly without risking either form of direct address.

Lee Thomas's full-length locker door stood open like the lid of an empty sarcophagus, its mummy having permanently donned a red tie and gold clip some time ago for display in the Hallway of Death. It would be worth voting in a new partner just to get that empty space reassigned, to see hooked there a jock strap that had recently harnessed a pair of live balls.

On his way through the lobby John waved to the security guards, one of whom said, "It's a good day for it." Pushing through the revolving door he squinted into the sunny chill of autumn, windbreaker weather. John's T-shirt, a gift from his son, was emblazoned with the MTV logo. His running shorts bore the signature of Frank Shorter, a personal hero.

Fresh, fibrous horse dung gave the southern end of Central Park a pastoral fragrance, adding to the illusion of actual nature. A horse sneezed, a tourist laughed and snapped a photo. John kicked at a fallen leaf as it skittered crablike across his path. He put a heel between the slats of a park bench and bent forward, toward his knee.

A thin young man trotted up to the bench and began stretching also. Belatedly he asked, "You mind?"

"Not at all."

In the younger runner's glossy new attire John detected corporate sponsorship. The guy was a living, breathing advertisement for Mercury Shoe, and his face looked somewhat familiar. His cheekbones were like a couple of marbles beneath skin burnished red by the sun and wind. The beard meant to downplay his weak chin did just the opposite by slanting backward to look positively vaginal. He was bald on top, just a few wisps left, and his forehead descended to a pair of deeply set eyes, dark as a couple of black marks on his soul. Squatting now, hands on his knees, the guy quivered with restrained energy like John's new Porsche when he first started it up.

"Do I know you?" John asked.

The guy looked up. "Doubt it. I don't run here very often. The air's not good."

"But you're a pretty famous runner, right? I mean, I haven't followed the sport closely, but you look sort of familiar."

"I've done a few marathons." The guy stared down the path, focusing on some unreachable horizon, his goal. "Sorry if I seem a little distant. I'm about to take a long run and I need to concentrate."

"Maybe I'll trot along with you for a while."

The guy shook his head. "You're welcome to try."

"If you're going really long, you must not be going too fast."

The guy looked John up and down, finally focusing on the slight mid-body paunch. "If you can keep up, fine."

"Great," John said. He was sure that he would be able to stay with the pro for a quarter mile or so. "You say when."

Now the guy smiled. "Okay? You ready? I don't want to catch you off guard . . . when!"

John kept up for about a half step, then was sucked along for ten feet or so in the guy's draft. The marathoner was gone with such speed that he passed surprised rollerbladers and bicyclists going in the same direction and finally disappeared over a rise in the terrain. By the time John got to the top of the same hill, the Mercury Shoe guy was nowhere to be seen.

He was amazed, first by the quickness of the marathoner and then by the fact that he himself was for the second time in three days running without pain, and his pace a bit faster, if his watch could be trusted.

```
┌─────────────────────────────┐
│                             │
│   C H A P T E R   4         │
│                             │
└─────────────────────────────┘
```

By January he was training at a 7:15 pace, and most of the small roll of fat had disappeared from his belly. He had to have all of his suits taken up, the tailor worrying the whole time. "I sink you bedda eat whole lot more food!" An amazing thing began to happen to his jawline and cheekbones. He'd known many older men to lose a lot of weight and look good from the neck down, but their faces! Unsupported by the fat of a fortunate life, the skin now shriveled in a sort of jump start on decomposition. But John's skin tightened up against his emerging cheekbones and strong jawline which for too long had been concealed by the pudge of prosperity. It was the damnedest thing, how good he looked. In line for the movies with Elizabeth just the other day he caught a woman staring at his ass. Thinking he must have sat on a piece of gum, he tried to brush it off. But there was nothing there. Just his ass. Amazing.

On Saturdays and Sundays after a good long run he would take the Porsche out for a couple of hours. Though it was too cold to put the top down and get the full effect, he still found that behind the wheel of the Silver Missile he felt like an independently wealthy gadabout en route from one immoral situation to another. It was an illusion he projected easily to people on the sidewalks, and in the Sensible American Sedans he passed, who did not know that in fact he had no life except as a money earner, and that running was his only real freedom from it. He had perfected the slight nod of acknowledgment and used it whenever he caught someone staring at him, wondering at the source of his wealth. Elizabeth was wrong, he thought. These people do not see just another middle-aged man in a Porsche.

One Saturday afternoon he drove to Seatowne and walked up and down the deserted beach with his hands in his pockets and the cold sea breeze in his hair, and then wandered over to a newsstand. In the sports magazines section he saw on the cover of *Distance Running* the unforgettable face of the marathoner who had blown him away in Central Park back in late November. The same vaginal beard, the same dark eyes and sharp cheekbones. His mouth was turned up in the shape of a smile, though you got the feeling this was merely an imitation of something he'd seen others do, that the expression did not come naturally to him.

Reynaldo Miller: Man or Machine?

He bought the magazine. Sitting in a pizza parlor with a beer and a couple of slices, he read all about Marathon King Reynaldo Miller. About to turn thirty-one, the guy had won every marathon he had entered for the past three years. But he had never run the New York or Boston races, always blaming some minor physical injury for his last-minute withdrawals. Running aficionados wondered, Was he not up to the challenge psychologically? Or was he simply getting too old? The general consensus was that he had only one or two good years left. If he wanted to secure his place in marathon racing lore, he needed to put Boston or New York under his belt soon.

If there was anything John was sure of, it was that the Reynaldo he had met in Central Park, with the deep-set, defiant eyes, did not lack the mental fortitude required to win. He had often recalled those eyes during his own training runs whenever he was tempted to slow down and just coast to the finish. He admired Reynaldo, envied the younger man's opportunity to win the New York Marathon. Perhaps he himself could have been a great runner if he had spent his twenties in training instead of in the law office. The article left him slightly wistful at the fact that there was no such thing as a fifty-year-old marathon champ.

He no longer thought of Reynaldo's chin as *weak*. Rather, it was *aerodynamic*. Looking at the training photos, which showed the marble cheekbones and the lithe muscularity of a determined runner, he found it hard to believe that Reynaldo Miller would ever be fifty, would ever die.

* * *

ONCE HE WAS returning from an errand just as Elena crossed the street to a pastry and bread shop. He waited, watched her re-emerge with a bagel and a soda. A pair of young men did simultaneous wing-tip pivots to stare at her from behind. The day was a spring tease, and Elena had left her overcoat in the office. She walked toward the Met in a skirt and blouse.

John had already entered the building and pushed the elevator button when he decided to go back outside and follow her.

He found her sitting on the steps of the Met with her knees pressed together beneath the hem of her skirt, most of the bagel still in her lap, the soda by her side, and in her hands a book. Ascending the steps, he saw that she was directing her intense effort at the pages of the same Baltazar Brantley novel which had been putting him to sleep in three minutes or less every night since Andy had given it to him for Christmas.

"That's a good book, isn't it?"

She looked up, using her hand as a visor against the sun. "Oh, hi! Have you read this?"

"Yes, a very powerful writer. One of my favorites."

She moved her soda aside so he could have a seat. "Well, you're full of surprises. All the things you find time to do—running, reading. I wish my father were as well rounded. As it is, he's just sort of round."

He had been aware for several days now that her admiration seemed to be approaching unusual levels and maybe even was becoming something sexual. Did she have a crush on him? At the very least their relationship had become more friendly than professional even as he had broadened her responsibilities to include doing some research, which he hoped would help prepare her for law school. He had no plans to push the relationship any further, believing it better to maintain the status quo with inaction than to jeopardize it with some grand gesture, some declaration of his obsession. The mere knowledge that he would see her every weekday morning made it possible to get out of bed without once hitting the snooze button. Driving into the city in his Porsche, he looked forward to asking how she had spent the previous night. Their various discussions were not always about law. The non-lovers found common outrages to denounce, common moderate ground on which to stand regarding hot political issues. Eventually the time they spent together would spill over into the after-work environment, or so John hoped. He was not calculating ways to get her into bed, yet at the same time he was doing everything possible to make her want to sleep with him. The mere thought of making love to her made his heart race like a teenager's. He kept thinking about the last time he had seen a woman naked, three years ago, Elizabeth surprised and outraged in the bathroom, covering herself.

There on the steps of the Met, John heard himself asking Elena out to dinner. His tone was casual, merely friendly.

"I'd love to!"

"Great!"

"But I can't." She frowned. "I'm supposed to meet this guy who's been sort of after me, the one I mentioned to you the other day. It's not really a date, though."

"David something? The Wall Street guy?"

She nodded. "He was one of my formal dates at Magnate. He's been working till midnight for the past several weeks, and now he's finally got a night off. I really couldn't turn him down. He's nice."

"Just dinner, right?"

"We might have a drink afterward." A moment later she said, "Don't worry, I won't be having breakfast with him."

"Well, I mean it's none of my business."

Picking at a cuticle, she said, "David's too young for me."

"Isn't he your own age?"

"A year older, actually." She smiled. "Maybe you should go back to Groveton and take your wife out to dinner."

"I don't know. Sort of felt like hanging out in the city tonight."

"Well, if you're still walking the streets at eight a.m., I'll probably be eating breakfast at Michelle's Café. Eighty-third and Third."

They strolled back to the firm together in easy conversation, strolled down the hallway to his office while associates and paralegals sprinted past, carrying rolled-up legal papers like relay batons.

Alone at his desk, John called up Andy over at MTV.

"Dad, what's up?" The kid sounded surprised, worried, bracing himself for bad news, so rarely did his father call him at all, and never at work.

"I was just thinking maybe we could go out and get some burgers or something." There was a pause. The phone lines conducted Andy's wince. To lighten the mood and cover his own embarrassment, John adopted an indeterminate foreign accent. "You know, I thought we could, how you say, hang out." Silence. Honor thy father, boy.

The kid gave in. "Sure, Dad, and then maybe I'll meet up with some friends later."

As ELENA PREPARED for her not-date she tried to imagine how John would spend the evening. In practiced refinement, no doubt, perhaps reading Baltazar Brantley or some other great writer in an antique leather chair until midnight or one, when he would pour himself a cognac and stand by the window musing up at the constellations, whose names and legends he probably knew by heart.

She on the other hand was about to go out for a cheap dinner with a guy who hadn't seen a woman socially since his management-training program began in August. He would have nothing to talk about except work. His main purpose would be to fill her full of margaritas to make himself more sexually appealing, and he was as refined as they got at that age, when their brains were suspended in a testosterone medium as if in formaldehyde. Compared to his peers, he was a nice, smart, civilized young man. And all he cared about was getting laid.

She stepped into the common area and asked her apartment mate to zip her dress. "You look beautiful," Shannon said. "I feel an attack of reverse lookism coming on."

"Don't tease."

"But it's true. I think you must be stupid."

"Oh . . ." Elena had conceded to herself that reverse lookism, although it obviously existed, was not exactly the hot cause of the nineties. That she had attached so much importance to it, that she had truly *believed* in the fight against it, now embarrassed her, and inwardly she resented her thesis adviser for not counseling her against the ill-conceived project. He probably hadn't even read the whole thing, but had given her the A-plus based solely on the manuscript's surprising length and—she could admit this now—because he had a crush on her. Working with John she had learned so much about the legal system that she no longer saw the need to create some new civil-rights field or even enter one of the existing ones. In fact, corporate law, which she had long eschewed as a heartless, boring trade, was turning out to be quite interesting.

She sat on the couch beside Shannon and watched CNN. The third roommate came in from the kitchen, the corners of her mouth pasty with powdered sugar. Donuts, probably. If Shannon lacked Elena's stunning beauty, she at least was not threatened by it. Kim, on the other hand, consoled herself by eating too much, thereby ruining her naturally plain looks. To prove her attractiveness to herself she slept with whatever blind-drunk boys would have her, and they slinked out of the apartment hungover at dawn vowing never to drink again. "Got a date?" she asked, wiping the powdered sugar from the corners of her mouth into her hairy forearm.

"Sure do. David Michaelson."

"He's cute."

"And what are you up to tonight?"

"Getting wasted, probably," Kim said. "There are a couple of parties, and this guy that likes me will be at one or the other. He slept with me last weekend."

"Has he called?" Shannon asked.

"His phone's not installed yet, I think."

ELENA ALMOST DIDN'T recognize David Michaelson, though his attire was typical Magnate casual: khakis and a button-down shirt. In the few short months since he had started his intense management-training program, working some eighteen hours per day regularly, his hairline had radically receded. Twenty-three now, and when he smiled there were deep crow's feet at the corners of his eyes. In the taxi she patted him affectionately on the belly, which had grown soft, and told him he needed to start running. "Tell me about it," he said, "but my job . . ." And that was it.

He talked about his job for the rest of the night. Occasionally he caught himself rambling, and asked her about her own work. Did she think it was preparing her for law school? How long was her workday generally? Did she like her boss? But every answer she gave served only to remind him of something he had forgotten to tell her, some subplot to a subplot (like this dinner date, she sensed: DAVE TAKES ELENA OUT) within the ongoing hit movie of his life and work. In keeping with his primary goal tonight, he did manage to pause at intervals to try to talk her into another margarita.

"No, but you go ahead."

"You don't mind? God, it's been so long."

He was hammered by the time they walked out of the restaurant. He threw his arms high and shouted, "I love New York!" They found another bar. As drunk as he was, Dave lost his deterrent factor. Other young men now began trying to engage Elena in conversation. Often they began with an ironic remark about her date, who, eyelids half shut, was carrying on an ill-defined, one-way political discussion with a bartender who was trying to ignore him.

She thought about her friend and employer. Had he ever, even in his youth, behaved this badly? What was he doing now? Cognac. Baltazar Brantley. Perhaps a fine cigar.

She would not have guessed that he was pickling his epiglottis in shot after shot of Cuervo.

WINCING, HE SLAMMED the shot glass down. Across the table Andy exhaled a cloud of cigarette smoke. "Feel better yet?"

"Yeah." But for the second or third time since meeting Andy outside Proof Required he had the sensation that the kid was eyeing his hair. "What is it, what are you looking at?"

"Nothing."

Was the bar called Proof Required because everyone was so young, or did young people gravitate here because of the name? The music was just loud enough to turn everyone into confidantes, forcing them to lean toward each other's ears and speak with a mild sense of urgency. Still in a lawyer suit, John pinched his briefcase between his ankles and tried to bob his head in time to the music as he watched his son expertly weave through the crowd to the bar. The kid made it back without spilling any of either beer. "That's why you sent me to college, you know. I sort of majored in Keg Access."

"I guess Dartmouth was good for that, huh?"

"It really prepared me for the future." The kid gave himself a foam mustache and wiped it into his shirtsleeve. "I've been thinking you should give me your Porsche, Dad. Seriously, what good does it do you? You're fifty years old and married. Now, if it were mine I'd look like the rich kid I grew up being, and you wouldn't look like some old guy in a midlife crisis. Not that I'm saying you're having one." He glanced up again at John's hair.

"If you want a Porsche, work your butt off for twenty-five years. How much they pay you at MTV?"

"Hell, I couldn't even afford a set of hubcaps for that car. In fact, I've thought about stealing yours. Doesn't matter that I'm virtually indispensable around the network, I'm quote low-level end quote, so my salary's low. As long as we're asking, how much do you make?"

The kid had never asked before. John almost told him to mind his own business but then decided to sock it to him. "Last year? After bonus? Seven hundred and fifty thousand."

He expected the kid to call such an income obscene and unjust, to repeat the weak anti-capitalist platitudes of some Marxist professor at Dartmouth from whom Andy had taken a single course. But instead the kid said something surprising. "You ought to at least be able to afford better hair coloring. You're making it too black."

It took John a moment to get the meaning. "You think I'm dyeing my hair?"

"I can see you're dyeing your hair, which I understand. It goes with the Porsche." He took a big swig of beer. "You're doing it a little at a time, right? Maybe most people won't notice."

"What are you talking about?" John glanced around. An attractive young woman who was crammed against him had overheard some of the conversation and was looking up at his hair. "I don't dye my hair," he told her.

"Fine," Andy said. "I take it back. It's just turning black again on its own."

"Watch my briefcase." John made his way through the crowd to the bathroom. Leaning close to the mirror, he turned his head to either side. Maybe Andy had a point: the ratio of salt to pepper seemed to have gone down a bit. But perhaps it was only that his attitude had simply become more youthful, making him seem younger, making his hair *seem* a bit darker. In a few days he would check it again for any further development.

Walking back toward his son, he scanned the crowd just on the off chance that Elena's date had been crude enough to bring her here. No such luck. But he was having a good time anyway— God, how long had it been since he had really *tied one on*, as he and his friends had used to say. Among all these young people he began to feel young again, just as a dog that lives only with human beings begins to imagine himself their equal. Or superior.

He and Andy had three pints each at Proof Required, and then Andy suggested another place for dinner. "You can meet some of my friends. Besides, it's probably been a while since you rode the subway, huh?" Years, in fact. The first car they boarded was nearly empty. Looking around, John saw why. Right in the middle of the floor was a huge red puddle, unmistakably blood. Huge! The Red fucking Sea! People had traipsed through it, leaving footprints all over the car. John and Andy would have retreated to the platform, but the doors closed and the train lurched forward, nearly spilling them both to the bloody floor. After a moment they began to laugh. "Look how it vibrates," Andy said. A moment later he said, "We can get off at the next stop and wait for another train if you want."

"Nah."

They met a couple of Andy's MTV co-peons down in the Village. Like Andy but to a greater degree they affected a sort of glamorous fatalism and a disdain for both past and future, the first because it was nothing but kitsch, and the second because no amount of kitsch could save it. Kristen Newton arrived. Not having seen John since that November cookout, she was shocked at his improved physical appearance. She patted his belly and said, "Wow. Andy, you're going to have to start doing some sit-ups, boy." The kid rolled his eyes.

"I've lost twenty pounds, mostly in my gut," John volunteered.

"I've been running a lot and even doing some lifting in the health club downstairs."

One of the MTV boys said, "Lifting? My God, what for?"

"Just to be in shape."

"But why?"

"How's your new paralegal working out?" Kristen asked.

"That's right," Andy said. "Is she really such a babe?"

"Well, I imagine someone her own age would find her attractive, yes."

"And you don't?"

"Hell, sure I do." He had added another beer to the healthy Cuervo base. "I'm a man. Things don't just stop working when you turn forty or forty-five or even fifty. Elena Conifer is a top-notch paralegal and a brilliant future lawyer who just happens to be drop-dead gorgeous. But she's so young. She makes me feel sort of fatherly to her, you know?"

"God help her," Andy said.

The cheeseburgers were tall and magnificent. John kept having to wipe the juice from his chin until his napkin looked like a castoff bandage. He ate all of his fries and then started in on Kristen's. "Take it easy, Dad, you're going to put all that weight back on." But he had lost the weight without cutting back on his food intake. Just the opposite, he had increased it, and without considering fat content, food groups, the new pyramid chart, or any quacky nutritionist stuff whatsoever. Three times in the past week he had eaten steak and eggs for lunch at a little diner three blocks from the firm. At a doctor's appointment recently he learned that his cholesterol level was down to one hundred fifty. "Must be all that bran cereal," the doc had said.

When the check arrived, everyone dug out their wallets. Andy inspected the bill. "All right, who had the side of slaw?" Only then did John realize what was happening, so long had it been since he had witnessed this ritual of the starting-salaried. He magnanimously waved his gold card at the passing waiter. "It's all on me." As if stunned, the others waited a moment before repocketing their wallets. He accepted the mumbled gratitude of the MTV guys. Andy thanked him, too, though he seemed to have expected such a move all along.

The MTV guys took off just as one of Kristen's roommates ar-

rived for the next leg of the journey. Almost immediately she
paired off with John as the four strolled around the Village, trying
to decide where next to drink. Jasmine was the girl's name, she
was a beautiful second-generation Chinese, and they talked on
and on about her publishing job. Finally she said, "So what's
your connection with these two? You work for MTV?"

The realization that she did not know he was Andy's father
warmed him. Suddenly everything she had said was transformed
retroactively from polite conversation to exploratory, flirtatious
banter. He glanced over at his son and saw the kid listening with
a big grin on his face.

"Wilt thou deny me?" the kid asked.

"I'm Andy's father," John admitted.

"Really?" She blushed. "How old were you?"

"Twenty-five."

"He's fifty now," Andy said.

Jasmine balked at the news.

"I run a lot. It keeps me in shape."

"How are your heels?" Kristen asked. "We're thinking about a
place a few blocks uptown, and it's a nice night, but we could
take a cab if you're having trouble walking."

"Are you kidding?" The suggestion embarrassed him. Jasmine
seemed to treat him as if he were suddenly more fragile, and her
conversation died into politeness. At the first opportunity she fell
in beside Kristen. Andy patted his father on the back. "I had no
idea you were such a flirt, Dad."

"Was I flirting? I didn't feel like it."

"Not feeling much of anything, are you?"

"I'm a little toasted."

"You're not driving that Porsche home tonight. I'd hate for you
to damage it. You'll have to take the train or else stay over at my
place."

From a pay phone they called Elizabeth and told her not to
expect him. She was not happy. John handed the phone to Andy.
"We're just having a good time, Mom. I'll keep him out of trouble, I promise." A moment later the kid said, "No, his heels are
fine, Mom." And then, "He's not going to have a stroke, and if he
does I'll take him to the emergency room myself." He rolled his
eyes while Elizabeth spoke, finally interrupting her. "If they're

only seeing gunshot victims, I'll borrow someone's gun and shoot him in the leg or something."

At one-thirty, John carried a round of tequila shots to their table in some other bar; he wasn't even sure what part of town they were in anymore. Andy and the girls looked at him as if he were crazy. "I really shouldn't," Kristen was saying. Jasmine said she simply wouldn't: "I've got to get up early."

"Me too, Dad."

"The night is young. I'm fine, aren't I?" He threw back a shot. "Jasmine, you're not going to drink that?" When she shook her head he picked up the glass with his lips and turned it straight up. Empty, it fell from his mouth, and he bobbled it with both hands, finally pinning it against his crotch.

"Drink up, son!"

Andy shook his head. "You're a very bad influence." He threw both remaining shots into his mouth at once and downed them in a single gulp. Only momentarily was his face contorted, and then it took on an expression of drunken pride.

"That's my boy."

Kristen and Jasmine exchanged a look: let's get the hell home. John and Andy waited with them while they hailed a cab. As the taillights pulled away, John said, "Do you think they had fun?"

"I think you scared the crap out of them."

He looked around the lively sidewalks, the brightly lit streets, and took a deep whiff of the city air—urine, sweat, carbon monoxide. "Ahhh! I'm hungry."

"Dad," Andy protested.

"We need protein. If we go to bed without eating, we'll be sick in the morning."

A few minutes later he was mopping egg yolk from his plate with a folded, buttered piece of toast. Andy had also opted for the traditional breakfast—three fried eggs with ham, hash browns, and toast—but didn't seem to be enjoying his as much. "Isn't this great?" John asked. "I used to do this all the time."

Andy's face had begun to sag from fatigue. He looked on with bewilderment as his father, in a state of alert intoxication, dropped an extra pat of butter onto his hash browns. "I'm impressed. I really am. You're an animal, Dad."

"I always thought I wanted what I now have—the house, the money and all that. Imagine my surprise. Imagine my surprise."

The kid sat back. "Now you're worrying me."

"You should've been worried long before. It's too late now. Now I'm getting to be okay."

He woke in a strange room to the sound of someone being sick into a nearby toilet. As he began to remember things he looked around for his briefcase. At first he did not see it, and a jolt of panic ran through his body. Then he realized it was beneath his head on the couch; it was his pillow.

He sat up into a shaft of sunlight coming in through a window. Turned his head slowly, first one way and then the other. He was not hungover at all. He felt like taking a little run.

Through the open bathroom door he saw the hunched back of his puking son. "How you feeling?"

The kid raised his head from the toilet. "I'm not as young as I used to be."

AND ACROSS TOWN, David Michaelson, the Wall Street guy, was slinking out of Elena's apartment.

CHAPTER 5

CABBING UPTOWN FROM Andy's apartment, John changed his destination from the garaged Silver Missile to a certain café at Eighty-third and Third. He stared at the front door for a moment, feeling foolish, and was about to turn around when Elena opened it, smiling brilliantly, her hair held back by a wide purple band. Much to his relief she really was eating alone—toasted bagel with jelly, small orange juice, and coffee in a clear glass mug. He had feared finding her across the table from David the Wall Street guy, both of them awkward with a sudden and total physical familiarity.

Instead it was John Ashe who got to sit across from her. He feigned disappointment at how poorly her date had gone.

"First he takes me out, he gets really sloppy drunk—it was embarrassing enough just being seen with him. Then we go to this party full of equally hammered people, and my roommate is there."

"Shannon?"

"Her, too, but I mean Kim, the fat one who sleeps around a lot. Anyway, I came out of the bathroom and found them kissing in the corner. So I just left. As I was getting my coat he waved bye. About two a.m. I woke up—there was this constant thumping sound. Kim's headboard banging the wall on the other side of my bed. This morning I got up early to get some water, and good old David Michaelson quietly opens the door to Kim's bedroom and steps out wearing only his boxers, holding his clothes in his hands."

"What did he say?"

"He got all sheepish and tried to apologize, but he wouldn't

56

talk at normal volume for fear of waking up his new woman and maybe having to have breakfast with her or something. She was snoring so loudly that he probably didn't need to worry. I just went back into my room and shut the door. I swear, John, young people are by definition philistines. I'm sure I would rather have been with you, doing something more . . . reasonable than running around getting drunk. And being stared at by everyone with a gram of testosterone in his blood, not that you don't have at least a gram. What did you end up doing?"

He gave her a watered-down account of the previous night, a quiet dinner with his son and his son's girlfriend, "who I think you know, actually. Her name's Kristen Newton."

She turned her head, smiling. "What does she have to say about me?"

"Nothing. She said to say hello."

"Really? I'm surprised. I lived with her sister at Magnate our first year. For about six months. I started going out with a guy named Jake Coates—"

"You went out with a guy named Jake?"

"Yes, a guy named Jake. Anyway, it turned out Pam Newton, Kristen's sister, had been secretly in love with him from afar all along. She couldn't handle it. She refused to eat, she had to be hospitalized. In the end they transferred her to a different room. But none of it was my fault."

They walked around enjoying the rest of the morning and then had lunch at the Barrister Bistro.

"I look forward to meeting Elizabeth someday. She must be fantastic."

"She's talked about having you over, too." He smiled. "She's a very admirable woman, pretty set in her ways, though."

She walked him to the garage. When he asked her what she was going to do that night she said she wanted to catch up on her reading. "I'm reading everything by Baltazar Brantley. Don't you just love *Unto the Seventh Generation?*"

"One of my favorites," he said.

ELIZABETH WAS SWINGING through the foyer, her glance stopping momentarily on the book in his hand. "What's that?"

"*Unto the Seventh Generation*, Baltazar Brantley. I've been meaning to get to it for a while now."

"Really? You don't seem to like the one Andy gave you for Christmas."

"Well, some people at work were talking about this one. I thought I'd give it a try."

She took the book and read the jacket blurbs. "I've not read this one, but I've heard it's good. I've always found him so adept at describing the private condition."

"What do you mean?"

Flattered by his sudden interest in her literary insights, she continued sharing them with him on the couch in the family room. He didn't reach for the remote control to turn on Larry King, but instead listened intently to Elizabeth's theories, hoping for some insight into the character of his new paralegal. Then she stopped in mid-sentence, staring through the window to the backyard. "William and Anne are getting a divorce."

"Hmm. I guess that's no surprise. Although Kristen was with us last night and she didn't say anything."

"Some of the teachers were talking about it. It's just *everyone knows*, it's got to be so humiliating for Anne." She suddenly hugged him tightly. His vertebrae, still slightly misaligned because he had slept on the couch, cracked back into place. The sound alarmed Elizabeth into loosening her hold enough that he could run his hands over her broad back. "I love you, John. I'm glad we'll never have to go through that."

"It would be nice to avoid."

She cooked that night, something she never really had time to do anymore, what with her administrative and pedagogical duties at GCDS. Broiled swordfish, lightly boiled asparagus, and angel food cake for dessert. "You just had a perfectly satisfying meal, and it was very low in fat," she said at the end. "I want you to keep that in mind, it *is* possible. Now that your cholesterol is finally under control, we don't want to backtrack."

He refrained from telling her about the steak and egg lunches he'd been having, the cheeseburger last night, his bedtime snack of fried eggs, ham, and hash browns.

"Did you drink too much last night?" she asked.

"No one counts drinks when they're in the city."

"It's okay." She struck a rare tone of permissiveness. "Every now and then you can have one or two extras without causing much trouble."

More like ten, he thought, topping off his lemon mineral water.

"Maggie Calloway stopped me in the grocery store tonight," she said. "She saw you somewhere, and at first she thought it must have been your younger brother. I told her you don't have one. She wanted to know if you've had plastic surgery or liposuction or called Jenny Craig or what. I told her no, I was just feeding you a very strict diet."

She reached across to touch his hair. "But she's right, John. You do look radically younger, so much younger it's hard to believe. You make me feel so old all of a sudden."

"I guess it's the running, now that my heels don't hurt. Maybe you should run or exercise or something, Elizabeth."

It was a risk. Her sedentary nature had long been a sore point between them. To his surprise she did not challenge the assumption that she should get some more exercise; she merely protested that no method suited her. Running hurt her knees, walking took too long, aerobics was too dangerous, lifting weights was silly, and she couldn't swim. But whose knees wouldn't creak a bit beneath such an untended bulk?

"It's not just the physical changes," Elizabeth said. "You've changed in other ways. Are you sure it's just the running that's doing it?"

"Just the running, Elizabeth. Nothing else has changed."

"Promise? You still love me and everything?"

"Of course. Listen to you." He reached across and touched her face.

"I had some silly dream about you having an affair. But I know that'll never happen." She paused, waited for him to second this. He merely stared at her, smiling slightly. "You had plenty of opportunity for that when you were young," she continued, "and you never fell for it then, which I appreciate."

The comment offended him. Though still smiling, his face darkened. She seemed to be saying that she had looked forward to his physical deterioration as some sort of insurance against his nonexistent philandering. He would stay with her not because of any promise he had made but because the wrinkles on his face,

the saggy chin, the tube of fat around his waist, and his bursitis
limp would make him too unappealing for anyone else. She must
have been feeling quite comfortable along about last November,
when her main responsibility was to keep old moneybags breathing for a few more years. And now that he looked better, she felt
threatened. Hell, she could lose some weight if she wanted to,
couldn't she? He looked at her, considered it, and decided probably not. She was just big, and it was no easier to imagine her any
other way than it was to imagine Elena at one-eighty. His wife
would lose no weight until she began to shrivel and hunch with
old age.

Staring at her, he realized that her comment carried a second
implication, that he had somehow missed his chance—or worse,
been afraid to take it. Did she imagine him stilted and tongue-
tied in front of beautiful women, comically befuddled like some
lovable old character actor, the fucking comic relief?

In truth, he had found faithfulness easy to maintain, but not
because of the various reasons she seemed to suspect, and not
because he loved her, though he did. He had simply been too
busy. Not just the days but the years had rolled by, and the train
had rolled in and out of the city, Elizabeth calculating all the
while that soon it would be too late, he was getting too old, *had
missed his chance.*

"I suppose you'd be a hell of a lot happier if I'd snap an Achilles, get fat, and have to hobble around on a cane."

"You weren't fat. You just looked your age."

"And now that I'm in good shape, you feel threatened."

"No, no, I'm happy for you."

He tried to relax a bit. There was no point in hashing this out
just after she had gained the moral high ground by cooking dinner. Instead he sulked into the next room, missed my chance . . .

She surprised him again, her hands encircling his waist from
behind. He felt her swordfish breath in his ear as she whispered,
"Let's go upstairs."

It had been several weeks. Upstairs, he stripped to his underwear before the mirror, observing his body's new youthfulness.
"It's amazing how running picks up your metabolism," he observed aloud by way of suggestion. Flexing his stomach, he could
just make out the blocks of muscle he had seen, in more distinct

form, on professional bodybuilders and eighteen-year-old lifeguards. As much puzzled as pleased, he stood on the bed. In the mirror he could see himself from the neck down, and when he ducked to make sure it was his head on that body, he had the sensation of looking at an obviously doctored photograph. Hair was growing on his legs again, dark curly hair, thick stuff that he had feared had been permanently rubbed off by years of wearing suit pants. The skin seemed healthier, stretched tightly over a supple muscularity of thigh and calf.

"Aren't you going to undress?" he asked. Elizabeth was weighing down the end of the bed, staring at the bend of her thick knees. He slipped his underwear down and stepped out of it. He was straight up, hard and tall, the head nearly purple with rigidity. This genital youthfulness was something he had first noticed a few nights ago when he found himself trying to suppress the urge to masturbate. Matter winning over mind, he had stood in the bathroom jerking off like a schoolboy to an imagined sexual encounter with Elena. The load he shot was startling in its thickness, volume, and range. He'd had to clean the mirror.

Now Elizabeth reached up to touch what she had not even seen in so long, most of their so-called lovemaking occurring in darkness, under the covers, as if the transaction were something shameful. She pulled her hand back as if his thing had pricked her. "It hasn't been that hard for years." She stared at it. "And it's lasting."

"Undress, why don't you?"

She got up on her knees and took him into her mouth, working it slowly for a couple of minutes while he clutched the back of her head and stared at the gray hairs sprouting up between his slightly parted fingers. What had gotten into her? Years since she had done this for him. Best not to question it. She pulled away, stood up. "Don't go anywhere." She took her neck-to-toe nightie from the closet and was about to walk into the bathroom when he sighed in disappointment. She whirled, tears in her eyes. "I can't undress in front of you!"

Once in the bathroom she refused to come out until he turned off the bedroom lights, and he refused to turn off the bedroom lights unless she just once, Elizabeth, forgot about the nightgown. Finally she agreed. He turned out the lights. Suddenly she was streaking past him, diving under the covers. He yanked them back, grabbed her by the ankles, and planted her feet far apart. He entered her in a single stroke, surprised at how wet she already was. For the first time since before Andy was born she was a noisy lover, clutching his back, kissing his chest. As he pumped away he closed his eyes and she became Elena.

He wanted to come on her, wanted her to see the volume. Just before the explosive moment he pulled out, surprising her at first. He grabbed his cock and pumped it a couple of times, Elizabeth watching wide-eyed. The force just kept building up at the root until he thought he might pass out, and then the thing recoiled. A wad of semen thunked against the headboard, loud as a spitball. The second spurt streaked her from hairline to belly button, and the final spasms left a thick white puddle on the cracked earth of her stretch marks. He squeezed out the last few drops on her thigh.

She sat up, a dollop of semen at the corner of her mouth and tears in her eyes.

"What's wrong?"

"You were thinking of someone else."

He almost asked, *What does it matter?* Instead he swore that he had been thinking only of you, Elizabeth, and after a while she said she believed him.

```
┌─────────────────────────────┐
│                             │
│   C H A P T E R   6         │
│                             │
└─────────────────────────────┘
```

NATHAN BARRADALE'S REACTION to Lee's heart attack had been to stop running altogether. Now whenever John saw his old buddy in the Hallway of Death, he teased him about the extra pudge he was putting on. Barradale would only laugh and cite another study. "They say alcohol is good for the heart, you know. So considering this new information I've restructured my workouts." He cited studies supposedly showing that very light exercise provided the same cardiovascular benefits as, say, running. "You only get one set of joints," he would say. "I don't want to have terrible arthritis when I'm eighty-five."

"Or even older," John said, "if you keep drinking all that alcohol and improving your heart."

"That's right."

The practical upshot of all this was that the Silver Milers had ceased to exist, which was just as well for John, since probably no one in the firm, not even the spry boys in the mail room, could keep up with him. The one person he was willing to slow down for was thirty-four-year-old vixen Kelly Epstein, who seemed to have developed a flattering crush on him.

During one of their outings she remarked that Elena didn't seem to like her very much. "I think she's feeling a bit territorial. Girls that age can be pretty unrealistic sometimes."

"What do you mean, 'territorial'?"

"Don't play dumb. Hey, if it wouldn't be too complicated, you'd be crazy not to sleep with her, right? I mean, she's beautiful and so young."

"I haven't even thought about it."

"John, don't even try. I'm not even saying you're a creep for wanting to, which a lot of women would say. I mean, it's natural to lust, right?"

Stunned, for he had never known her to discuss such issues, he just let her continue.

"The trouble with her is that she'd want it to turn serious, and you've already got a wife. You need a more mature woman who wouldn't get things all jumbled up and expect you to leave whatsername."

"Elizabeth."

"Oh, yeah, Elizabeth."

There was only one way to deal with this turn of conversation. He increased the pace to the point where Kelly was too winded to speak. With a mile left he asked her if he could run on ahead and wait for her at the end. She nodded, wheezing, and slowed to a walk.

Darting ahead, John felt again as though his life was not passing him by, time was not defeating him. He was running just ahead of the tip of its arrow, so fast the people on the benches stared after him, this lunch hour athlete sprinting by like a high school boy with no fear of injury or heart attack, no mental register of pulmonary pain or muscular exhaustion. He made a strange sight, he knew, for despite the improvements in his physical appearance it was still clear that he was no young sprite, but an affluent white man racing nobody in particular through Central Park. At the Met he stopped, checked his watch, and realized that he must have misremembered his starting time, because there was no way he could have run a mile in five minutes and fifty-two seconds.

Some three minutes later, Kelly trotted up huffing and puffing. "Wow, that was fast. You should maybe consider entering a race or something."

"I've thought about it."

She patted his flat belly through his T-shirt. "You'd probably win your age group."

It was an unseasonably warm day for February, and they decided to walk rather than jog back to the firm. Kelly was finally catching her breath. "So how are you and whatsername getting along?"

"Elizabeth? She thinks I'm crazy for running so much. Other than that, we're getting along."

Kelly was about to say something, stopped herself, and then after a moment of consideration proceeded. "I'm generally pretty happy with the life I've made for myself in New York. I mean, everything's here. You can do almost anything you want . . ."

"But."

"But. Let me put it this way. I just got a nice new apartment but there's no one to share it with, even for just a few minutes right after work, say. I mean, the dating scene is so scary, all these diseases going around. But people are sexual creatures, and they need that little extra oomph sometimes just to keep their sanity. I'm not saying I'd like to get married or even have a long-term serious relationship. I guess what I'm saying is I just need someone who'll give me that little extra oomph every now and then."

He understood it to be a proposition, but one made in such a way that he could choose to let it go over his head. "I'm sure someone like you would have no problem. You're young, very attractive and all that, seems like you could get that little extra oomph whenever you wanted it."

"But I want it from someone I'm attracted to, someone who hasn't been sleeping around all these years and who is therefore safer." More bluntly she added, "Someone who doesn't want to leave his wife, but just needs a little extra oomph sometimes him-self."

A moment later she asked, "You really think I'm attractive?"

"Absolutely."

There was a moment when Kelly could have gone into a pout at being denied. She seemed to consider it, lowering her head, but then she raised it smiling. "Just let me know if you think of anyone who falls within the parameters of my description."

He laughed, nodding, the cool air drying the sweat on his face.

WITH JOHN'S TACIT approval Elena began to neglect her clerical and administrative tasks in favor of her research duties, so that the message light on her phone was always blinking and her stack of unopened internal mail was always precariously high.

She would often begin the day by studying a case obviously relevant to John's current work, but then stray into questionable precedents and minor rulings, sometimes from provincial foreign judges. The discussions she and John had about her discoveries often lasted through lunch and most of the afternoon, as the work piled up, and as various associates and assistants to other partners came for his signature on this or that document, many of them remarking that his office always smelled of Chinese food. In early February, vaguely aware that his partners were beginning to resent his new work habits, John halfheartedly promised himself to do better. But it was so much more fun to sit on the leather couch and talk with Elena, occasionally trading a little lemon chicken for a forkful of her hot *kung pao.*

Valentine's Day he found a heart-shaped card on his desk. When he opened it, a subscription notice for *Distance Running* fluttered to his feet. There was no preprinted message inside, Elena not being one for store-bought sentiment. She had written:

Dear John,

I just want to thank you for giving me the chance to work with you. I've learned so much about law, as expected. But I could not have guessed I would learn so much about life, or that you and I would become such good friends. Thanks.

Love,
Elena

John looked at the clock, then looked out the window. The roses he had ordered were supposed to be here already. As he reread Elena's note the suspense he felt at the impending delivery was momentarily overcome by a feeling of joy. Then he checked his wristwatch. Where was the damn florist?

Finally he heard Elena's excited voice through his closed office door. "Who from!" And then his door opened. She was holding the vase away from her body, but the red roses, on long stems, still grazed her smile. She put them down on the edge of his desk and threw her arms around his neck, moistening his cheek with a brief kiss. "No one's ever sent me a whole dozen before."

"No one's ever given me *Distance Running* before."

Acting of their own accord, his hands clasped the narrow small of her back. Her breath, through the straight white teeth of her smile, displaced a lock of his hair. They held the hug for a few moments. He pulled away just as his rising cock was about to nudge her abdomen. He sat down to conceal the bulge.

"So who's taking you out tonight?"

"I'm just going out with Shannon."

"Good. I don't want to have to get protective." He shuffled some papers. "Elizabeth and I will probably go out. Someplace healthy."

"That's nice."

She sat in one of his guest chairs, and they began a rambling conversation which arrived via multiple tangents at a discussion of *Unto the Seventh Generation*. "I've always found Brantley to be so adept at describing the private condition," he said, beginning a lengthy repetition of Elizabeth's impromptu lecture about the novelist. He wished he could say something of his own, or at least credit the source of his words. He finally got the chance when Elena disputed one of his points. "Yeah," he conceded, "I don't really buy that myself. Elizabeth got that in her head for some reason. She's generally such a good reader, too."

He had a road race coming up in Groveton, a ten-miler organized by the Kiwanis Club, and Elena wanted to come see him run.

"Well, my wife will probably be there. Of course, the only reason she's going is so she can cart me to the hospital afterward if I need it, which I sometimes think she half hopes I will. To teach me a lesson."

"Oh, I doubt it. It's okay if I go, too, isn't it? I'd love to meet her."

"Yeah, it's just at this point she's not too confident in how she looks. And if she sees how beautiful you are . . ."

A moment of silence, which she broke. "Why, thank you."

"My wife, the years have been sort of hard on her. I still love her, but we have a lot less in common now than we did when we first married. That's one of the reasons I like talking to you so much. I feel more connected to the younger generation sometimes."

"It's because you really are young, John. Know what? I think you should enter the New York Marathon."

He made a self-deprecating grunt, which he hoped didn't make him sound too old. "I wouldn't mind it. But I really am fifty. I don't want to push my luck."

"Watch you win the whole thing."

"Oh . . ."

"Well, Kelly Epstein says you're really fast."

He smiled at the thought of actually running the New York Marathon.

BACK AT HER desk, Elena received florist after florist, each making paltry deliveries of one to six roses. David Michaelson sent a dozen carnations and a note about his "mistake" last fall. Nice try. She kept looking at the dozen roses her boss had given her.

Elena's main complaint with the boys who pursued her was that they were too immature. There were cute guys her own age, sure, but they cared about only one thing, and they weren't even very good at it yet. An older man would likely be a more patient lover, would not express himself in foolish ways like the boy who had overnighted a series of love letters to her parents' beach house while the family was on vacation. Every morning her father had to get up early to open the door for the FedEx guy, who became increasingly sheepish and apologetic with each of his five consecutive deliveries.

And that suitor's behavior was not atypical. They didn't all send FedEx love notes, but they all did equally strange things that revealed their compulsive desperation rather than any actual personal value, about them or her. Perhaps worst of all was that she had to put up with the bar scene even to meet one of these well-meaning types. Straining over bad, loud music to hear liars exaggerate the importance of their entry-level jobs was not her idea of a good way to spend an evening. She preferred to discuss books and legal cases and life in general with a Renaissance man like John Ashe.

Yet she told herself that she didn't want John—wasn't ready to admit that—but someone *exactly like* John, some other considerate, handsome, established man of experience. Not that if John weren't married she wouldn't go for him. She told herself how lucky his wife was, and tried to make herself happy for Elizabeth, whom she had never met but who seemed to cause John so much constant, minor aggravation. She felt he deserved better.

THREE DAYS LATER they both worked late, and John decided that a meal on the firm wouldn't be out of order. Le Cirque, perhaps. But Elena wasn't dressed for it and very likely John would have run into one or two colleagues surprised to see him with a woman so clearly not his wife. Now that he thought about it, years ago he had once run into Elena's father at Le Cirque.

The Union Square Cafe, then. Elena seemed to fit in so naturally, long and elegant at the table, that she might never have slurped up ramen noodles in her college dorm room. She ate her grilled salmon with relish. John went for the red meat, filet mignon rare. So insulated and self-sufficient did the two non-lovers seem that John was surprised when Elena said someone two tables away looked familiar. Between laughing at his jokes and staring into his eyes, when had she had time to notice?

He glanced over at Marathon King Reynaldo Miller. The runner was eating the grilled salmon. His companion was a full-figured woman about his age whose gentle, lilting voice—though John could not make out a single word—bespoke her southern roots.

"That's Reynaldo Miller, the marathoner," he whispered. "I've run with him in the park before."

"You know him?"

"Nah, we just see each other in the park now and again."

He ordered another bottle of wine. "Are you sure?" Elena asked, and for a moment he worried that she had been counting his drinks like a wife. "It's seems a bit expensive."

"You're kidding, right? First of all, the firm's paying. But even if it weren't, why did I work so hard every day for so many years and ride the damn train back and forth if not to enjoy evenings like this one without worrying about the bill?"

"Well, in that case . . ." She smiled. "This is really nice of you, John."

For dessert Elena chose something tall and chocolate. She had said that she never worried about her weight, just as she rarely wore makeup and then but a touch. Her exercise program was sporadic and varied, and sometimes nonexistent for stretches of four or five days. When he discovered this, his suspicions grew that she was not susceptible to deterioration. Unlike the carefully forged, precarious attractiveness of so many young women, her own longevity of beauty was not dependent on a time-consuming exercise program.

Coincidentally they stood to leave at the same time Reynaldo Miller and companion did. On the way out John caught the Marathon King's eye. "How you doing?"

The Marathon King smiled warily. "All right."

"Reynaldo Miller, right?"

"Do we know each other?"

"We ran in the park once."

Miller smiled more warmly. "I must have been warming up." The woman he was with smiled at Elena and then said, "Rey, honey, we got to get goin'." Apologetically she explained, "Rey and I are goin' to a play."

"Sounds great," Elena said.

And that was it. "He didn't seem to remember you," Elena said as he walked her home.

"I know. We ran together for a while, too."

"Did you see his cheekbones? They looked like table corners."

"I wish I were that young sometimes."

"But you're so much better-looking than he is."

"Thanks."

The stares of the young men reminded John of that first day he had walked with her up Fifth Avenue, stopping in at Godiva for that box of chocolates. She noticed it too this time, and took his arm to quash any hopeful speculation that he was her father.

At her building they stopped a few yards from the watchful doorman. "My dad says walk-ups are for guys."

"He's right."

She glanced over at the doorman. "Victor's a good watchdog."

"Yes, well, I can feel him staring, all right."

It was a relief that she wasn't going to ask him up. What the hell would he have said? But now she stood on her toes to hug him and buss his cheek. "Thank you for a wonderful evening."

As he drove home, the ridges on his steering wheel reminded him of Elena's spine through her blouse.

When he opened the door at one a.m. Elizabeth was swinging through the foyer in her nightgown, carrying a glass of water. She said that no, she had not been worried about him. She assumed he had a business dinner or something. Which of course was technically the truth.

CHAPTER 7

WARMING UP FOR the Kiwanis Club Ten-Miler, he kept a close eye on the other men he guessed to be in his age group. What he saw and heard annoyed him—guys who'd done a lot in their lives now saying things like, "I just want to finish," and "I may have to walk a bit." They huddled around together, nervous and chattery, telling stories about their chronic injuries and the treatments that had failed to heal them. John felt no connection to these guys at all. It was a conscious effort not to let his contempt show. He did not act on his one moderately charitable impulse, which was to warn a squat old man who was built exactly like Lee Thomas that perhaps he should take up leisurely walking instead of road racing.

In being apart from the crowd, in being generally serious, John attracted attention to himself. They stared at him with a sort of boyish admiration for the best athlete at recess. His physical appearance had changed so much that in a department store the other day he had inadvertently greeted his own reflection as it passed across a huge mirror.

Knees locked, he leaned over and pressed his palms to the asphalt until his hamstrings were nice and loose. While in that position he heard his wife's cautionary wail. "Johhhn! Be carefuuul!" She sounded so far away. Even when he looked up and saw her, an anomalous large person in this crowd of exercise enthusiasts, he could no more speak to her than to a character on television. He turned away toward the starting line, glad that he had finally been able to talk Elena out of showing up, and half hoping that she would be waiting for him at the finish line anyway.

The young people lined up first, high school cross-country runners and recently graduated college athletes. They bounced on the chalk starting line, pulling their heels high to touch their buttocks, throwing their elbows back and forth as if they expected to have to vault a wall at some point during the race. John imitated them, even the way they breathed, making a circle of the lips and hollowing the cheeks. The runners up front began to settle down, planting their feet on the chalk line. The rest of the group fanned back in sections chalked off according to projected pace. The view from front to back provided a time-lapse picture of deterioration. Postures began to curl, hair turned gray and then white, legs began to look like whittled balsa.

This being his first race, John lined up in the eight-minute section though he knew he could run faster. He reasoned that it would be a kick to begin by passing a bunch of people. Then he decided that he was not being fair to himself—from this far back it would be twenty seconds before he even reached the starting line, and what if the eight-minute label became a self-fulfilling underestimation? He moved up to the seven-minute section. He planted one leg forward and clenched his fists. Someone kept brushing up against him, and he could smell the guy's old, unwashed running outfit. Depending on which way the breeze blew, he could also smell sun screen and Ben Gay.

The president of the Kiwanis Club, a prosperous-looking younger man, stepped up to the podium, his starter's pistol in hand. "Ladies and gentlemen, welcome to this year's Groveton Kiwanis Ten-Miler." He raised the gun. "On your mark, get set . . ." The gun sounded a percussive crack, the crowd cheered, and as a unit the runners surged forward, trying not to step on each other. The smelly guy kicked John twice within the first ten yards, and then the contenders began to spread out. The kicking stopped. No one passed John.

He ran at what felt like an easy pace, though people he passed glanced over at him with genuine concern. "You know this race is ten miles?" one guy huffed.

"Oh, right."

"Well, you better pace yourself."

The word "yourself" came at John from behind. Now he was up with several people he recognized from the 6:30 section, and they were all falling behind him. Still he did not even feel winded.

The route took them by Kurt Vermiel's house. The Nobel prize winner was taking a break from croquet to sit in a lawn chair and watch the runners pass. He recognized John and raised a hand in greeting. "How's it going?" John yelled.

Vermiel gave him the thumbs-up sign.

On the eighth mile it got a little tough, but not unpleasant. In his physical soreness and near exhaustion John felt a gratifying affirmation of being. His muscles tightened ever so slightly, and it was no longer pure, painless reflex to keep putting one foot in front of the other. At nine miles someone was calling out splits. John's group of four was at fifty-eight minutes. On that news one of them dropped back.

John looked at the other two. "Let's pick up the pace."

"Go for it," one of them said.

The word "it" came at John from behind. He passed people who looked over at him with puzzled expressions, sometimes glancing at their own wristwatches as if to make sure they had not slowed down.

At the finish line the runners were funneled into a chute beneath a giant digital clock displaying their times. John crossed the line in 64:45 and was given a Popsicle stick on which was written the number 75. So seventy-four people had beaten him.

Still, it had been a good race. Clutching his Popsicle stick, he walked over to the water table and gulped three paper cupfuls, some of it trickling down his chin and through the chest hair beneath his tank top.

A hand closed around his sweaty forearm. "Good run!" It was Elena, with another girl. "This is Shannon, my roommate. Not the one who sleeps around."

"I've heard a lot about you," Shannon said.

"All good, I hope."

"Actually, yes."

John looked at the finish line, where younger men were still huffing across, claiming their Popsicle sticks. "I thought about what you said awhile ago, Elena. That I should run the New York

Marathon. I don't think I will, but just the suggestion made me run faster."

She beamed at him. "I know you could do it if you really wanted to."

Shannon was scrutinizing John and Elena as if they were two characters on *Melrose Place*. Then her alternating gaze stopped between them, and her eyes widened as if at an oncoming train. "Who's that?"

Elizabeth. Coming through the crowd she smiled at the girls and frowned at John's heels. He kept shifting his weight from one foot to the other, not in demonstration of his lack of pain but with the obliviousness reserved for all well-working body parts.

She reached for his shoulder. He felt her grip slacken against his unexpected sweatiness. "Are you all right?"

"Sure. I feel great."

"You did really well." She smiled at Shannon. "I'm Elizabeth Ashe. You must be John's new paralegal."

"I'm just her roommate, but nice to meet you anyway."

"Oh, well, it must be you, then." She extended her hand to Elena.

"I'm Elena Conifer. It's a pleasure to finally meet you."

"Oh, well, of course we knew your father decades ago in law school. We have pictures of John holding you when you were a baby."

"Really?"

"Oh, yes. Your father used to help sneak me into the dorms. This was back when even in grad school you technically weren't supposed to be doing that sort of thing. That'll tell you how long ago it was."

John watched, fascinated. Was she consciously trying to remind the girls how old he was? "John and I really have to get you over to the house to meet our son," Elizabeth said. "I'm sure he'd love to meet you. He works for MTV, you know. They don't pay much, but I guess there's what he calls the 'glam factor.' He gets invited to neat parties and meets people like, oh, what's that rem guy, Michael something?"

John said, "R.E.M. Michael Snipe."

"Stipe," Shannon said.

Just then a chubby, smiling member of the Kiwanis Club approached holding a clipboard. He was staring at John's racing number. "There you are, number forty-two! You can stay for the awards ceremony, can't you?"

"I won something?"

"Oh, God," Elizabeth said.

"You won your age group. Fifty to fifty-five."

Elizabeth asked the official if he was sure about this. "I mean, you're responsible if you give him the encouragement that snaps his Achilles' tendon."

The race official checked his clipboard and looked up at John. "You're John Ashe, right?"

"That's right."

But the official was looking at him more critically now. "You wouldn't have a driver's license on you, would you? I should take a look at it just to confirm your age. There may be people who question if you're really fifty."

Elizabeth said, "We're real careful about what he eats." And from her purse she produced his wallet, which she had held for him during the race. "You know, low fat generally, not too much sugar or red meat."

Holding the driver's license up beside John's face for comparison, the race official said, "You're dyeing your hair."

"No. I am not."

Elizabeth said, "I haven't noticed any hair-coloring products in his bathroom."

The awards ceremony didn't start for another hour or so, and the only people left were those who had won something and those who knew them. Going up to the podium for his trophy, John detected among the few remaining spectators a slight attitude of condescension. *Guy's pretty good for his age. Hope I can still get around like that when I'm that old.*

It bothered him. As well as he had been running lately, he still knew that he could not go much faster, and there was an element of truth in Elizabeth's warnings about how much longer he could expect to train without injury. Logically the best he could be was age-group champ on the local level. Fifty-year-old men simply did not win races outright, something Reynaldo Miller would learn for himself soon enough. From the awards podium he gave Elizabeth, Shannon, and Elena a wink. Walking toward them with his trophy, he glanced at the winner of the next oldest age group and caught himself thinking that the guy looked pretty good for his age.

"YOU CLEARLY HAVE a crush on him, *bella*. I guess I can see why, he is pretty handsome." Shannon pulled out of the race site in her blue Miata, the car behind her honking. "What the . . ." In the rearview mirror she saw a carload of men emboldened to catcalls by the fact that they were turning the other direction. "I don't like them older myself, you know that. I'd rather be the teacher than the student. But I must admit, he's pretty handsome for a fifty-year-old *married* guy."

"Isn't Harrison Ford in his fifties?" Elena asked.

"Well . . . good point."

"I know you think it's strange, but you saw him. You saw how well we get along."

"Yeah, and it's probably even better when his *wife's* not around."

"Stop that. I can't tell you how much leeway he's allowed me at work. Sometimes he'll just take a couple of hours to answer my questions. I really feel so much more prepared for law school because of him. I just wish we were closer in age and he was single. Do me a favor. Tell me I'm being stupid."

"You're being stupid, *bella*."

"I can't help it, though." A moment later she asked, "Didn't you see how his wife sort of limits him? Is that normal, is that what happens? Because I never want to be that way."

Shannon nodded. "I admit he could do better. I just think he should have affairs with women closer to his own age."

"We're not having an affair."

Shannon looked over, eyebrows raised.

"Well, it's true," Elena insisted.

"So far," Shannon said.

BACK IN GROVETON that afternoon, John and Elizabeth sparred over whether or not he could have a celebratory martini. He finally gave up. Better to be dry than to try to enjoy a drink while

Elizabeth detailed for him the horrors of death by throat cancer. He lifted weights in the garage for forty-five minutes on a set of Olympic equipment he had purchased just a few days before. She didn't like that either—he might have a stroke, or at least injure his back and have trouble getting to work. Lying in bed that night, he felt her hand on his chest. She was sitting up beside him.

"Don't you understand how much I love you?" she asked. "The whole reason I hate to see you doing all these weird mid-life things is that I really think it's bad for you in the long run. I figure your body has got to last three or four more decades, and it still bothers me that you don't seem to be thinking that far ahead. Like the Porsche. That was expensive. Our money's got to last, too."

He considered pretending to be too tired to discuss it. She wouldn't let him. "John? Didn't you hear me?"

"We're worth several million dollars. Hell, we could split it and we'd both be fine for the rest of our lives."

"Why would we split it?"

"That's not what I meant. I meant we could lose half of it somehow and still be fine."

He lay there terrified that she would pick up on that revealing error of diction and neither he nor she would get any sleep that night. He tried to take the conversation in another direction. "I've done everything I was supposed to in life, you know that? Just like Lee Thomas. Good college, good law school, good job, nice family. Thinking back on all these years, I hardly remember anything. I hardly have any memories, Elizabeth. It's like I remember some good times in law school, some important cases in my career, and the bad parts of a few vacations, and now I find myself at this age suddenly able to run pretty well. I can't explain why my heels don't hurt, but damned if I'm going to pretend like they do. I'll run till one of the tendons snaps. As for the Porsche, yes it was . . . uncharacteristic, I admit, but nothing we can't afford. Okay, darling?"

He sat up. The curtains were pulled back and the moon was high. In that blue light his face did indeed look very young. She reached up and touched his cheek. "I just wish I were looking younger, too," she said. "That we were both looking younger together."

"You look fine."

"Do you still love me, I mean the same as before?"

"That's the wrong question, isn't it? Don't we both love each other differently now than when we started? All this stuff I'm doing, Elizabeth, when I get senile and I'm just floating around in the past, I want there to be something there besides the train and the office. I'm just trying to save up a life to remember."

```
┌─────────────────────────────┐
│                             │
│   C H A P T E R    8        │
│                             │
└─────────────────────────────┘
```

AT WORK THE next day he was limping slightly, but the pain was a pleasant muscular one unrelated to tendons or bones. It was more a young man's soreness and a reminder of his surprising physical accomplishment. He thought it unusual and was even slightly disappointed that Elena did not talk about his successful race, and when he commented on this, as casually as he could, she reminded him that discretion was an important part of her job. "I'm in the habit of keeping secrets." He was forced to resort to a theatrical limping in front of his colleagues so they would ask what was wrong and he could say, "Tough race yesterday." The conversation would go from there. Nathan Barradale was particularly impressed. "Maybe I should get back into it," he kept saying. "Maybe I will."

By the end of the day, word had reached Kelly Epstein third-hand. In his office she was hyper-complimentary. "Let's go out tonight and I'll buy you a dinner to celebrate. Plus, you still haven't seen my new apartment." She smiled at Elena. "Don't you think he should let me treat him?"

"Sure, if he wants."

"I'm not working late tonight," John said. "I should go home."

Kelly looked at the piles of paper on Elena's desk and around it on the floor. "From what I hear, John, you have plenty of work to do. I hear you're running a little behind in that particular race."

He shrugged it off, but she was right. He couldn't get any work done. That Kelly had felt the need to warn him meant that some of the other partners were annoyed by his recent subpar contribution to the firm, something he meant to correct as soon as he got over his schoolboy crush on Elena. But for now, how could he concentrate with the ever-present option of talking with her, taking her out to eat, perhaps touching the warm, smooth flesh of her elbow as they crossed the street at noon?

"I enjoyed meeting Elizabeth," Elena said over a plate of pasta in Little Italy. "She's got such a . . . solid presence."

"Yes, I suppose she does."

"Twenty-five years you've been married?"

"Afraid so." He smeared some extra butter on his garlic bread and crunched into it. "I don't mean I dislike admitting that I've been married that long or married to Elizabeth that long, just that I'm old enough to have been married to *anyone* that long. It's sort of depressing."

"I don't know. You've done pretty well for yourself, and your family."

"I don't think you get an obituary for that."

Her face lively and radiant in the light from the plate-glass window, she said, "Who cares about obituaries?" And suddenly the postmortem write-up seemed irrelevant again, as it had when he was in his twenties and immortal.

Later that afternoon, they were both in his office when the phone rang. Closest to it, Elena answered. Next Saturday was supposed to be nice and sunny, and Elizabeth thought it would be fun to have Elena over for a cookout so she could meet Andy. "I really think he'd be interested in meeting you, in any case."

"Oh, I'd love to," Elena said. "I'll be there."

"Great! Can you transfer me to John? I actually thought I dialed his direct number."

"Oh, you did. I was just bringing him some things to sign when the phone rang. Just a minute, here he is."

She handed John the phone.

THAT NIGHT WHEN he got home there was a huge cardboard box on the porch. In the living room he found Elizabeth trying to put together a treadmill. "I can't stand you being in shape without me," she said, as if "shape" were a location and the treadmill her means of conveyance to it. She held up a screw. "Can you help me get this in?" It took him most of the evening to get the contraption assembled, and as he neared the end she went upstairs to get into her new exercise clothes. She wore shorts and a T-shirt, perhaps to blunt the specificity of the leotard beneath. New walking shoes. She bent over and let her arms dangle toward the carpet. "I still don't know how you can touch your toes," she said.

The thing had cost five thousand dollars; it was the Porsche of treadmills. John tried it out and thought it was all right. Running indoors didn't give him the same feeling of freedom, but it might help him maintain his training schedule during snowstorms and thundershowers.

Elizabeth refused to get on the thing while he was still in the living room. "You're not going to watch," she said.

"Why not? I might be able to correct your form or something."

"Precisely what I'm worried about. I can handle it, okay?"

He calculated that he had thirty minutes while she tried out the contraption, so in the kitchen he made a stiff martini. On the door of the refrigerator was the newspaper clipping listing him as the winner of the fifty to fifty-five age group. The trophy he had won was on top of the fridge, beside the box of Colon Bran. Already the thrill of victory had diminished, and now when he read the inscription all he saw was the embarrassing qualification of his age.

From the doorway he peeked at Elizabeth as she pounded the treadmill, her back hunched slightly from the force of her determination. He felt toward her an overwhelming sadness and concern that approached, but fell short of, love. She *was* important to him, yes, and she deserved his respect, but having given her the first half of his adult life, did he really now owe her the second—?

She whirled. "What are you drinking?"

"Keep going. Don't let me distract you."

She stepped off the treadmill. "I'm tired anyway. That thing works up an appetite."

"You've only been on it for five minutes." He took a big swallow of his drink. "You're not even breathing hard. You just burned about twenty calories, and now you're going to eat five hundred, right?"

"What does it matter, you don't even like me anymore."

"That's obviously bullshit."

Later both would regret many of the things that were said during the ensuing argument. It ended with her in tears in the bedroom and him with another martini on the couch, where he woke up the next morning when the sun shone through his closed eyelids.

THAT AFTERNOON HE took Elena out to lunch and confided in her, over ravioli in a heavy garlic sauce, what had happened the previous night with his wife and the treadmill. She commiserated. Elizabeth shouldn't have snapped at him like that. Was she maybe under some sort of pressure that was making her behave that way? Elena reached across the table for his hand.

"I'm glad we've become friends," he told her.

"Me, too."

"If the treadmill thing had happened before you came along, I'd be grousing around the office feeling old. You've really come to mean a lot more to me than you ought to. In some weird way I think you've helped my running."

She shook her head. "Oh, come on."

"No, I mean it. I think the fact that my Achilles' tendons don't hurt anymore has something to do with you."

"Right."

He covered her ringless hand with his beringed one and left it there two or three seconds longer than was considered appropriate by the nosy pair at the next table.

BACK IN THE office they found Nathan Barradale on the couch and Haley Wilson standing with his hands clasped behind his back as he scanned the untended quilt of papers covering Elena's desk. He seemed reluctant to touch anything. He pointed to the blinking message light and said, "I've left three voice mails here over the past three days."

Barradale said to Elena. "I guess John here is keeping you busy? Because I've left a message or two myself."

"I'm keeping her so busy she doesn't have time to check voice mail, that's for sure," John said. "I'll have to ease up."

Smiling, Haley Wilson extended his hand to Elena. "I don't believe I've had the pleasure."

John handled the introductions. "Just out of Magnate," he said. "She's brilliant. Best thing I ever did was hire her."

Barradale said, "All the same, it's not common for an office to be completely unresponsive and, it turns out just now, completely vacant of human beings. We thought you'd been kidnapped or something."

"We should step into your office," Haley said.

The men sat around John's desk, Haley glancing down at the folders of unfinished work stacked on the floor. Barradale kept readjusting his tie. "We understand that you didn't hire Maxine Estep."

"Felt like I needed some fresh blood. I can hire who I want, right?"

"Theoretically, yes," Nathan said. "You and I both know otherwise."

John leaned back in his chair. "How'd you know I didn't hire Maxine Estep?"

Haley said, "Her lawyer told us by way of a lawsuit he filed on her behalf. She's got Brenna Fryerson as a witness that you didn't want to hire Maxine because she was too old."

"Brenna? I gave her a thousand bucks!"

Haley said, "Maxine might win a lot more. Of course, the firm is less concerned with the potential monetary loss than with the possible damage to its reputation. The Jordy Hamilton foot-fetish incident notwithstanding, we've made great strides in recent years in the promotion of women within our ranks. We've handled several important sex-discrimination suits."

"I told her we'd be happy to pay her salary," Nathan said. "All she had to do was drop the suit and sit at home collecting her pay until retirement, which would've been in two or three years anyway. But she's been around the block a time or two. She knows she can take us for a lot more than that. I don't think she'd be doing this unless she had a pretty clear-cut case. Like you hired someone with no experience." He cocked his head toward the closed door beyond which Elena sat. "She did have some paralegal experience, right?"

John said, "I couldn't just not hire Elena because she's so

young and happens to be beautiful. That would be a double case of age discrimination *and* reverse lookism."

Nathan glanced over at Haley, whose mouth had gone crooked with verbal restraint. "I'll take it from here, if you'll excuse us." Haley got up, walked stiffly across the room. When he opened the door, they could hear his voice on Elena's speakerphone; she was finally checking her messages.

Nathan waited until he had shut the door. "John, cheating on your wife is one thing. Cheating on the firm is more serious."

"I'm not cheating on my wife or the firm, Barradale. I've just got a good-looking paralegal and a work overload."

"You seemed more productive when Brenna was around. Look, I'm your friend. I just want you to work on it, okay? You said she's Bill Conifer's daughter. Maybe she helped him in the office one summer, making copies or even just making coffee, okay? That counts as experience. Follow that angle. Maybe Conifer would be willing to help us out by embellishing her job description a bit."

THE ESTEP DEVELOPMENT required that he spend the afternoon making notes about the hiring process and collecting any paper data he had produced during that time. It also required close work with Elena. "Are you sure you never helped out in your father's law office?" he persisted.

"Well, I guess once I cleaned up a coffee spill. I spilled it accidentally one day when I stopped in to borrow Dad's credit card."

He snapped his fingers. "Well, there it is, your past experience. You were a paralegal before I hired you."

He explained the entire situation to her, and she felt at once guilty for being the source of his problem and grateful to him for having risked such consequences in order to hire her.

"She was more qualified than you on paper," John said. "But I knew you'd be better. I also liked you, I wanted to give you a shot." His stare faded out; now he was looking somewhere beyond the mahogany walls. "I guess this is what happens when you try to go against the grain."

She placed her hand momentarily on his shoulder. He called up the answering machine in Groveton and told Elizabeth he was going to have to stay so late that he might as well spend the night in the city.

Hanging up, he said, "Elena, you don't have to stay late. You can leave at five. This is my problem, not yours."

"No way. I'm going to help you get out of this."

In her mind the night stretched out before them in a sort of montage of preparation. Reading, writing, brainstorming, coffee rings on critical documents. The pain, the pleasure, the ideas.

But by seven o'clock John was finding it difficult to concentrate. He suggested a short break, perhaps a brisk walk around the block with a cup of coffee. It turned into dinner with three bottles of wine and a spirited discussion about everything but Maxine Estep.

It was that special period of a relationship between the awkwardness of getting to know each other and the awkwardness of knowing too much, so that everything either one said was utterly fascinating. John began to imagine that even as he held this girl as a baby he had known, felt that he had been born too early. Ridiculous, but the thought was there. And Elena remembered the day he had hired her, how desperate she was feeling when the phone rang, how gloomy were her prospects, how sternly her father had begun to insist that she move back into her childhood room with its pop-music posters and its dried corsage from the prom. That John had helped her out was more than enough to earn her gratitude. That he had damaged himself in the process earned at least her loyalty. And love? She wished there were some way to repay him.

His tie was loose, his hair mussed, and he was walking through the Upper West Side holding the hand of his twenty-two-year-old paralegal. He half hoped someone would see him and word would get back to Elizabeth. Why not? His marriage was dead, wasn't it? He had a pang of fear at the thought of being spotted by his son, but that was very unlikely. They stopped at a bar, and each had a martini. The sharp angles of the glass seemed to flow naturally from her wrist and hand.

"I don't want to go back to the office," he said. "And I don't want to go home, and I don't want to get a hotel."

"My roommates won't be back till late. Sometimes the apartment's spooky when I'm by myself."

In the taxi he kissed her. She parted her lips, and he felt the hot, soft tip of her tongue in his mouth. And in that moment some horizon toward which he had been moving since first meeting her finally stopped receding, and he had burst through it to the other side. He felt the way he had at seventeen when Becca Pearson stripped off her panties and hung them on his stick shift and he realized that this was it, it was finally going to happen.

They composed themselves just barely for the watchful eyes of Victor the doorman. But before the elevator doors closed, John cupped her breast through her shirt and she pressed up against him, wrapping her leg around his. They ran down the hallway, and in her impatience to get the door open she delayed them further by dropping her keys. "Damn it," she whispered.

Inside, she dimmed the entryway light with one hand while already unbuttoning her blouse with the other. In the middle of the living room, in the moonlight beaming through the sheer curtains, they stripped.

Now they began taking their time. He rested his hands on her hips and brought her forward for another kiss, then held her gently at arm's length, the better to admire her. A thought of Elizabeth made him, for a moment, consider reconsidering. But once he realized the choice was irrevocable, Elena filled his mind as completely as she dominated his vision.

She pushed her fingers up through the hair on his chest, then reached down to cup his balls, a handful. The tip of his shaft dented her tender forearm.

"This is impossible," he said.

"Apparently not." Her breath tickled the hair on his balls. And then he felt her tongue nudging them, running up the shaft, and her lips suddenly closing around its thick base, her mouth amniotic in its wet, comforting warmth. He sank to his knees; she pushed him onto his back and straddled his face. Years since he had smelled and tasted the possibility of pregnancy, children. He rolled her over to get a different angle on it, flicking his tongue against her clit as if it were a piece of hard candy. When she began to tremble he glanced up and saw that she was running her fingers around her nipples, tweaking them just slightly. She wrapped her legs around his head, something else he remembered happening years ago. Her body was so tight that it seemed a single, solid muscle; and then her back arched slowly to maximum tautness. She loosened all at once, moaning and driving her heels into his shoulder blades. "Stop, stop," she said, her hands buried in his dark hair, pushing him away. "Get on up here."

He started in the missionary position. Elena ran her tongue around the shell of his ear. Her breathing was so loud he was certain that anyone passing in the hall could hear it. Then she pushed him away and rolled over. He entered her from behind and pumped steadily. The side of her face was mushed against the carpet, and each thrust gently bumped her head against the padded sofa leg. Her lips were parted, eyes closed, face red. "Stand up," she said. When he withdrew his cock, it sprang back against his stomach with a wet thwacking sound, leaving a column of her glisten. She stood against the wall. "Pick my leg up."

He grabbed her by the ankle and stood holding it out to the side. "Are you sure?"

"Put it on your shoulder."

He did. Her left foot was flat on the ground, and her right ankle was pressing against an ear that was still wet from her tongue. He entered her and she began to whisper encouragements. He got over being amazed at her flexibility and just concentrated on what he was doing. Then his consciousness ceased to be a factor at all. There was something wet on his chest, and he was surprised to discover that it was a string of his own drool.

"I'm going to come soon," he said.

"I can tell. Put my leg down."

He did. It made her feel even tighter.

"Just before you come, pull out, okay?"

He did as he was told, expecting to send his load into thin air. Instead she pushed him away, dropped to her knees, and closed her lips around his base again. He shot so hard against the back of her throat that her eyes suddenly opened wide and glistening, and she made a little squeal, as if her epiglottis were a bell he had rung. She held the load in her mouth for a few seconds, gulped it down, then licked some more off the tip.

His knees were so weak that he slid to the floor. She sat slumped against the wall with her feet drawn toward her buttocks and her knees spread wide. Her eyes were closed. In the moonlight he stared at her open vagina, its shellfish taste still on his lips. For John Ashe, acutely conscious of having just fucked a girl whom he had held when she was a baby, the surely impossible had become the incredible.

When he awoke, nothing was the same. He was staring at an unfamiliar ceiling, and there was a head of lush, blond hair on his chest. His hand rested between two perfect shoulder blades. One of Elena's thighs crossed both of his. On the wall at the foot of her single bed hung a Magnate pennant above a corkboard collage showing Elena partying with her friends. All the girls were prosperous-looking, if not genuinely attractive, and the boys' square jaws were softened by beer fat that might someday turn into outright commuter pudge.

He rubbed a hand over Elena's smooth ass. She mumbled something, squeezed him tightly, and then pushed herself up, squinting against the sunlight that beamed through the thin curtains. She pecked his lips and stood beside the bed, perfectly comfortable in the nude. He told her he'd been looking at her photographs, and she stood at the corkboard to give him the story behind each one. "Here's David Michaelson, who ended up going home with Kim. Here's Jake Coates, my first boyfriend." John looked a little more closely. Coates was movie-star handsome, taller than the others in the photo, with wider shoulders and a narrower waist.

"Where does he live now?"

"L.A. He's one of those waiter slash actors."

Good, a whole continent away. John was hard-pressed to feign convincing interest in the other photos beside which the true object of his attention stood naked and so beautiful. She looked down between his legs. "My, my."

It was alive again. Without another word she climbed onto the bed and straddled him, supporting herself on the balls of her feet and maintaining her balance by grasping the top edge of the headboard. He held his cock up while she lowered herself onto it and pretty much took over. It didn't take long. She ground herself slowly against him, the better to feel him come.

"There, now. Feel better?" she asked.

Dressed in yesterday's rumpled clothes, his hair awry, he

walked out into the living room and found Shannon there watching cartoons. She glanced up at him, did a double-take. "Whoa! That's a surprise."

"How you doing?"

"I'm all right. The question is, how are you?"

"Never been better."

"I bet."

Her hair was mussed, her face puffy from sleepiness, and she wore a large T-shirt that came down to mid-thigh of her bare legs. She wasn't nearly as pretty as Elena, but he had a sting of desire for her just the same. He felt attractive, felt that it was actually possible that Shannon, too, would be available. Slightly embarrassed at her appearance, she made a sleepy effort to mash down a fountain of hair which plumed oddly from her crown.

"What's going on here?" It was the third roommate, the one who slept around, a chubby little woman with a donut in her hand. She looked from Shannon to John to Shannon.

"Actually, he's here with Elena," Shannon said.

"Well, well, how interesting. You must be the runner guy she works for. She talks about you all the time. How old did she say you were?"

"I'm fifty."

"Really?" Her shock was genuine. "I'd put you at late thirties, tops."

In the bathroom he took a long look in the mirror. He did look significantly younger than he had even just yesterday. The crow's feet at the corners of his eyes were less pronounced, the stubble on his face a bit darker. He raised his shirt and flexed his stomach. Blocks of muscle. Amazing.

Hoping to win some roommate loyalty, he decided to cook breakfast for the whole group. Kim's frequent trips to the grocery store had left the refrigerator well stocked, and she agreed to donate the ingredients if John would donate his labor. Loaf of bread, carton of eggs, a stick of butter, three different flavors of jam, and a cylinder of orange juice concentrate. Kim cleaned off the dinner table, which was so completely covered by magazines, old mail, scarves, empty purses, and other refuse of city life that John was sure they had never before used it for an actual meal. Elena traipsed through the living room wrapped in a towel, blushing under Shannon's knowledgeable scrutiny, and a moment later John heard the shower running. Her hair was still wet and her skin luminous when she sat down at the newly cleared tabletop.

John cooked up the eggs to order and served his guests as simultaneously as the two working stove eyes would allow.

"We like your new boyfriend," Kim said. "Will he do this every morning?"

"Isn't he great?" Elena asked.

Shannon said, "You tell us, *bella.*"

After breakfast John went back to Elena's room and scanned her bookshelves. She had all the Baltazar Brantleys. He picked up *Whiter Than Blood, Redder Than Snow,* and lay down on his back to read it.

Elena woke him minutes later. "Don't forget about the cookout."

He checked his voice mail at the firm and found that Elizabeth had called twice already, wondering where he was and how his work was going, and would he please stop on the way home for some mustard?

RIDING INTO GROVETON in the Porsche was a lot better than taking the train, waiting for some madman like Colin Ferguson to come along and cure your nagging headache. It was an unusually warm day for early March, and John had put the top down. Elena had a scarf tied over her hair, and she wore large, dark sunglasses. Yes, Grace Kelly with a nineties body, and a bit of Jackie O as well.

There was none of the self-conscious embarrassment that sometimes follows a first fuck. Instead John and Elena were so at ease with each other that neither felt the need to speak. She changed the radio station from Alltalk 91.4 to WROC 105, and he drummed the steering wheel in time to the music.

He forgot about the mustard until he was well into Groveton. Too late now to stop somewhere on the edge of town, where he wasn't likely to run into someone he knew. He pulled into the parking lot of Davidson's, where the butcher and the baker were mildly terrified of Elizabeth. Most of the checkout people knew her, too. It was a small store catering to people whose tastes New York had made forever eclectic. A half aisle was devoted to varieties of gourmet mustard. He picked out three kinds and headed to the express checkout.

In line ahead of him, buying cigarettes, none other than William Newton of prostitute-sting fame. "Hey, you're looking great!" Newty said, breaking his prolonged leer at Elena with irregular, unfocused glances in John's general direction. "You haven't changed a bit."

John introduced him to Elena. "She lived with your daughter for a semester at Magnate."

This information gave Newty some justification for his staring. "I thought I recognized you. And how do you know John here?"

"He's my boss. We're going to a cookout at his house."

John held up a jar of mustard as proof positive of what she said. "Your daughter's going to be there. Apparently she and Andy have been seeing each other."

"That's what I heard, too." He paused for a moment. "I'm sort of on the outs with the family, don't know if you've heard anything."

"No," John said. "What happened?"

"Big misunderstanding, really. I was doing research, boning up on my Spanish for a novel I was thinking about writing and, well, it was a wrong place, wrong time sort of situation for me when the cops broke the damn door down." He glanced at John. "It was a bad day all around."

AT THE ASHES' house Kristen and Elena put on a good show of getting along. They talked about mutual friends and said they should all get together sometime. But Kristen was irritated at the attention Andy kept lavishing on Elena, the way he kept clowning at the grill and being extra solicitous of her cooking preferences. Since when had *medium* been such an engrossing art?

This was just what Elizabeth had hoped would happen. Her son was a red-blooded American boy like any other, with no major commitments to Kristen. And the thought of being drawn back into social relations with the Newtons after William's public disgrace was not easy to stomach. Anne was okay, she supposed, but William was obviously a pervert. What if Kristen and Andy got married and had daughters? William Newton could not be trusted alone with the children. And of course for Elizabeth there was also the matter of her image. It would not do for the chair of the Department of English at the Groveton Country Day School to be seen about town with a convicted john.

"She really is pretty," she said to her husband as they both stared at Elena. "You don't think she's too young?"

He suffered a momentary stab of fear. "Too young for what?"

"Well, for Andrew, of course. I guess she's not. It's only three years' difference. It just always worries me to see too big an age spread because I think the cultural reference points aren't there. You know, like I could say to you, 'Remember when "Hey Jude" came out and you would remember."

" 'Hey Jude'?"

"Remember when we first heard it? Andy was still in the crib, and your hair was longish because you hadn't started at Masterson, Grandissime, and Barradale yet. And we were in a coffee shop and that song came on and you said, 'Elizabeth, I don't think I want to do it. I don't want to be a lawyer.' Fortunately, I was able to convince you to change your mind." She looked over at the house. "Or we wouldn't have all the things we have now."

" 'Hey Jude,' " he said, thinking back.

"Remember the Beatles, John?" She sang the nah-nah part, even the ow-wow part, but still he couldn't quite place it. Finally just to stop her up he claimed to remember the song, but it worried him that he really didn't.

In the living room he flipped through the record collection and found some old Beatles LPs. When Andy came in, he found his father standing dumbfounded before the stereo while Paul McCartney belted out "Hey Jude."

"This is a great song," John said.

"Duh. Just because I work for MTV doesn't mean I don't appreciate the golden oldies." The kid looked out the window at Kristen and Elena, who were chatting at the patio table. "Jesus, Dad, why didn't you tell me to stop by your office or something? If there was ever an excuse to fabricate some sort of fatherly summons, she is it. Share the wealth, Pops."

"I thought you were happy with Kristen. She's a good solid girl."

"Sure, Kristen's all right."

John cocked his head at the music again. "So 'Hey Jude' is a pretty well-known song, you'd say?"

"Dad." Andy just shook his head. "Where have you been?"

"I guess I've been on the train for twenty-five years."

Andy scrutinized his father's hair. "I checked the bathroom. You don't have any dye up there. You're really not coloring it, are you?"

"No, son."

"It's pretty weird."

John was proud of Elena for not signaling their mutual attraction. None of the others could have guessed that he had spent the night with her, had screwed her with a sort of college-boy gusto, and had been made a bit younger, perhaps, for doing so.

His only real disappointment came at the end of the day when he tried to drive Elena back to the city and his son preempted him. "She can ride with us," Andy said. "You don't mind taking the train, do you, Elena?"

"Of course not. It would be silly for John to drive me all the way back."

"Besides, John, you need your rest," Elizabeth said.

The Silver Missile being too small, John drove the three to the train station in the Sensible American Sedan, with Kristen in the front passenger seat and Elena in back with a flirtatious Andy. The kid wouldn't shut up, just kept babbling and babbling while his girlfriend up front became more and more sullen. As they finally got out, Elena let her hand brush across John's neck, her signal that last night had really happened, that she wanted it to happen again.

```
┌─────────────────────────────┐
│                             │
│    C H A P T E R    9       │
│                             │
└─────────────────────────────┘
```

THE MILD WINTER ended early that year. On the first day of spring it was clear and sunny and would stay that way except for an occasional cleansing shower. Walking to work with Elena that morning he thought about the run he would take during his lunch "hour," which lately had stretched to seventy-five or ninety minutes or even longer.

At the corner of Sixtieth and Lexington he fingered a crumb of sleep from the corner of Elena's eye and clasped her hand in his. "I wish we could take the Porsche out. Perfect day to put the top down."

"Maybe it'll still be nice this weekend and we can take a little drive."

"Yeah, head south for a few hundred miles. We could take the Maxine file with us so we don't get behind."

"As if that would work, John."

They stopped at a bagel shop for coffee, took it outside, and continued walking, sipping occasionally and squinting up at the sky, a watercolor blue. It was going to be a beautiful day, and perhaps this was the best part of it, when you could enjoy the lingering nighttime coolness in anticipation of the coming warmth.

Everything was perfect with Elena. The coffee John was drinking gave him good breath. He no longer farted during his sleep. He found himself making fewer stupid remarks perhaps because Elizabeth wasn't around to hear and disapprove. Sleeping in Elena's single bed, the lovers were a warm entanglement of pulse and breath. Recently he had been waking up with a stiff hard-on, something which had often happened when he was much

95

younger but never in recent years until now. The amazing thing was how matter-of-factly Elena would straddle him and take care of it, and how, as her gyrations accelerated, her lovely face would develop a wicked sneer of pleasure. Over the years he had begun to believe that only in the movies did women make noise during sex. But Elena often had to muffle herself against the pillow or the dark hair of his chest to keep from disturbing her apartment mates, who must have heard her gasps anyway, and strange thumps, and the universally understood squeaking of bed-springs. John imagined Shannon in the next room with her ear pressed to the wall and a hand down her panties. He loved to walk out into the common room and find her and Kim staring glassy-eyed at the television and picking popcorn from bowls in their laps, trying to pretend like they didn't know where he'd just been, and how deep. But this pleasure would not be available to him for long. He and Elena had already started looking for a "love nest," they were playfully calling it. There was no more room in her closet, and so his suits hung from the curtain rod, and his wing tips and Bolt! running shoes lay wherever he happened to step out of them.

Up ahead was the building, the law firm, that would remove the lovers from this perfect day and separate them from each other, that maddening wall between John's office and the reception area. For a moment he thought about cutting, as in *cutting class*, and was surprised at the sudden resurfacing of that term. He let go of Elena's hand. "See you at the office," he said.

"Okay, careful driving in from Groveton."

He strolled around the block in order to approach the firm from the direction of the parking garage, as if he had just arrived from Connecticut in the Silver Missile. How he longed for the day, not far off, when some means of scandalous exposure would render pointless this weak discretion.

He glimpsed his reflection in the dark window. He had made it out of Groveton with four of his most recently altered suits, and now they were too wide through the belly again. It was time to get a new wardrobe, perhaps from Brooks Brothers, so he would continue to look like a lawyer even if he didn't feel like one anymore.

He felt like a runner.

*   *   *

FOR WEEKS NO one had passed him on foot. He ran along in Central Park passing everyone else, slowing down sometimes to chat for a moment before moving on. "Good day for it, huh?" Regulars had begun to notice him. People had even started asking him for training advice.

"Damned if I know," John would say. "I just like to run."

One day he felt a little pulse of alarm at the sound of a runner approaching from behind. Virtually impossible. He checked his watch to make sure he hadn't dropped the pace. He hadn't. Refusing to turn his head and look, he waited until the guy caught up. It was Reynaldo Miller, dressed to please his corporate sponsor. Every piece of clothing displayed the Mercury shoe logo. They would have put him in sandwich boards if possible.

"How you doing?" Miller asked. "Pretty good clip you're maintaining."

"I guess you're faster."

Miller remarked upon the beautiful weather, discussed training schedules and minor, nagging injuries almost as if John were his athletic equal. Did he recognize the older man? Probably not. At their first meeting Miller had been pestered by a fifty-year-old lawyer out for a trot, and at their second, weeks ago and so brief, he had been in a hurry to get to a play. So it was not familiarity which had led to this casual chat between near equals. It was John's new speed.

"One thing I'm glad of, man," Miller said, "is I've never had a problem with my Achilles' tendons. You get that and you're pretty much screwed. One day it just snaps. Happened to a friend of mine. Said it felt like his whole muscle rolled up like a window shade. Flap flap flap. They opened him up, stretched it back out and sewed it on again, but he'll never be back to normal. Not even close."

"Is that right? Achilles' tendons almost never heal?"

"It's a career ender. All I gotta worry about is my knees, you know. That'll end your career, too, but it's usually more wear and tear. Not a sudden snap. Say, how old are you, anyway?"

"Fifty."

Reynaldo raised his eyebrows. "No, tell me for real."

"I'm fifty. Honest."

"What's your name?"

"John Ashe."

"How come I never heard of you in the masters division or anything? Where'd you come from, man?"

"The New York Bar Association. I've been a lawyer for twenty-five years, or maybe I would've had more time for training."

They were running so fast. At the sound of their footfalls people walking ahead of them jumped out of the way protectively clutching purses and videocameras. They passed a group of wobbly rollerbladers and a fat couple on rental bikes. Miller said, "I usually train out in Utah, but my girlfriend, she's here. Plus I want to win the marathon this year, so I better get used to breathing all the pollution, you know? Man, you're moving really fast."

"Am I wearing you out?"

Miller chuckled. "I'm Reynaldo Miller, man. Nice-ta-meetcha." And with that he floated on ahead. As easy as he made it look, he might as well have been strolling through the front yard in house slippers to get the paper. John tried to keep up but there was no way. Not yet.

WHEN JOHN RETURNED from the locker room, freshly showered, he found Andy sitting on the corner of Elena's desk, arms folded, and on his face the remnants of a rapidly disappearing grin. "Hi, Pops."

"Andrew. How are things at MTV?"

"Cue cards galore. Been in touch with Mom lately?"

"We met last week to discuss finances."

"Ah, that's nice. She's doing okay, in case you're interested. She's really throwing herself into her work. I think she'll be fine without you."

"Glad to hear it, she's a tough lady."

John hurried into his office and closed the door behind him— not wanting to witness directly this odd interaction between his old and new lives. It had not been Elizabeth who had compelled him to ride the train every morning for so many years, not really. It had been Andrew, and John's hopes for him: private schools, semesters abroad, undergraduate degree from an Ivy League school. Andrew Ashe was not going to fail for lack of opportunity, not as long as John Ashe rode the train.

John pressed his ear against the door and listened to the kid try to chat up Elena. "I don't want you to think all Ashe men are like Dad," he said. "Dad's not even like Dad right now." And here John knew the kid ran a hand through his hair, his usual gesture of noble suffering and perhaps one of the reasons for his premature frontal hair loss. "I know you know who she is."

"I can't tell you," Elena said.

"I'm not asking you to. I'm just saying, it must make you kind of sick to be drawn into the middle of all this and have to pass messages back and forth and whatnot. I think you'd be within your rights to tell him to screw off. It's not part of your job, arranging sordid little trysts and whatnot. I just hope your opinion of him doesn't affect your opinion of me."

"I like your father, Andy. He's a good guy."

Behind the door John raised a finger to his lips and willed her to be more careful. Of course, Andy was going to find out sooner or later, just like everyone was going to die sooner or later—but it was best to put it off as long as possible. He and Elena had been extremely careful to avoid Proof Required and other Andrew haunts—that whole quadrant of town, in fact—and Elizabeth had promised not to reveal to Andy the identity of the other "girl," she had pointedly called Elena. "But he's going to find out very soon," she had said. "He's a smart boy."

Well, at the moment his ordinary powers of perception were blunted by infatuation. "What I was hoping is, and I promise not to use the occasion to pry for information, what I was hoping is you'd go out to dinner with me."

"I have a boyfriend. He lives in Colorado. He's in grad school in anthropology."

"What?" John imagined his son's wide-eyed disbelief, the mouth hanging open just slightly. "You're waiting around for an anthropologist? You'll end up in the middle of some third world revolution trying to save gorillas and shit. So let's go out tonight. Just friends."

"I have plans."

John opened the door and stuck his head out. "Andy, can I see you for a minute?"

The kid looked like he might bolt altogether but finally acceded to his father's request, perhaps for the chance to yell at him in close proximity. He followed John into the office and closed the door.

John sat behind his desk, which ordinarily afforded him a physical and psychological advantage over his visitors. Unfortunately, the desk effect didn't work on his son. The kid paced as he delivered a speech that he must have been going over in his head for days. "You know what gets me, Dad, is how this is all so contrary to the example you set for me. I mean, you laid out a foundation of expectation and behavior that I was supposed to follow because you followed it, and then you just shrugged and walked away. Where does that leave me? None of this is good for you . . . your rapid weight loss, this complete refusal to follow doctors orders as far as your Achilles' tendons go, the apparent natural change in your hair color—which is impossible, by the way. I looked it up. I just think you should sit back and take a look at a couple of things, like how old you are, like what they call this period of a man's life. Namely, a midlife crisis. I'm not saying it's right—but I'm saying you can be forgiven for it because it's a documented phase, you know, like puberty. I could talk to her, Dad. I bet I could. I could explain some things about what you're feeling from a man's point of view, and you could dump your new woman and go beg for forgiveness. Mom's so upset, Dad, don't you *care*?"

"Of course I do. Of course." Momentarily shamed, he broke eye contact. And of course he did care for Elizabeth. It was sad that their two paths had so clearly diverged, but it was also undeniable. He squared his jaw and stared at his son, who, apparently satisfied with his own fervor, had sat down to observe its effect.

John leaned forward. "I want you to stop being so selfish."

"Huh? That's a nice twist, Dad, a really nice twist."

"Basically it's none of your business, Andy. Do I come over to MTV and ask you who you're sleeping with?"

"It's Mom I'm thinking about."

"You love your mother, sure. I hope you don't hate your father. But the person you're thinking about here is you. You want a pretty picture in your head of your dear old mom and dad sitting on a porch swing and getting heart palpitations whenever you pull up in the driveway with the wife and kids. Guess what, Andy, I don't see myself in that picture. My girlfriend would never see me in that picture, either."

"*Girl*friend? What is she, seventeen?"

"Not quite, but she's pret-ty young."

"Shit, Dad. That's ridiculous. She must be an idiot."

"Basically what I'm telling you is it's none of your business. I've done everything in the world for you, and now my obligation to you is through. If you want to be friends, fine. If you can't handle that, I'm not going to cry about it. Someday you'll kick yourself. I'm the only father you'll ever have, and the simple fact is we're blood. Sooner or later, whether you like it or not, you're going to understand me." John lifted his chin just slightly and tightened his jaw in preparation for the counterattack.

But the kid lowered his head. Surrender for now. "I just hope you and Mom can still work it out."

On his way out he stopped and turned. "Say, you don't know anything about her boyfriend, do you?" He was pointing at the door beyond which Elena sat. "What is he, some Magnate grad or something?"

John shuffled some papers. "I think so, actually. She seems pretty serious about him, too. I hear her on the phone sometimes."

After Andy left, John tried to put in some good work on the Maxine question, but he kept thinking about sex and Elena sitting out there in the next room. He wanted to go pound a few brews. All those nah-nah-nahs from the end of "Hey Jude" kept going through his head. And he kept thinking about his next race, a 10-K in Stamford.

It was only a mile from Groveton Junction to Andy's boyhood home, and Saturday morning he walked hungover through the same streets where years before he had taken his first bike ride without training wheels, his father running along behind him.

Now as he passed a certain stop sign he could not suppress a grin. This was the spot where, at the age of sixteen, he had rearended Mrs. Crabtree's new Beamer. When she walked back and looked in his window, she saw not only the Ashe boy sheepish behind the wheel, but her own daughter in the passenger seat stuffing beer cans into the glove box. Young Lisa Crabtree would have done better to remove the empty condom wrapper from the dashboard. A few years later Andy had enjoyed a secret feeling of primitive triumph, shaking hands with the groom at her wedding. Mrs. Crabtree even got a bit tipsy at the reception and made several cryptic references to what she called the "wrapper incident."

Most of the people who lived in these houses were professionals of some kind who worked in the city and left twenty bucks on the kitchen table so the kids could order pizza or Chinese for dinner. For the kids this slightly monied independence facilitated their high school, white-bread idea of the fast life, and walking through these streets now Andy smiled at no particularly memory but at all of them together. Growing up had been cake; the ingredients were mostly forgotten.

His house was just around the next corner. Was there something to what his father had said? Did he really just want to keep a pretty mental picture of Mom and Pop on a porch swing even if it meant they would be miserable? They wouldn't be miserable, it was that simple. They belonged together.

Approaching his house now, he could see his mother squatting in front of the shrubbery, pulling up weeds. The rigid curve of her back gave away her static anger. She yanked the weeds violently and threw them over her shoulder without regard to the dirt crumbs that fell into her hair.

"Mom?"

She whirled. "Oh. Hi, Andrew." Standing, she shook the gloves from her hands and then stared at them on the ground. "They're John's, they're way too big for me."

What he found most alarming about her new sullen demeanor was its potential permanence. She was starting to look like those bitter old ladies he would see in New York walking along with their well-groomed little kick dogs while the world passed them by. Their main occupation now was to harass people in service positions—the dry-cleaning man, the butcher, the baker, the mail carrier, everyone—because it was the only way to be noticed anymore.

"I'll be all right by myself," Elizabeth said at the kitchen table, her fingers curled loosely around a glass of iced tea. She stared through the window at the two backyard trees between which John had always talked about stringing a hammock.

"I'm not worried about that." Andy sat across from her. "I know you can handle living alone if you absolutely had to. I just question whether things have to work out that way."

She looked at him. "Have you seen John?"

"Yes . . ."

"Did he seem happy?"

Andy waited too long to deny it. "He's delusional," he finally said. "He only thinks he's happy."

He already could tell this wasn't going to work, yet he felt the inevitability of his words as keenly as he felt their worthlessness. "Mom, I don't know how it is for women, but I swear, and this is hard to talk about with you, my own mother, but sometimes I lust so much that I do things I later regret, like make a fool of myself or something. I'm not saying that what Dad has done can be taken so lightly—obviously it can't—but, well, it comes from the same source, and it's exacerbated by the fact that he's just turned fifty. It's a midlife thing. A cliché guys say is that the penis has no conscience."

Silence. He blushed. Would she get mad? Break down? Had he embarrassed her? Well, it was for her own good.

Her body convulsed once with laughter, then twice. It was a slow buildup, like an old engine trying to turn over in sub-zero temperatures, but eventually Elizabeth put her forehead on the table and laughed so hard that she had to dig a fist into her side as if to prevent some sort of internal rupture. She sat up again with her head back and her mouth open. Stood and kissed her baffled son on the forehead. "I love you," she said. "It's amazing the things moms pretend they don't know, that their sons have to come along and enlighten them."

"Would you consider taking him back?"

She sighed, choked off more laughter. "I met him at the Wharf House last week to talk about the money situation. It was cordial. But his obvious happiness really hurt me. I think I could've forgiven him for sleeping with another woman once. Even twice. As long as he felt guilty about it and hated himself for it and all that. But, Andy, he moved in with her."

"You know who it is?"

She nodded. "But I won't tell you."

"Do I know her or something?"

"I can't say."

"So I know her, then." He ran his hand through his hair. "Who?"

"They've been public, Andy. A lot of people have seen them out together and reported back to me—and you'll probably find out some way soon yourself. Just try to keep *your* cool, okay?" She raised her eyebrows. *Promise?*

"Okay," Andy said.

"It would be hard to take him back without sacrificing the last remaining smidgen of my dignity. People would just think she dumped him and I didn't have enough pride to tell him to stay lost."

Andy said, "So I guess you're going to divorce him."

She was still smiling a bit about the penis comment. "Oh, I think I have to. But I'm sort of worried about him, about his mind. It seems to me like he's forgotten a lot of stuff. Because if he remembered it, he would never have left me. I don't understand how he could've spent so much time with me, shared so many experiences, and then just turned his back." She tapped her temple. "I wonder if he's okay up here."

"Jesus, Mom. You're talking like you think there's a medical reason for him leaving you. The midlife crisis isn't caused by a tumor or something. It's a weakness that allows the amoral penis to run things for a while, that's all. It's caused by a nostalgic hard-on." He saw her again trying not to laugh. "Don't laugh. Come on. It's not funny."

But laughter reddened her face. "It's so . . . ridiculous!" She wiped tears from the corners of her eyes.

ELIZABETH WAS A firm believer in the principle of situational competence. Kurt Vermiel, winner of the Nobel prize in physics, in the laboratory a genius, was said to be incapable of balancing his checkbook. She might have been a blithering idiot at home, pulling weeds all day and spending her evenings bawling into the Public Service Helpline, but she was a rock of stability at

Groveton Country Day School, where if anything her teaching seemed to become more energetic and inspirational.

"Who is the narrator, Caitlin?"

"Jacob Barnes."

"That's right." Elizabeth focused on a disturbance in the back of the room. Class beauty Julianna Bach had dropped her pencil to the floor. As she leaned over to pick it up she extended her long bare legs into the aisle as a counterweight to her enormous breasts. Sitting two seats behind her, lacrosse star Ken O'Brien was wagging his tongue in an act of air cunnilingus while his boyserfs snickered at his cleverness.

"Kenneth, can you tell me what injury Mr. Barnes suffered during the war?"

His mouth dropped open and his eyes went blank. "Vietnam?"

"Mmm, let's see." Elizabeth paced to the back of the room and stood beside Ken at his desk. His copy of *The Sun Also Rises* was in pristine condition, the spine smooth and uncracked. She lifted up his notebook and saw a copy of Cliff's Notes, also obviously unread. "The novel was first published in 1926, so we know right away we can rule out several wars which occurred after that, right, Kenneth? Just think, if Jacob Barnes had suffered an injury during the Vietnam War, then *The Sun Also Rises* would be some sort of science-fiction time-travel book, and Hemingway must have been a prophet." Now the class was on her side, but half-heartedly, still reserving an unreasonable, by her lights, measure of sympathy and admiration for King Kenneth.

Elizabeth paced back to the front of the room, smiling. "We can be reasonably sure that the war occurred before the story being told, which would rule out Vietnam. I'm surprised you couldn't get at least that much out of your Cliff's Notes, Kenneth."

"I didn't have time, I just sorta skimmed 'em."

"Just sorta skimmed"—in Ken's jock-stud cadence—"your Cliff's Notes? Next time why don't you just skim the title?" Then she called on the meekest girl in the class, Lisa Shelton. "Tell us, Lisa, during what war was Mr. Barnes injured?"

"World War One," she whispered.

"And Lisa, loudly now, what was his injury?"

Lisa looked down at her desktop. "I can't."

"Help me out, Lisa."

The girl looked up. "Mrs. Ashe, I just can't."

"Well, I can." Elizabeth held eye contact with Ken O'Brien until some of his smugness disappeared and he glanced away. She said, "Somebody shot his penis off, that's what."

Recent events had given rise to one flaw in her attitude. She liked the boys less. In every smart-ass comment she saw the seeds of their middle-age failure, their destiny to disappoint themselves and their families. Even here at this upscale school she had before her, she suspected, several future wife beaters. A higher percentage, the little John Ashes, would simply leave their wives for younger women. For the girls she felt a sense of pity, because right now they were buying into the myth that if you were pretty or maybe even just smart and clean, with good sweet breath and a pleasant disposition, you'd eventually marry someone who would never, for the rest of his life, tire of you. Together you would raise a family. If the current socioeconomic trends were any indication, you would both have to work, but you could deal with the stress because a bad day in the office could never take away the solid bond of your marriage. The great American dream for women of Elizabeth's mother's generation was to bury the husband shortly after he retired and then become a widow fixture about town, frugal with his pension. Mail would still be addressed to Mrs. Dead Husband. Though Elizabeth had overtly rejected that life plan when she was younger, perhaps she had covertly embraced some of its principles later. It was a mistake she hoped she could save girls like Lisa Shelton and even Julianna Bach from making—Julianna, two years earlier a stick figure, so beautiful now she probably stood naked before the mirror puzzled at her sudden *body*. But Elizabeth labored under the growing conviction that no matter what she did, her students were all doomed—the boys to disappointment, the girls to being blamed for it. They had only a few more years of happiness left, and basically it was all because of the penis. Why couldn't it whither and fall off like an umbilical cord along about forty-five or fifty? The wounded Jacob Barnes seemed to her the perfect man.

It was in her office that she felt most comfortable with herself, performing her duties as chair of English. If the framework of her marriage had collapsed after twenty-five years, well, the school's stone walls had been around for a hundred and seventeen. Far from suffering because of her well-known but only whispered-about marital difficulties, her administrative skill seemed to increase. Conflicts between feuding teachers were dispensed with in ways that were unexpectedly satisfactory to both parties, who often began eating lunch together in the school cafeteria and socializing on weekends. Scheduling difficulties seemed to work themselves out if she simply gave them a few moments of her attention. Before John had left her, she had been putting off a series of conferences with parents of "troubled" (public university–bound) juniors, and she finally got those out of the way, managing to exonerate the school in every case. She even met with the students themselves, and three were making such substantial improvements in their grades that if they kept it up, the peripheral Ivies would be a distinct possibility or at least Duke or Chicago, or if it had to be public, then hopefully Virginia, though they partied too much down there. Ken O'Brien was going to Virginia, enough said.

After her seventh-period literature class she ordinarily took a half hour for herself to read the *Groveton Gazette* in her office. The departmental secretary usually propped it against her door, but today it wasn't there.

"Linda, have you seen the paper?"

Linda looked up from her computer. Beneath her orange bangs her pale blue eyes were wide with guilt. "The paper?"

"The newspaper? The one I read every day."

Linda glanced around the room, without lifting her fingers from the keyboard. "No, I don't see it."

Elizabeth peered into the circular file, and there it was, covered in wood shavings and graphite powder from the recently emptied pencil sharpener. She brushed it off and wiped her fingers on a tissue plucked from Linda's desk.

"The local paper's so worthless anyway," Linda said, staring at her computer screen. "I don't know why you bother. I don't know why we subscribe to it. I mean, how their deciding something is newsworthy or not, I'll never know."

In her office Elizabeth saw what had concerned Linda. On the bottom of the front page, smudged a bit from the graphite in the trash can, was a photo of John Ashe crossing the finish line of a ten-K race in Stamford. LOCAL RESIDENT SETS MASTERS RECORD. The bastard. He wasn't even a local resident anymore, not really. Elizabeth read the accompanying article for any possible mention of the hero's girlfriend. Nothing. It turned out that the record wasn't official until John passed a drug test and his age was confirmed. As the fawning author noted, the runner looked no older than thirty-five.

There was a knock on the door. "Come in."

It was someone she knew she should recognize. A disgruntled parent? A former employee? A college admissions counselor from somewhere small but respectable? But then Elizabeth saw in the woman's face a sign of true understanding rather than the cloying sympathy of women like Linda and the rest of the yet unscathed. Memories began to return of this former fellow teacher who, with her husband, had spent many hours restoring a dilapidated Victorian they had bought for a song back before the eighties housing boom. This was Anne Newton, whose husband had recently been nabbed in a prostitution sting. Elizabeth gulped at the petty, gossipy way she had reported that news to her own husband—probably giving him the impetus to do something similar, men often imitating one another in their competitive resistance to decency. She quashed a ridiculous sense of superiority arising from the fact that John had left her for a beautiful young Magnate graduate and not an actual fee-charging whore.

She crossed the room for an embrace. "Anne, Anne, Anne, it's so good to see you. It's been so long."

"I've been meaning to call ever since I heard."

"Me, too."

"You've held up well," Anne said.

"A lie, but thanks."

Elizabeth folded up the *Groveton Gazette*. "John set the age-group record for the ten-K this weekend, if you can believe that."

"What's a ten-K and who cares?"

"Oh, thank you."

They went out to dinner, arriving at Fellini's thirty minutes before the kitchen would open. Nothing to do but sit at the bar and drink wine. "Something good," Anne instructed the bartender. To Elizabeth she explained, "My lawyer says I should run the credit card up as high as it'll go to demonstrate my expensive lifestyle."

"How does one go about finding a good divorce lawyer?"

"Don't tell me you don't have one yet. Still thinking there's hope for your marriage?"

"I know, it's stupid."

"Take him to the cleaners."

They were just finishing their first bottle when the maître d' arrived to escort them to the dining area.

Elizabeth scanned the menu for something fattening and finally settled on cheese tortellini in alfredo sauce, a dish so evil that watching her eat it would have put John in a funk for the rest of the week. Anne ordered triple cheese lasagna. "And another bottle of that, whatever we were drinking."

They talked about how unfortunate it was that Andy and Kristen were no longer seeing each other, a development both women blamed ultimately on their husbands. "I suppose our kids will be a little shy about marriage after what's happened to their parents," Anne said.

"Good. I want Andy to be shy about it."

They talked about the old Victorian, how charming it was, and the incredible profit the Newtons had made upon selling it in 1989. They talked about their old days together at GCDS, before Anne had taken time off to work on the Victorian, raise the kids, and generally run the household while William got to ride the train into the city every day and have a life. As she spoke of William Newton gallivanting about New York City, her face took on a determined cast. "I've got a lot of catching up to do," she finally said. "Don't you see how ripped off I feel? Finding out he doesn't love me, that he's been sleeping with someone else, I feel like the only one who went through with a suicide pact, the one dumb enough to go first." She shook her head. Since the turpentine days of the Victorian restoration her once blond hair had turned golden, and the sharp angles of her face had blurred somewhat—but her blue eyes were sharper, smarter.

Although it had been years, the two women fell as easily as sisters into a pattern of reciprocal confession and understanding. The wine helped. By the end of the meal they had finished three bottles and were working on number four. After the waiter took the plates away there were just a bottle of wine and two glasses between them, and they weren't sisters anymore. They were a couple of old war buddies getting schnockered and sentimental.

"I mean, she is only twenty-two," Elizabeth was saying. "So I don't blame her. Still, I hope she dies."

They dinged their glasses, sloshing wine onto the evergreen centerpiece and attracting attention from several nearby parties. Anne said, "Well, all I can say is you can be glad he's not paying for it." When she noticed someone from the next table looking over, she smiled at him. "The cops caught my husband in flagrante delicto with one of those Mexican whores from Lincoln Avenue. Maybe you saw his name in the paper? William Newton." Leaning toward Elizabeth, she said, "I'm getting an HIV test."

"Do you really think—"

"Sure, it's possible. Most of those prostitutes are crack addicts. I haven't had sex with William for over six months now, so my doctor says I can get the test. To tell you the truth, I'm almost convinced I've got it. Every little sniffle is the beginning of the pneumonia that will kill me in a few days. I've been writing a long letter to my daughters just in case." Her eyes filled with tears.

Elizabeth reached across the table and held her hand. "I'm sure you'll be all right," she lied. Having been monogamous since before the rise of so many sexually transmitted diseases, she couldn't understand how young people like Andy dealt with the new dangers. From reading the magazines it seemed likely that you would almost always pick something up, if not AIDS, then something else inconvenient—herpes or warts. The very thought made her shiver. She was only fifty. Sooner or later she was going to have to resume her sex life.

Anne's eyes were dry and sharp now. "You know what he said to me? He said"—she stifled her laughter—"he said he always used a condom. Therefore it didn't really count because—ready for this?—'because there was hardly any actual skin contact.' He said it was like masturbation. I said, 'Why didn't you just jack off and put the money in the bank?' "

Trying to stifle her laughter, Elizabeth managed only to convert it into a snort. People three tables away were watching her.

"Sorry," she said to the group at large as she daubed the tears from her eyes with a napkin stained with alfredo sauce.

The manager, who had been watching from across the room since Anne's loud use of the word "whore," marched over and asked if everything was all right. Elizabeth blew her nose into her napkin.

"We're fine," Anne said. "Except our wine is out."

"I'm afraid you've had enough," the little man said. "How will you be paying?"

"We're not." Anne pulled out a gold card, the sight of which went a long way toward restoring the manager's politeness. "William Newton is. My faithful, steadfast husband."

While they waited for him to bring the card back, Elizabeth said, "Am I mistaken or did we have a good time?"

Anne considered it. "You know, I think we did. How did that happen? I thought we were supposed to cry on each other's shoulders."

"You know what?" Elizabeth leaned forward and lowered her voice to a windy stage whisper. "Fuck our husbands. No, wait, that came out wrong."

"Fucking is not what they need, apparently."

This last exchange had occurred during an untimely softening of the music. Elizabeth recognized across the room young Lisa Shelton, the meek thing from her class today, sitting with her still nuclear family. The girl's eyes were wide, her ears unusually red. Elizabeth tried to summon the competence that came to her so naturally in her office at school, but it was impossible. In the end she waved across two or three tables to the Sheltons and flashed a smile that she hoped looked more jolly than drunken.

Outside in the parking lot, they stood on either side of Anne's car. A moment of hesitation. It was irresponsible to drive in their condition, not at all something you'd expect from two locally prominent women who had taught so many of Groveton's sons and daughters. But what the hell, they both got in.

Anne pulled up at Elizabeth's house, switching to the left side of the street. The front wheel hooked over the curb, and a four-foot sapling John had planted last fall disappeared beneath the fender. "Ooops." Anne put the car in reverse. They could hear the grinding, snapping sound as she backed off the tree. It sprang up to a forty-five-degree angle, missing about half of its branches and a long strip of bark. "I guess those last several glasses hit me harder than I thought."

"I know. It still feels like we're moving." The car was rolling backward. "Brakes, Anne! Brakes!"

Anne stomped a pedal, fifty-fifty chance. The tires squealed and smoked, and the rear fender smashed into the brick mailbox, toppling it across the driveway in an avalanche of broken mortar and dust.

After the car had rocked to a stop, Anne said, "I better have those brakes looked at."

Elizabeth knew she had never laughed so hard in her life, at least not in her married life of twenty-five years. She got out of the car, staggered into the yard, and collapsed, laughing and pounding her fists into the grass, which was just turning green again. The air smelled of brick dust and burnt rubber. When the water cleared from her eyes, she saw Anne on the ground also, her body heaving as she tried to regain control of herself. Some of the neighbors were turning on their porch lights, stepping outside in pajamas and bathrobes. "Come on," Elizabeth managed to say, "we're not being very discreet." She crawled toward the front door.

In the kitchen they popped aspirin and drank tall glasses of water like a couple of college boys trying to prevent a hangover. Anne slept in the spare room.

CHAPTER 10

AT A BOOTH in back of a loud, fashionable deli, a thin man, late thirties, spoke into his palm-sized microcassette recorder. "June seventh. I am waiting here in the Midtown Deli to meet the new men's masters record holder for the ten-K, an unknown named John Ashe. No record of him placing in the top twenty-five of any major race, ever."

This was Jeff Sutton from *Distance Running*. He had called Subscriptions and learned that John Ashe had just recently started taking the magazine. One Elena Conifer had given it to him in February right around Valentine's Day, interestingly enough. On the morning in Stamford when Ashe had set the record, he had yet to receive his first issue. So where the hell had he come from?

The situation was very unusual. Most masters champions were former stars who had managed to deteriorate at a slower rate than other former stars. It was a function of relative injury, pure mechanics. Sutton, for example, had once placed sixth in the Boston Marathon and then had declined slowly enough that at thirty-nine he could beat three of the top 5 finishers, including the now bloated winner Gil Stevenson, owner of the Hot Foot chain of running shoe stores. Jeff's injuries were simply less bothersome than those of his former betters. One thing was for sure, though. Almost everyone who mattered in the racing world had been taking *Distance Running* since their teens or twenties when someone made a subscription gift of it—usually a relative, sometimes a lover.

Sutton compared a photograph of John Ashe crossing the finish line in Stamford to a man who had just entered the deli and was looking around. No way the guy was fifty, and if he was willing to lie about his age, then maybe he was willing to use performance-enhancing drugs. Sutton smelled fraud, and a scoop.

"There he is," he said into his microcassette recorder. "Looking far younger than I expected. Sort of a cross between a cocky athlete and a smug lawyer." He stood and waved the man over.

"How you doing, John Ashe?" They shook hands. "Jeff Sutton. Thanks for agreeing to the interview. That was quite a run you had up in Stamford the other day."

John scooted into the booth. "At the end of the race I was kicking myself for holding too much back. I could've gone faster."

"Hey, man, what drugs are you taking?" Sutton placed the microcassette recorder on the table between them.

John stared at him for a moment. "Alcohol, mostly. Aspirin sometimes. I've recently discovered the pleasures of a good cigar. I was hungover in Stamford. I almost didn't run. I really think they should've spotted me a few minutes on the race." He took a sip of ice water. "That was a nice try, though, get the old man to trip up and confess to something. I'm not using steroids. I've had a blood test, and I've had my birth certificate authenticated." Just then a waitress touched his shoulder with one hand while describing the various sandwiches on the menu. "Thanks, darling," he said.

Sutton was slightly taken aback by the force of the man's presence. Excepting the big-thighed, broad-shouldered sprinters, most decent runners were mere whiffs of humanity, so thin they often seemed to be life-size posters of themselves. You had to get them excited about something to even notice they were actually sitting with you at the banquet table or awards podium. Reynaldo Miller angry was the Marathon King. Reynaldo Miller in a good mood just sort of disappeared. This man Ashe was charismatic, calling the waitress "darling" like that *without* offending her, and attracting the attention of patrons at nearby tables apparently by sheer personal magnetism. If everyone in this restaurant were suddenly dropped on a desert isle, John Ashe would be king. They could all tell that some sort of interview was taking place, and there was no question about which man was the subject. Sutton felt himself losing control, becoming a sidekick to the garrulous star.

In some attempt at recovery he simply blurted out what had been bothering him. "I'm thirty-nine. Ten years ago I took sixth in the Boston Marathon. Peak of my career. But I got older, and now I have some nagging injuries." He stuck a hand under his shirt. "And my belly's getting soft. It's not too bad, I guess. But see, what's happening to me is normal, it's what's supposed to happen. As people get older they sort of fall apart, like cars."

Ashe thanked the waitress for his food, and she managed to squeeze his shoulder again. In addition to dyeing his hair, he had obviously had some plastic surgery done. No fifty-year-old had skin that tight around the jawbone, Sutton was convinced. John took a large bite of his Reuben sandwich and chewed slowly, eyebrows knitted together in thought. "See, in your mind they've taught you to think one way. You expect deterioration, therefore you get it. For a long time I expected it, too, and I got it. Let me tell you something, Jeff, off the record." He reached out, turned off the microcassette recorder.

"The average fifty-year-old man doesn't produce much semen. That's a medical fact. It's not that he's infertile or even necessarily impotent—another issue altogether. He still produces billions of sperm. Four or five ejaculations and he could fertilize the whole damn planet, theoretically, of course. But he doesn't really want to. He thinks less about sex, his wife thinks less about it, and he's so tired all the time from riding the train in and out of the city. The sense of urgency has gone out of him because he's in the process of giving up. His balls sense this, I think. It's as if they know the guy's through making babies, so hey, let's kick back and relax a bit. Let's just give him the minimum amount required to have a visible orgasm, it's not like he really needs the stuff."

Sutton said, "What the hell are you talking about?"

"Simple." John drank half a glass of water. "Proof I got my youth back. These past few weeks I've been shooting huge loads. Thick handfuls and mouthfuls."

"Whose mouth?"

"Let's leave her out of this."

"You're married, right?"

John held out his left hand. His ring finger still bore the ghost

of a constriction from the wedding band he had so recently removed. "Do you think that dent is permanent?" he asked.

"I just don't know. So you're getting divorced?"

"I imagine. It's up to her. I can't really fight it in good conscience or try to screw her over financially. It's not that I want to
marry someone else. That's probably the last thing I want to do."

They kept talking. Sutton was amazed at the subjects John was
willing to discuss, everything from his improved semen load to
the new ease with which he pissed. His prostate, which must
have been slightly enlarged back in the "old" days, must now
have shrunk back down to normal size. "I drink and piss like a
college boy. No waiting, no starts and stops."

"Congratulations."

John sat back and looked hard at Jeff. "What do you really
think of me, Sutton?"

"I find you . . . interesting, if somewhat crude."

"Yeah, I wasn't crude before all this started happening. I
would've had lunch with you, and you would've been bored out
of your skull. You wouldn't have written a story about me because you sure as hell wouldn't have found me interesting. Are
you offended by me?"

"No, the funny thing is, I like you."

Sutton felt that the interview was going poorly, but he couldn't
say why. The guy was answering all his questions, sometimes in
amusing ways, and some of what he said on the record was
printable. There was no serious hostility between subject and in-
terviewer, just an unusually high degree of give and take. Then
Sutton realized why he was so bothered. John Ashe was upset-
ting his values and expectations. The guy was a living refutation
of what was supposed to happen and how you were supposed to
behave at fifty. There was something unnatural about it. Frustrated by the inexplicable nature of the man's physical improvements, he almost brought up the subject of drug use again. But
no, it would be better to investigate that on his own.

The interview moved outside. John led them to a tobacco shop,
where he selected a Macanudo cigar. "Want one, Jeff? My treat."

"No, thanks. I don't smoke."

"Bad for you, huh?"

John shouldered the cigar with his teeth while the clerk

counted his change. Out on the sidewalk he lit up before the door had closed behind him. "So maybe I'll miss out on the Parkinson's years."

He walked toward the park, Sutton a half step behind him now and trying to catch up. Ashe was making eye contact with women walking in the other direction. Several of them smiled back at him. Most were much younger than he.

"Yeah," he was saying, "I did some calculations. If I just keep up my Stamford pace for twenty more miles, I'll win any marathon." He blew a cloud of smoke toward the sky.

"Oh, well, the marathon." Here Sutton felt himself on firm ground at last. "The marathon's a completely different animal altogether. It makes the ten-K look like a quarter-mile sprint."

"I'm running in New York this November. I got a special invitation." He turned around to observe the rear of a young woman they had just passed. "I don't know what's gotten into me lately, but every women I see, it's like I'm nineteen again. You know what I mean?" He held the cigar between his teeth. "Say, how about an easy fifteen through the park? Is there someplace you could change?"

"No, thanks," Sutton said. "My knee has been bothering me a lot lately . . ." And he kept talking, explaining the intricacies of his chronic injury, but John had withdrawn into a different, better world. His spirit had turned inward, leaving his body to walk along staring at Jeff Sutton with a slight smile, from which protruded the glowing Macanudo. Don't talk to me about injuries.

ELENA AND REY advised him not to run through the park after dark, but of course sometimes he did it anyway. Let the shadowy figures come at him, the packs of kids so bored they would break your head for entertainment. Let them come at him, if they dared. However much Elena tried to convince him otherwise, he felt that while running he was invincible. She knew he was just the kind of fortunate white man whose senseless murder would, for a day or two, dominate the Metro section of the *New York Times* and perhaps, after a few editorials, become a fleeting campaign issue for local politicians.

John ran through the park anyway, scanning the bushes for shadowy figures. They were in there—sleeping, smoking, drinking. Three or four times during the past few weeks he had been approached by a couple of potential muggers who, seeing his sharp eyes and his unusual swiftness, decided to wait for easier prey. Hell, he wasn't carrying a wallet anyway. Once Elena had insisted that he carry twenty dollars of "mugger money" in his fist. "They'll get mad at you if you don't have any."

"I'll get mad at them if they try to mug me."

"Just take it."

On his way home after that particular run he stepped into a bar and unrolled the twenty from his sweaty fist. It was good for four pints of beer, which took him an hour and a half. Elena had already called the police by the time he returned.

"The police?" John said when she told him. "What'd they say?"

" 'Lady, he's probably in a bar somewhere.' "

"Those guys know a lot about human nature. I guess that's why they're cops."

He continued running at night whenever he felt like it, and without the mugger cum beer money. In early May he finally encountered someone crazy enough to take him on—and the circumstances of the assault were somewhat unusual. John had already left the park. He had turned west on a side street and was within view of his building, sprinting toward it, when suddenly his feet were kicked out from under him and he was airborne. His palms skidded along in the sharded funk. He stood, whirled. With his body in a defensive crouch he saw his fists rise like a gun sight, and between them—unbelievable—the face of his only son.

Andy said, "You even brought her to our house." His voice shook and his eyes were red. "I asked her *out*, for chrissakes." Reaching out to shove his father's shoulder, the kid seemed all the more frustrated by how solid the old man was.

"I wasn't really involved with her when she came over to the house," John said, lowering his fists.

Andy's reply was a blow that glanced off his father's cheekbone. Acting on reflex now, John landed a punch and was clear-headed enough to be grateful that Andy's eyes were set so deeply, a trait from Elizabeth's side of the family. The kid stepped back for a moment, swaying a bit. He pressed a hand against his eye and then checked the fingers for blood.

"Are you all right, son? Please, let's—"

The kid charged, screaming at him. John sank to one knee and drove a fist into Andy's stomach. Andy doubled over, exposing his back. John was about to lower an elbow, but his reflexive intentions were thwarted by an unexpected sight—the pattern of Andy's ribs, visible through his T-shirt. The torso was heaving a bit without expanding and contracting with breath. Andy went down on one knee, making a high-pitched gasping sound. Clutching his stomach, he fell over onto his shoulder.

"My God . . . Andy!" John knelt beside the boy, rubbing his hand over the ribs. Blood from his palms soaked Andy's shirt. "I just knocked the wind out of you, you'll be all right." The sight of his son lying there trying to breathe brought back the horrible moments just after Lee Thomas had fallen to the pavement of the jogging path, still conscious though his lips were turning blue. John had lamely tried to joke with him and put him at ease. "What's the matter, I guess we're too fast for you, huh?" He had uttered hollow reassurances immediately belied by his fearful expression and unsteady voice. "You'll be all right, buddy, everything's fine . . ." Meanwhile Nathan had been yelling into his cell phone for the second time. "He's dying, where's the goddamn ambulance? I think he's having a heart attack!" A speeding teenage rollerblader had seen Lee at the last second and managed to jump over him, shouting "Jesus!" and looking back in annoyance.

"Oh no, son, I'm sorry, I'm sorry." John rubbed Andy's back.

The kid sat up, his eyes red-rimmed, lips coated with spittle. He still clutched his stomach, though his breathing was a bit easier now.

"Let me see your eye." John put a thumb on his son's cheekbone and turned the face toward the glow of a distant lamp. "We need to get some ice. Elena and I live not far from here—"

"I *know* that."

"So you were just waiting for me?"

A small crowd of gawkers had gathered around.

"What are you looking at?" John yelled as he helped Andy to his feet. They walked together toward the new love nest.

JOHN AND ELENA'S place on the Upper West Side was still barely furnished, and when he and Andy walked in that night they could see their colors smudged and reflected in the gleaming hardwood floor. Elena made an ice pack for Andy and, at John's signal, excused herself to the next room. Andy sat on the floor with his back against the wall and held the ice to his blackening eye.

"You got a couple of good punches in," John said.

"Right."

"No, really, I was just kind of lucky." He sat on the floor next to Andy. "I knew you were going to find out sooner or later."

"Why didn't you just *tell* me?"

"I knew you'd want to kick my ass . . . this isn't about money, is it, son? You're not worried that I'm going to leave it all to Elena, which I might at that, but I mean that's not why you're so upset, is it?"

"Jesus, Dad. *No.*" The kid looked disgusted. "I don't sit around thinking about my inheritance. I had hoped you and Mom would spend it all traveling or something, *with each other*. I'll be sixty by then anyway. I don't want *your* money. I want my *own* money." Groaning, he stood up.

"I think you need to stay here and rest for a while."

Andy was moving toward the door. "Thanks for the ice."

"Hey, are you going to keep attacking me like this, or can I relax about my own son?"

Andy paused in the doorway, looked back. "It was stupid, I shouldn't have done it . . . and someday you'll be saying those exact words."

"Ah, the grand exit. Well, be sure and slam the door."

Andy did.

Elena came out of the bedroom. "Are you okay?"

"Why wouldn't I be?"

"Because your son appears to hate you."

"No. I think he's frustrated that he really can't." Or so he hoped.

*   *   *

NOW JOHN AND Elena had their own place on the Upper West Side. The polished marble foyer, the gleaming hardwood floors, the sparse furnishings—it all seemed so bohemian to one who had spent the better part of his adult life in a fully nested Groveton home. Signing that lease, he felt as he had on his first day of college when his parents finally drove away. Liberated, time to *live.*

His new alertness rendered sleep a mere formality. Sometimes he would wake at five, Elena's head on his chest, and spend the next half hour stroking her smooth back and wondering how the hell all this had happened. Sometimes she would wake up and shuffle to the bathroom, the sight of her nude body in the moonlit room never failing to stun him. Even groggy and cranky, nearly tripping over his running shoes, she was such a beautiful little baby. "John!" She kicked his running shoes out of the way.

"Sorry."

She climbed into bed and laid her head on his chest. "I'm not going to pick up after you like a wife."

"Please don't."

His days since the affair began . . . he didn't think of it as an *affair*, not at all. That word implied something tawdry, something peripheral to some other more substantial relationship. Nathan Barradale had *affairs*. He would mislead the target woman into thinking there was a possibility of becoming his second wife, a delusion he would nourish over sneaky, candlelit dinners at second-rate restaurants to which he would never have considered taking the formidable Mrs. Nathan Barradale. When the woman demanded a commitment, Nathan pled confusion. He was very sorry, but she must have misunderstood his intentions. Through it all, Marni's position was never at risk. Very likely she even knew of the affairs and accepted them as something husbands were supposed to conduct, and the most you could ask was that they be discreet about it. Several biographies of her ambassador father detailed a history of philandering that covered three decades and ten countries, and produced for Marni several unconfirmed half siblings who sometimes wrote to her asking for money.

This relationship with Elena, it wasn't an affair. If he were to screw some other woman, like the waitress in the deli who had kept touching his shoulder, that would be an affair and it would hurt Elena very much. He could never do that, but there was no harm in looking. Elena had resurrected his sexual awareness. When he considered it, the image that came to mind was of those paramedics trying to jump-start Lee Thomas' heart, Lee's body arching into the air and then falling dead as clay to the sidewalk. Well, if Lee had suddenly opened his eyes . . . that's how John felt. Back from the dead. Every moment of every day was to be savored.

At six a.m. he would slide out from under Elena's head, if possible without waking her. He would reach into the shower for his jock strap and running shorts.

During this time he found it incomprehensible that as recently as last November he had been unable to run in the mornings. Now there was nothing to it. In the new suppleness of his lower limbs he found no resistance to the will of his mind. Days since he had even thought of his Achilles' tendons.

He usually ran five miles in the morning, just a little wake-up. Leaving the building, he would wave to the doorman and head east toward the park. He liked to run by the deserted Met and remember that day months earlier when he had followed— stalked—Elena out there during her lunch break. It had been a moment of courage or foolishness worthy of celebration. At six a.m. there was always one old bum on the steps, in his fashion a resourceful fellow, for he was always drunk. And what did he say? Same thing that Kurt Vermiel said. "Good day for it!"

Thirty minutes and five miles later, John would sit on the edge of the bed and jostle Elena, sometimes bending down to kiss her neck or back. "Wake up, babe."

Breakfast had become so much more important to John since his discovery that he could eat eggs with impunity. No more Colon Bran. He and Elena usually stopped in at the Sunrise Diner, where she had a toasted bagel to his three-egg omelet with hash browns and a buttered, jellied biscuit. Then the walk to work. Now they no longer parted ways a block before reaching the law firm, their affair being apparent to all who considered the possibility. People had begun to talk. So what?

Work was the worst part of the day. Barradale and Haley Wilson were all over him about Maxine Estep, who was all over them with her damn lawsuit. None of the other stuff John was supposed to be doing got done. On only a few occasions was he able to muster a sustained period of concentration. It didn't last long. He kept looking out the window. Hell, it was probably lunchtime anyway, and he would spend the next two hours running, or chowing Chinese take-out with Elena.

In the old days, when the train ride to Groveton awaited him at the end of the day, he had often worked until seven or eight. Now he was out by five to get his evening run in while Elena sometimes went to the gym or met her old roommate Shannon for a drink. John and Elena would rendezvous at obscure restaurants and hold hands across the table, just talking, repairing whatever slight damage the necessities of the day had done to their relationship. Sometimes John would smoke a cigar on the way home, Elena breathing in deeply the rich smell of contraband Cuban tobacco. They were increasingly unto themselves.

SHANNON LOOKED AT Elena over the rim of her wineglass. "So tell me, are you really happy?"

"I really am."

The bar was crowded with various young people just off from work. Someone kept bumping into Elena's back. "Sorry," he would say. "Guess you've got gravity." She did her best to ignore him.

Shannon continued. "I mean, I must say I was pretty surprised when you actually moved in with the guy. I thought you were just going to have an affair with him and get his help with law school."

"I didn't anticipate how strongly I'd feel."

"I'm not saying I can't understand why you're attracted to John. But I just think maybe someone a little closer to your own age . . ."

Just then someone bumped into Elena again. The same guy. "There goes your gravity again. You're attracting me."

She gave him a fuck-off smile and said to Shannon, "What were you saying about guys my own age?"

"If you just do the math."

"I can't think of it that way. It's not an equation."

"He's going to be an old man in a few years. And what *about* law school? Is he going to follow you to law school?" She paused for effect. "Or is he going to try to talk you out of going?"

"He wouldn't."

Yes, everything Shannon said about May-December relationships made sense in general, but of course it didn't apply to Elena and John. "In the first place, I've always pictured myself married to an older man." Not twenty-eight years older, she conceded to herself, but at least ten and perhaps even fifteen. "Is it better to have the right person? Or a person who's the 'right' age?" For that Shannon had no answer. "And the sex is absolutely great."

"So I remember hearing," Shannon said. "Those walls are pretty thin, *bella.*"

"I mean, he wants it more than nearly any other boyfriend I've ever had"—even more than Jake Coates, her first, when they were both nineteen and he was so constantly excited that she was surprised one day to catch him sleeping in the nude and see that his cock could be so soft and small. She merely blew on it, and it sprang to life while its nominal master kept snoring. That moment was somewhat of a revelation for her, illustrating the sometimes hilarious, sometimes alarming independence of the penis. John was almost the same way, as randy as a college boy, but his lust was not so scattered as had been poor Jake's, whose desire attached itself to whatever woman happened to cross his field of vision, until another one did, and so on. In the library it had amounted to a learning disability.

Shannon listened intently. Elena tried to describe what John was like as a lover, and kept coming up with unlikely oxymorons: ardently patient, expertly reckless, and so on. "What do you think *he'd* be like?" she asked, pointing a thumb over her shoulder at the guy who kept bumping into her. John, on the other hand, relished every part of her body. Sometimes she would go for days without touching his penis with her mouth or even her fingers. He wanted to work on her, not the other way around. The guy behind her now probably thought foreplay meant pushing his girlfriend's face toward his crotch. John would rub his big hands all over her body, kneading the skin and the muscles beneath, smelling her hair. Sometimes he would oil her down. Often he brought her to orgasm with his tongue. He was such a slow lover that he rarely entered her before she begged him to. Sometimes she suspected that this was his goal, to make her beg for it. She would grab him by the hair and pull him up to face her, at the same time trying to catch the tip of his swollen penis on the lip of her vagina, whereupon she would thrust her hips upward, sheathing him completely. Once inside her he would begin steadily, still trying to maintain control, and then as he pumped and pumped, all indications of intelligence would drain from his face and he would fuck her with an urgency which in her experience had always precluded such maddeningly slow foreplay. Jake Coates used to just stick a finger in to see if she was wet enough. At nineteen, staring down at his reason for existence, she usually was.

Shannon said, "I don't really want to hear all this, do I?"

"Oh." Elena's face reddened slightly. "Guess I got carried away."

HE WAS SCHEDULED to fly to Boulder on Friday, May 23, to run the famous Bolder Boulder Roadrace.

Also on May 23 he was scheduled to be in court for a preliminary hearing regarding the Maxine Estep lawsuit. Barradale was excited. Walking down the hall with a hand at the small of his old jogging partner's back, he said, "Some of that stuff you and Elena came up with was great. I wish you could've gotten her father to agree to appear voluntarily—"

"Bill won't even talk to me. What little we got, she got."

"What little. He gave us a deposition swearing he'd employed her as his paralegal. We can always subpoena him for the actual trial."

The two men passed through the Hallway of Death, both glancing up briefly at Lee Thomas. Red tie, gold clip. Barradale steered John into his office.

"Hello, Mr. Ashe." From Nathan's secretary he detected a coolness indicative of his diminished status within the firm. Barradale himself had remained friendly, though his exasperation with

John's indiscretions appeared to be growing. He had yet to lose his Christmas bloat. Perhaps this year it was permanent. If he looked a bit older, sitting there behind his desk, he also looked perfectly competent, and his voice sounded even more stentorian than before, as if the extra poundage had improved the acoustics of his chest cavity. "Now, John, say you're in court. On the witness stand. I'm Maxine Estep's lawyer. I ask you if you're romantically involved with Elena Conifer. What do you say?"

"I wasn't romantically involved when I hired her."

Barradale handed over a manila envelope. "Take a look at those."

It was full of photographs of John and Elena out on the town, holding hands, kissing. In one, her hand was clearly on his crotch. "Maxine's lawyer gave me those yesterday in the hopes that I would settle with him. Should I settle with him?"

"Well, this is pretty strong stuff."

Barradale said, "If I were Mr. and Mrs. America on the jury and I saw these, you'd be cooked. I'd know you wanted to sleep with her from the moment you saw her."

"But, Barradale, don't you see how ridiculous that is? Didn't you want to sleep with her from the moment you saw her? Doesn't everybody? I don't want to go to this hearing thing. Something's come up."

" 'This hearing thing.' " Barradale spoke very slowly, as if trying to understand the words. "Don't want to do it." He shrugged, raised his eyebrows. "Matter of fact, I don't, either. I think we should settle. Otherwise your wife might see these pictures. You know Court TV is considering covering this trial. Big sexist lawyer versus grandmother paralegal. I think if there's no celebrity murder between now and then, you're on the air, old boy. Elizabeth will see these photos . . ." Barradale inhaled, was about to speak, but seemed to think better of it.

"What?" John said. "Go ahead."

"John, a divorce is expensive, and a mistress is expensive." He threw his arms into the air. "To begin with, you're doing this all wrong. You don't *marry* the women you have affairs with! Hell, I've cheated on Marni, you know that, but I still love her. As a rule you shouldn't even spend a single night at another woman's place. You should just sort of get them out of your system. Think of your assets, how they'll be divided up. I like Elizabeth, John. She's all right. Think of your grandchildren having to visit you and Elizabeth separately, it's ridiculous. Yes, Elena is a beautiful woman, girl. She's a beautiful girl. But you honestly think this is going to work? Come to your senses. She's bowled over right now because of your position and your wealth, and okay, the running thing. Congratulations, by the way. But what if you lose your position and half your wealth?"

"Why would I lose my position?"

Barradale pressed his fingers together. "There's been some talk, just talk so far, of asking you to take a leave of absence."

Ah, there it was, the threat. Clauses in some document somewhere provided for a partner to be forced to take a leave of absence—to be fired, essentially—for various vaguely worded infractions. A couple of coarse gray hairs were curled around Barradale's nostril rims. Horrified, John tried not to stare. But gray nose hairs . . . it would soon be portrait time.

He said, "I don't want Elizabeth to see those photos. No point in rubbing her face in it."

Barradale said, "It's a shameful period in a man's life. But so many of us go through it. We're friends. Listen to me, go back to Elizabeth. Cut down on the running. You've already got the masters record and that's great. You're fifty years old, you're not getting any faster. Or younger. Stop acting like a teenager." He saw in John's face that his words weren't registering. He sighed, shook his head. "I don't know what to say to the other partners."

John stood up. "Before Elena, I was just like part of a machine, Nathan. I rode into the city and I rode back out again with a bunch of cash. And that's all I did, and that's all you do, only I can't do it anymore. And as far as getting old—Elena makes my body younger."

"She makes your mind feeble, I think." He paused. "And can you tell this guy Jeff Sutton to stop snooping around? He keeps accosting people in the lobby and asking about you."

THE NURSE LED Jeff Sutton into an examination room. "Just take off you shoes and socks, please. The doctor will be right with you."

When the door opened again, Dr. Dowling stood there glancing over his clipboard at Jeff's still shod feet. "You'll have to take those off," he said. "And your socks."

"Actually, I don't have a problem with my feet," Sutton said. "I'm a reporter. I just wanted to buy a few minutes of your time to ask you about a patient of yours."

"All records are confidential," Dowling said. But he closed the door.

Jeff opened his own clipboard to a series of articles about John Ashe setting the masters record in the 10-K. "You must be quite a podiatrist, Doc. I understand he used to limp all day after running just a few miles." This information he had obtained from bribable paralegals at Masterson, Grandissime, and Barradale.

"Really?" The doctor held the photographs up to the window. "This is incredible. Unbelievable. I mean, it was only a matter of time before one of his Achilles' tendons ruptured. I told him, watch yourself, remember what happened to Al Gore."

"So you have no way to explain this?"

"I'm still not even sure I *believe* it."

MAXINE'S LEGAL TEAM stalled on the settlement. They weren't interested in settling out of court, they said, when they could expose such a pervasive problem as age discrimination to the public at large via Court TV. John got the call Friday morning.

"The hearing's definitely on," Barradale said. "Two o'clock."

"My plane leaves at two."

Across the room Elena had just finished zipping the last suitcase. Now her shoulders sagged. It had been months since the cookout at John's house, and since then she had yet to escape the complexity of Manhattan even for just a weekend. She put her hands on her hips. "No way." John put a finger to his lips, shushing her.

"Okay, okay," he was saying. "Fine, fine, I'll be there."

They managed to get their tickets changed to the five o'clock flight. In order for them to make it, the hearing would have to start on time and end quickly, and Elena would have to keep a cab waiting out in front of the courthouse with their bags in the trunk.

When John walked into the courtroom and took his place

among team Masterson, Grandissime, and Barradale, Maxine Estep leaned toward one of her lawyers to speak. John read her lips. She said, "Who's that?"

Was it possible? Had he changed so much that she did not recognize him? The thought was not as comforting as he would have expected. Now Maxine's lawyer pointed at the prescription glasses that she held in her hand. She put them on, and her eyes widened as if at some grotesque physical anomaly. John winked at her. When the other side complained to the judge, Barradale said that John had recently developed an unfortunate twitch of the left eye due to the stress of being ensnared in such a frivolous lawsuit. The judge banged his gavel.

Maxine Estep had also changed. Flanked by lawyers, she looked much older than when she had first stepped into John's office to assume command. Now she looked good-hearted, too, grandmotherly, though she didn't have any kids.

The proceedings began at 2:45. John played tic-tac-toe against himself on the back of a dollar bill. He kept grabbing Nathan Barradale's wrist and twisting it around to see the time. Barradale told him to stop it, to sit up and square his shoulders and try to look interested. At four o'clock the judged called a ten-minute recess.

Fifteen minutes later, everyone was back in place but John Ashe. Barradale, expressing concern for his friend's health and safety, won permission from the judge to go check the men's room. As he walked down the hallway he half expected to find his old friend lying on the tiled floor in the last stages of a heart attack, and he half expected the truth, that this irresponsible runner, this burden to the firm, had simply left.

IN THE RENTAL car with the windows down and the radio loud, riding north along the front range of the Rockies, John and Elena were amazed at the pleasant dryness of the air, the brightness of the sun, and the monumental beauty of the mountains. "And what the hell song is this, this is great."

"It's the Band, a song called 'The Weight.'"

"I don't see how you keep up with all this new music."

"This is like twenty years old, John."

"Really?"

"Guess you were on the train."

They crested one last hill and there, spread out below them, was Boulder, a town that might have been designed in reply to New York City. There were two tall buildings, which John later found out were dormitories for the University of Colorado. Otherwise, everything was low, as if in deference to the mountains. "Let's move here," he said. "I'm probably not going to have a job when I get back anyway."

"You sure about that?"

"Pretty sure." Did he feel guilty for taking off from the courtroom? Maybe he should have, but in fact he didn't. Besides, they'd do as well or better without him—he was, after all, the source of the suit.

She looked west toward mountains, which were golden in the glow of the sunset. "I guess I could apply to law schools from here."

John had already been considering a move. He had learned that Anne Newton had moved in with Elizabeth. That his wife now had some good company went a long way toward assuaging his feelings of guilt. But there was something depressing about the thought of two so-to-speak spurned women resorting to a roommate-type relationship of shared grievances. He wanted to get away from such thoughts, and Boulder was perhaps farther from Groveton than any sense of guilt could reach.

The most important reason for moving to Boulder would be that it was a great place to train, according to *Distance Running*. The thin air would be great for building up lung capacity, the mountains great for inspiration. He and Elena could hike all around and make love outdoors. He also understood that Boulder had an extensive network of off-road trails which were said to be easier on your feet, knees, and ankles than was concrete. Not that he needed to pamper himself, apparently. Indeed, he felt an almost superstitious fear of taking certain precautions, lest his mind and body conspire to justify them.

THEY STAYED AT a turn-of-the-century inn called the Hotel Boulderado, located just a block from the shops and restaurants of Pearl

Street. They followed a baggage-laden porter up the stairs, running their hands along the ornate wooden banister. Though Boulder was a city of nearly a hundred thousand just thirty miles north of Denver, the Hotel Boulderado still had about it the elegance of an outpost on the frontier. With its thick, hand-carved woodwork and its sparkling chandeliers it must have once been a honeymoon destination for the heirs to ranching and agricultural fortunes. At the top of the stairway Elena leaned out over the lobby four stories below and pronounced the place "wonderful, John."

After tossing their luggage onto the bed, they walked out to Pearl Street and stood there for a moment trying to decide which way to turn. Finally Elena dragged him by the hand west toward the silhouette of the mountains. In her jeans and Bolt! T-shirt she fit in seamlessly with the younger crowd and attracted the attention of several scruffy looking males. Trustafarians, she called them—as in trust fund and Rastafarian. She kept her arm around John's slim, tight waist, rubbed his belly. "We've got to get you some food, get you to bed."

They wandered from restaurant to restaurant, reading menus in the windows. The Fourteenth Street Bar and Grill specials that night included grilled beef tenderloin and several seafood dishes. Inside, they drank martinis at the bar and discussed the upcoming race with a man who, it turned out, would be in charge of one of the water stations at the finish in the University of Colorado football stadium. "It's a party, I'm telling you. The Kenyans usually beat everyone, and then a few more foreigners, and then a few Americans, and then finally all the normal people who just want to go out and have a bloody Mary brunch. I'm not saying foreigners aren't normal," he said. "I hope you didn't think that. Nobody thinks that in Boulder."

After a long pause, Elena said, "So, what do you do?"

"I'm a recycling volunteer. Except I have to drive to work, isn't that ridiculous? I'd sell my car, but it wouldn't be enough to get the mountain bike I really want."

The hostess tapped John's shoulder. "Your table's ready."

John and Elena followed her to a table by the window. John had the beef tenderloin special, Elena the shellfish medley over linguini in a cream sauce. She ate with relish and, no doubt, without detriment to her figure. Back in the hotel, they took their time with each other, and John woke up at six a.m. feeling totally re- freshed. Took a little training run along the Boulder Creek Path, dodging all forms of wheeled recreation, some of which he had never seen before and could not name.

Elena had earlier on told Andy she had a boyfriend in Boulder. In fact, she had a female friend, a former Magnate suite mate pursuing an M.A. in anthropology. Zoe Gordon was a thin girl with a beautiful, angular face and hair out of a Botticelli painting, thick, dark rings spiraling down to her shoulder blades. Sunday they met for a late lunch at Buscon's on the west end of the mall.

Being a graduate student anywhere in the country meant you were too poor to eat out in style, and Zoe for months had lived on pasta, peanut butter, and porous Midwestern bagels. So at Buscon's she stared at the menu as if it were a winning lottery ticket. The martini glass, when she raised it to drink, accentuated the fine angles of her face and her smile drawn back in laughter. Her knee brushed John's under the table—was that intentional? Her expression gave no clue. She was nodding her head while Elena told the story of going hiking the day before with John up in Chautauqua Park.

Within a few minutes John had decided that the sub-table con- tact had been accidental, but he was still thinking about it. "Boul- der's a great town," Zoe was saying. "But I haven't met any guys yet that really excite me. They've got no ambition out here. All they want to do is ski and ride their bikes and climb rocks. That's fine for a year or two, but you're twenty-eight years old, do something with your life."

John thought about that for a moment. "Just be careful. You're beautiful enough that you could probably get one of those guys to quit skiing and go to law school. But that's not what he really wants to do. He wants to ski, and so if he goes to law school it's just an act. Even if it lasts twenty-five years."

Elena was looking at him somewhat critically. "I don't know about that."

"I speak from experience."

The knee brushed his under the table again. Again pure accident, he told himself. The martinis were getting to Zoe, and very likely she did not even feel the contact herself. She was as beautiful as Elena, but in a completely different way, darker. John tried to imagine what her life was like, what she would look like at thirty, forty, fifty . . .

If one was good, were two better? Sophomoric, he told himself. But logic didn't stop him from wanting Zoe, too. That night, making love to Elena, he confessed this to her, and was surprised at her reaction. "She's not really into that. I have other friends, though. Maybe if you're a good boy, I'll surprise you someday."

"Have you ever slept with another girl?" Why did he ask *that*?

"Once," she said quickly. And for the next five minutes she told him the things she had done with the other girl. When he finally came, a massive load, he found himself wondering if his wise lady had made it all up just to enhance his momentary pleasure.

HE ALWAYS LOST her at race time. She was in the crowd somewhere. A cursory scan of heads failed to reveal her new Boulderado hat, which she had bought for protection against the sun. Frank Shorter, who had founded the race, was no more than ten feet away, and John was wondering if he should introduce himself when Shorter spotted him and walked over. The veteran hero of the 1972 Olympic marathon clapped John between the shoulder blades and congratulated him on the Stamford run. "Saw your picture in *DR*, quite a race." Despite all that had happened so quickly during the past few months, John still could not believe he was receiving the congratulations of Frank Shorter, an idol of sorts. Often as he rode the train into the city during the seventies he would think of Frank Shorter out in the wilderness somewhere, alone in a setting of natural beauty, every unphotographed step a missed poster opportunity. Yet meeting Shorter also brought out John's competitive side. "You know, I'm going to have to beat you today."

"In that case," Shorter said, "do me the favor of beating your own record."

"Deal."

It was at the Bolder Boulder that John first saw the three Kenyans who had been winning all the major road races lately. Rumor was that they weren't even trying, that they were merely using the races as training runs for the New York Marathon in November. They were equally curious about the old man everyone was talking about, and they gathered around to shake his hand. Their English was passable but sounded a bit perky and fast.

Elena stood with Zoe at the five-mile mark, both of them amazed when the three Kenyans appeared in the distance, so far ahead of everyone else and in the middle of some sort of argument or debate. The one on the left yelled at the other two, pounding his fist into the opposite palm, all the while running with his knees high. His running shoes skimmed the asphalt at nine-foot intervals. The Kenyan on the right disagreed at full volume and with expansive movements of his lanky arms. They weren't even out of breath. The one in the middle saw Elena and Zoe and elbowed his adjacent companions into awareness, the women were so beautiful. The argument stopped. All three Kenyans looked up smiling, and then—whoosh!—they were gone. A titter of amusement rippled through the crowd of spectators gathered near Elena and Zoe.

John was not far behind the next pack of runners. "This is Frank Shorter!" he yelled, pointing at the man next to him.

Whoosh, they were gone. Another titter of amusement rippled through the crowd.

John felt great. This was his best race so far. Maxine schmaxine. The lawsuit issue lifted whole from his mind like a hat knocked off by the wind.

Everyone had warned him about the altitude in Boulder. But his lungs felt fine. And Frank Shorter wasn't there anymore, he was somewhere farther back.

The race finished spectacularly in Folsom Field, the runners doing their last quarter mile around the University of Colorado's track while spectators in the stadium cheered. For John it was an all-out sprint. He passed two more runners, both much younger. He rounded the far turn, his knees high and his lungs for the first time today beginning to ache. He sprinted to the finish line, grabbed his Popsicle stick.

People were slapping his back. He had just broken his own

record by three seconds. He made his way to the water station and said hello to the guy he had met at the Fourteenth Street Bar and Grill. A minute or two later Frank Shorter shook his hand and called him remarkable.

```
┌─────────────────────────────┐
│                             │
│  C H A P T E R    1 1       │
│                             │
└─────────────────────────────┘
```

"IT'S AN M.D. slash Ph.D. program, and it's pretty self-explanatory. It takes seven years, and then you're an M.D. who also has a Ph.D."

John had agreed to this examination when young Steven Fiske called him out of the blue a few days after the Bolder Boulder. The not-yet-a-doctor was writing his dissertation on a theoretical phenomenon called *youthing*. He admitted quite frankly that even his most tolerant advisers thought he was wasting his time. The old guard, the same bunch that had driven the famous Dr. Hurvitz out of practice and into virtual poverty, thought Steven Fiske was as crazy as that crackpot had been, and maybe the two so-called theorists should get together somewhere, preferably in a rubber room. "Some people have had HIV for ten, fifteen years and still haven't developed full-blown AIDS," Fiske told John, "which conventional medical wisdom says is impossible. Similarly, a very few people like yourself have done some remarkably youthful things later in life and they all feel, as you said on the phone the other day, like they got their youth back. I want to find out how and why."

They were in a laboratory at the Cornell University Medical School. Despite his youth—Fiske was just twenty-seven—he had the haggard look of someone who has sacrificed his health in the relentless pursuit of discoveries. A small blue vein ran from the corner of his right eye back along his temple and into the thin hair above his ear. He was already thickening up across the middle, and his cheeks had a sort of Lee Thomas softness to them. He stood behind John and pressed the cold circle of the stethoscope into the older man's muscular back.

"Ah," John said. "Little more to the left."

"Breathe deeply, please. Basically what I'm telling you, John, is that this is all impossible. What you're doing, a fifty-year-old man just up and running this fast after a life of inactivity, it's totally impossible. What I'd like to do is find out why, so I can help others be more productive later in life."

"Some sort of serum you can extract?" John shook his head. "I don't know. I hate to tell you this, but I wasn't totally inactive all those years. I jogged fairly regularly."

Fiske grinned. "I know. I have the records from your podiatrist." He opened a folder and held a series of X rays one by one up to the light. The severe inflammation at the backs of both heels was readily apparent. "I can't believe he didn't tell you to stop running."

"He did tell me to stop running. It's a good thing I didn't listen to him." He counted the points off on his fingers. "I'd still be unhappily married. I'd still be riding the train in to work every day, eating Colon Bran for breakfast, getting fat anyway, spending all day in an office, riding the train home at night, falling asleep in front of Larry King. I'd be dead."

"Colon Bran?"

"It's what I call it."

Fiske patted his own stomach. "I should run, I guess. Let me tell, you though, John, if we took, say, one hundred fifty-year-old men and put them in a running race, first of all it would be impossible for any of them to run as fast as you, and if they did manage somehow to do it they'd probably have a heart attack."

"That happened to a friend of mine."

"See?"

That John was running so well seemed an anomaly that Fiske wanted to attribute more to virtually unique physiological events than to some training routine which others could theoretically emulate to obtain similar results. John was here out of charity for Fiske and curiosity about himself. What the hell *was* making him run faster?

There was one big change in his life, in the before and after pictures, and her name was Elena Conifer.

Fiske was drawing a few cc's of blood now. "I'm going to test you for everything from steroids to cholesterol. I'll need a swatch of your hair, from the temples, to satisfy myself that you aren't coloring it." Wrinkling his forehead, Fiske ran a finger around the outside corner of John's eye. "And what moisturizer are you using?"

"Moisturizer?"

"The skin around your eyes, it's too smooth."

"Too smooth," John repeated blankly. "I don't know. I think it got that way because I started eating a lot of eggs and greasy food, and all that moisturizer just went in there and smoothed things out."

Fiske smiled and jotted a few lines of scribble into his notebook. "I want you to help me out," he said. "Assuming all the drug tests come back negative, as you say they will, I'd like you to please come back every week so I can monitor your progress, or regression, as the case may be. And maybe you'll learn a little something about yourself." Fiske smiled. It was too early to tell yet if he had found a corroborating case to Hurvitz's landmark study of 1961, which had gotten the brilliant researcher laughed out of his job and stripped of his reputation. But he could hope.

THERE HAD BEEN no absurd drunkenness since the night Anne backed over the mailbox, though they did split a nice bottle of wine every evening with dinner.

There was always an arrangement of flowers somewhere—the kitchen table, the living room coffee table, the vanity in Elizabeth's bedroom, or Anne's. She had taken the spare room and done it over in a less conventional color scheme, with such impressive results that Elizabeth was considering having the whole interior of the house transformed as radically as her own notions of love and marriage recently had been. Funny, though, despite the emotional upheaval she was only rarely depressed anymore, and fewer and fewer were the moments when she caught herself wishing John were snoring in bed beside her.

Living with Anne was a revelation. In a marriage, a favor done several times becomes a regular chore. To stop doing it is a form of negligence. But Elizabeth and Anne tended to notice and appreciate each other's contributions to the household rather than simply getting angry when for one reason or another something didn't get done.

Anne was cleaner, neater than John. She didn't spatter the bathroom mirror with the product of her flossings. She didn't spit toothpaste onto the consequently ever gleaming faucet. Whereas John had viewed the house simply as a sort of camping site away from the daily Battle of New York, for Anne it was more of a home, to be improved by small, frequent gestures of courtesy as much as by rare, large-scale weekend projects. One of Anne's most considerate renovations had to do with the stair climber, which she felt John had used as a prop for reminding her of her expanding dimensions. Anne pushed it outside next to the patio and planted ivy around its base. "In Florida they're doing the same thing with old tanks and things," she said, "dumping them in the ocean for the coral to grow on. They become things of beauty."

Anne didn't spend her evenings complaining about having to go back to work the next day, the way John had. *Know what it's like riding the damn train all the time, sitting in my office all day?* Or: *Lee Thomas had a heart attack.* The way he had turned that awful news into a rhetorical sledgehammer, making her feel petty and insensitive to his needs! And Anne didn't fall asleep in front of Larry King with her shoes off and her swampy socks emitting the events of the day in a sort of olfactory replay.

Dinners were the best part of this new life. Elizabeth and Anne would shop at the overpriced, organic-obsessed Davidson's Market, the kind of grocery that didn't look like a grocery but perhaps an architectural firm or a software company. No gaudy sales banners hung in the tinted windows. You could even miss the sign itself, which was but one nondescriptive word anyway: DA-VIDSON'S. No need to announce GROCERY. Those who could afford Davidson's prices already knew about it; in its aisles were no trailer wives in curlers and sweatpants with a fistful of food stamps and a passel of children trailing behind the squeaky cart. Snobbish thought, Elizabeth told herself. Well, what the hell . . . Even the employees were well educated, failed academics mostly, and if you cared to listen to them they could be quite eloquent, as they unpacked the fruit crates, about their thwarted expectations and how academia was a scam similar to but on a grander scale than that of the local Groveton Secretarial School, which couldn't guarantee you a job, either. Elizabeth and Anne knew all about thwarted expectations and how sometimes you were better off with a life you had not anticipated. They were an encouraging, motherly audience for the disenchanted.

Every other day they walked out of Davidson's with some of the finest meats, fish, and produce, and the best breads, oils, and spices to be had on the east coast of the United States. Eating well had become a source of healing, and a source of comparative satisfaction. John and William no doubt were clogging their arteries with the fat of cheeseburgers. Not that Anne and Elizabeth were eating with their own arterial health in mind, but wasn't it better to die clogged up with the fat of beef tenderloin than with that of ground chuck? Didn't you get some sort of extra points for that?

One night as Anne opened the wine she said again, "I guess I have to move back soon. I hate for this to end."

"Sell your house," said Elizabeth, stirring heavy cream into a madeira and tomato sauce. "Move in permanently."

"You really wouldn't get tired of me? Not that I would get tired of you, I wouldn't. But I think I'm hard to live with."

"Who told you that? William? You can't move out, I'll be lonely." She stirred the sauce briskly, the wooden spoon clacking against the sides of the pan. "What am I going to do, cook for one? Within three days I'd be microwaving frozen burritos."

They talked about it. The truth was that neither had been looking forward to coming home night after night to a big, empty house, monument to a failed marriage and a spent youth. There would be that horrible moment when the kids gave you one of those medical-emergency transmitters to wear around your neck.

Both were broad of shoulder and through the middle, with thick thighs and back-heavy upper arms. As they ate the same foods and began slowly to put on weight, they became so nearly identical in figure that each could wear the other's clothing. In the mornings they would traipse back and forth between their two homes, trying things on and soliciting opinions. One day they literally bumped into each other in the hallway, each in a bra and panties, each holding two possible dresses in either hand. Elizabeth laughed. "We're starting to act like a couple of dykes."

"People probably do think that, don't you imagine?"

That evening they watched a talk show featuring women who had left their husbands for other women. All spoke generally of how much more satisfied they were with their new partners, how much more fun it was to cook, to shop, how much nicer the house was. Elizabeth turned up the volume. During a commercial break she said, "I really wish I had thought of that. Can you imagine the crushing blow to his ego?"

"It *would've* been a good idea." Anne seemed about to say something else but instead filled her mouth with wine.

"What?" Elizabeth asked.

"I have an extremely embarrassing confession to make. I really, really miss sex, though I don't miss having it with William. He always seemed so bored with me."

"Little did you know."

"That's right."

The show came back on. They watched attentively. During the next commercial break they resumed their conversation as if it had not been interrupted.

"John and I didn't do it much, either. He had a very low sex drive. I'd be thinking about it during the day, you know, maybe thinking about grabbing him in the foyer as soon as he walked in. But he always seemed so tired. He was always asleep in front of Larry King. Sexy, let me tell you! Mouth open. Shoes off." She waved a hand in front of her nose.

A moment later she continued. "That's what I don't understand about him and Elena. I can't imagine he's doing it enough to please her."

Anne refilled both wine glasses. "Suppose I want to . . . get laid, I believe is the term. How do I go about it? I really don't know any desirable men. I can't go to a bar and pick up a stranger—I mean, I've already tested negative for HIV and there's no way I'm going to put myself at risk again. You see, the thing is, Elizabeth, I don't want a relationship with a man. The most I'd want is his penis for a few minutes."

"I sort of feel like I'm running a penis embargo," Elizabeth said. "But I guess we could go out and try to meet men. Insist that they wear condoms."

"You think anyone would pay attention to us?"

The show continued. Most of the lesbian relationships had begun in friendship and then proceeded to lust only after a firm mutual respect had been established. Often two women lived together for a time and shared the household chores such as cleaning and cooking. Then one night an accidental touch became a purposeful one. Or a glance suddenly deepened. Or the conversation simply turned to sex and how they missed it, while dreading the insensitive man that the operation would necessarily involve. Or would it?

By the time they got around to a physical consummation of their mutual love, said first-time lesbian couples on the show, the act was a cathartic pleasure, long overdue.

Anne opened another bottle of wine. She refilled both glasses. "Have you ever had a lesbian experience?"

"God, no." Elizabeth blushed. "Can't say I've never thought about it, what it would be like. Oh, this is good wine." She took a long drink. "Part of it is I think women are expected to be more intimate with each other generally. Remember in college sitting around in your panties and doing those breast exercises and talking about sex and what it would be like with this or that guy? It crosses your mind, what would it be like with *her*? Have you ever seen—and I'm not going to say when I did—have you ever seen a pornographic movie with two women doing things to each other? Oh, I can't believe I'm telling you this, you're getting me drunk."

Anne feigned shock. "Has the chair of the Department of English at the Groveton Country Day School just confessed to being turned on by a porno flick?"

"Don't tease."

"Sorry." Anne moved closer on the couch. Their thighs were touching. "I can honestly say that I know the feelings you're talking about."

Elizabeth tossed back the rest of her wine and set the glass on the coffee table. "I don't know how I'd be coping with this divorce stuff without you." When she threw her arms around Anne's neck, her foot rose, swatting the wineglass to the carpet.

She didn't bother picking it up. "I trust you completely," she said.

"I trust you, too."

They moved into the bedroom, dimmed the light. They were less nervous than they would have been undressing in front of some strange man after more than twenty-five years of being seen (or not, in Elizabeth's case) by an unimpressed husband. The strange man might laugh. He might be diseased. He would almost surely be drunk. In the morning he would slip away without a word, feeling as though he had defiled himself, yet later that night would tell the story to all his bar buddies. *Hey, you remember those two old fat women who were here last night? Well, I got sooo drunk . . .*

None of those fears was in play now. Elizabeth and Anne understood the stretch marks, the mild cellulite, the low-hanging breasts, the random gray pubic hair. All the signs of aging which generally drove men away Elizabeth and Anne celebrated, and they discovered that the clitoris did not age, was an everlasting nub of youth. This was glorious defiance, like having sex for the first time when everyone from the preacher to the P.E. teacher and of course your mom warns you against it. Elizabeth and Anne were grabbing late in life at forbidden pleasure and enjoying it.

Both had known what it was like to be young and attractive, to be pursued by boys you liked, boys you didn't, to be harassed by bosses, whistled at by construction workers. Elizabeth's boss at the movie theater when she was twenty had told her that if she didn't want to work Christmas day, she could meet him in the back room after closing. So she worked Christmas day. Anne had once received a C in college rather than boost her grade by the extra-credit activity suggested by her married, yellow-toothed professor. All their lives sex had been something to trade for something else, and this was the first time it had ever come without the power play.

After that night whatever small desire remained for marital reconciliation vanished. If Elizabeth could take John for half of the defunct union's assets, and if Anne could take William for half of theirs, then the new couple could live well just off the interest from their combined divorce settlements. Neither, though, would quit their jobs for a few years. Work was good for you; it fed you the outside world in measured, familiar doses.

When Elizabeth woke up the next morning, Anne beside her, she felt confident, attractive, and capable for the first time since John had told her—over the phone, the coward—that he wasn't coming home again.

She shook Anne. "Did I snore?"

"Mmm?"

"John always said my snoring kept him up."

"No, you weren't snoring."

"He said I snored like a cow."

"It must have been because you weren't sexually satisfied. You sure didn't snore last night."

CHAPTER 12

THE HOT FOOT was owned by Gil Stevenson, who had won the Boston Marathon the year a never-was has-been named Jeff Sutton placed sixth. Stevenson had managed to parlay his fame into the multimillion-dollar shoe store chain, of which this downtown store was the flagship. On the wall was a poster-size blow-up of the *Distance Running* cover showing Stevenson's thin chest breaking the tape that year in Boston. Six minutes behind him, way out of camera range, lost to history, was Jeff Sutton at the peak of his career.

He sat down in a chair waiting for John Ashe. This would be the second of three, perhaps four interviews.

The great tragedy of Sutton's life, he felt, was that as a young man he had chosen a field in which only the very best ever made any money. Suppose he had spent as much time and effort trying to become a lawyer. Hell, he'd be as rich as John Ashe right now and have a big house in Connecticut with a Pawley's Island hammock in the backyard. Instead he had sacrificed his twenties in an effort to be number one, and he had been number six, which might as well have been number six thousand. He thought of other professions. What if he had become the sixth best doctor in the nation? He'd have money, position. The sixth best tax accountant, the sixth best chef, the sixth best anything, for chrissakes, the sixth best waiter! Even the sixth best sportswriter, which he unfortunately was not, in part because his sport was not the sixth most popular.

Gil Stevenson himself walked in with John Ashe and the two men stood at the cash register talking. Sutton lifted his microcassette recorder. "He's looking even younger now. Part of it is his clothing. He's a more youthful dresser, his hair is longer, darker. He looks like a poster boy for the Gap or Banana Republic." He checked his slightly contemptuous tone. "Talking with Gil Stevenson, Stevenson the younger of the two, though his career is over, Ashe the older man whose legal career is over but whose running career appears to have just begun." From his various inquiries Sutton knew that in the wake of the million-dollar Maxine Estep settlement Ashe had taken a "voluntary" leave of absence from Masterson, Grandissime, and Barradale—voluntary in the sense that he hadn't objected to the loaded suggestion that he do so.

"Hey, Jeff," John called, "get over here. You know Gil, don't you?"

Stevenson said, "I don't think we've met." Over the years he had put on enough weight that now he might have been a retired bowler or golfer.

"Sure we have." Jeff pointed to the blow-up of the *Distance Running* cover. "I got sixth in that race. Jeff Sutton."

"Rings a bell," Stevenson said. "But you know, I beat so many people!" He burst into laughter, slapping John Ashe's back.

A young kid, maybe nine or so, was in the store with his parents. The father recognized Ashe. "Hey, I've been following your recent accomplishments," he said. "It's just great, it's a real inspiration."

The kid pulled on his father's hand. "Dad, what's a second wind?" He had read the term from a Mercury shoe poster.

"Second wind? I bet Mr. Ashe knows."

John bent over to look the kid in the eye. "When you're running along, kid, and it's about two-thirds of the way into your run or race, if it's a race, and you just feel like dying. Or you feel already dead. There's no reason to go on anymore, and you wouldn't mind just quitting. Well, suddenly something happens and you feel great. I don't understand what it is really, maybe your body releasing chemicals or something, but you could go on forever, it feels like. You're as fast now as when you started, you're totally rejuvenated. That's what a second wind is, son."

"Thanks," said the kid's grinning father.

Sutton and John walked down the street looking for a café. But John veered into a bar and ordered a beer.

"So I guess you've run already this afternoon?" Sutton asked.

John drank half the beer at once and then wiped foam from his lip into the hair of his forearm. "I thought I'd skip it today, actually. Hey, would you look at that?" He was staring into the mirror at the reflection of a waitress crossing the room behind him. Slapped Sutton between the shoulder blades. "Why was I in the office all these years, huh? You, you're doing it right, being a reporter. You get out more and see more things."

Jeff said, "John, look, I know I've been injured and out of competition for a while, but I think I know what I'm talking about. You can't just start skipping your training runs."

John shrugged. "Why not skip one every now and then? It's not about hard and fast rules, you know?"

Ashe still had the same force of presence, Sutton thought. If anything, it had increased with the glow of his recent accomplishment in Boulder. But Sutton had the odd feeling, as he watched this fifty-year-old man steal glances at himself in the mirror, that John Ashe was becoming increasingly immature the faster he ran. Ogling women like a kid . . . He also sensed that the older man was slightly contemptuous of him for having been so weak as to acknowledge an injury. Sutton put the microcassette recorder on the bar and started to drink.

After a couple of hours John said, "Let's bag this interview, Jeff. We'll go get Elena and get something to eat." And sober you up, he added to himself.

EVEN GIVING ELIZABETH half his fortune, that still left John two million dollars. Which raised the question in his mind now as to why the hell he had been working so hard. To leave it to Andy? The boy would probably move to the beach or something. He remembered the anxiety buying the Silver Missile had caused him, the melodramatic family conflict, Elizabeth stalking around the house offended that he hadn't consulted her so she could tell him no. During John's voluntary leave of absence from work the Porsche fast had become the great vehicle of his new life with Elena, and he was embarrassed for men his age who drove Sensible American Sedans. That he had ever been a commuter baffled him, in much the way commuters tend to be skeptical of a Time Before the Train. And Elizabeth? He bore her no ill will whatsoever. Wasn't her fault he had been a sap for twenty-five years. Hell, if someone was willing to work like a slave to bring in great sums of money, who could blame Elizabeth for letting him? Yes, he had reneged on his marital vows, but he had also been betrayed by the promise of marriage.

In the Silver Missile with Elena in the passenger seat, her hair tied back and her sunglasses on, he drove south through New Jersey on Route 1. Earlier that day he had run fifteen miles. In just a few days he would run the famous Peachtree Roadrace in Atlanta.

Elena was punching buttons on a pocket calculator. "You realize we've spent a thousand dollars this week just on dinner?"

With a flick of the hand he dismissed her worries. "So? It's not like I'll never make any more money. Look at Gil Stevenson. Guy wins one little race and ends up owning the whole Hot Foot chain."

Picking at her cuticles, Elena said, "You don't want to do that, you lack the—"

Discipline, she was about to say. She stuck her elbow on the windowsill and closed her eyes. Why ruin this lovely day by speaking the unattractive truth? Fact was, since leaving the law firm John had become something of a goof-off. Occasionally there were flashes of the stable maturity, the avuncular protectiveness that initially had made him so appealing, but in general the competent symbol of magnanimous power that she had fallen in love with was now more a sort of late-blooming party boy, even more handsome than before but not as dependable. To the extent that she could join him in this phase without feeling that she was sacrificing her future, she still enjoyed his company. Unfortunately, this meant a virtual end to any dealings with her father, who now refused to talk to her even on the phone. "Great profit potential," John was saying. Every now and then he could come up with a term that reminded her who he had been, but it was so much talk.

She looked out at the diners and factories and car dealerships of Route 1, then the blankness of I-95. Once they got past Philadelphia she began to recognize various landmarks she had last seen through the tinted windows of the Magnate Airporter, on her way back to school after spring break in Florida. "Can we stop at Magnate?" she asked. "You've never seen it, have you?"

"Sure, why not?"

He smiled, tilted his chin up so the wind could blow his thick, dark hair back. He was growing it out. It already came down past his earlobes. In a 7-Eleven on the side of the highway someone asked him if he was famous. Something about the way he carried himself, something about the beauty of his girlfriend. His cheeks had hollowed with the increased training so that from some angles he looked like a rock star, from others like a Hollywood leading man.

But the physical changes were also mirrored by mental ones. She wondered if he really had never heard any of the popular music of the seventies and eighties—if he really had been "on the train," as he said—or if there were some other reason, perhaps some glandular malfunction, that could also explain his remarkable talents on the running course and in bed. And now he was telling her not to worry about law school.

She interrupted him. "Law school's not like it was when you got out. It's not a guarantee you'll get a job. That's why I'm so concerned about it. I have to get into a good school and do well there."

"The paralegal experience was really helping," she said a moment later, his voluntary leave of absence being hers also.

"Don't try to make me feel guilty about that, okay? I said I'd help you find another job." He gunned it past a tractor trailer. "I just don't see why you'd want one. Let's just concentrate on me and you right now and the road and this great day right here."

She tried. But within ten minutes she was asking about Elizabeth. "Wasn't it fun being married, at least for a while?"

"I imagine. I don't remember, I was on the train."

"Maybe you should say something to Dr. Fiske about your memory. Maybe something's wrong with you."

"Look, Elena, if I'm sick and it feels this good, I don't want to be cured. If he cures me, then what? Do I go back to Elizabeth? You don't want that, do you?"

"No."

They rode into Magnate on Jefferson Avenue and parked on Magnate Street in front of Irwin Library. Campus was full of boys who knew Elena and felt the need to hug her while John stood by with his hands pocketed, grinning with restraint. No one mistook him for her father, but the age difference was apparent enough that several students were surprised to learn he was her boyfriend. After strolling around for a couple of hours, he managed to get her back into the Silver Missile.

Through Wilmington with its landscape of industrial collapse, through Baltimore, which looked good from the road but John knew better. Around the Capital Beltway. The conflict back in New Jersey was miles behind and long forgotten. John was smoking a Macanudo, downshifting to pass car after car. She enjoyed the smell of his cigar and the sight of him smoking it. It was midnight when they saw a sign for Virginia Beach. "What the hell," he said. "Let's get a room."

"It feels like we're criminals on the lam, doesn't it?" Elena was grinning. "Like *Getaway*." She picked a small hotel built in the fifties, worthy of a film noir tryst. "We don't even have a reason to go back tomorrow or even Monday, do we?"

"Hell, *no*."

They slept late in the cheap hotel, waking just in time to beat the church traffic to a seaside brunch. With the salty breeze whispering through their hair, they ate poached eggs and English muffins and drank a succession of bloody Marys to the scandalization of a nearby family that kept talking about God's will for an upcoming congregational vote on a proposed addition to His church. Everyone was pretty sure He would be for it.

"I want you to know how sorry I am about how your father's taking this," John said. "I guess it's understandable. Technically I'm a lot older than you are."

"What about Elizabeth? I'm pretty sorry about how she's taking it."

"What she's taking, Elena, is half the money. Don't worry about her. She's also got Anne Newton there, and that's good companionship at least. And sex never meant much to Elizabeth, even when she was young."

"I just feel like a home wrecker sometimes."

"Our home was already wrecked."

She waited for the waiter to take the plates away. "John, do you think you might ever settle down again? It might do you some good."

"You mean get married."

She shrugged. "I'm not saying I think we're ready for it or anything."

"You want to rescue me. How did that happen?"

"I'm not saying that."

"I've *been* married, it's not so great. I'm not saying the same thing that happened to me and Elizabeth would happen to you and me, but you never know." He sensed that his equivocation did not disappoint her. "It's not like I don't love you, you know I do. Marriage is just such an . . . old guy's thing. I need to feel a little freer. Not that I'd ever cheat on you. Tell you what, let's just never mention marriage again."

"Fine," she said, so surprised at the degree of relief she felt that she took his hand.

ANDY RANG THE doorbell to the love nest on the afternoon of July 3. He tried to look through the one-way peephole. He wore jeans and a white button-down shirt, with his hair swept back to flaunt his widow's peak. He could hear music playing beyond the door, and the whisper of sock steps on a hardwood floor. Elena's voice: "Andy?"

He waved at the peephole. "Hi, Mom."

She opened the door. "He's flying down to Atlanta. He runs the Peachtree Roadrace tomorrow. Why aren't you at MTV?"

"That's what I came by to talk to him about. I guess it can wait. Or I could tell you and you could, I don't know, whisper it in his ear."

She sighed. "Let's go get a drink."

In the bedroom she threw on some jeans and sneakers, and when she came back out again she found him admiring John's various running trophies and newspaper clippings, which were arranged atop the entryway table. "I didn't mean to be such a jerk," he said, staring intently at one of the trophies. "I shouldn't take it out on you." By the time they walked past the doorman together, Andy was in a state of reflective contrition. "I've been trying to understand people more lately, trying to understand my dad, you know? And mom, for that matter. Boy, that's a tough one."

"Hard to understand Elizabeth?"

"I don't even want to talk about that one. Does Dad ever say anything about her living arrangement?"

"He's glad she's got some companionship."

"That's one way to look at it."

It was mid-week at Proof Required, and they had their pick of the bar stools. Andy ordered a margarita, Elena a martini. At his gestured suggestion they clinked glasses. "Cheers," he said.

"Let's try to be friends."

"Okay, okay." He was quiet for a moment, obviously considering his next words. "I understand," he began slowly, "and please don't take this wrong, I'm not making a move on you." Slowly he began again. "I understand why he's attracted to you. I don't understand so much why you're attracted to him. He's not *that* rich. He's not *that* handsome."

"He's extremely handsome." She sipped her martini. "But that's not why. I don't know why, you can't quantify it like that. He's an older handsome man. He . . . adores me."

Not looking at her, he said, "Elena, there aren't enough hours in the day for you to sleep with everyone who adores you."

"Well, that's not really why, either. I never set out to do any harm, I just fell in love. Nobody can control that, and if they can they're not very interesting to me."

"Just couldn't help it," he said, sounding slightly more hostile. "Just couldn't help it. And Dad, too, I suppose. He's such the creature of passion."

"You'd be surprised."

"Oh, come on, I don't want to hear that."

"Surprise, your father's human."

He ordered another margarita and watched the bartender make it. Traded a five-dollar bill for it, took a few sips. "What I came by to tell Dad, I had an audition at MTV this morning. They gave me the afternoon off."

"Andy, that's great! Congratulations! I was worried you were going to say you'd quit or something."

"I won't get the show, though." He ran a hand through his

hair and shook his head. "The ironic thing is, the producer is this running fanatic and he's actually heard of the great John Ashe. So, damn if I don't owe Dad. I thought I'd picked the one field in which he couldn't possibly help me. It was just a courtesy to Dad that I got the audition, I think. There were some real pros there, people you'd recognize, even."

Later, on his third margarita, he abandoned that defensive self-deprecation. "I was definitely the best one there. I mean, I really understand what the show's going to be about. This'll be oriented toward bands and musicians and whatnot—and nobody too commercial, it's not like Pearl Jam needs my help. It's an off hour, like eleven-thirty or midnight, 'cause you know a lot of kids out there just don't think Letterman and Leno speak to them. We want those kids. We will have those kids. And the format would be that I would ask the guests a few questions and then invite them to play a song or two unplugged—so it's a way to keep that whole thing going. It's like unplugged meets Letterman meets Leno, and it only lasts a half hour, so they can get back to the Sega channel or whatever."

As enthusiastic as he was being about his new and improved prospects at MTV, he began to remind Elena of John when he talked about running, setting records and so forth, opening a shoe store chain. The minor epiphany she culled from the observation was that John was, in his fashion, acting no more mature than his son. Or perhaps maturity was the wrong word here, when what both father and son were exhibiting was enthusiasm about some great success just within their grasp. Her own father's vision had narrowed. On his horizon the most promising thing he saw was a palm tree in Florida, and himself hog fat in a chaise longue, a tiny umbrella in his pink mixed drink.

Andy was getting more drunk than she would have liked. But perhaps she could turn it to her advantage. For a long time she had wondered about Elizabeth, because she was not without sympathy for the other woman who had worked so hard building up the Jericho walls of her marriage. "How's your mother doing?"

Andy slurped his drink. "Fine. I still can't believe she's a lesbian."

"What?"

"But it is another reason I got the audition. People think it's so cool."

"What makes you think she's a lesbian? Just because she lives with a woman?"

"It's funny, you know. When I started seeing Kristen's mom at the house all the time, I was happy. They were always drinking good wine and cooking a big meal. I thought it was good for Mom. I was glad to see her having a little fun."

"That doesn't sound lesbian to me. That sounds like friend-ship."

Andy spoke with his face tilted up so the melting margarita ice wouldn't drip from his mouth. "I went over there early one morning . . ." Finally he swallowed and turned to face her. "Found them in the same bed. Mom explained to me how much better this was than trying to find another man, et cetera, et cetera. Women are less judgmental, more understanding, et cetera, et cetera.

"God," he said, shaking his head at Elena, "who would have thought it . . . my family is so postmodern."

```
┌─────────────────────────────┐
│                             │
│   C H A P T E R   1 3       │
│                             │
└─────────────────────────────┘
```

THE PEACHTREE ROADRACE. Forty thousand people were registered that year to run the famous Fourth of July 10-K through Atlanta's sweltering streets. The top finishers would come from all over the world—including John Ashe from New York. But the field would be made up mostly, as in years past, of good old Southerners from places like Columbia, South Carolina, and Auburn, Alabama. Often they were lawyers or businessmen whose commitment to office and family pushed all athletic endeavor to the weekends . . . but also made it financially possible to jet into Hot'lanta just for the Peachtree. If a man could run the race as fast as he had the year before, he could be sure that for twelve months time had overlooked him, leaving him free to enjoy a theoretically permanent state of arrested deterioration.

Circling the airport, John Ashe caught a glimpse of the skyline rising up through the haze. This was the first time he had seen any city burned by Sherman. It just rose up on flat ground, no real reason for it to be there, though he supposed it must have started up around a river or something.

The man beside him seemed fairly sure that the plane was going to crash on final approach. Silent until that moment when the left wing dipped and through the window he could count cars on the interstate, the man suddenly burst forth in drawly eloquence. "Never did trust these things. Well, machines in general but particularly ones that ferry me from city to city at this rate, this high. It was foolish of me. I usually just drive, but I wanted to get back for the Peachtree."

"I'm running the Peachtree," John said.

"So'm I." The man looked doubtfully through the window at the wing. "Is it supposed to be shaking that much?"

"I'm sure it's okay." John reached across, drew the shade.

"The Peachtree's something else," said the man. "So many people it took me seven minutes just to get to the starting line last year. But it's fun, you get a T-shirt, and I usually go out with some friends afterward for brunch. Boy, do I hate flying. You sound like you from up North." Nawth, he pronounced it.

"I live in Manhattan."

Just then the man noticed John's Bolt! tote bag and his Bolt! T-shirt and running shoes. "You must like Bolt!."

"They're sponsoring me."

"Isn't that something!"

"I've got a contract that says I have to wear this stuff traveling to and from athletic events." John pulled from his carry-on bag a copy of the current *Distance Running* and was about to show his co-passenger the latest write-up about himself.

But at the electric humming of the landing gear being lowered, the man pressed his head against the back of the seat and closed his eyes. His knuckles were white on the armrests. "I just went up to New York on business," he said. John considered responding but then realized the guy was praying. "I hope I didn't do anything to offend you and if I did, oh, God, I take it all back. Bless my mother and father and my wife and kids and everyone in the world. If you call me now, then fine, but I'd really like to put it off for a little while longer, if that's all right with you."

It was unusual for a masters champ to get more than a few items of clothing from any so-called sponsor, but the folks at Bolt!, sensing that the rise in John's popularity had just begun, were paying for his plane ticket, his hotel room, his meals, and they were even throwing in a little discretionary cash. The deal was enough to raise the sparse eyebrows of Mercury shoe spokesman Reynaldo Miller.

The current issue of *Distance Running* carried a photo of John training in Central Park with the Marathon King, who looked strangely older than the masters prodigy. Beside the smiling, handsome, long-haired John Ashe, the Marathon King looked downright emaciated and angry, his eyes psychotic above the burnished, bony knobs of his cheekbones. It was unfortunate for Rey that when he sweated he looked, if possible, more bald.

Also in that issue was an oversize reproduction of John's driver's license with the D.O.B. circled in red. In the photo his hair was almost completely gray and his skin loose beneath the eyes and across the cheekbones.

The wheels thumped against the runway. John was amazed at how completely the color drained from his troubled co-passenger's face. Then there was the great noise of the reverse thrusters, and finally the plane began to slow down. The man opened his eyes to find his prayer answered.

Looking around the plane, he said, "I just cannot get used to these things." To hide his embarrassment at having been so afraid, he grabbed the copy of *Distance Running* from John's lap. It was already open to the relevant article. He pointed at the D.O.B. on John's driver's license. "We were born the same year. How's that possible?"

"Read the sidebar about the kid who's trying to figure it out for me." The sidebar, entitled "The Human Doctoral Thesis," reported that John Ashe was meeting with medical researcher and Ph.D. candidate Steven Fiske twice a month for the benefit of science. "You can keep that magazine if you want. There's a good article about the Peachtree."

He made his way down the aisle wearing Bolt! everything and carrying a Bolt! tote bag full of his actual Bolt! racing gear. Said good-bye to a flight attendant who had been particularly attentive, gave her a big smile which she returned in kind. The praying Atlantan chose that moment to say, "So you gonna try to set another record?" He flashed the issue of *Distance Running* at the flight attendant. "There's a whole article in here about him." She stared at John with reinforced admiration.

"I'll try to do my best," he said.

The collapsible tunnel contained a sample of Atlanta's damp July heat. John felt it again between terminal and taxicab and between the cab and the Atlanta Grand Hotel. His face took on a sheen as if he were leaning over a pot of boiling water. Through the automatic doors flowed an a/c gust powerful enough to give him a pleasant shiver.

The manager met him halfway across the lobby. "Mr. Ashe?"
"Yes."

"Bolt! called ahead. Your check-in is all taken care of. They were concerned that you not be hounded by autograph seekers."

"I'm flattered."

"And I'm to tell you to rest up for the race. Last year's winner stayed here, you know, so we do have a good track record, so to speak." He took John's bag and walked with him to the elevators. "Do you know Atlanta well?"

"I will soon, I'm going to take a little run."

"There are some areas I would advise you not to go." The manager was one of those clerks who resent their own polite servility to the point of seeming snobbish. "We at the Atlanta Grand like to keep our guests among the living." He named several places to avoid. Wearing an expression of feigned interest, John nodded. Suddenly he said, "Atlanta makes me want to eat a cheeseburger, you know that?"

When he left the Atlanta Grand in his running outfit, one of the valets said, "Man, you gonna sweat worse than a Coke bottle."

He was drenched within five minutes. At street corners he would shake his head and watch the sweat rain down on the sidewalk around him; then he would peel the strands of long, dark hair from across his face. He ran by bars and restaurants, wishing he were inside looking out instead of the other way around. Atlanta women puzzled him with their friendly staring, which arose in part from that fabled southern hospitality, he supposed . . . but it went beyond that. They flirted with him at stoplights. If you gave them a slight smile of vague meaning, they gave you a big one whose meaning was clear. Their thick, lilting accents, which he heard several times literally in passing, made them sound somehow inherently kinder than the average Northern woman. At one street corner a beautiful woman held her McDonald's soda out to him. "You want the rest of my Coca-Cola?" She had just begun to sweat through the belly of her cotton dress.

"Sure, thanks." John drank it in front of her.

"There's a certain pleasure in seeing people's basic needs satisfied, don't you think?"

Still drinking, he nodded. It was nice, in a way, to be away from Elena for a little while, he decided. Not that he didn't love her completely, but still, two people needed a break from each other every now and then.

BACK IN HIS hotel room, fresh from a shower and still wearing nothing but a towel around his narrow waist, he sat in front of the plate-glass window high above the city and called Elena. She told him about Andy's visit, starting with the big news: Elizabeth and Anne.

"Lesbians!" he said. "Are you sure?"

"That's what Andy said."

"Well, that explains a lot!" His first reaction was anger, but it quickly dissipated with the realization that this development might retroactively justify his infidelity to those who had yet to forgive him. "It just seems like a long time to pretend to be heterosexual, you know? No wonder she never wanted to do it." He laughed. "I always said she was a strong, brave woman. I didn't know it was because she's got a pair of imaginary *cojones*."

"I thought it turned you on."

"If they're young and pretty and they want me involved, sure, I guess that's the universal male fantasy, if we can admit it. I bet Elizabeth wasn't even really bisexual, now that I think about it. Why else wouldn't she want to do it with me, you know? Well, what the hell, I'm happy for her. It actually makes me feel good. It makes me feel like in doing the right thing for me, I also, unintentionally, of course, did the right thing for her. I guess I sort of liberated her."

He was also excited about Andy's new opportunity at MTV. After he got off the phone he found the channel and contemplated the vee-jays. Andy really was just handsome enough to be one. The kid was lucky to have that receding hairline, which saved him from the kind of too good looks that would have undercut his intellectual credibility. He would have women all over him if he managed to get that hosting job. He'd be coming into his own. Maybe once he started feeling a little more comfortable about himself, he would be able to reconcile with his dad. John was fairly sure of it. That the kid had come by to visit at all was, he felt, a good sign in itself.

John pulled on a pair of faded Levi's, his Bolt! shoes, and his Bolt! T-shirt with its huge lightning bolt logo on the front. He stepped out into Atlanta again, which was cooling off slightly as the sun went down.

A thirty-minute walk later, he planted his elbow on an oak bar and ordered a beer. Soon he was sinking his teeth into a cheddar cheeseburger with lettuce, tomato, and a whole slice of onion. He unrolled his napkin and wiped the juice from his chin. He mopped up ketchup with his fries and ordered another beer, his third. "I don't care what anyone says," he told the bartender. "No food has been invented that can top the simple perfection of a cheeseburger." He turned to a couple of late-twenties semi-beauties occupying the stools to his left. "Right, ladies?" They were dental hygienists, it turned out, Kim and Savannah, blowing smoke toward the ceiling between bites of cheddar-filled potato skins and sips of bottled beer.

"What's with all the Bolt stuff?" Savannah asked.

"They're my sponsor."

"Right."

"Seriously, I hold the masters record for the ten K."

Kim said, "Then why aren't you running the Peachtree?"

"I am."

She looked at her watch. "It starts in like ten hours."

"I'm carbo-loading." He slid his empty glass toward the bartender. "I'll have another."

"How old are you?" Savannah asked, stubbing out her cigarette.

"Fifty."

"Huh. If you're fifty, I'm an octogenarian."

"What a wonderful word for a Southerner to say. Say it again."

"Octogenarian." She sounded a bit like Carrington Calhoun, Rey's girlfriend, but without the rich depth of tone that bespoke generations of diminishing but still viable wealth. No, this lady lived paycheck to paycheck. For a dental hygienist she had, he observed, surprisingly bad teeth, a mouthful of silver when she laughed.

"I really am fifty." He handed over his whole fat wallet. Savannah and Kim saw his gold credit cards, his business card from when he was still at Masterson, Grandissime, and Barradale, his photo of Elena.

"Who's this?"

"That's my girlfriend."

"She just needs to tease her hair up a bit."

Savannah was the cuter of the two. After a few minutes he let Kim fade from his consciousness like all thought of physical injury. He did not want to go home with either woman, but he found that he wanted the clear option. After two more beers he was satisfied that he had it. He checked his watch. Nine hours until race time. Pushing away his empty beer glass, he said, "Well, I guess I've had enough carbohydrates."

"Where are you staying?" Savannah asked.

"The Atlanta Grand."

"That's so far. Can I give you a lift?"

"I'll enjoy the walk."

"My apartment's close, you could stay there." She smiled, a mouthful of silver.

"No, thanks." He was pinching his ring finger, where the constriction of his wedding band was still visible.

"You're not married, are you?"

"Not anymore. Marital difficulties."

"I bet."

He slapped a five-dollar tip on the bar and stood up. As he was leaving, Savannah called after him, "Good luck, John! We'll be watching you."

Two or three blocks from the bar he stopped and looked around, slightly disoriented. Was this the way he had come? He stood in front of a boarded-up house against which an old bum was urinating. From an open window across the street came the sounds of a man and woman arguing. A carload of black kids drove by slowly. "You must be lost, senator."

"Yeah, can you tell me wh—"

But the car just kept going. Nothing here looked familiar, but perhaps on his way to the bar, preoccupied with thoughts of Elizabeth and Andy, he had not taken note of his surroundings. He decided now to keep going the same way in the hope that it would lead to a major intersection with a gas station or convenience store where he might ask for directions. The cheeseburger and fries were sitting well in his stomach, and he enjoyed the invincibility that came with a good beer buzz.

The farther he went, though, the higher the percentage of houses that were boarded up and sprayed with graffiti. An old man was picking through an overflowing dumpster in the parking lot of a pawnshop, right across the street from a stand-alone liquor store with iron bars on its windows as if for a jailhouse effect, to make customers feel more at home. Virtually one-stop shopping for a bottle of booze and a good, cheap gun. There was music coming from a low cinder-block building on the next block. A handpainted sign above the doorway read, DA GANGSTA DIN. There were no windows. From the back parking lot a few eyes looked at him. Should he go over and ask where the hell he was? Offer a little self-deprecating laugh for being such a stupid white guy? His instinct was to hail a cab. But this was not New York, where they were just cruising the streets waiting for your jacketed arm to rise and your white palm to flash in the gloaming. He told himself that he wasn't really lost. The Atlanta Grand, he was pretty sure now, was off to the left. He turned at the next block; now it was just a matter of putting one foot in front of the other. This section of town wasn't really that bad, was it? Not all young black men wanted to punch him in the face, did they? He breathed deeply of the thick, humid air and kept putting one foot in front of the other.

A half block ahead of him a young black woman pushed a baby stroller out to the street and turned onto the sidewalk ahead of John, going in the same direction. Thirty seconds later he was close enough to the house she had left to admire the well-tended flower boxes along its white porch railings. The whole place had been freshly painted. The trimmed grass lawn stopped neatly at the property line, giving way almost immediately to the dusty brown moonscape of the neighboring lot. He was touched. It was one thing to keep your house and lawn looking good in Groveton, where if you didn't, you would face the wrath of the neighborhood association and your kids would stop getting invitations to their friends' birthday parties. But here in this virtual shantytown it took real effort, pride in the best sense of the word. Looking ahead at the young woman's muscular hips shifting beneath her pink dress, he imagined her doing the yard work while her baby slept in that stroller on the porch and the teenagers next door lit crack pipes and drank quarts of malt liquor. They probably berated her efforts, threw beer bottles into her azaleas as casually as someday one of them might put a bullet through her brain.

The stroller wheels were squeaking. John's admiration for the woman had energized his stride; now he was only twenty or thirty yards behind her and could see the pleasant effect of a distant street lamp on her shoulders, bare but for a white purse strap which she shifted occasionally from one to the other. Every three or four feet the squeaky stroller wheel turned sideways, and she would fix it by tilting the cart briefly onto its back wheels. She glanced back at John and seemed to increase her pace. He wanted to tell her not to worry, he was on her side, but wondered how she would react to the sight of a slightly drunken white man hurrying to catch up with her, and on his chest a big costumish lightning bolt, the tip of which reached beneath his waistband as if to electrify his crotch.

For her own peace of mind he slowed down to let her get a few more paces ahead of him. She walked briskly, clinging tightly to the stroller handle and pinching her shoulder bag protectively between elbow and narrow waist.

John let himself start thinking about tomorrow's race. He wished Rey had registered for it. It would have been interesting to see if the Marathon King could run any faster than his marathon pace. John had been keeping up with him lately during their shorter training runs.

Several houses ahead of him now he saw the silhouettes of two young black men step out from the shadows of a dilapidated porch and move slowly toward the street. It registered in his mind that they were trying to look casual, uninterested in the beautiful woman with the white purse glowing like a star against her pink dress and pushing a stroller which squeaked like wounded prey. They turned toward her. Their hands were deep in the pockets of identical dark, hooded jackets. John was far enough back in the shadows that they did not see him. Something about the time of night and his slight drunkenness activated a certain college-boy invincibility, those times when he had felt like a superhero waiting to happen.

"Yo, baby," one of the young black men said. "I need a little cash, you gonna help me out?"

The other one grabbed his crotch and dipped his knees. "It ain't money I'm wanting right now, ho."

"I wonder if she in a giving spirit."

"Go on home," she said. The squeaky wheel rotated and got stuck sideways. She rocked the cart back to fix it. Cash grabbed her purse; Crotch grabbed her stroller. In the faint light coming from a distant storefront John saw that the kids were grinning, enjoying this. Crotch smacked her buttocks. She yelled—and would've hit him, but she couldn't let go of the stroller containing her baby. She probably would have *given* Cash her purse had it not depended from the unbreakable link between herself and her now crying child.

John had never felt like someone's last and only hope. He was standing there watching and listening—they were calling her "ho" and pawing at her dress—and as he began to believe his eyes there flowered within him a deep rage which left him blind with the desire to do harm to these vermin. He wanted not just to prevent the mugging or rape or whatever was about to happen, but also to squeeze in his two bare hands the hearts of the would-be perpetrators. He wanted to turn those kids back into clay or die trying. He moved forward in a swift crouch just as they reached into their jackets. Now their right hands glinted silver. Only question now was *guns or knives*? Wearing quiet Bolt! running shoes, John was closing in.

"Leggo, bitch!" Crotch jammed a glint of silver into her side. If it was a knife, he had just cut her lung. Cash yanked the purse strap again; the stroller tipped up on two wheels.

Not knives, thank God, so the woman's lung was still whole. On the other hand . . .

John rammed his shoulder into Cash's rib cage. He heard a snapping sound and felt the wind leave the kid's body as they both tumbled to the sidewalk. He hopped up and whirled to face

Crotch, found himself staring down the barrel of a pawnshop .38 just beyond which was an eat-shit smile. He grabbed the kid's wrist and ducked sideways just as the gun went off, the bullet whizzing by so close that he felt the wind on the side of his neck. Now it was a struggle to keep the gun pointed away from him.

The woman was free to run now, but she didn't, or couldn't. Her screaming attracted the attention of a group passing on the other side of the street. A car squealed sideways to a halt, the headlights blinding Cash, who, still sitting on the sidewalk, had leveled his gun at John's heart through the back. He covered his eyes with his forearm and fired anyway.

John felt a sudden absence of resistance. Crotch looked down at himself, amazed. There was a new hole in his sternum. He looked over at Cash. "You dumb motherfucker."

John said, "Now, now, I'm sure he feels just terrible about it." He took the gun from Crotch's hand and spun away. Pointed his gun at Cash. "Don't move."

He had always wondered what it would be like to kill a man for unimpeachable reasons such as rescue and self-defense. He had thought about it often while reading those shocking stories of kidnapping, rape, and murder—how he wished he could have stumbled upon the remote cabin where a couple of white trash scumbags were torturing some young girl; he would kill them both before her eyes. What a wonderful release for his pent-up commuter outrage. But would he have the balls, could he really pull the trigger?

Cash hopped up and was raising his gun to John's chest. John blammed away at the kid, who was maybe eighteen and should have had six decades of life left to enjoy, and the last shot before the gun clicked empty put a red dot in the center of his forehead. An umbrella of blood sprayed out the back; over the ringing in his ears John barely heard it spatter to the sidewalk. The kid was still standing there, already dead but looking as though he wanted to whine about it, *This ain't right, man.* Instead he fell flat on his face.

Lying on the sidewalk, Cash was in shock, almost gone. He had stuck a finger into the hole in his chest in a futile attempt to stop the bleeding. John squatted before him, looked into his eyes, and counted down: "Ten . . . nine . . . eight . . . seven . . . six . . . five . . . four . . ." Suddenly the light went out of the kid's eyes, and his expression was something like that of a supermarket fish on ice.

Already there were sirens audible in the distance. John looked around, surprised at the size of the crowd that had gathered. They were all black. Had they seen everything? Did they know it had been self-defense and the rescue of mother and child? He set the empty gun down and walked over to the stroller. He wanted to get a good look at the baby before the crowd tore him apart, and even crying and screaming the infant girl was beautiful. Her mother clutched the baby to her body, unable to catch enough breath to say thanks. In fact, the hyperventilation weakened her, and John had to help her sit down.

"You all right?" he asked.

She nodded, her breasts heaving with emotion.

John turned to face the crowd. After a moment of silence the witnesses started cheering and clapping. It all sounded slightly muffled to John because his ears still rang from the gunshots.

Cop cars squealed up to the scene. Cops got out, guns drawn.

"You're too late," someone yelled. "That man there's a real hero."

The first news van pulled up, and soon the entire scene was so awash in cameras and lights that it was hard for the ambulance to get through. Two emergency medical technicians carried a stretcher and a huge first-aid box through the crowd. They made John sit down while they took his blood pressure.

"I'm fine, I'm all right," he said.

"You ordinarily have a hole in your neck?"

The bullet he thought had barely missed him had in fact grazed his neck. The left side of his shirt was soaked with blood. When they got the wound cleaned off they agreed that it wasn't serious but still insisted, against his protestations, that he be taken to the hospital right away.

"I can't, the race starts in eight hours."

"Not for you it doesn't."

A reporter yelled across the tape. "Hey, Boltman!"

It took a moment for John to realize the woman was talking to him—the Bolt! logo on his T-shirt.

"Hey, Boltman, how you doing?"

Pissed off, thinking about the Peachtree Roadrace, John yelled, "I've had worse splinters."

And the only two people who did not laugh at that were dead on the sidewalk.

THE DAY WAS already heating up. Not yet seven-thirty and Jeff Sutton already had sweat stains under his armpits. He was sitting up on the grandstand with some local race officials, a few select members of the media, and various representatives of the corporate sponsors of the fastest runners and the race itself. The Bolt! rep was driving him crazy, screaming into the phone. "I thought you said he was responsible, a former *lawyer*, for chrissakes." He looked out over the crowd. "Yeah, well there's forty thousand people here. You want me to mill around and see if I can find him? Look, he was supposed to have checked in an hour before the race. We were going to take photos of him in Bolt! gear."

Sutton leaned back in his folding chair. "Maybe his brethren from outer space beamed him back up."

"What?" Still on the phone, the Bolt! rep seemed to consider it.

"Sure, or maybe he had to get his pre-race infusion of plutonium."

The guy got off the phone and sat down beside Sutton. "We had the hotel check his room, made it sound like we were worried about some sort of health crisis, which to tell you the truth I am at this point . . . anyway, he checked in yesterday afternoon. His bags were in the room, his bed showed no signs of use. He'd obviously taken a run because his jock strap was hanging from the shower knob."

"Interesting," Sutton said. "The jock-strap factor, what does it mean?"

"This is a very serious matter!"

But the news of John Ashe's Bolt! contract had thrown Jeff into annoyed reflection. Even at the height of his career, when he had placed sixth in the Boston Marathon, he had never had what might legitimately be called an endorsement contract. Oh, sure, he got a lot of free shoes, but so did the top fifty or so runners.

Probably the top hundred. Company reps figured okay, this guy's a nobody, but he might get lucky, and if he does he might as well be wearing our shoes.

John Ashe doing endorsement contracts. Once you fucked up like this, missing a race, they started looking for ways to drop you. Maybe John had gotten a little too big for his britches. "I'll tell you where he is. He went out to get a cheeseburger some-where, probably ended up partying all night with some woman, not his wife, not even his mistress. He's waking up right now to take a piss, and he's looking around at the cheap apartment and the woman in bed next to him and he's wondering why he feels like he's missing something important. 'Oh, shit, the race!' " Sut-ton clapped his own forehead in a dramatization of that hypo-thetical moment.

The Bolt! rep was not encouraged. "I thought he was an ex-*lawyer*, a responsible guy!"

"He is an ex-lawyer. Unfortunately for you, he's also an ex-adult."

Sutton crossed his arms behind his head and stretched his back. The move shifted his line of vision to a small television that had been set up on a table to his right. It was time for the 7:25 report, local Atlanta news, and Jeff was curious about how much hotter it was going to get in this paved-over swamp. Suddenly there was a videotape of a crime scene—and John Ashe was sit-ting in the middle of it. A couple of paramedics were bandaging his neck.

Sutton nearly tipped his chair backward. "Hey, hey!" he yelled. Some race officials and sponsors and local reporters gath-ered around him, staring at the television. Apparently the station had devoted its entire 7:25 report to John Ashe's heroics—in his Bolt! shoes and T-shirt. The company rep was overjoyed. "Look at that sweet logo, oh, my God! Look at those shoes, yes!" Sutton was shaking his head—some guys had all the luck. There were interviews with several eyewitnesses to the incident, all of them praising "the white man in the Bolt! shirt," or "the Boltman," or simply "Boltman." They spoke of his damn fool courage in cap-ping the bad guys and saving the lady and her baby girl. Sutton was clenching his fists as if in anger.

On TV, John yelled, "I've had worse splinters." Sutton and the others had to laugh.

Now the television showed the district attorney answering questions from the press.

"You gonna file charges, sir?"

"Charges?" the man said. "Against a coupla dead guys?"

"No, sir, against Mr. Ashe."

The D.A. looked genuinely puzzled. "File charges against Mr. Ashe? What for?"

The news anchor said, "John Ashe's neck wound is not serious, but doctors have ordered him not to run in this morning's Peachtree Roadrace anyway. He should be out of the hospital by this afternoon."

Sutton turned to the Bolt! rep. "Guess you're bummed."

"I'm thrilled."

Some of the local race officials were amazed that John had managed to get out of that part of town alive, much less a slightly wounded hero. Of course, it was too bad that the masters champ was going to have sit out this famous race, but perhaps arrangements could be made to present him to spectators at the awards ceremony anyway. It would be good publicity for the event. *Not only does the Peachtree Roadrace pump millions of dollars into the local economy, it also brings in the occasional crime-fighting hero like Boltman!*

THE BANDAGE ON his neck was awkward and scratchy, and his left ear kept ringing no matter how hard he jammed his index finger into it. From his hospital bed he had already called Elena to let her know he was all right. "Yeah, I was just out getting a cheeseburger, minding my own business, and I go to walk home, I must've taken a wrong turn out of the bar." He took in the excited concern in her voice. "You must be in shock or something. John, you *killed* two people."

"Well, actually, I only killed one."

"Don't you feel bad?" From her tone he could tell she was smiling. "I wish I could be with you right now." She sounded, more than anything, a little bit horny.

"I don't feel bad about it. Maybe it'll sink in later. I did what I had to do, Elena. He was going to kill me."

"I know, I know. I'm not saying you shouldn't have." She lowered her voice. "What did it feel like?"

He lowered his. "You wanna know the truth, it felt good." Just then the nurse came in to check his blood pressure again. "Gotta go, hon."

He wanted to be in the Peachtree, he felt fine. But here he was, thirty minutes before the race, flat on his back with his arm extended for the blood-pressure gauge. True, if the bullet had hit two inches to the left, he'd be dead or paralyzed. But it hadn't. It had just sort of blasted a piece of flesh from his neck without touching the jugular. He had not lost all *that* much blood. What the hell was he doing here? They were practically keeping him prisoner. Because of the circumstances of his hospitalization he found the nurses and doctors to be a lively, friendly bunch, but their concern was stultifying and overdone.

"How's my blood pressure?" he asked the nurse.

"Normal, surprisingly enough."

"Great. So I can go?"

"Goodness, no, you need your rest."

After she left, he sat up in bed. His shoes, jeans, and his blood-stained Bolt! T-shirt were all folded neatly on the chair beside the door. He stood, pulled off the ridiculous skirtlike pajamas, and slipped back into his street wear. The shirt reeked of smoke, perfume, blood.

Standing before the mirror, he tugged the oversized gauze bandage and got a peek at the wound. Minor but unappetizing. The gauze ran through the scab in some places so that to peel it off would have restarted the bleeding. Damn, he was going to look pretty strange running a road race with this huge white patch stuck to his neck. Well, he had no choice.

As he ran past Patient Registration, one of the young doctors yelled, "Hey, Mr. Ashe!" By the time the guy decided to give chase, John was already climbing into one of the taxis out front.

The driver, a black man about forty, held his hand above the start button on the meter. "You Boltman, ain't you?"

"Yeah, I guess so. You think we could bolt to the Atlanta Grand and then to the Peachtree Roadrace?"

The driver retracted his hand without starting the meter. "This one's on me." He stomped the gas. "That was amazing, what you did! I saw it all on TV. Lotta white guys, they would've been too scared or maybe plain indifferent. But you helped out that lady, man, you helped her out good. Lotta white guys would've been afraid the crowd would tear them apart."

"Never actually crossed my mind."

"Yeah, I know, like we'd rather have some lady get robbed if saving her means having to thank some cracker like you."

The man was a magic-carpet driver; the taxi floated through turns at impossible speeds. Maybe the physicist Kurt Vermiel could have explained it; John could not. He just sat in the middle of the backseat and let the carpet take him. The doormen and valets at the Atlanta Grand, unimpressed with the outward appearance of the magic-carpet taxi, approached it with complaint on their faces—*get that thing outta here.* But then John popped out and said, "He's going to wait right here."

They recognized him. "We've been looking all over for you. Hey, you're all bloody."

Racing through the lobby, dodging guests, he attracted the attention of the hotel manager. "Mr. Ashe? Mr. Ashe? Mr. Ashe!" John hopped on the elevator and waved to the little guy as the doors closed. Thank God for high-speed elevators. Within twenty seconds he was unlocking his room. Twenty more and he was in his running shorts and sprinting back toward the elevators. There had not been time to change his bloody Bolt! shirt. He came out of the elevator like a horse from the starting gate, nearly dominoing a group of old folks who stared after him in a consensus of bewilderment.

One of the valets grabbed his arm. "Take the limo. The driver's good."

John looked at the limo with its Atlanta Grand logo on the driver's door; so they wanted a little free publicity for ferrying Boltman to the race. He looked at the magic-carpet driver, apparently anticipating rejection. "I'm with you," John said. He hopped in back. Bolstered by this affirmation of his skills, the driver stomped the gas so hard that the force of acceleration slammed the door, muffling slightly the sound of squealing tires.

Unfortunately, the route he picked was cordoned off because of the race. "Shit! Where all this race go to anyway?"

"Just get me as close as you can."

"But you'll have to run it." He held up his wristwatch. "Look at the time."

The driver maneuvered to within three-quarters of a mile of the starting line, but by then it was 7:55 according to his watch, which he conceded was a bit slow. John dropped a fifty-dollar bill over the front seat and ran off while the driver called behind him. "Hey, hey, I said this was on me!"

ENVIOUS THOUGH HE was, Sutton began to feel a little more charitable when he learned that the Boltman would not be able to run the race. Very likely that light gunshot injury had caused a deeper psychological wound that would upset whatever mental balance had allowed him to run so well. Fiske would not be able to explain the sudden end of Ashe's career, but Jeff would write about it eloquently and even, after a while, sincerely. The Boltman had been a great runner, an inspiration to that group of men for whom P.E. no longer meant physical education but prostate examination.

He recognized several famous runners on the front row, their toes on the chalk of the starting line. A few had already stopped talking and were staring down the great, empty street before them as if at a gate they had to get through before it closed, and anyone who did not would perish.

The man who would fire the starter's pistol kept wiping his forearm across his bald pate. The platform on which he stood was draped with a banner featuring a peachtree of the same design that appeared on the runners' T-shirts. The three Kenyans were already wearing theirs. Apparently they were having some sort of argument, too, arms rising and falling, mouths open. One of them suddenly pointed wide-eyed down the empty street through which this entire horde would soon be running. On the grandstand, the news crews swung their cameras that way. Jeff Sutton stood up in his chair to see what was going on. Some nutcase was sprinting toward the starting line, his shoulder-length hair trailing behind him, some sort of white bandage on his neck, and his white Bolt! T-shirt stained with blood. Guy jammed a finger deep into his left ear and wiggled it around.

Jeff Sutton's pen fell out of his mouth.

JOHN SQUEEZED IN among the Kenyans on the front row. Their long, thin arms reached out to pat his back. "How you feel, man?" Pronounced *fill.* How you fill? "We heard what happened, very dangerous!"

"I've been pampered by nurses all night. I feel great, I'm ready to beat you guys."

They laughed at that. "Sure, sure."

Rushing toward him from the direction of the grandstand were the race physician, an official of the Peachtree, Jeff Sutton, and several other people John did not recognize. "Don't make a big deal out of this," he said. Reluctantly he surrendered his arm to the blood-pressure gauge.

"I feel great!" he told them all. "The beer's worn off, the time I spent in the police station and the hospital was no problem. I didn't get much sleep—oh, Jeff, the nurses here are really fine. When I finally do have my heart attack, I'm coming here for recuperation. What's the read, Doc?"

"You seem healthy, but—"

"But I wouldn't advise allowing him to run," said a man stepping forward, briefcase first. On that hot morning at this outdoor athletic event, the guy wore a suit.

"Ah, the damn lawyer," John said.

The guy shrugged, apology in his eyes. "It's my job to recommend that you be disqualified for health reasons."

The Bolt! rep said, "We saw it all on television. You were great, John. Or should I say Boltman?"

"You should all step back and start the race. You're making me nervous here." He extended his arms toward the crowd behind the starting line. Those up front could see what was going on, the reason for the delay, but there were forty thousand people here, and toward the back a collective murmur of dissatisfaction had arisen. They had become restless like drivers caught in a traffic jam of distant unknown cause.

The lawyer convinced the doctor to alter his professional medical opinion, and now the sawbones spoke flatly, "It is my expert opinion that you should not run the race."

"If I had listened to you guys, I'd still be fat and old, watching my cholesterol. Jeff! What the hell are you doing skulking around back there?"

Sutton said, "I'm taking notes, that all right with you?"

John was bouncing now on the balls of his feet. Every few seconds he hugged a knee to his chest. "We gonna get this thing started or what? You want me just to yell mark set go?"

"But you've been shot!" the doctor argued. "You haven't slept in over twenty-four hours."

"I know! I want to get this thing over with so I can take a little nap, if you don't mind. People shouldn't be afraid of living— makes you younger."

Sutton wrote furiously as the entire contingent withdrew in glad defeat—the Boltman was going to run.

JOHN CRUISED PAST the five-mile marker in a flat twenty-four minutes, up there with the young guys. The gauze bandage irritated his neck, and he kept tilting his head sideways against it. Every few yards he would try to dig the ringing out of his ear. His legs were springy and strong, his heart was racing, and he was slightly hungover, tired, and handling it all. A quarter mile ahead of him were the three Kenyans, who would again take one, two, and three in a major American road race despite the fact that they were apparently telling jokes up there. One of them was in the middle of a long-winded story that had the other two holding their sides with laughter. What the hell did they have to talk about in the middle of a race? John touched his neck to make sure the sweat, which was stinging his wound, was not also loosening his bandage—no need to gross everyone out by exposing the hole in his neck. He kept putting his finger into his ear, trying to get rid of that awful ringing.

He was cruising, thinking about Elena and about how he was able to kill that boy. He remembered how the bullets had made red splotches on the kid's shirt and pants and the way the kid kept swatting himself as if he were being bitten by mosquitoes. Thought you were going to kill me, didn't you, you fucker. Then the kid had stood there with a hole in his forehead and a strangely puzzled expression that you might expect to see in a classroom. Teacher, am I dead? Eighteen years old, according to the news reports. Well, if John the Boltman could have had that him-or-me moment back again, he was sure he wouldn't have behaved differently. He'd *had* to act.

With Elizabeth's admission that she preferred women, and with Andy's improved prospects at MTV and the kid's surprising visit to the love nest, John's conscience was rapidly clearing. His thoughts lately were mostly of eating. And sex, of course. Often a good bout of one would lead to desire for the other. And then, of course, he thought about running.

John Ashe felt downright immortal as he crossed the finish line perhaps a bit later than he would have if he had not been shot the night before, but still four seconds faster than his own masters record. There was no limit to how fast he could run. He believed it.

THE AWARDS CEREMONY was still going on, but there were no reporters left to record the event; the winning Kenyan accepted his trophy to lukewarm applause and a few camera flashes. Most of the reporters had followed the hero of the day to a large orange thermos nearby. John Ashe, Boltman—they were using both names to address him—drank shot after shot of water from a softening paper cup while answering questions from the crowd of reporters. He spotted Jeff. "How ya doing, Sutton? I keep expecting to see you in the race one day."

"Maybe once I get young enough."

"There you go."

A spectator in the crowd stepped forward and presented John with a cigar. "I heard you like to smoke them."

John ran it under his nose, closing his eyes. "Why, thank you, the aroma is great."

And a moment later, having shouldered the cigar with his teeth and borrowed a light from one of the reporters, he was recounting, between puffs, the story of what had happened the previous night, downplaying his heroics. "Anybody would've done what I did, or else they'd be spineless cowards. All I did

was what I was obligated to do. There's no heroism in that."
When asked how he had felt about killing that boy, he said,
"Very sad, to tell you the truth. I assume he's got a mother somewhere who's really unhappy now, and I don't feel good about
that." When asked how it was that he had been able to run the
race so well, breaking his own masters record despite the extenu-
ating circumstances, he said that it just hadn't "occurred" to him
to be tired. "Maybe now I'll get around to it. But really, who
wants to sleep all the time? You waste too much of your life that
way. I had this friend, Lee Thomas, guy had a heart attack just
out running one day. You think as he was lying there dying, he
was fondly recalling the various naps he had taken? I doubt it."
He blew smoke into the still, humid air. Some of the reporters
actually applauded. He downed the rest of his water and threw
the empty cup at the winning Kenyan, who had swung his way
in hopes of some media attention. The Kenyan picked it up and
threw it back.

John yelled, "I'd like to get you in a snowball fight, Henry."

Mugging for the crowd, Henry said, "Snow? There is no snow
in my village."

John brought the Kenyan over to the water thermos, which had
become the de facto awards podium, and threw an arm around
his neck. "I'm gonna make a bold prediction," he said. Henry
coughed in the cigar smoke. "I predict I'm gonna beat Henry and
his countrymen one of these days."

The Kenyan rolled his eyes. "I don't think so, man."

Among the reporters, Sutton was the only one who took the
challenge seriously. "This season? You going to beat him this season? Or you going to wait for one of them to get injured?"

"Oh, no, I'll beat them fair and square."

Sutton said, "Get some sleep, Boltman. I think your head's
foggy."

IN HIS HOTEL room, packing for the next morning's return flight,
John turned on CNN and heard himself lauded as a hero. First
there was a clip of him receiving medical treatment beside the
two dead assailants. "Less than six hours later the same man left
his hospital bed, ran the four miles from the hospital to the start-

ing line of the Peachtree Roadrace, and then proceeded to break his own masters record in the ten-kilometer distance." Now the footage showed him crossing the finish line, Boltman, his shoulder a red badge of courage. "For those of you who are wondering, we do have confirmation that he really is fifty years old."

"And single," said the female anchor.

He sat in front of his hotel window sipping a beer and watching a fireworks display in the distance.

CHAPTER 14

"I KNOW I signed a contract, but that was before I got so damn famous because of the Boltman thing." John kept his voice low so as not to give himself away in this restaurant. He had considered inviting the Bolt! rep to the love nest, but in the days following Atlanta the love nest had become his and Elena's only shelter from his growing fame. Even here in this out-of-the-way restaurant he probably would've been recognized if not for the baseball cap and dark glasses.

He had never really liked the Bolt! rep, who was now shaking his head sadly as if to say, "I'd like to help you son, but . . ." Not a former runner, not a former athlete of any kind from the looks of it, the guy was a short, squat, pasty-faced man with thick glasses and thin hair. He had some sort of MBA, and he could have ended up working for a perfume company just as easily as he had landed at Bolt! For just a moment John felt like reminding the guy that he wasn't the only educated person at this table. But let him think what he needed to think in order to deal with the world. Let him think John Ashe was a naive jock. "You see, John, when we signed you we took a risk. Did you ever take a risk, John? Maybe you played a slot machine. Well, we had no idea whether or not you'd pay off. We just put in our quarter and pulled the lever. Sure, we hit the jackpot, and it's ours because we took the risk. Suppose you had bombed every race after you signed the contract. Do you think we'd be asking you for our quarter back? See? So why are you trying to get your hands on our jackpot?"

"It wasn't exactly a long-term risk." No, the contract would barely take him through the New York Marathon, the Bolt! people had been so skeptical of his long-term prospects. "I'm just putting you on notice I'm going to sign with someone else when the contract's over, someone who has a little more faith in me."

The Bolt! rep was shaking his head again. "We have the option. We can keep you for as long as we feel like signing you up."

"You're saying I gave you a perpetual option? I hope so, 'cause I'll beat that all over the place in court."

"You'd argue that you, a lawyer by training, didn't know what you were signing?"

"I *didn't* know what I was signing. I'll say I thought Bolt! was a reputable company and I was surprised to discover they were trying to rip me off. How's that for publicity?"

When the food arrived, the two men ate in silence. The Bolt! rep knew he'd have to fork over more money at the end of three months to avoid a legal battle, but he didn't really care, though he had to put on an act for John. Boltman was as good as gold for the shoe company, which had been struggling for market share in recent years. Finally he asked, "How much would it cost to keep you? I mean, you're no Michael Jordan, John."

"No, but I'll have a lot of other offers. I expect it'll cost a bundle to keep me."

Relatively speaking, of course. His endorsement income would have been a windfall for any young man—Reynaldo Miller, for example—but it was nothing compared to what John had made as a law partner. If he spent it all and spent all the interest from his small fortune, he could just about tread water without sacrificing any more principle than Elena had already spent on furnishings for the love nest. He wasn't worried about it, though. Boltman didn't worry, he won.

THAT NIGHT HE and Elena went out on a double-date with Rey and the woman who kept the Marathon King in New York when he should have been out in Boulder or Utah running on soft trails at high altitudes. Rey was stupid in love with Carrington Calhoun, direct descendant of John C., and in love with her past. That he could ever date and perhaps marry a woman who had been a real live debutante in Greenville, South Carolina, was a sort of coup for the bastard product of a mixed-race fornication in a northeastern public housing building. A year younger than Rey, she had already been through marriage and divorce within her social set and now seemed to want to try again outside it. As John and Elena approached the door, they heard the voice of Carrington's son behind it. "May I stay up past eleven tonight, Mother?" The kid had a flawless private-school accent, his mother a flawless Southern one. "Did you do your homework, sugar?" *Sugah.* Carrington was the woman who had been with Rey at the Union Square Cafe months ago, when John had stopped them to chat but they were "goin' to a play." The two couples had since laughed about that encounter, and John's account of his and Rey's first meeting in the park.

"Is it really the Boltman?" Carrington asked across the threshold. "You keep knocking Rey off the headlines."

"Every dog has his day," Rey said. "Look, if we're out tonight and there's any trouble, just stand back and do not fear. Boltman will handle it."

Cooper Calhoun Cannon, Carrington's boy, thrust a copy of *Distance Running* and a pen up toward John's chest. "Will you please sign?"

As John complied, the kid said, "What happened to your neck?"

"Mmm? Oh!" He had trimmed the bandage down so that it no longer tickled his chin. Now he sometimes forgot about it. "That's where the guy shot me."

Carrington rolled her eyes. "He's been so excited to meet you. Now, Cooper, I told you not to bother him."

John signed the magazine over to "Cooper, the Junior Boltman," and returned it. Suddenly the boy yelled "Junior Boltman!" and ran across the room to dive onto the couch. The baby-sitter, an older woman, said to John, "Thanks a lot!"

As the foursome piled into a cab, Rey announced that he had already decided to skip his morning run so he wouldn't have to count his drinks. John made the same commitment, and the four directed the cabbie to a faux cowboy bar where they had very real margaritas. When the bartender realized who John was, the next two rounds were free. "What about me?" Rey asked. "Don't you recognize me?"

"This here's the Marathon King," John said, throwing one arm around Reynaldo's neck as if to hold his face still for a punching. "The Marathon King!"

They talked with an older Italian man, well dressed, very drunk. Wouldn't tell them his real name. "Just call me Luciano." John and Rey huddled with Luciano, listening to the guy's life story, which was probably mostly made up but who cared? If the story was compelling, did it matter one way or the other whether Luciano really had killed three men in 1961 and then married one of the widows? As he and John compared notes about killing, Carrington and Elena detached themselves from that conversation to talk about everything from private schools to the problem of racism in the North. "I mean, here they are," *heah they ah*, "all self-righteous about the South. Look in the *New York Times*. There'll be a story about discrimination in the South on the front page, and in the Metro section you get to read about blacks beating up Jews, Italians beating up blacks, on and on. And everyone up here says, 'At least we're not as bad as the South.' I beg to differ." *Diffuh.*

Elena grabbed John's hand and pulled it away from his ear. "You're going to have to stop that," she said. "It's the gunshot," she explained to Luciano. "Now he has tinnitus in that ear. It rings forever."

"Tell me about it!" Luciano said. "I got tinnitus in *both* ears, all the guys *I* shot!"

Walking down the street, Rey pried for details of the Bolt! contract. "They only signed me through the New York Marathon," John said, "for a pittance, too. What about you?"

"Subsistence money. Most of my food I eat over at Carrington's. She's great, huh?"

"Yeah, sure." John glanced ahead at her fine, ample ass. "Bit old for me, though."

Rey give him a little punch in the shoulder. "Yeah, you wish."

Later they found one of those high-backed circular booths good for group photos and dinner scenes in movies. Carrington and Rey were lovely people, John thought, and the night was beautiful, and the waiter recognized Boltman. Soon there was a bottle of champagne on the table, compliments of the owner.

About the only thing that could have ruined the night did finally happen. On their way out, as John and Elena held hands and gave each other a quick smooch, they nearly ran into her father, who, with some of his law partners, was waiting for a table. John felt like a high school boy caught feeling up the principal's daughter. "How you doing, Mr. Conifer?" The old bastard looked down at the lovers' intertwined fingers, and his gaze was a laser beam that separated them.

"Not as well as you, from the smell of things." Conifer waved his hand in front of his nose. "You're not driving, I hope."

"Of course not."

Elena tried to intervene. "Daddy—"

But Conifer kept it up. "How long has it been since you cut your hair? At first I thought, *I was hoping,* you were someone else. You look like a has-been rock star, John, you know that? And get your finger out of your ear." He turned to his daughter. "How are those law school applications coming?"

Bill Conifer had that spent look common among the fathers of beautiful women, as though raising Elena, protecting her, had taken all of his energy. And now that she was, supposedly, an adult, a Magnate grad, a future lawyer if she would get her applications in, she did *this*! Starts going out with John Ashe! And unfortunately, the guy had money, so Conifer couldn't resort to the purse-strings gambit to regain control of her. John Ashe, whose vow to love Elizabeth Baxter for life Conifer had witnessed. Conifer was visibly upset.

Rey stepped forward to patch things up. "Hey, I've known John and Elena for a while now, and they're great together. Really great." He was too drunk for such diplomacy. "John may be a little older, but he doesn't look old, and he's young in all the important ways. Right, Elena?"

Carrington was pulling him back. "Rey?"

"I mean, I don't hear her complaining about their sex life."

Conifer would have thrown a punch at someone then if Elena had not grabbed his forearm and pulled him out onto the sidewalk. Through the glass door John could hear her. "Dad, you stay out of my life!"

"He's fifty years old! You gonna marry him? Is he gonna call *me* Dad? Is his son gonna call you *Mom*?"

She said she was her own woman now and thank you very

much for your thoughtful advice, Dad, but the day you start directing my dating life is the day, is the day . . . her anger rose up in place of words. John, Rey, and Carrington heard Bill Conifer, taken aback, trying to appease her. "Now, look, darling, of course you're right, it is your life, but think about it like this— would you be happy if I left your mom and started living with, say, Shannon?"

"That's not fair, Dad."

Silence. Then the door suddenly opened and Conifer stormed into the restaurant. Catching sight of John in the corner of his eye, he turned, raised his finger, opened his mouth to say something, but that silencing fury of his daughter's took over. His face turned red and his jowls actually began to quiver, and then he pivoted on the front sole of one wing tip and joined his party at the table John and the others had just vacated.

The incident galvanized Elena. Now she was going to stay with John no matter what. In this state of mind it became almost incidental that they really were in love. Still, her father's throwaway scenario of himself dating Shannon or Kim did kind of sicken her, no matter how much she tried to deny it.

ANDY ASHE TOOK a seat at a table on the sidewalk and ordered a beer. His father showed up minutes later, a spry-looking man of indeterminate age. Shoulder-length hair, high cheekbones—and a trimmed-down bandage still on his neck. The waitress checked him out as he passed by.

Sometimes when he saw the way other people reacted to his father, or when he felt himself succumbing to a sentimental pride in the old guy's accomplishments, Andy had to remind himself to stay angry.

"Hi, Dad. Thanks for coming."

"Thanks for inviting me." John scooted up in his chair. "Did you note that waitress checking me out?"

"Come on, Dad."

"What, I'm not supposed to notice? I'm not supposed to like it?"

"That's not what I meant."

His attitude toward his father had softened for several reasons.

Scanning the menu, he considered the fact of his mother's new sexual preference. How could he demand that his father go back to her if she didn't want *any* man? If she had been leaning that way all these years, the stress on the marriage must have been incomprehensible to anyone outside it. Maybe the old man didn't deserve scorn for abandoning the marriage, but pity for sticking with it so long.

"I saw you on MTV the other day," John said. "You were interviewing some white-trash guys."

"Oh, yeah. Actually, two of them went to Choate."

"Choate? No shit?"

"Now somehow they're punk rockers."

"Those assholes went to Choate?"

"When did you start cursing so much?"

"It's funny, Andy," John said, "but it seems my son has a sort of priggishness that runs counter to this MTV hipness you're trying to cultivate."

"Yeah, well, don't tell anybody."

The turmoil in his family had continued to be good for Andy's career—the new show was his. "Is it true what I hear about your mom?" the so-cool producer had asked before making his decision. "That's so cool," he said, "and your dad's still running well?"

Now Andy wore a black cotton jacket and wire-rimmed glasses with circular lenses to accentuate the angularity of his cheekbones. His attitude, cultivated, said that nothing surprised him, nothing bothered him.

And in fact his best efforts to remain merely perplexed by his father's recent actions had begun to give way to a degree of understanding. To call it a midlife crisis would have trivialized this rebellion of his father's, this abdication of responsibility which, paradoxically, had come responsibly late, after his son was through college and the house was paid for and there was finally time for the luxury of questioning the twelve-hour workdays and the packed commuter train. Still, it made Andy sad that both of his parents seemed so happy with their new, separate lives; it left him secretly wistful for the myth of the everlasting nuclear family.

"So, Elena said you stopped by."

"Yeah, we went out for drinks a couple of weeks ago."

"Still got a crush on her?"

Andy shrugged. "She's a bit young for me, Dad." This time he almost smiled when he said it.

John appreciated it, but felt he had to point out, "A lot of girls her age would like to go out with me, or some other wealthy older man. I know that's still hard for you to imagine, Andy, much less accept."

The waitress returned to take their orders. "I saw you down in Atlanta, on the news," she said, touching her own neck where John had been shot. "At first I didn't put two and two together."

"That's me, darling. And what do you do in this great city?"

"I audition for parts."

John and Andy chuckled dutifully at the joke and gave her their orders. John turned to watch her walk away.

"You think you and Elena will get married?" Andy asked.

"Made that mistake once." John shook his head. "Marriage can bring out the worst in people, keep that in mind. Imagine this, you're going out with a girl and you know she can break up with you at any time. So you're nice to her. Well, after you get married, she can't break up with you so easily, and you can't with her, either. It's a legal matter. So you can start leaving your aromatic socks everywhere, and she can decide, for example, only to have sex on alternate Saturdays and then only in the missionary position, and so you start being a jerk, and so does she, and pretty soon you're just sort of living together, estranged roommates, and it sucks, to borrow one of the many terms I have adopted from your show on MTV."

"That is so cynical, Dad."

"Just the opposite. Even sex is boring if you do it the same way for twenty-five years. You don't think you'd lose interest?" John paused to let the point sink in. "Now, if your mother had behaved like that before we were married, I wouldn't have married her, and if she thought about it she would know that. But it's not just her. I'm sure I did things that pissed her off, too, not in spite of the fact that we were married but precisely because of it, since she couldn't very well get rid of me. When two people aren't married, there's a greater sense that things could end at any time. Everything you do seems to matter so much more to the relationship. Pain and pleasure are so much more acute. Life itself takes on greater swings of good and bad, pain and pleasure. A more casual relationship may well bring out the best in two people, or else it simply ends. All of which is why I'm not really interested in marriage at this point."

"Do you regret marrying Mom?"

"I'm damn glad I helped bring you into the world. And, of course, there were good times . . ." How many, really? he asked himself.

The waitress set down the cheeseburgers. John said, "If I take my bandage off, you can see the food going down."

"Dad—"

John proceeded to gulp down an unchewed chunk of cheeseburger.

"Chew your food, Dad."

"Yes, son." Smile. "You see that public-service spot I'm in?"

John took another bite and swallowed immediately. Because of the incident in Atlanta, he had become the television spokesperson for a general campaign against violence. Dressed in his Boltman outfit, including his still necessary bandage, he would give statistics about violence while, in the upper right corner of the screen, they ran the clip of him being treated by the paramedics in Atlanta. At the end of the spot he said, "I know about violence firsthand. It's not pretty. Give peace a chance." The spot ran on TV regularly. Just the other day a semi-famous rocker had stopped Andy in the hallway. "Dude, I didn't know your dad was Boltman."

"And to think I used to find it embarrassing," Andy said, although to a degree he still did.

John was quickly done with his cheeseburger. With his few remaining fries he sponged up the film of grease which coated his plate. Sensing Andy's disapproval, he said, "My cholesterol's one-twenty. Lower than yours, I wager. Say, do you still see Kristen Newton around? She's a good solid girl."

Andy shook his head. His father seemed determined not to be a father, to neither worry about the things a father worried about nor be the subject of the condescending worry of his own progeny. "She detected my crush on your former paralegal, and it made her sort of bitter. But I agree, she is a good solid girl."

"How's she taking it about her mom being a lesbian?"

"She didn't know as of the last time I spoke with her. A month ago, maybe. She kept talking about how wonderful it was that our two mothers were spending so much time together. 'In the sack,' I was tempted to say."

STEVEN FISKE, NOT yet a doctor, had been inspired by his regular study of John Ashe, a.k.a. Boltman, to start jogging. He was up to a mile now, and it usually took him about ten minutes. He found that it had a beneficial, stimulating effect on his bowel movements. And the exercise was invigorating, if not rejuvenating. He still looked much older than his twenty-seven years, not that he regularly took stock of his appearance, vanity to him being a waste of time.

"Nice to have you gracing us with your presence, Boltman," he said. "This is my dissertation we're talking about here. This is my life, okay?"

"Sure, sure."

There was really no excuse for having missed the last couple of sessions, but then again there was not much reason to be here now, either. In fact, the novelty of the study was beginning to wear off, and as Fiske examined his rapidly healing gunshot wound, John glanced with dread at the treadmill. He had considered arriving in jeans and a T-shirt rather than his usual running outfit in order to avoid the contraption.

"Up and at 'em," Fiske said. "Come on, it's in the interest of science. Shirt off so I can hook you up."

With all those wires attached to his body John felt like a monster—which was not far off, he thought, from how Fiske felt about him. But *in the interest of science*, okay. He'd read somewhere that they had preserved Einstein's brain for study. Maybe his body . . . He ran on the treadmill while Fiske jotted down readings from various instruments.

"There are no steroids in your bloodstream, you're not coloring your hair. Your metabolic rate is that of a man in his early twenties. When you were in college, you could probably drink all night and then go find an omelet or a hoagie and you never really gained much weight. Your cholesterol's gone down. Your prostate's smaller than mine. If you start getting zits, I'm turning you over to the government."

The little guy stood in front of the treadmill. "I think we've got a case of *youthing* here. It's a totally theoretical concept based on only one precedent. In that case an older man's *youthing* seemed to coincide with his relationship to a much younger woman."

Jogging at a six-minute pace, John was barely winded. "So what are you trying to say?"

"Jeff Sutton stopped by here the other day—"

"I know him."

"Yes, well, he was talking about your mistress."

"She's not my mistress. She's my girlfriend. I live with her."

"It doesn't matter. All this speed you've picked up, did it start before you met her?"

"I hardly think that's why I'm running faster." The suggestion would not have annoyed him if he had not already thought of it himself. He was aware that the forcefulness of his denial probably revealed his fear. "I thought this was a scientific study. What are you saying, my girlfriend's got some sort of healing powers?"

"Well, we're not sure. If this is a legitimate case of *youthing*, then I would be inclined to think that it's your reaction to her. There's something about the way you respond to her, perhaps in a spiritual way, and it affects your body." He paused. "Let me ask you to describe something. Describe for me how you felt on the day when you and Elizabeth brought Andy home from the hospital after his birth."

"Why?"

"Do you have trouble remembering things? Or admitting to yourself that you remember things?"

John stepped off of the treadmill, the electrodes coming untaped from his body. "This isn't about my memory. I thought this was a physiological study. Fact is, I train very seriously, and I like to think I owe my speed to my dedication to the sport."

"And the cigars and beer, right? Come on, John, you're a fifty-year-old world-class runner because you try real hard? I don't think so."

John was pulling on his shirt.

"You'll come back next week, right? You promised."

"I'll think about it."

"John, I need your help."

John walked out the door. Fiske hoped, believed, what he had here was a legitimate case of *youthing*. Of course, it would still not be accepted by the mainstream medical community even with the corroboration of the Hurvitz precedent. But perhaps over time the concept would win acceptance. His own career would be made.

But he was worried about his subject. In measurable ways John had become younger, or at least more youthful. There were factors that could not be measured, though. The hormonal shifts and spurts of a young man, such as John's glands apparently now thought he was, required a young man's body to deal with them. Fiske worried that John's condition might be weakening him the way continuous pressurization and depressurization weakened the hull of a jetliner until the metal flaked away in midair. Sure, he could run fast. His heart seemed fine. But it was still fifty years old. So were all those little veins in his brain that could clot up and end his life instantly, and so was his liver, which was processing alcohol at a rate that would have jaundiced most fraternity boys.

The Boltman case had proceeded far enough that Fiske now felt he had a legitimate excuse to call the ostracized Dr. Jeremy Hurvitz, who lived in Los Angeles. Or at least he'd lived in L.A. as of his most recent publication some twenty years ago. In a field where reputation was everything, Hurvitz's placed him just a few notches above Jack Kervorkian and the carbon monoxide death machine.

After some telephone detective work involving calls to Hurvitz's former places of employment and the various medical associations that had sanctioned him, Fiske finally tracked down the researcher in San Diego.

Hurvitz at first seemed irritated and distant, but when Fiske explained himself the old man was aroused and acute in his responses. He had read about John Ashe. "Someone brought me clippings from some sort of magazine for runners. Next they'll probably have a magazine for people who just like to walk!"

Fiske withheld the news that there already was such a magazine, and the two men arranged for Hurvitz to fly to New York for several days of research. "It really was my most interesting case," Hurvitz said of his unique 1961 study. "Robert Timmerman was an athlete, too, of course, a surfer dude, he called himself. It was wonderful seeing the change that came over him. Of course, it turned out badly. You're familiar with the study?"

"Yes."

"Tell me how it ended, then," Hurvitz demanded. A test to see if Fiske was worth his trouble.

Fortunately, Fiske had reread the study the night before, and the ending was particularly memorable. The surfer dude had won several competitions, displaying in each one an unlikely dexterity and stamina. He seemed to look very young. People couldn't believe how old he was. Suddenly his youthfulness began to vanish, and it was gone within a few days. He wasn't young anymore, but he kept surfing. On a day when the waves were so small that several weeks earlier he would not have bothered, he surfed for the last time.

Hurvitz's annoyance at his patient's disappearance finally gave way to concern, and he went out looking for him. He found a group of kids taking turns on Timmerman's trademark purple surfboard.

Hours later the crew of a fishing boat pulled in their nets and found, among the gasping fish, the broken-backed body of an old man dressed in surfer garb.

WALKING FROM FISKE'S office toward the love nest, John wondered if perhaps there was an unpleasant side to this *youthing*, or whatever it was called. Fiske seemed to be implying that one symptom of the phenomenon was a certain kind of memory loss. Facts of the past were retained but inspired no emotion. Just the other day John had watched a television movie in which a woman brought her child home from the hospital and laid him in a crib, and she and her young husband leaned over the railing making faces and talking silly. The scene had moved him. Yet when he thought about the day Andy had first come home from the hospital he remembered only the bare facts of the event and none of the emotions it had inspired. He could even remember getting sentimental about Andy's childhood, often on the train when he was ostensibly staring out the window or reading the *New York*

Times. And just a few months ago he had sat in his law office remembering the kid's reaction to the news that the whole family was moving to Groveton. Just six at the time, Andy had asked what language the Groveton people spoke. And at the memory John had felt not just the sweet pain of loss and the sorrow of the passage of time, but also the joy of having had so much. Now, though, his memories failed to rise up and be real; they were multiplication tables or the capitals of all fifty states. Everything after Elena was bright and clear, but it was as if nothing important had come before.

CHAPTER 15

AFTER WEEKS OF neglecting her daughterly duties, and feeling guilty about it, Kristen Newton took the train into Groveton one Saturday to surprise her mother with a visit.

She had about a mile to walk from Groveton Junction to her childhood home, where she still parked her Honda Accord. Older people were working in their yards, and occasionally someone would stare at her in a moment of imperfect recognition. She had played jump rope on these streets, hide-and-seek in these yards, and in some of these houses she and boys like Andy Ashe had sought and found what back then had seemed so hidden. She had learned to drive here, riding around in her father's Audi while he, in the passenger seat, kept stomping an imaginary brake pedal to the floorboard. Hard to believe what Dad had done. A prostitute. A *hooker*—that word from the TV cop shows of her childhood. She hoped someday to be able to forgive him.

Blocks away she could see several cars parked in front of her house, and she wondered if her mother was having some sort of brunch party. Closer—what?—a Toni Moldoni FOR SALE sign in the yard. A bunch of strangers were traipsing through the house, which smelled of fresh popcorn and oranges pierced with cloves. Kristen stood in the foyer, her mouth agape. She was beset by a heavily perfumed, badly dressed fat woman with a broad smile. "How are you? I'm Toni Moldoni."

"This is my house. Is my mother around?"

"Oh, dear, it is so nice to meet you. That must be your little Honda you've been keeping in the driveway. I'm afraid you'll have to move it if your mother and I have our way. We've been

192

having such a wonderful time getting the house ready for listing." She was digging around in her purse. At last she came up with a notepad. "I've got her number where she's staying right here."

"I know the number."

In the kitchen of her childhood, sterile now for showing, Kristen called the Ashes' house. Anne answered. "Mom! I'm at our house. What a surprise that you're selling it!"

"Well, I've been meaning to tell you."

"Where are you going to live? You can't keep living at Elizabeth's, you'll wear out your welcome."

After a moment her mother said, "Why don't you come on over, dear? We're putting together a lovely summer salad."

What she found at the Ashes' house put her in a state of shock. A man answered the door. No, it wasn't a man, it was her *mother*, dressed in sweatpants with a purple paint roller in one hand and a roll of tape in the other. Her mom had a butch haircut—that hair which she had so fastidiously curled, sprayed, and teased for so many years—and she had begun to fill out in a sort of squarish way. "Hi, darling, what do you think?" She pointed toward the living room. The walls were purple. "Elizabeth and I thought the old color scheme was just so, well, nuclear family."

Rounding the corner from the kitchen, it was Elizabeth, also with a butch cut and noticeably chunkier than she had been just a few months earlier. Kristen retreated just slightly and then, embarrassed by that reflex, threw herself into a hug. She backed away, grinning fiercely at her mother and Andy's mother standing side by side. Clones. If she had seen two other women like this, with matching butch haircuts, restoring a house together somewhere, she would have assumed . . . But in this case there had to be some simpler explanation. Two bad haircuts, too much good food, that was all.

"I love your new haircuts," Kristen said, still grinning too widely. "You must save a lot on shampoo." Weak joke, she knew.

In the kitchen she helped Elizabeth prepare the salad. She chopped vegetables for a while, pulling ripe tomatoes from the Davidson's grocery bag. "I hope Mom's not wearing out her welcome," she said. "It's very kind of you to put up with her so long."

"Put up with her! I'd be miserable without her. We have such good times together, much nicer than having a man around."

"Speaking as someone who's lived with women since first year of college, I can say that I'd like to have a man around." A moment later she added, "A horny one, if possible."

The older woman said, "Well, we all march to a different drummer, dear."

Now, what the hell did that mean? Kristen kept washing tomatoes and chatting about various innocuous events. A few minutes later she excused herself to go to the bathroom.

"Go upstairs, dear. Annie's still painting the one down here."

"Okay." *Annie?*

Walking quietly down the hallway, she looked in every bedroom to see which was her mother's. Maybe there would be a suitcase or something, some sign that this arrangement was both platonic and temporary. But room after room was spotless, the beds perfectly made. Only the master bedroom showed signs of use. There were two feather pillows, each retaining the dent of a sleeper's head. Kristen leaned close to one of the pillows and picked from it a short strand of her mother's golden blond hair. On the nightstand on that side of the bed was a framed photograph of Kristen herself. On the other nightstand, a photograph of Andy.

They had already divided up the closet. Elizabeth had one side and "Annie" the other. No sign of the lawyerly suits Mr. Ashe had once kept there, none of his wing tips on the closet floor.

She opened the dresser drawer and found panties of two different brands and slightly different sizes mixed together. Noticing at the bottom of the drawer the corner of a book, she cleared the panties from on top of it. *Making Love to a Woman: A Guide for Women.* Complete with pictures.

Lunch was awkward. It was hard for Kristen, who considered herself quite open-minded in matters of human sexuality, to accept the conclusive evidence. Her mom and Andy's were shacked up together. They were a couple of . . . well, they were living together and they were a couple of *dykes*, is what they were. Her discomfort was so obvious that at the earliest polite moment Elizabeth excused herself from the table.

Anne said, "I thought Andy would have told you."

"I haven't seen much of Andy since he developed a crush on his father's girlfriend."

"Which just proves our point about men. You need one to have a child, and it's nice if they're around earning money to help you raise it, but you can't really count on that anymore. And once the kids are through college, well, who needs a man?" Anne shrugged. "I've been meaning to tell you myself, Kristen. I'm really happy with this whole situation. I want you to understand that."

"How could you be? Have you always felt this way? Because if so you must've been really miserable before." And now she was thinking, no wonder Dad went to a . . .

"Your father had no reason to complain."

"That's not what I said. Oh, I can't talk about this."

Anne said, "I don't really have much experience in this matter. If you recall, most of my adult life was spent raising you and taking care of my supposedly faithful husband. By the time I was your age you were three, so I didn't have time for the sexual experiences you've probably had—"

"Mom!"

"Let me just say that sleeping with Elizabeth—"

Kristen turned her head away. Anne continued: "Living with her, making lunch with her, *all* of that, is a hell of a lot better than sleeping with your father, living with him, serving him dinner. He was far less appreciative, I assure you. And even years ago he was a rushed lover."

"I don't think I want to hear this."

"You need to know I enjoy *being* with Elizabeth more than I ever enjoyed *being* with your father, more than I can imagine enjoying *being* with any man ever again."

Kristen nodded. Get a grip. She reminded herself that she had always believed sexual preference was a private matter. But it was different when it was *her own mother*. She could sustain only a semblance of civility for the rest of the afternoon.

"You can leave your car here, if you like," Elizabeth said toward the end of the visit. "I don't think we'll have any trouble selling that other house."

"Thanks," Kristen said. "I really can't afford to rent a spot in the city."

When offered a ride back to Groveton Junction, she quickly accepted.

She felt the need to get back into the great jumble of the city. There everything was *supposed* to be screwed up. That was part of its charm, in fact, just as part of the charm of Groveton was supposed to be the solid normalcy now revealed as a facade she could barely believe or deal with.

REYNALDO MILLER STOPPED by the love nest with about fifteen copies of the August *Distance Running* in which Jeff Sutton had written up the Boltman incident. There were a few still shots of the videotape at the crime scene, John being treated for the neck wound, and then there was the shot of a bloodstained, neck-bandaged Boltman running down the broad, empty street toward the field of forty thousand runners poised to stampede over him. "These are for in case you've got any family still speaking to you," Rey said. "Carrington's little boy, Cooper? He took this issue and the autograph you gave him to school to show all his friends. He still calls himself the Junior Boltman."

John was stretched out on the couch, still groggy after a nap. He picked up one of the magazines and looked at himself on the cover. "I'm glad Sutton's getting some good copy out of this. I feel bad for him sometimes."

Rey was heading for the fridge. "You got any orange juice?"

"Help yourself. Bring me some."

John turned on the television.

Rey came in from the kitchen and sat in front of the television, spread his legs, and tried to put his forehead on the carpet. Being a runner, he was too inflexible to do it, but the attempt was part of his stretching routine. "I feel like it's getting better," he said, massaging the knee in question. "It still hurts but through a smaller range of motion, you know? My doctor says I'm just getting old. I told him about you. He says he's heard of you and you don't count." He lay flat on his back. "There's not as much snap to my legs, John, and the marathon's so damn soon. You know when you find a green twig in the woods, how it's real flexible? When I was a kid we used to try to make bows out of those things for shooting arrows. And then over time they'd dry out.

One day when you tried to bend it as far as you used to be able to just fine, the thing snaps." Reynaldo pressed the sides of his fists together and then broke them apart.

More injury talk. John phased out and started flipping channels. In Rey's voice he smelled the smell of the end of a career, the metamorphosis into Jeff Sutton, except that Rey probably couldn't write. Rey seemed resigned to the loss of his youth and talent. He seemed almost to *want* the loss, almost as if keeping up the speed and being young were too much for him now. He seemed almost to crave has-been status so he wouldn't have to work as hard to be the best at something. Corporate sponsorship and occasional prize money did not a fortune make, especially if you spent so much time in New York courting a certain Southern debutante, and for Reynaldo's tendons to go brittle would also mean the sudden uselessness of his ATM card. He would have to get a real job, perhaps at Hot Foot with Gil Stevenson for a boss.

"I shoulda had a career in law first, apparently. Saved up some money before I started running. What was a typical day like for you at the office?"

"Tell you the truth, Rey, I can't even remember."

Rey chuckled. "Must not've been that great."

"That I can promise you."

"I'm going to have to get a real job," Rey said.

"Go to Boulder, get in some altitude training. Go somewhere they got hills, at least."

"Carrington likes it here."

"You love her enough to give up your career early?"

"It's not that early," Rey said. "I wouldn't mind getting on with my life, going on to the next stage."

John didn't want even to consider such a thing.

HE HAD NO races scheduled for August, just some good distance running and a few store appearances he could forgo.

They stayed in a suite in the Boulderado, and John spent the mornings and afternoons running with Frank Shorter and others along various trails through the mountains. His limbs had never felt so supple or his lungs so massive and healthy. Shorter introduced him to one of the University of Colorado track coaches, who had him doing speed work in Folsom Field, the same stadium which contained the final quarter mile of the Bolder Boulder. It was incredible to the coach that John had neglected this part of his training. "You mean you've been heading out and running a few miles at always roughly the same even pace and that's it? No wonder you've got no real kick. We're going to give you some speed, buddy." On the last day of the week John raced every heat of the forty-yard dash with the members of the University of Colorado football team. Only the running backs, receivers, and one particularly quick linebacker were able to stay with him to the finish line. The track coach pulled him aside and handed him a piece of paper on which were written three speed workouts. "You should be getting one of these in every week. You think those Kenyans don't do speed workouts?"

"They've got a pretty good kick," John admitted.

That night on Pearl Street, he lit up a Cohiba that a friend of Rey's had smuggled back from Cuba. "I could live in a place like Boulder," he said. "You've got an application for the University of Colorado, right?"

"Yes," she said, "but why would I come here when my LSATs could get me in anywhere?" Bill Conifer, who had partially reconciled with her for the purpose of law school consultations, of course was pushing for Harvard if the school would take her, and then, as backups, northeastern schools in order of decreasing reputation.

"It really doesn't matter where you get into law school," John said. "Wherever's best for you. Because I could live anywhere except maybe Boston or L.A."

"There are hills in Boston. You could run in the countryside when the leaves change."

"Well, just don't go to UCLA. I couldn't live in Los Angeles."

"Nor I," she assured him.

At first he was not sure that there was a connection between his fine cigar and the hostility he felt from various Boulder locals. Perhaps his fly was gaping. He checked and it wasn't. He blew a puff of smoke out in front of him and then walked through it. Someone behind him coughed theatrically. Someone else said, "We should get a petition and put this kind of air pollution on the ballot."

John turned around to face a man and woman about thirty, pushing their child in one of those hi-tech jogger strollers. "That is very inconsiderate," she said, pointing at the cigar. "It's a health hazard for me and my child."

"So is getting all pissy about it," Elena said. "You're going to give yourself a stroke."

John said, "Look, you're going to be really surprised when you get to be about sixty-five, and despite all the jogging and all the salads and no smoking you get cancer and die anyway. Live a little." Still, he took his cigar to a side street and puffed it in an alley as if he were a crack addict. "Did I say I could live here? I take it back."

Leaning against a brick wall and watching John smoke, Elena was still thinking about law schools. After having spent her whole life within seventy-five miles of Manhattan, she wanted to escape its radius of influence. In fact, she wanted out of the whole Northeast. Boulder had opened her eyes to the fact that the world did not stop spinning if you left New York. The sun still rose and set. The colors were just as bright, in most cases brighter, and the people could be just as interesting. Still, Boulder was sort of an oasis between the true, flat Midwest and the true mountains. Thirty miles farther east and it would be a milk-white town of beauty contests and prize pigs. Thirty miles farther west and it would be a paramilitary survivalist camp full of cross-burning racists. Michigan had a good law school but was too cold. UVA had a good law school but was too far south of the Mason-Dixon line. That left . . . California. If she eliminated L.A. at John's request, that left only northern California. Stanford, she felt, was probably the place. She could venture up and down the coast with the wind blowing through her hair, riding in the passenger seat of John's Porsche. But did she really see herself that way? In the passenger seat? Or even with the Boltman at all? Boltman—the nickname had seemed cute at the time but now was growing rather tiresome. Just before making love he would actually say something like, "The Boltman's coming at you!" And—she knew this shouldn't bother her, he couldn't help it—but the way he kept trying to dig the ringing out of his tinnitus ear had begun to gross her out. The thigh of his jeans was stained with excavated ear wax.

After making love that night, John said, "You wore the Boltman out."

"Please don't call yourself that, John, okay?"

It was dark, she could not see his face. A moment later he said, "A few months ago, early in our relationship, did I ever say much about my marriage?"

"Of course."

"What did I say about it?"

"That it was boring, stultifying, your wife didn't understand you."

"I can't imagine it being that way if I were married to you."

"I guess it would be nice. But don't you think there was a time when you were in love with your wife?"

"I hadn't met you yet." He propped himself up on an elbow. "Elena, I've been thinking more and more about the possibility of us getting married."

She smiled, touched a finger to his lips. "Let's not talk about it just now."

IT SEEMED THAT Elena was of two minds about everything lately. Developments over the past few months had moved along so swiftly that when she did find a moment to contemplate them she was all the more baffled. Last November her father had been about to make her move back into her old room in Connecticut. Now she was sharing a spacious apartment on the Upper West Side with a handsome older man. That he was *much* older she tended not to remind herself, and that willful ignorance was easy to maintain in light of what John was doing on the running course. His speed was impossible—everyone thought so—except that apparently it wasn't. Races that he entered with the intention of loafing he would wind up winning the masters division. Later the same day he might take a training run and then go eat a big dinner, and on the way home smoke a cigar. She loved his success, and enjoyed her status as the bedroom beneficiary of his rejuvenation.

But she found it alarming that he had begun to see a connection between those lovemaking sessions and his racing performance, his new youth.

One morning soon after their return from Boulder, there was an ominous discussion about it. John had hugged her and said flat-out that the only difference between the time when he couldn't run well and now was that he was having sex with her. "I don't know if I want that responsibility, John. That's mental blackmail. It's your attitude that's helping you."

"But what changed my attitude?"

"What if . . ." *What if we break up?* she was thinking. "What if something happens to me? Are you saying you won't be able to run?"

"I don't think another woman would have the same effect on me."

"It's not the sex, John."

Later that morning he seemed to feel threatened by the fact that she was going out for lunch with her ex-roommate Shannon, who had called to suggest the idea. "I never see anyone my own age anymore, John."

"Don't beat me over the head about my age!"

"I wasn't."

"That's what it sounded like!"

"I haven't seen Shannon in a while—"

"I'd been thinking we could walk down to the Village, get something to eat."

The purse-strings gambit of her father? "Can't we do that tomorrow? I mean, we *live* together. It's not like you won't see me." She grabbed her purse and walked out the door, leaving him staring after her with a perplexed hunch to his shoulders.

She was also increasingly irritated by his attitude toward physical pain—*it's all in your head.* The contempt he sometimes showed for his nominal best friend whenever Rey complained of being injured was bad enough. "He's wavering mentally, is the problem," John would say. "He's mentally weak. I ran the Peachtree with a bullet wound in my neck." But then he turned that same irrational scrutiny on her one day when she had a light cold. "Stop coughing so much. It's all in your head." Right, he ran the Peachtree after getting shot, didn't see him coughing. Part of his problem seemed to have to do with the experiments this Fiske was performing. Apparently Fiske was verbally reinforcing John's notion that she was the source of his rejuvenation.

Elena and Shannon met at Juanita's and had a couple of margaritas. Never in particularly good shape while they had lived
together, Shannon had since slimmed down thanks to an exercise
regimen that included aerobics and weight training. "I felt so
hard up when you and John still lived with us because, *bella*, of
all those sounds you were making. No wonder you make him
feel so manly—my God, a couple of times you almost gave *me* a
hard-on." She paused to watch Elena's blush. "I met this guy in
the gym, he's older. Well, not older like yours is older, he's
twenty-five. He's got the most perfect body I've ever seen, ridged
stomach and everything, and I've been having a great, great time
with him." She stuck her tongue in her cheek and raised her
eyebrows.

"Good sex?"

"Let's just say I understand what all the noise was about.
Derek—that's his name—I wouldn't care if he never spoke. He's
not that bright, really, but his thing is like constantly hard, it's so
amazing. He's like a gorilla or something. Sole purpose is to eat,
sleep, and fuck. And I've had enough sensitive men to last a
lifetime."

"Zero?"

They laughed. Throughout college Shannon had been the kind
of drunk who would have to ask her one-night stands the next
day whether they had used a condom. She could remember the
fact of copulation but not the specifics. That she finally thought
enough of herself to stay relatively sober during the act was encouraging, and Elena found herself jealous of her new friend's
enthusiasm for this new relationship. It had been nearly a year
now since she and John had first laid eyes on each other during
that job interview . . . and there had been some sort of dangerous, undeniable chemistry in that first handshake, but you built
up a tolerance to it over time. Now Shannon was asking about
Boltman, wanting to know how things were going.

"Great."

"You don't sound as excited as before."

"I've been doing law school applications. It causes some ten-
sion because we've got to pick a place that's good for both of us."

"Really?" This time Shannon's eyebrows stayed up for a long
time. "Co-relocation?"

"I'm sure it'll work out. You didn't think I'd just move in with him for a while and spend a bunch of his money."

"Oh, no, of course not."

"I really love John. He's older, sure, but you'd never know it from the way he runs or the way he lives or the way he, you know, makes love . . ." Her turn to stick her tongue in her cheek. "I think we have a good life ahead."

Shannon had the annoying look of someone trying not to speak her mind. Rather than criticizing John openly, she opted to damn him by comparison to her new humpman, who not only was a good lover but also shared her "timetable of life." Elena kept silent as her friend continued: "If it turns serious, I've got it all worked out, where we'll get married and how far apart we'll space our kids and how old we'll be when they get out of college. We both agree that it would be better to get rid of the kids while we're still young enough to travel. But you know what? If it doesn't work out that way, if we break up in a month or two, it's still the best sex I ever had. I think he's made me a better lover, put me more in touch with my physical side. I mean, there are times when I feel like I'm in a National Geographic video, you know what I mean?"

Elena said, "And if you break up, you can always find someone else who shares your 'timetable of life.' "

"You noticed that, was that too much?" Shannon grabbed Elena's wrist on the bar. "I just worry about you, *bella*. By the way, Jake Coates got a part in the new Walt Stacker movie!"

"No way!"

"That's what I heard. He's a bad guy, a hitman. And Walt Stacker was pissed because Jake is just so damn good-looking. He's got this minor part, but he's stealing all the attention from Walt Stacker. So Stacker's agent forced them to shoot it all over again and forced the makeup people to make Jake uglier, which must've been hard."

"That's great!"

"And who knows?" Shannon said. "He could be famous soon. You know, I don't think Jake ever got over you."

Jake had gone to L.A. after graduation to be an actor, a move generally considered foolish by his classmates. Other Magnatians had found success in Hollywood, but they had done it the Magnate way—that is, by making use of connections that were already in place. And Jake's connections were in St. Louis, where he could have had a cushy job in a field related to what, as far as everyone could tell, was his great personal interest, beer. Instead he had gone out to Babylon, a prodigal son with no more connections than a corn-haired fraternity boy from Ohio State. Elena remembered what a hurried lover he had been and how curious she herself had been to get the first time over and done with. God, they were both a couple of bumblers. It brought out a smile now beneath faraway eyes.

Shannon said, "Uh-huh, I didn't think it was all gone yet."

Elena shook her head. "I'm happy with John. We actually have a very similar 'timetable of life.' "

For dessert they both had another margarita. It wasn't until they had walked through the park in a pleasant tequila haze that Shannon happened to mention that she knew of a sort of mini Magnate reunion taking place at the Palm Bar. "I just remembered it, let's go."

In the Palm Bar, which was decorated like a travel brochure for some Caribbean island, they found eight or ten college acquaintances, including Jeanie Grover, who had arrived at Magnate with blue hair and a clove cigarette dangling from her chapped lips, and after three weeks had morphed into the perfect sartorial expression of Anne Taylor, Inc. Also here were a couple of kids whose surnames were not coincidentally the trademarks of a major home-appliance manufacturer and a food-company conglomerate, respectively. Elena had had a couple of brand-name friends in college, but generally she could not relate to their baronial sense of entitlement. If every salesman in Sears and Montgomery Ward and J.C. Penney was trying to sell a refrigerator with your name on it, and you got a cut of their business, it sort of tended to quash your ambition for anything but stylish play. And how to justify it? You found yourself falling back on some theory of genetic superiority perhaps coupled with a belief in divine right. She preferred the sons of middle management, scrappers like Jake Coates, and cases of relaxed admissions standards and generous financial aid like basketball point guard Ed Battle, who was also there at the Palm Bar. He had worked at the circulation desk at the library. Like nearly every other male with the self-esteem to do so, he had asked Elena out on a number of occasions after she had finally broken up with his best friend, Jake Coates. Now Ed worked for a senator in D.C. "What are you doing up here?" she asked.

"I probably shouldn't tell you this," he said. "It's not in my best interest, but I'm here visiting Jake, who's visiting New York."

"What a coincidence, we were just talking about . . ." She looked up at Shannon, who performed a you'll-thank-me-later shrug. So this was all a big setup. Did they disapprove of John *that* much? She should just walk out of this place right now without even seeing Jake, who had just gone to "take a whiz," according to the genteel Ed. She stared at the rest room corridor from which her first lover would soon emerge. She ought to just leave right now. Right this very minute before . . . Jake appeared in the doorway and looked around the bar as if fairly sure some tourist group might snap his photo. He looked great. He'd filled out a bit, and he had about him the glow of imminent success. When he saw Elena, his face lost the narrow-eyed action-hero look and went a little bit buffoonish with the momentary resurfacing of his virginal confusion. He crossed the room in about three long strides and took her by the shoulders. "When are you gonna get fat and ugly so I can get on with my life in peace? And what's this I hear about you and this old runner guy I've been reading about? Did I turn you off young guys forever? Was I that bad? I mean, I know I wasn't exactly an expert or even very considerate, and I was only faithful until I got the chance to cheat with . . . but never mind about that, you never found out about that, did you? Anyway, I just gotta know, was it my fault?"

He was attractive, playful, and she had to smile. "Yes, Jake. All of my decisions since we broke up have been my pathetic attempts to deal with it, to in some way arrange my life to fill in the great void you left."

He put his arm around her neck and whispered. "I'd like to fill in your void again. Interested?"

"No." Anyone else, she would have been offended. But after what she and Jake had been through, what was the point? She wondered if there would ever again be the thinnest glaze of formality between them.

"Come on, I've got a hard-on right now just thinking about it. Feel it, no one's looking."

She kissed her fingertip and touched it to the perfect cleft of his broad, square chin. "You'd better go find a bathroom stall and relieve myself—*yourself*," she quickly corrected.

"Revealing Freudian slip, though, don't you think?"

They stuck together for the rest of the afternoon in the Palm Bar. He told her that if she ever came out to L.A., he expected a call. "I'd love to show you around, and hell, why pay for a hotel when I can put you up?"

"You've got an extra room?"

"No, but I've got an extra pillow."

She watched him run a hand through his hair—such cheekbones, such smooth skin, such broad shoulders. It seemed clear that he was going to be successful out there. Someday, she supposed, she would say, "I used to know that guy" whenever his name came up.

"You've got to come out and visit UCLA Law School, right?" he said.

"I've been thinking about it."

"Sure, come out there for law school."

"I might. Maybe I will."

Later Shannon pulled her aside. "Do you realize when you're forty John's going to be sixty-eight?"

"I won't care."

"Do the math. You do care. You think he's going to be a great lover at sixty-eight? You're going to have to help him pump up his penile implant. Take my advice, have your fun with him, get the older man thing out of your system once and for all. He's an interesting character, and it'll be cool someday to be able to say you used to know Boltman, but that's *it*.

"On the other hand, *bella* . . ." Shannon smiled across the room at Jake. "Over there's your soul mate."

GENTLY, ELENA RAISED the age concern that night. Before, it had always been a source of amusement. ("When I made partner you were five years old!") But this time John sensed an alarming, genuine concern about what Elena called the "age chasm." He'd never even heard her use the word *chasm* before.

"I don't think you should go out with Shannon anymore, if this is what happens."

"I can go out with whoever I want, John."

What a thing to say, and in such a spiteful tone, like a teenager rebelling against her father. She had never before questioned the basic premise of their relationship. There had been arguments, that was normal—but over small things like the color of the new sofa or where to go for dinner. He did manage to make love to her that night, but there was a sadness to it, as at the end of the summer when the beach shuts down. She felt it, too. "I didn't mean to ruin tonight," she said.

"It's okay." He was sitting against the headboard, rubbing her back. "You were just worried. If you can't talk to me, who can you talk to?"

A minute later he said, "So what happened out there today? What made you act like that?"

"Shannon and I ran into some old Magnate friends."

"Like an old boyfriend?" An unpleasant edge had crept into his voice. "Or should I say, a young one?"

"John, please don't get upset. I love you, okay? I just found out today I miss my friends, that's all."

In the middle of the night he woke from a fitful sleep and hobbled toward the bathroom to take a piss. Halfway there he realized his heels were hurting.

THE NEXT MORNING he was scheduled to run a little ten-K charity exhibition race in New Brunswick, New Jersey. This was his distance, and people were eager to see him break his own masters record, but he told them all to keep their expectations in check since he would be using this race simply for training. He did not also admit that his Achilles' tendons were nearly as stiff as in the days of the Silver Milers. How strange to think that until last night, getting up to go to the bathroom, he had forgotten the very existence of those strands which connected his calf muscles to the bones of his feet in such a way that permitted walking, running.

He jogged through the Rutgers campus, hiding his limp. The

fastest women in the race were so far ahead of him that he could no longer see them anymore, even here on this relatively long straightaway bisecting downtown. Some old guy, early fifties maybe, plodded along beside him. "Hey, you're that guy who keeps setting all the records, aren't you?"

"Yeah."

"Well, what's wrong now? You're not injured, are you?"

"No way. Injuries are all mental."

But finally he pulled over and started walking. He cut across several blocks to the finish line and found Elena there waiting for him to cross. Watching her for a moment, he was touched by the worry in her face. She still cared, the way she kept standing on tiptoe in an attempt to spot him among the middle-of-the-pack runners who were approaching the finish line, holding their stomachs, wheezing, staggering, their faces turned up as if in final appeal to heaven.

His heels felt a little better for the concern she was showing. He approached her from behind.

"John, what . . ."

"It's my heels," he whispered, taking her hand. "Let's get out of here."

JOHN AND FISKE decided to give Hurvitz another five minutes before proceeding without him. "He's an older guy," Fiske said when John sighed and checked his sports watch again. "And like I said, his plane just flew in. When he gets here, you better be nice to him, okay?"

"Sure, sure. I had a grandfather once." John hugged first one knee and then the other to his chest, limbering up for the treadmill. For Fiske there seemed to be about this coming event the significance of opening night, the hour of judgment.

There was a knock at the door. Fiske opened it, nearly genuflecting at the sight of an old man shabbily dressed, sporting a poorly groomed beard and carrying an old-fashioned doctor's bag. "Dr. Hurvitz?"

"So I'm in the right place, then."

"I can't tell you what a pleasure it is to meet you, Dr. Hurvitz."

Turning eagerly to John, he said, "Dr. Hurvitz is the world's foremost expert on youthing."

"You might say that." Hurvitz shook John's hand. "You might also say I'm the only one who believes in it, except for young Fiske here."

Despite his aged, fragile appearance Hurvitz had a strong handshake, and resolute eyes in a face otherwise slack with time. His obvious competence John found reassuring—here was a man who might be able to explain things—and almost immediately he wished he could exclude Fiske from the rest of the session. Fiske suddenly yanked John's Bolt! shirt up over his head. "Hold it here while I get you hooked up. You won't believe this, Dr. Hurvitz."

"I've been fully briefed. I've seen the printouts of his heart rate and so forth. Let him put his shirt back on."

John lowered the shirt.

Hurvitz said, "Fiske here tells me you had some trouble in a race the other day. Your Achilles' tendons were inflamed."

"That's right."

"Was there anything unusual about the night before? Some sort of mental stress resulting, say, from an argument with your Elena?"

Not wanting to have to explain, too embarrassed to admit that he had been worried about his age and that this had made him unreasonable, leading to an argument and unsatisfying sex, he denied it altogether. He could tell Hurvitz did not believe him.

"How old is Elena?"

"She just turned twenty-three last week."

"It's young for a man your age, isn't it?"

"She and I always say, is it better to have the right person or a person who's the right age?"

Hurvitz sat down in a utilitarian steel chair and opened the doctor's bag across his lap. "I've brought you something I want you to fill out." He pulled out a form several pages long on legal paper. The space between the questions was about four inches.

"You want me to write?"

"You're a lawyer, aren't you?"

John took the form and read the first question out loud. " 'What is your most cherished experience with your ex-wife?'

Oh, come on, that's not important to me now. You know, memory is overrated anyway."

Hurvitz said, "What's your most cherished experience with Elena?"

John sat down on the examination table. His voice grew quieter, more soothing. "I remember the first time I saw her. I was interviewing her, and it was all I could do not to stammer. You work in a law office all day every day for two and a half decades, you forget that people like her really exist. It was a revelation for me. She was a revelation. She was perfect, and she didn't know my faults and flaws. She'd never seen me snoring in front of *Larry King Live*—which I don't do anymore, by the way. I can't even imagine doing that."

"So," Hurvitz said, "is that an overrated memory? Would you like to forget it?"

"I'll never forget how she made me feel."

"So tell me, can you remember anything so pleasant about Elizabeth?"

"I was married to her for a long time."

"But that's just a fact. Yes, you loved your wife once, of course, you did. But all you can remember now is that for a certain number of years you were married to her. Available to you are none of the perceptions which make your life *your life* as opposed to a time line on a page. Your life began the moment you met Elena, is that how you feel?"

"Or the moment we first had sex. Take your choice."

"How are your heels? Take off your shoes."

John did as he was told, slowly. "They still hurt a little."

"Have you made up with Elena completely? Because that's my prescription. Take her out to dinner, some place very nice. Take her home and make love to her like the first time. Your heels will be fine after that."

After John had left, Fiske, who had been taking copious notes as Hurvitz spoke, said, "So I was right? It's *youthing*?"

Hurvitz nodded. "Very similar, at least. The surfer I was telling you about began his transformation when he became infatuated with a young girl . . ." Of course, Fiske had repeatedly read the study that was the foundation of his own dissertation work. He listened only when Hurvitz deviated from the documented story of Robert Timmerman and his young girlfriend. "I was quite good friends with them," Hurvitz said. "He used to flirt with my wife. We would have him and his girlfriend over for dinner. They had nothing in common whatsoever. Just that they were both emotionally incomplete. Maybe somehow if they joined spiritually they would both be whole. But they didn't really join spiritually, just physically with their interlocking parts."

"And then he broke his neck one day, the surfboard," Fiske said.

"Yes, but in my study I was perhaps too coy in describing the precipitating factor. I wanted to protect the identity of the young girl in question. What if everyone tried to copulate with her to get younger?"

Fiske laughed. "Then she'd be just like every other mid-twenties woman with old guys after them."

Hurvitz said, "She's a grandmother now, by the way. Hearty and happy. Been married to the same man all this time, someone from her college class.

"Anyway, she grew tired of Robert Timmerman for one reason or another. He had become somewhat crude and immature. She began to see someone her own age, and Robert couldn't handle it. All the beneficial effects of his relationship with her—and we still can't really explain their existence—just disappeared."

"Is there something about the young woman?"

"No. Very unlikely. You mean to ask if I, for example, were to copulate with this Elena Conifer, would I begin to get young? No. No woman would work for me because I am at peace with my own age, not averse to dying soon, really, and I'm still as much in love with Ruth as I was on our wedding night in 1930."

"What about me?" Fiske asked. "I don't want to die. I don't want to get old. If I had sex with Elena, would I suddenly become younger?"

"No! For your salvation you've got to believe so deeply that this girl will make you younger that it wouldn't even occur to you not to believe, or that you do believe. See? It's such a deep belief that at least at first it is not even a conscious one. Very likely if you copulated with a young woman, the only thing it would get you is divorced. The stress of which would probably make you age even more quickly."

Fiske was still puzzled. "Why don't we tell John all this?"

"I just gave him a big hint, didn't I?" Hurvitz shook his head sadly. "There's a danger. I told Timmerman outright, and he behaved rather badly around *his* girlfriend after that . . . it led to their falling-out. He began to demand sex like medicine, and she gave it to him that way for a while, and it worked for a while . . . but the magic was going out of it. It's not just the sex, it's the love, it's the uncontemplated faith. If I knew what it was, I would be rich."

"And young," Fiske said.

Hurvitz grinned. "Probably not. It looks like too much trouble to me."

JOHN THOUGHT HE would stop and have a drink on the way home. A couple of mid-thirties guys in their cups recognized the Boltman and started buying him shots. It went on for hours. He achieved a sour inebriation and became convinced that at home he would find Elena in bed with some boy with zits on his back, some Magnate kid with an entry-level job somewhere, some *kid*. He talked himself through an imaginary argument with her in which he said all the right things, left her quivering on the floor in tears, and then in his infinite wisdom forgave her, giving her an experienced screwing by way of apology.

By the time he got home, he was blind drunk. He limped around the love nest checking all the closets and under the bed. Elena watched him from the bedroom doorway, a look on her face that seemed to him both superior and incredulous, which only served to anger him further.

"Are you looking around for someone, John?"

"Should I be?"

"No."

He approached her. "You sure?"

He got louder and more inane as his last tequila shot kicked in. He pestered her for sex until she finally agreed to it. "You undress and get in bed, John. I'll be there in a minute." He lay down and immediately passed out, snoring so loudly that Elena had to sleep on the couch.

The next morning, he tied up the bathroom for two hours being sick, a middle-aged man sunk to the floor. Occasionally Elena came in and touched the back of his head. "You all right?" He nodded and kept on.

He slept all day. Whenever he got up to go to the bathroom, he had to limp on his swollen heels. Despite the insignificance of that last race, rumor of his failure to finish it had already made it back to the Bolt! rep, who kept calling. "Well, when will he be in?" he asked Elena. She said she didn't know. Jeff Sutton also tried two or three times to get through, and when at four o'clock the doorbell rang it was Reynaldo. "The old man in?" She let him into the bedroom. "Hey, man, should I call a priest or what?"

"Got drunk last night. Said a lot of stupid shit. I didn't call you or anything, did I?"

"Nah. What'd you do, say stupid shit in front of Elena? 'Cause she's been taking care of you all day and fielding your calls, so you're gonna owe her."

His stomach felt better by early evening, but not his heels. A good hot shower cleared his head, and he began to comprehend the breadth and seriousness of his misbehavior. He limped out and begged Elena to forgive him. She ran her hand through his hair, which seemed a positive gesture, but she also kept shaking her head no in a sort of slow exasperation. "Elena, you've got to forgive me. I know you never want to be with anyone but me. I was just out of my head drunk." She just kept playing with his hair and shaking her head.

He opted for a different strategy, shift some blame. "I was so embarrassed because of the way I ran. During the race I kept thinking about how unhappy you were because of our age differ-ence, and I started thinking, maybe she's right, maybe I'm too old for her and too old for everything. My life is over—"

"I didn't say that—" She was sitting forward now, concerned.

"—and I should just quit. If I haven't been as attentive to you lately, if I've let all this . . . *fame*"—he rolled his eyes to show how ephemeral, how unimportant it was compared to her—"go to my head, then I'm very sorry. Let me tell you something. I don't only love you. Elena, I need you."

She closed her eyes. It was the last thing she wanted to hear.

He clapped his forehead. "I forgot to follow Hurvitz's prescription. Yesterday Hurvitz told me to take you out to dinner, be very nice to you, then make love to you."

She smiled. A way out. "So follow it."

They went out. In some ways their conversation at dinner was that of a couple on a first date, so much damage had John done to the relationship. He remembered what he had said to Andy about how you had to be on your best behavior when you weren't married, that only afterward could you safely start taking your partner for granted. Well, maybe he had begun to take Elena for granted, to assume that he no longer needed to deserve her. She could, after all, leave him at any time, what was to stop her? So he was extremely *appreciative* that night.

She kept talking about law school and her life beyond. "I guess I just see the degree as a good thing to have. It only takes three years, but I'm still unsure about what kind of law. There are so many options." John encouraged her in every way he could imagine.

"Didn't you tell me once that you lived in student housing when you were at Virginia Law?"

"Yes, I did."

"That must've been valuable, making all those connections."

"I don't know." It was where he had met Elena's father, but no need to remind her of that.

"What was it like living there?"

Precisely the sort of thing that had drained like blood from the corpse of his memories. Sure, he had lived in student housing, but he couldn't remember what it had been *like*, not really. He had studied a lot, made coffee in the mornings. He and Bill Conifer had driven to a topless bar in Richmond once. "I imagine I must've thought it was okay. But I'd rather have had a real house or an apartment like we'll be able to afford. You can still make connections."

Things seemed normal again. They walked back to the apartment holding hands. The sex was as good as ever. She gave him a long, slow, expert blow job. For a moment he thought of his heels and how they weren't hurting anymore, and then his mind was blank as if from the effect of a powerful narcotic.

When he came to, he found that they had moved to the bedroom. She lay beside him in post-orgasm alertness. He was still catching his breath. His appetite had returned. He was so damn hungry he could have eaten two or three steaks. His limp had disappeared in favor of his old swaggering gracefulness, and he danced toward the kitchen to make a sandwich.

CHAPTER 16

HEADS TURNED WHEN Andy Ashe walked into Proof Required. He waved and smiled at a few cronies across the room and then headed toward the girl he had come here to meet. "It's been months, hasn't it?" When he gave her a brief hug he felt, through her thin blouse, the backs of her ribs and the muscles of her lower back. "And you've been working out."

"Check this out." She raised an arm, flexed it.

He pinched it between his fingers and thumb. "Feel da burn."

"So congratulations on your shift in fortunes at MTV."

"Yeah, well, when I heard it was going to be called the *Andy Ashe Show*, I figured I had a lock on the hosting job."

"Oh?"

"There's only one other guy there named Andy Ashe, and he's a retard. Excuse me, mentally challenged. He cleans the bathrooms."

They squeezed up to the bar and ordered a couple of beers. "So I guess we're cousins now," Andy said. "Or half siblings or something."

"Does that mean we committed incest?"

"Didn't feel like incest to me."

Kristen was good-looking in a preppie sort of way, which was to say that there was in her sturdy, sensible face a comforting social competence and, he thought wryly, the suggestion of a trust fund. There was almost something narcissistic or incestuous about loving her—she *was* the streets of Groveton and the nice houses and the proper order of things in Andy's childhood. At kindergarten recess he had once chased her from the sandbox

216

brandishing an earthworm. Within a year he was playing doctor with her, and then Anne Newton had caught them and called his mother to come retrieve him from the Newtons' grand Victorian house—seemed particularly funny now in light of recent developments. With Kristen Newton, Andy didn't feel out of his league, as he did with a true beauty such as Elena, or on another level, as he did with some of the urchin-waifs, the music tramps who had recently begun pursuing him. Getting laid wasn't a challenge anymore. He could have it anytime simply by swapping out his true personality for his new celebrity status. Already he had been treated once for chlamydia.

Well, no thanks. If he was going to go through the stress of having his own show, he at least wanted a normal, trustworthy girlfriend. Like Kristen. He even thought he might like to go home with her tonight. She would insist on the missionary position, fill herself full of spermicide, and would of course make him wear a condom. It was a routine he had gone through with her several times during their brief relationship last year, and once when they were both eighteen, and if there was nothing particularly spontaneous or novel about it, at least he wouldn't spend the next three weeks checking himself for signs of disease. "I mean, I'm excited about the show," he was saying, "but I ask myself, am I really contributing to, you know, society by working at MTV? Or am I part of the problem? Should I sell all my possessions and move to lower Moldovia and teach them to cook their pork all the way through? Or should I stay in my own culture and try to make a connection with the kids in America today?"

"God, cousin, does that kind of talk get you laid?"

"Actually, yes."

"Don't forget who you're talking to, I know you too well."

After a moment he said, "Want to see if we can go catch our mothers playing doctor?"

Kristen pinched her temples, shook her head. "Say no more. I wouldn't mind if they were living together, even if they slept together sometimes, but do they have to get the haircut and everything? Why don't they just put signs on their backs?"

"Actually, last time I was back home your mom was wearing a 'Yes I Am' hat."

"No."

"Yes."

Some of Andy's new sycophants came over to pry him away from this rather plain-looking lady. He introduced her as his cousin, which she thought was so funny that she buried her face in his shoulder in a decidedly uncousinly manner. Then Andy announced that he and his cousin were going to hit a few more bars "without all you guys."

The hangers-on were disappointed, but it wouldn't do to run after him. Sure, early ratings for his new show had been promising, sure, he was in a position to help some of his former fellow cue-card holders, but there was still the possibility that his might turn out to be the wrong ass to kiss.

It seemed his incipient fame had already given him a new posture of confidence. Walking down the street, holding hands with his "cuz," as he was now calling her, or half sister or whatever she was, he felt as though everything in life was going to work out—movie career, the house in Malibu, it was all coming.

"Have you seen much of your father and Elena the blond goddess?"

"He was sort of embarrassing last time I went out with him. He got hammered and kept talking to the waitress. He was wearing his Bolt! T-shirt, too, and she kept calling him Boltman."

"And to think you asked Elena out."

"Well, I didn't have my own show then."

THAT SAME NIGHT John and Elena were out for a walk after dinner, holding hands for the first time in weeks. He felt the jealous eye of nearly every man who glanced his way. Him with her? Why, he must be thirty-five! And yet they couldn't have been surprised, not really, as good as he looked and as rich as he probably was. "I still can't get over Andy getting that show. It's great. I'd say he's got a lot of me in him, the way he rebelled against us by not going to law school and then showed us up anyway. I remember I told him not to take that cue-card job. I think I even yelled at him. But now I'm glad he didn't listen to me. I think he'd be a terrible lawyer. But a talk-show host? Talking's what he's good at."

"Look." Elena stopped at the window to a travel agency. Displayed there was a poster of Santa Monica beach. "Sure you couldn't live in L.A.?"

He shuddered. "No way."

"We could travel around a lot. You could run in the north."

"Maybe. If you get into Stanford."

"When are you going to tell me what law school's *like*, John, and not just when you went and what you did there? What was it *like*?"

"That was a lifetime ago, Elena."

He kept thinking about how quickly he had recovered from his recent swollen Achilles' tendons; it boded well for the New York Marathon. Yesterday in the park he had gone fifteen hard miles with Rey. The Bolt! rep, who had heard about John dropping out of the recent ten-K, had decided not to invoke the "continued excellent performance" clause of the contract. Still too early for that. What he was more concerned about was the wife/mistress problem. A role model had to keep his image up. Which was yet another reason John had let the thought of marriage cross his mind recently. Make an honest woman out of Elena? After these occasional considerations he would always decide against asking her. She was great, but was she the only one for him? It was not beauty that he craved. There Elena had no peer. It was variety. In a perfect world he would never get completely tied down and women would always want him, so there would be no need to engage in that mutual entrapment known as marriage.

"Look," Elena said.

Andy and Kristen were walking toward them.

"Well, well!" said John. "I was just talking about you, son."

Kristen said, "We were just talking about *you* two."

"Should we all go get a drink or something?" Elena suggested. The ensuing silence answered her question. There was no animosity among them, but it was still too early to go on a double date.

Finally Andy said, "Not right now, but we'll take a rain check."

"Okay, son. You let me know when."

Sure, Dad, just don't lose any sleep waiting for the word.

C H A P T E R   1 7

BOLTMAN LANDED IN Pittsburgh October 16 wearing full Bolt! attire. Surrounded by autograph seekers in the airport, high school runners mostly, he told them all that he was treating this fifteen-miler as a training run for the upcoming New York Marathon. "You'll have to watch that one on television if you really want to see what I can do. Look for me out front." He felt good. Cocky. He was conscious that his penis was flaked with Elena's now dried secretions.

Now he was jittery at the starting line. He had learned to say, "Hello, I hope you have a good run" in Swahili, and the three guys he now referred to collectively as "the Black Wind" were impressed. They grinned and patted his back. The fastest one, Henry, said, "You too, old man," running the last two words together so that it sounded like a surname: "Oldman." Rey was there, too, explaining the intricacies of his slight injury to anyone who would listen. Covering his ass for what would be a poor performance. John filtered out that whining attitude, which lately had led poor Rey to believe the predictions of his own professional demise. What, in fact, was Reynaldo Miller qualified to do? Lately John and Elena had been double-dating regularly with Rey and Carrington, and he had noticed that love seemed to dull rather than sharpen Rey's competitive edge.

Rey approached him at the starting line with an exaggerated limp. "You think I could hang out with you the first few miles? I don't want to go out too fast and blow the knee."

"Sure." John only slightly resented the reminder that Rey, for all his injuries, was still faster. Hell, he was also twenty years younger. And he wasn't that much faster anyway, not anymore. In the back of his mind John suspected he would beat the Marathon King at his own game in New York.

"On your mark! Get set . . ." Bang!

Three or four out-of-shape crazies sprinted out ahead of the field. Their wheezes were audible within a twenty-yard radius. Their feet slapped the pavement so hard they might have been running in scuba flippers. John and the Black Wind had to smile. At every race there were always a few runners who so badly misjudged their own capabilities that they fantasized about the impossible, winning. And they sprinted out ahead like this. Two hundred yards later the real runners glided by effortlessly. Rarely did you see the jackrabbits at the finish, because they never arrived.

John, Rey, and the Black Wind stuck together at a pace designed not to exacerbate injuries or even cause enough soreness and fatigue to put a crimp in anyone's training routine. John waved to people shouting "Boltman!" along the route. He and Rey dropped back a bit and ran along in the draft created by the Black Wind.

Rey said, "Everything's fine but the side of my knee. Unfortunately, a chain is only as strong as its weakest link."

"Why don't you drop out? Save yourself for New York?"

"I'm fine at this pace."

"You're not going any faster?"

"Nah."

"Then, buddy, this is the first time I'm going to beat you."

"Don't hurt yourself."

John pulled on ahead. He caught up to the third-place Kenyan and ran with him past the eight-mile marker. "Easy race," the Kenyan said. "Save for marathon." The slight fear in his voice spurred John's competitive spirit.

"Oh, but I feel so good, I don't think I can restrain myself."

At mile twelve his legs started turning over at a rate which amazed the spectators and surprised even him. It was almost as if his body outran, in those moments, his spirit, leaving it scrambling to catch up. He had never gone this fast, had never run with so little pain. He wasn't even in oxygen debt yet, could've probably even sung most of "Hey Jude." He had to shake his head at the thought. He wanted to turn his legs over even more quickly. And . . . whoosh! What was that? He just passed another Kenyan.

Now no one was saving himself for the New York Marathon. Everyone ran hard. The Kenyan that John had just passed tried to catch him but only managed to slow the rate at which he was losing ground. The only one left out front was Henry, the one who called him "Oldman," and the one who had the reputation for the strongest half-mile kick.

But since his most recent trip to Boulder, every week John had been putting himself through a speed workout—and now his final kick was a secret, unexpected weapon. He ran along in Henry's draft, waiting for the right moment. The Kenyan was clearly not loafing this race. This had turned into a serious competition. Their speed now was such that it gave a noticeable Doppler effect to spectator cheers. The Kenyan checked over his shoulder to see who was pushing him. His eyes opened wide.

John ran parallel to him. "I thought we weren't going to race."
"Me too, Oldman."

John considered dropping back until the last half mile and then kicking, but despite his recent speed work he was not confident that he could take Henry in such a short distance. He needed to make his move now. While he was thinking about it, Henry pulled ahead with just under a mile to go. The Kenyan's kick was indeed ferocious. Before John realized what was happening he was ten yards back, floating along in the wind.

It took him a quarter mile to make up those ten yards, and then the two were sprinting side by side, both too winded to speak. The Kenyan tried another kick, but this one won him only a step or two. With great effort John made it up. The finish line was visible a quarter mile ahead, and John's knees rose high, his stride long and his elbows tight against his body. For a hundred yards the Kenyan was a lingering threat in the back of his peripheral vision, and then receded and was gone.

On the grandstand, Jeff Sutton. Mr. Sixth Place. His pen fell from his mouth. What had happened to all that talk about just loafing it through this one? The important contenders appeared to be trying to catch John, but they just couldn't.

Boltman's chest broke the tape in record time for the masters class. He had just come close to the open American record for fifteen miles. Now he was hugging his bombshell mistress, who did not seem to care how sweaty he was. She toweled his face dry, handed him a cup of water. Sutton couldn't believe it when she handed Boltman a cigar. Too much.

Later a race official at the awards podium introduced him as American's fastest fifty-year-old. When John got to the microphone, he removed the cigar from his mouth long enough to say, "Actually, today I'm fifty-one."

IT WASN'T UNTIL he got home that night that he realized he had missed a specially scheduled appointment with Fiske and Dr. Hurvitz. The answering machine memorialized the irritation in Fiske's voice. "As you recall, *Boltman*, Dr. Hurvitz was all the way out from California. His wife's not well and he goes home tomorrow. By the time you hear this message, I will have left for a previously scheduled research conference . . ."

John tracked down Hurvitz at the Sheraton and begged for a few moments of his time. "I just have some questions to ask you, okay?"

Hurvitz relented. An hour later, wearing his Bolt! T-shirt, John met him in the hotel lobby. The old man looked small, hunched, and pale as a mollusk in the open shell of his high-backed leather chair. John rushed forward to keep him from getting up to shake hands. "No, no, don't bother." He took the adjacent chair. Except for the elevator traffic behind them and the pedestrians passing out front, just beyond the glass, they might have been in Hurvitz's personal library or Nathan Barradale's office. "It's my memory that I want to talk to you about," John said. "It's like you told me, I can remember things, but I can't *feel* anything about them."

Hurvitz seemed not to have heard him. "I have an old friend who lives in Groveton. Kurt Vermiel."

"You know Vermiel? I used to see him all the time when I'd go out running. He played croquet in his yard, and he'd always wave." John shook his head, smiling. "Guy's a genius."

Hurvitz began to tell the mildly interesting story of how the two men had first met at a conference in Miami. Impatient, John interrupted. "Doc, why can't I remember what it *felt* like to hold my son for the first time? Why can't I *feel* that again?"

"But then you'd be . . . old, wouldn't you? And that's not what you want." Hurvitz smiled. "Ah, that was a moment, when I first held my son in my arms. I remember it well . . . but then, I am very old."

"That doesn't make sense."

"Doesn't it? The truth is, Mr. Ashe, you don't really want to remember everything, do you? You want the best parts of the life you left behind and the best parts of the one you've got, and it may turn out that you can only have one or the other, not some preferred combination."

"The problem is, I love Elena."

Hurvitz laughed. "I saw a photo of her the other day. I love her, too."

"So you're saying I can't expect to remember everything if I stay with Elena? Because I intend to do both."

"But you can't. It's not Elena's fault; it's a question of your attitude." Hurvitz tapped his temple. "In here you're suddenly very young. It seems impossible to you that nearly twenty-six years ago you first held your baby boy in your arms. It seems impossible that you were ever in love with a pretty young woman named Elizabeth who helped you through law school. That wasn't you, was it? All those years ago? How can that be?"

"No, it's my body that's gotten younger."

Hurvitz just shook his head. "No. What I'm telling you is, there's a connection between how you think of yourself and how old your body seems. And in your case there seems to be a connection between how you think of yourself and the woman you're seeing."

"Wait a minute, you said you saw a picture of Elena. Who showed it to you?"

"A young sportswriter named Jeff Sutton. He's very interested in my study."

"The media. What can a guy do to protect himself?"

"Stop wearing that Bolt! T-shirt, for one."

"But then no one would recognize me."

Hurvitz smiled. "The study that Sutton is interested in is not

just Fiske's study of you but my study years ago of Robert Timmerman."

"The surfer," John said. "His girlfriend made him younger—"

"That was my guess. Maybe I was wrong."

John leaned forward, elbows on his knees. "I gotta know for
sure, is it Elena that's doing this for me?"

Hurvitz shrugged. "That's not the kind of question I can answer with certainty."

"At least tell me how it ends. What happened to Timmerman?"

Hurvitz paused for a full minute, staring out through the glass.

"You all right, Doc?" John asked.

"Yes, thank you." Hurvitz looked John in the eye and said,
"Robert Timmerman moved to Australia with his girlfriend. I believe they are alive and well today with a big family. He seems to
be living happily ever after."

"That's good to hear."

So John resolved to quash even the desire to remember former
desires and feelings, the better to preserve his current youthfulness. Everything in life was a trade-off; this was just one more.
Yet he still doubted his decision some. He was surprised at how
painful it was to try to shake his *thought* that he and Elizabeth
had once shared wonderful moments which now might as well
never have existed. Would he someday feel the same way about
Elena? Would she grow too old for him, and would he shack up
with someone who was now thirteen or fourteen? He finally realized toward the end of the week why he could not completely
put Elizabeth out of his mind. It was because he was jealous of
her for being able to remember holding Andrew for the first time.
Jealous that she could remember what it was like to be twenty-
three for real. Perhaps she even remembered the excitement of
making love to him for the first time. On a golf course, actually.
She was a bridesmaid and he a groomsman for the wedding that
had taken place just a couple of hours before. Everyone else was
partying in the clubhouse. Must have been something, though no
telling now.

In fact, the only spot of color he remembered from his now
black-and-white twenties was that moment when he had held
baby *Elena* to his chest. He remembered how precious she was,
how purposefully she had gripped his shirt in her tiny fist, and

how when he kissed her forehead she smiled and cooed . . .
sadly . . . as if at the inconvenience of having been born twenty-
eight years too late.

THE LAW SCHOOL essays were not easy, but Elena found it easy to
make herself work on them. For her twenty-third birthday John
had given her a new Toshiba notebook computer and a Hewlett-
Packard laser printer, the equipment adding to her enthusiasm
for the project at hand. She was so grateful for the computer that
she all but convinced herself to rule out UCLA. While John and
Rey drove away from the city in the Porsche, looking for more
interesting places than Central Park in which to run, she would
sit at her new toy and dream about life in law school and beyond.
The intensity of it, the acid dialogue in class, the friendships, the
betrayals, the Paper Chase. The romances, too. Well, not the romances. John, of course, would be with her. He loved her, she
loved him. Of course.

Her mornings would begin when John and Rey headed out.
She would rise, make a pot of coffee, and look over what she had
written the day before. Often there would be some glaring error
in a section that she had already dismissed as brilliant and finished, or she might suddenly realize that an essay needed a paragraph or two on this or that. Dressed in a pair of shorts and a
wrinkled T-shirt, she would wash her face and get back to work.
Sometimes it would be noon or later when she first looked at the
clock and realized that she ought to eat something and maybe go
to the bathroom. Sometimes Rey and John would blunder into
the love nest and break her concentration at the end of a four-
hour stretch. Hunched over the keyboard, she would mutter,
"Goddammit, you guys." Oblivious to the distraction they were
causing, they fumbled around in the kitchen for glasses and water or orange juice, talking about some scenic feature of their
training run.

"That third hill, remember that one?"
"Was that the one with the UPS truck on the left?"
"No, man, I mean the row of trees, the dogwoods."
"Oh, yeah! That was a hill, all right."
Such intellectuals. Both were in peak marathoning condition.

John had never been so thin and muscular, and Rey's cheekbones were so sharp as to have gone beyond looking tough to looking fragile, a match for his weak chin.

Her excitement at having the new computer and printer notwithstanding, turning twenty-three had forced Elena to think harder about her future. By the time she got out of law school, she would be twenty-seven. Thirty-four when she finally made partner—Kelly Epstein's age! She could finally have children without risk to her career, and John would be . . . in his sixties. But he loved her, she reminded herself. That counted for a lot. And the love nest was nice and this lifestyle they were leading was like an endless summer vacation during which the most important decisions were all about where to eat.

Then why did she feel so . . . uneasy? Trapped? She sensed the dangerous possibility that the ease of it all would diminish the force, the drive, the *hunger*, which had forced her to write a three-hundred-page A-plus senior thesis at Magnate; to go after the job with John as she had . . . What was happening to the Elena that had achieved things for herself? She was going to go to law school and get into the world. Let it try to wear her down, let her look a little older in a few years, but be more accomplished, more mature, more in control of her own life and, if she dare think it, less dependent on John.

John. He had grown almost superstitious about her curative powers, insisting on having sex before any race and any hard training runs. So the act itself had taken on a sort of sterile, medicinal quality that didn't seem to lessen his enjoyment, but did hers. Well, she was content to continue administering her special medicine at least until the New York Marathon; he had worked so hard for that race, and she would not have it that he fail because of some psychological trick he might play on himself if she were to tell him her concerns beforehand. If he failed, she wanted no part of the blame. If he succeeded, she would take a little bit of the credit. Either way, when it was all over they were going to have a serious talk about her role in his training routine; more, in their entire relationship.

As she labored over one phrase in the final paragraph of the Harvard essay, the front door opened and she could hear John and Rey in the foyer talking about the route they had just run.

For them, the past stretched back just two or three hours, and the future was a marathon just days away.

That night she was surfing the television channels and saw Jake Coates on *Entertainment Tonight*. There he was, Mr. Permanent Hard-on, talking about his "next project" and how he had always wanted to work with this particular director. She called him in Los Angeles and left a message on his machine.

"I AM SITTING on the steps of the Met," Jeff Sutton said into his microcassette recorder. "This is where John Ashe, a.k.a. Boltman, insisted that we meet for this, my final interview with him before he runs the New York Marathon. Apparently the steps of the Met hold some sort of sentimental significance for him, though he won't say what, and though I know from talking to the scientists who have studied him that any emotion he remembers feeling must have occurred after meeting his current girlfriend." Sutton put down his recorder and took another bite of a corned beef sandwich. He picked up the recorder and began again. "I have seen pictures of Ashe as a much older man than he is now. You will find that hard to believe, but it is true. But I have also noticed—and I'm not making this up—a corresponding regression in his maturity level. The surfer Hurvitz studied was arrested at the age of fifty for mooning people out the window of his Dodge. The question about Mr. Ashe is, through what great sex-related adjustment of attitude can he perform these feats? I doubt that he is sure of the answer himself." He put the recorder down and was still chewing his next bite of corned beef when John appeared in the distance, looking suave and young and wearing a cotton sports jacket over his Bolt! T-shirt. His hair was swept back, and his confidently tilted head was suddenly enshrouded in cigar smoke. The vision was marred only by the sudden jamming of a finger into his ear, but then again, the gesture only served to remind people of the Boltman incident that had made him a hero.

"How's it going, Jeff?" The two men shook hands. "Jeff, what do you say we bag this whole interview and go knock back a few?"

"But the race is coming up."

"No problem," John said.

"It's not so easy for me to recover from booze. I'm thirty-nine, John. What are you, thirty-two now?"

"Probably. Come on, Jeff, it won't kill you."

"Can we stay here for the interview at least? I don't think I can record you in some noisy bar, everyone recognizing you." He sensed that this appeal to the runner's ego was his best chance of preserving the original purpose of the meeting. "And I really need to get this on tape. People want to hear it."

"Well, okay." John leaned back on his elbows and crossed his feet at the ankles. Blew a series of smoke rings. "I hear you've been talking to Hurvitz."

"He has interesting theories."

"But they're just theories, you know."

"So tell me what your training schedule's like so close to the big race."

For a moment it looked as though Boltman might give a serious answer. Then he said, "Sex. Running and lots of sex and beer." Said with a straight face.

"So Hurvitz was right. You do need Elena."

"I didn't say that. It would just be unnatural not to have sex with her whenever possible, that's all I'm saying."

Still in denial, Sutton took a bite of his corned beef sandwich, chewed it very slowly. "Do you think there's any particular advantage to starting a running career so late in life?"

"Well . . ." Boltman blew a cloud of smoke toward the sky. He was a philosopher now. "People ask me that. I don't know. I guess if you start when you're older, then people make more of a big deal out of it when you do well. Plus, you get to be an inspiration." He looked at Sutton. "People seem to need me, Jeff. I guess I give them a sense of possibility. If you look out at this city, just think about how many quote middle-aged men end quote there are, and they're believing all the myths. And the myths are that the big annual event in your life from now on is when the doctor pulls his finger out of your ass and says your prostate is still okay. I represent possibility."

"But, John, a fluke isn't representative of anything. Although I guess you do realize you have a chance to break the masters record in this."

"Masters? I wouldn't be in this if I didn't think I could *win* it."

"Okay, you're crazy. I got sixth place in the Boston Marathon when I was in my peak condition, and I was young, and that's what it takes. That's who wins marathons, young men in peak condition." As he spoke he grew more exasperated, more emphatic, because his words seemed to have no effect. John seemed to be studying his cigar. His face was virtually lineless and the jaw was square, with a recently developed Cary Grant–like cleft. There was now a pink scar where he had been shot in the neck. And suddenly it did seem possible that this *young* man in peak condition might win the marathon. Still, Jeff resisted the notion. "You've got no idea the quality of runners they've got coming in from all over the world. It's not just the Kenyans. It's not just Rey Miller, it's everyone."

"And who are they all going to be talking about?" John asked. "Each other? No. They're all going to be talking about me, the quote old man end quote they're all afraid of. You can think whatever you want about who's going to win. You can be a doubter. I won't hold it against you when I break the tape. I'll just feel sorry for you because you've got a mental block or something that affects your health."

"It's just impossible," Sutton said. "You will not win the New York Marathon."

No response from Boltman. He had been distracted by the sight of three college girls walking along the base of the stairs.

Sutton tried to take control of the interview again. "One thing that would be very helpful to me and interesting to my readers would be for you to answer some questions about your past. When you were in your twenties, say, didn't you feel like running then?"

"I was on the train. My heels hurt whenever I ran, but since that wasn't very often it wasn't really a problem. My twenties. I don't really remember them very well. I suppose I was a loving father. I don't think I could handle the responsibility of fatherhood now. It almost feels like—and this is strange to say—I'm not *ready* for fatherhood. That's what it feels like. Fortunately, Elena doesn't want to start making babies yet anyway. She wants to go to law school. A mistake, I think. I've got enough money.

We could just live together and have a good time until the next truck bomb is a nuke."

Spoken like an adolescent, Sutton thought. "What's your biggest fear as far as running goes?"

"I'll tell you what it used to be. I used to fear that my Achilles would snap. But it wasn't just that. The pain I thought I could deal with. But I didn't want Elizabeth, my wife at the time, to find me crawling around so she could say I-told-you-so all the way to the hospital."

He laughed as if to show how far removed he was from that possibility now. "Enough talk about me. Let's go pound a few brews."

Pound a few brews! A young jock's jargon, and a fifty-year-old's, Sutton thought.

JAKE COATES RETURNED her call. They talked for forty-five minutes about what possible jobs he had coming up, and about her situation. "All I know for sure is I'm going to law school," she said. "I'm having big second thoughts about any kind of civil rights law."

"Ah, so there will be no groundbreaking work in reverse lookism?"

"Oh, Jake, it's embarrassing, I can't believe you remember that."

"Tell you what you do if you're worried about reverse lookism. You come out here, where it doesn't exist. It's just plain old lookism out here, and obviously you'd be on the right side of it. This town is full of well-paid lawyers, too. You should come out here. I mean, it's a risk—you've got a pretty good setup with Boltman, I guess. You call him Boltman at home?"

"Don't tease."

He suggested that wherever she went for law school, she consider coming to Los Angeles afterward. Not only would he love to have her nearby, he also thought she would do very well indeed for herself in L.A. "It's so much more a democratic town. You'd be leaving your father's Manhattan connections, but you'd be coming to a place where if you work hard and work smart, you're going to advance no matter *who* you are. Look, half the producers and studio execs, probably more than half, they're all lawyers. It's like the president's cabinet, or Congress, for that matter."

"I'd probably do well to go to UCLA, wouldn't I?"

"Sure, it's a good law school. And I just bet, and this is just a hunch," said Jake Coates, "that you could hook up with a rising star, sort of a boyfriend-girlfriend thing, be seen about town . . ." Of course, they both knew who he meant by a "rising star."

"I promised John I wouldn't go to UCLA," she said.

"Promises are a sometime thing, Elena. Look at him. Wasn't he married? Didn't he promise to love, cherish unto death do you part?"

She decided to visit L.A. but not until after John ran his all-important marathon. She would not take from their joint account a dime more than necessary to finance the virtually forbidden trip at its cheapest possible level, even if she had to economize by sleeping on Jake's couch. There wouldn't, she told herself, be anything sexual about the visit. They would be just two people early in their careers helping each other out.

Did she really believe that?

SUTTON FOUND BRENNA FRYERSON in Queens. The former paralegal was flattered to have a reporter recording her every word and was more than willing to ramble on about John Ashe as she had known him. "I feel sort of bad for Elizabeth. Some lawyers' wives are unreasonably suspicious of the secretary, but Elizabeth always trusted me implicitly. She knew I had no designs on her husband, and I didn't." Not, Sutton thought, that Brenna Fryerson was the kind of bombshell who was going to test a marriage. They sat together in her small living room. On the coffee table at their shins was a plate of store-bought cookies and two cups of black coffee. Occasionally grandchildren ran through holding toy trucks and action figures. "I quit to spend more time with them," she said. "Now they're driving me crazy."

She talked about John's obvious and instant infatuation with Elena Conifer. "When he saw her on paper, he wasn't even considering hiring her. The interview was just a courtesy to her father. When he saw her in *person,* I saw a man smitten, and I said to myself, poor Elizabeth. There's no way you can compete with this girl. But I'm a very discreet person, Mr. Sutton." With her thumb and forefinger she pretended to zip her lips. "So I just went on about my business, tried to make the new girl feel comfortable. I didn't warn Elizabeth or anything. Next thing I know after that is I'm getting subpoenaed for the age-discrimination trial, which I'm very glad they settled out of court."

"The firm lost a million dollars," Sutton said.

"Is that right? Well, I told him not to hire that Magnate girl."

It took three hours, and Sutton was glad he had brought extra microcassettes. This was all good background for the book he had decided to write. Maybe he could be the sixth-best sports biographer.

"YOU KNOW YOUR son turns twenty-six next week," Elena said to John one day in bed.

"I know. I should call him up."

"Maybe the four of us should go out somewhere?"

"Things would be tense, wouldn't they?"

"No doubt. Things were tense with Dad"—this is a reference to her recent visit to Bill Conifer on *his* fifty-fourth birthday. "But all in all I was glad I went. Besides, you've been getting along with Andy all right."

A few minutes later John called his son. "Sorry, Dad," Andy said, "the all-female branch of the family already has Kristen and me reserved for my actual birthday. How about the next night?"

"Fine. That's fine . . ." Said hurriedly.

ANDY LIVED IN the East Village in an apartment the lease for which bore the names of four people, all of whom had moved out since signing. Now they were represented by the junk they had left behind and the indeterminate number of others they had convinced to assume their rental burden. A place of pizza boxes and half-crushed beer cans. The tar-stained bong in the center of the coffee table was cleaner than any of the mismatched dishes stacked about the kitchen. And from the walls came the smell of marijuana smoke which had clouded the place daily.

As John and Elena stepped across the living room floor, she said, "Nice place. I mean, for a bunch of guys."

Boltman said, "Yeah, I could see myself in digs like this if Elena didn't keep me penned up." He winked at her, and instantly knew he was not being wonderful or winning. Why did he say such dumb things . . . ?

"You could just move in here, Dad. Nobody checks."

As if in illustration of this fact a pile of rags on the couch suddenly coughed and sat up. Andy asked it who it was.

"Zack. I'm a friend of Tom's."

"Who's Tom? Well, never mind. Just don't take anything."

Zack lay back down, a pile of rags once more.

"Kristen won't even come up here," Andy said. "We're sort of looking for our own place."

"That's great!" Elena put in.

"Yeah, son, she's a good solid girl."

THE GENERAL MOOD at dinner was mostly a matter of diplomatic moves. The conversation skimmed along just deeper than surface pleasantries until an unspoken assumption arose that it would be all right to discuss Elizabeth and Anne. "I still have a hard time dealing with it," Kristen said.

"Don't you think women are more comfortable showing each other affection?" Elena asked.

"Well, there's affection and then there's affection," John said.

"Dad—"

Kristen said, "I guess if it had to happen, I'm glad it was Andy's mom and not some earth mother guru type. This makes it easier for us to visit our respective mothers, for one thing."

"I've been talking to some of my lesbian friends about Mom and Anne. It apparently is a fairly typical scenario, I didn't realize. The husband, who the wife thinks is the best man she could find, which is why she married him in the first place, turns out to be sort of, excuse me for saying so, Dad, turns out to be sort of . . ."

"Unsettled?" Kristen suggested.

"Yes, that's good. Since he's the best representative of the male sex, and he's 'unsettled,' she sort of writes off all men and naturally falls in with similarly disillusioned women."

John said, "Maybe your mom drove me away because she was a lesbian all along. Ever consider that? Lord knows, she didn't want to have sex much, not for like the last ten years. That's why I don't think she should've gotten so mad at me for sleeping with someone else." He glanced at Elena. "Your mother was always into safety, protection. If she were here with us right now, she would've already checked for the fire exits. A person like that gets *more* like that with time." Looking at Kristen, he said, "I just hope your mom knows what she's getting into."

Andy stared at his father for a few seconds. "Was any of that really necessary?"

"She wouldn't undress in front of me, son. Not ever."

Elena said, "John, cool it. Please."

The other three worked to change the subject, but it was like doing a one-hundred-and-eighty in an ocean liner. Finally the discussion moved on to MTV, politics, and things unrelated and insubstantial. Andy was stunned at how his father seemed, well, superficial, in a way immature, in comparison to his mother, who had grown wiser and seemed really to be at peace with herself and her life. He couldn't imagine them together again in their current incarnations, and, conceding his father's point, it seemed unlikely that they had ever really been compatible.

CHAPTER 18

IN THE HEADY few days before the marathon John was forever Boltman. At Gil Stevenson's special request he and Rey stopped in at the flagship Hot Foot—John to sign a special Boltman poster in which he wore goggles and a cape, Rey to give free training advice to anyone who asked. Not many did.

Rey stood beneath a poster of himself running down a long, empty, wet highway toward a sunrise. The caption: YOU DON'T GET TO BE MARATHON KING BY DIVINE RIGHT. True running aficionados, the purists, gathered around Rey to speak to him, to perhaps collect tidbits of wisdom he might throw out like bread crumbs to a cluster of pigeons. But all the action, the celebrity seekers, the young girls popping bubble gum and those whose physical ordinariness gave them away as poseurs in running shorts—they all gathered around Boltman as if around a rock star. He signed himself over to them "forever with love," and the Boltman posters, he knew, were going up in high school lockers and the pinkish bedrooms of teenage girls, *To Tina, forever with love.*

Reynaldo—who was not all the time the Marathon King; there were still moments when he was himself—was frustrated by the lack of appreciation these people seemed to have for his sustained contribution to the sport. Oh, he could tell them stories dating back to when he was twenty-four and was just beginning to distinguish himself from all the other former collegiate runners. Most of his old teammates from high school and college had gotten jobs and had cut back on their running in order to become pudgy, successful family men. Maybe they'd done the right thing. Maybe he, the Marathon King, had missed the appropriate turnoff and now still sped down the same path that had first appealed to a teenage Reynaldo Miller from the projects.

His injured knee had gotten worse. Worried about the possibility of losing to the old man, he had pulled on himself a common trick of the mind. If I run faster, train harder, if I just ignore the pain, then I can work through this injury. Well, apparently not. And even as he smiled today he was bitter at the waning promise of his career.

In high school he had been the state champ in cross-country, good enough for a decent scholarship at a state U with a great cross-country team. A year or two out of college he discovered that he could run fifteen or even twenty miles at about the same pace he could run five. So there had been marathon victories over the years—but he had always had a block about running New York or Boston. They seemed so *final*. If you won them, then what? The Hot Foot? This year, though, he would force himself to run the New York Marathon and do his best to win it. Soon he would be pushing forty, living with Carrington somewhere if she would have him, the trophies on the fireplace mantel but the scrapbooks entombed in a dusty trunk under the stairs.

After the store appearance, Boltman suggested that they walk back uptown, which suited Rey just fine. He wanted to ask some questions of his young older friend. He heard himself rambling on, getting around to a question, but John wasn't looking at him, was barely listening. Instead Boltman was watching passing faces for any sign of recognition, nearly strutting down the sidewalk, as though to display himself to all who would behold his nature-defying condition.

ELIZABETH AND ANNE turned on a talk show and saw none other than young John Ashe, in his Bolt! T-shirt, sitting on a panel otherwise composed of middle-agers. The theme of the show was: "They said it was too late." The woman to John's left had started a drug-rehabilitation program which had reduced the heroin addiction rate in St. Louis by thirty percent. The man to his right had set up a foundation whose eventual goal was to feed every

needy child in Chicago. In fact, all six of John's co-panelists had
taken on some sort of social problem that was particularly acute
in their respective cities. These were big-hearted go-getters, gray-
haired do-gooders, the kind of folks who, the host of the show
said, "by their own actions bring out the best in others." And
then there was John "Boltman" Ashe, chewing on an unlit cigar.
"They made me put it out, there's no smoking in here," he explained to an audience member who asked.

The female panelist who had pushed through a smoking ban in
a northeastern beach town said, "I really have to take issue with
you for smoking cigars in the first place. I think all athletes have
responsibilities as role models to our children."

"How do you respond to that, Boltman?" asked the host.

John shrugged. "I say beware of anyone who wants to ban
something, generally speaking." Turning to the anti-smoker, he
said, "Isn't that what our generation was all about? Did you ever
do drugs? I bet you did in the sixties. Well, I was in law school, I
didn't. This cigar is a lot less harmful than that acid you were
probably dropping, right?"

The audience hooted and clapped.

Watching from Groveton, Elizabeth said, "I can't believe I was
ever married to that man."

Anne said, "He must've had plastic surgery, don't you think?
Look at his face."

One of the other studio guests, a corpulent woman in a big,
loose flower-print dress, had just finished explaining the condom-
distribution program she had founded in Seattle.

"Condoms!" John put in from the other end of the table. "They
make a man feel half alive."

The woman replied, "Half alive is more alive than you'll feel
after you die of AIDS."

"Or lung cancer!" said the anti-smoker.

A few minutes later, when asked about his typical training
schedule, Boltman was something less than a role model. "I usually start with a few beers the night before. When I wake up, I
feel guilty and have to go running, and that not only soothes my
conscience, it also gets rid of the hangover. By afternoon I'm recovered, and I get in a long run at a nice pace and it makes me

thirsty, and I feel like going out and having a few beers." He stuck a finger into his ear and wiggled it around, wincing.

Elizabeth said, "Not only can I not believe I was ever married to that man, I also cannot believe he was ever responsible enough to earn all the money I just took from him."

"Thank God he was," said Anne. Her own William had made bad investments in recent years, or had spent all the money on whores. Who knew? She got half, but half of not much left. Of course, they still both had jobs. Financially the couple felt stable, prosperous, even, so that money worries never impeded the development of their growing mutual affection.

"Oh, God." Elizabeth rolled her eyes at the spectacle being staged on television. In the talk show audience was the woman John had saved from the purse snatchers in Atlanta. She stood, cradling her baby, and told the story while John blushed and lowered his head. At the end of her story she said, "So I don't care how many cigars he smokes, I say he's a *real* role model."

The host asked Boltman how he had felt about killing the muggers.

Boltman said, "It was a them-or-me situation, and I was the only one standing between them and the lady with the baby. What was I supposed to do? Organize a safety patrol? Pass out condoms? Tell them not to *smoke*?"

In Groveton, Anne presented Elizabeth with a mailing tube encircled several times with purple ribbon. "I was saving this for our anniversary, but I can't resist." As Elizabeth opened the tube, Anne explained, "I had one of my students go up to him in the Hot Foot and tell him her name was Elizabeth."

It was a Boltman poster—John in his Bolt! T-shirt and a cape and goggles.

> *To Elizabeth forever with love,*
> *Boltman*

Great heaves of laughter sent Elizabeth to the carpet.

"HAVE YOU SEEN the credit card bill?"

"No, why?" Elena asked. "Is it late?"

"Yeah. I think next time I'll just send my payment in late and we'll see how they like it."

He was lifting sofa cushions and looking under magazines. He stared at the pile of law school applications on the kitchen table.

"The bill is not in there," Elena said, leaning against the stove. "So please don't go rummaging through my applications. I'll check around for it, maybe I put it somewhere. You've got to just concentrate on your training."

Later—he was finally out of the apartment—she removed the credit card bill from its hiding place beneath the UCLA application. It showed her purchase of a plane ticket she didn't want him asking about—especially where she was going. Having already sworn that he would never live in L.A., he would find very irritating her planned exploratory visit. Perhaps he would begin to doubt their relationship, which in turn would harm his performance in the marathon. So she was going to hide the bill and send in the check herself. It was best for all concerned.

But that wasn't all she was going to do to help boost John's marathon speed. She hoped to arrange a little surprise for him the night before, if Sophie Peters would help her out.

She couldn't deny it any longer—chronologically John was way too old for her. Before, it hadn't mattered. Now, he had regressed to a kind of jejune youthful behavior, even speech, that went with his body. Her initial attraction to him had been in part due to the distinguished way his dark hair was salted with gray, his winning sobriety of demeanor, his nearly paternal attitude toward her. Now that he was a dark-haired, youthful beer drinker, no longer paternal but possessive—well, staying in love with him was beginning to be a chore, an obligation not especially wanted.

Sophie Peters was the Magnate classmate with whom Elena had had her one lesbian experiment. Although okay at the time, no sooner was it over than she and Sophie felt the burden of complication that it added to their already stressful lives, full of papers and assignments and boys. By mutual agreement the incident was never repeated, though the two remained mutual confidantes for the rest of their Magnate years, meeting every few days in an off-campus coffee shop to gossip.

Sophie, in fact, lived in Manhattan. She was pleased to hear from Elena. "Through Magnate gossip I've been following your adventures. What can I do for you?"

"Let's meet for drinks and I'll tell you."

JOHN THOUGHT HE would take Elena out for dinner early the night before the race. He needed a couple of beers, a good steak, and a good session of lovemaking to be at his best at the starting line.

"Why don't we try Meme's?" Elena said.

"It's Italian. I'd rather have steak."

"I've really had my heart set on it."

"It's the night before the race, Elena. I ought to have what I need . . ."

"I'm sure Meme's has steak, let's go there."

John's filet mignon was excellent, and halfway through it he was thanking Elena for suggesting the place. Toward the end of the meal a young blond woman passing by looked over, and her face seemed to brighten. "Elena! How are you?"

"Sophie!" Elena hugged her tightly, and they cheek-kissed each other.

"I'm looking around for my date," Sophie explained. "He's an hour late. I'm just taking a swing through the dining room in case he's been in here all this time while I've been at the bar fending off weirdos."

"That's one stupid guy, your date," Boltman said, taking a chair from the next table without asking. "Join us for a drink."

"A Bombay martini," she said to the waiter. "Up, extra dry, two olives."

"One for me, too," John said. "Lubrication for tomorrow."

"And mine makes three," said Elena.

Sophie was a petite blonde, slightly smaller than Elena, her body hardened by aerobics. She was pleasantly flirtatious, but with whom was she flirting? Twice her knee brushed his under the table. But on top of the table Elena seemed to be her choice. The two kept letting their hands and fingers touch, kept gripping each other's forearms in the excitement of some new gossip.

"I'd love to see your apartment," Sophie said. "I know that building, and I hear it's just lovely inside."

"I'd invite you over tonight, but John has to run tomorrow. He needs to get to bed."

"Don't worry about me," he said. "If she wants to see the place, let's go."

WALKING WITH THEM he noticed once again not just the obvious friendship between the two women but its physical nature. Apparently they had not seen each other in quite some time. In the cab he sat against the door while they drew their legs up, facing each other, and squeezed each other's hands to emphasize the exciting points of their continuing gossip.

Back in the apartment, he stood at the kitchen sink drinking a couple of glasses of water. Could he suggest that Sophie spend the night? It was getting late, after all. Ah, what the hell, he told himself to stop thinking about impossibilities. Told himself to concentrate on the race.

Suddenly Elena was in the kitchen, her arms encircling his waist.

"What does your friend think of our apartment?" he asked.

"She likes it. Especially the bed. Especially you." With her hand on the small of his back she steered him from the kitchen sink.

Sophie was in bed covered to her smile by one white sheet through which he could see her dark nipples and the mound of pubic hair. Later he would realize that she was as aroused by his reaction to the vision as he was by the vision itself. His eyes were as wide as a schoolboy's at his first glimpse of a centerfold. Elena's arms were around his waist again, under his shirt, her fingers toying with the button of his jeans.

And the best part about this, he thought, was that it was unplanned! They had run into Sophie by accident in the restaurant and now, ninety minutes later, she was naked in his bed, pulling him toward her by his cock. Elena too seemed so overcome by his attractiveness that she wanted to watch him work his sexual ways on another woman. If only he could bottle whatever chemical he was emitting tonight . . .

Sophie was a good sport and relished every minute of the frolic whether as secondary or primary participant, or spectator. The only drawback was that she sometimes hogged Elena. She was impressed with John's flat, muscular belly and his twelve-noon hard-on, which barely deflated and soon recovered after each of his ejaculations. "You're like a nineteen-year-old," she said, fingering some cum off Elena's belly as if swiping frosting from a cake. "You produce so much of this stuff." He fought his exhaustion and screwed Sophie one last time while Elena rubbed his shoulders and flicked her tongue into his good ear.

By midnight they all sat with their backs against the headboard, eating Chinese food, watching Letterman, and drinking beer. "You think you'll be able to run well tomorrow?" Elena asked.

"I can't wait."

He woke at five, entangled with both young women and feeling as though God Himself had exempted him from all physical limitations, perhaps even from death.

It was Elena's gift, and the beginning of her move to separate herself.

In a cab on the way to the Verrazano-Narrows, the largest suspension bridge in the world and site of the marathon's starting line, Boltman read a front-page story about himself in the *New York Times,* and his "unlikely rocketing" to the top of the world of running. The article predicted a top fifty finish overall and a masters victory, no more. "These people have no faith," John said.

"Huh?" said the driver.

"I want you to remember my face. Remember this moment, okay? And then look in the paper tomorrow."

"Sure, okay."

Elena was not with him in the cab. She would meet him at the Central Park finish, or so she had told him.

THE GREAT RUNNERS were all kept together before the race so none would be lost in the confusion. So many were from remote areas of different countries that it was a wonder none had been mugged or beaten while exploring the city unsupervised in preceding days. As he mingled with them, trying his Swahili on anyone who looked vaguely African, Boltman felt like the only one really alive. The rest seemed props, witnesses to what he was about to achieve. He felt it, felt sure of it.

Reynaldo had finally gotten up the nerve to run the race. He hopped up and down on his toes. "I tried your advice, man. I had sex with Carrington last night, and I think my knee *does* feel a little better, even though she wasn't that into it because Cooper was in the next room watching TV."

Boltman wanted to relate the story of Elena and Sophie but decided to refrain. "So you're going to run on a sore knee?"

"I'm not getting any younger."

"Why the hell not? Maybe if you'd stop whining so much, you know?"

He wandered away through the crowd of elite runners. He recognized face after face from the pages of *Distance Running*. He spoke briefly to the famous Irish marathoner Ian Ghallagher, only twenty-seven years old. They shook hands and wished each other well, the moment recorded by several photographers almost as if the two men were heads of state. The three Kenyans were hard to find among the representatives of other African nations. There were also several famous runners from the mountains of Mexico. According to rumor, since childhood their ordinary method of travel had been running. "Run down to the store and get me some eggs" was a training command, and the store five hilly miles away. Their lungs were like scuba tanks, their hearts like water-treatment pumps.

But Boltman was not worried. His relaxed demeanor seemed to leave his competitors all the more agitated with pre-race excitement. Hell, he wasn't even bothering to stretch. He was just walking around introducing himself and suggesting places where people might go to celebrate after the race.

For the first time ever in his short racing career he did not feel like an old man who could run as fast as the young ones. He felt instead, if not younger than them, simply exempt from the question altogether. Ageless. He lined up in the second row behind the Black Wind, who for once looked as though they were taking a race seriously; there was no joking, no arguing. Behind Boltman were legions of inferior runners. Several yards to his left on the front row, Marathon King, Reynaldo Miller, was still fuming about the suggestion that he "stop whining so much." To Rey's right were a couple of those Mexicans with scuba tanks for lungs. There were Japanese, Chinese, Australian, and European marathoners on the front row. "Why is everyone so tense?" Boltman asked aloud to nobody. A few people behind him laughed, but no one fast enough to be on the starting line was so appreciative. They didn't even glance his way.

Bang! Caught slightly off guard by the starter's pistol, it took Boltman a few yards to elbow himself some running space. He had nearly been plowed and trampled, a thought which left him chuckling for the next few yards.

He was in no hurry at the moment. He waved to people lined up along the sidewalks, his grin and posture indicating that he could take the lead at any moment. He just didn't want to seem eager about it. He was running behind a couple of those Mexicans. They didn't look like they were really enjoying this, their postures were so serious. When one of them glanced back at him, Boltman winked. *"Hola, amigo,"* he said. *"Soy* Boltman."

UP IN GROVETON, Elizabeth and Anne were cheering for him despite themselves. The Boltman poster was up on the wall. For Elizabeth, who no longer believed she had ever really known John Ashe, cheering for him was almost like cheering for a total stranger or someone she had met maybe once or twice.

She once had seen the first husband of a famous movie actress interviewed on television. An insurance salesman, he told how he had met the young woman when she was only sixteen, and had married her against the advice of his cautious parents. The following year a Hollywood scout spotted her behind the J.C. Penney perfume counter in Boise and flew her out to L.A., where she did well both on the screen test and the casting couch. The woman changed her name and never went back to Boise. Later her first husband, on vacation in L.A. with his second wife, accidentally came across the ceremony honoring her with a star on Hollywood Boulevard. Pure coincidence. Watching her thank her fans, he had felt no more animosity toward her than he would have felt toward any stranger—which was none. Nor had he felt any love. Certainly he felt no desire to speak to this stranger that his first wife had become.

Until that moment when Elizabeth found herself cheering for John, she had not believed the man from Boise could have possibly been so detached. But now she understood.

At MTV, Andy was watching his father on a small monitor, amazed that the old man was in the lead. In the middle of a taping of his own show he said, "I just got to interrupt everyone right now. My father has the lead in the New York Marathon. He's fifty-one!"

In Atlanta, the fat man who had sat beside John on the flight down for the Peachtree Roadrace called his wife in from the next room. "There he is again, that's the guy! I sat by him on the plane."

The guy who had driven the magic carpet taxi in Atlanta, kids for whom John signed autographs, managers of shoe stores, the Bolt! rep and his family—all were watching and cheering.

Even Sophie Peters, still sore from the previous night, watched Boltman's progress on television in a bar, smiling in physical remembrance.

BY MILE FIFTEEN the pack had thinned. Remaining were two Kenyans, one Mexican, one Irishman, Rey, and John. Boltman was content to hang back in third place for a while, let someone else have a turn at the lead. He ran along just feet behind Henry the Kenyan, who for the first time since Boltman had known him was losing to a compatriot. Over his right shoulder he could hear Rey's footsteps and heavy breathing.

He still felt great. He felt as though the race had just begun and five minutes ago he had been lounging around the starting line, joking. Now he decided time to pick up the pace a bit. First he dropped back and said hi and good-bye to Rey. Then he was off.

Most did not even try to catch him. It was well known that the old man had never run a marathon before and could not possibly anticipate the afflictions that would befall him in the final miles. This ill-advised, premature burst of speed they considered akin to a lesser runner's decision to sprint from the starting line. Inevitably the unwise contestant would succumb to the realities of his physical condition or, in this case, his age. Only the two remaining Kenyans decided to stay with him, since they had learned not to doubt his capabilities, though in truth neither considered him a serious threat to win the race, even now, running strong past mile eighteen.

Because of the article in the *New York Times* that morning, many of the spectators recognized him. They knew how old he was, and that he was supposed to be satisfied with a top-fifty showing. When they saw him out front they went wild, and their yells carried him along like a favorable breeze at his back. The cheers seemed to work against the Kenyans, who glanced at one another, worried.

ON THE GRANDSTAND at the finish line in Central Park, Jeff Sutton had been watching the race on a miniature television. He knew John had been in the lead as late as mile twenty-three, and he knew what kind of pace the old man was running. It put a lump in his throat and water in his eyes, and Mr. Sixth Place could no longer look at the monitor. He walked away from the grandstand and into the pleasant anonymity of the ordinary spectators down at race level. There was no way any of this was happening. John's Achilles' tendons were going to pop, or his heart explode, or *something*, maybe a stroke.

When the first runner came into view, Sutton turned around and read the digital timer above the finish line. Where was the Marathon King, where were the Kenyans? John Ashe was alone, sprinting with both arms in the air. On both sides of the course the crowd shouted in gratitude—and Jeff Sutton, too, with tears in his eyes, cheered madly. When Boltman's chest broke the tape, Jeff looked up at the clock. No way. He walked toward it as if toward a shaft of light from heaven. No way.

Still in running mode, John nearly plowed over the various race officials who had converged to congratulate him. Someone was shouting something about a new world record.

"What?" John asked.

"How's it feel to be the fastest marathoner in history?"

AT MTV, ANDY interrupted his interview again. "I just want everyone to know that I am the actual son of the actual man who just made the New York Marathon the fastest in history." . . . In Groveton, Elizabeth and Anne opened a bottle of wine so they could toast the old bastard. . . . Back in Central Park, John was smoking a cigar someone had given him and peering over the shoulders of his congratulators even while signing autographs and giving answers to questions shouted by reporters.

He repeatedly shouted one question back: "Has anyone seen Elena?"

CHAPTER 19

THAT RACE CHANGED everything.

What had been a healthy, store-appearance type of celebrity, with a burst of minor news maker fame afforded by the Boltman incident in Atlanta, was now full-blown sports heroism. Mark Spitz. Bo Jackson. Michael Jordan. Mohammed Ali. John "Boltman" Ashe. Laughing and joking with David Letterman, having a little cigar talk, Boltman seemed altogether comfortable on television. Letterman kept referring to him as "the man who ages backward, ladies and gentlemen." He'd jab his elbow in Paul's direction and get a little drumroll. "So John, or Boltman if I may, why don't you tell us how you go about preparing for something like this? Did you do anything special the night before the race?"

"Just drank lots of milk and went to bed early."

"And tell us again, Boltman, how old are you?"

"I was born fifty-one years ago." John looked at the camera. "Elena, if you're watching this, I love you."

"Hey, no using my show to pick up chicks. And how fast did you run this thing again?"

At the answer, Dave shook his head slowly and tossed his number two pencil into the air. "You know, I too do a little jogging sometimes . . ."

Across the channel-surfing nation there were those who stopped on *Letterman* and exclaimed, "I know that guy!" Becca Johnson, née Pearson, now in Seattle, had heard the name of the new marathon champ on the car radio while her husband was driving her to yet another chemotherapy-treatment session, and it made her think of her John Ashe, her first all-the-way lover, her panties hanging from his stick shift thirty-four years ago. Not until she saw him on *Letterman* did she realize they were one and the same. Suddenly her nausea lifted like a fog, and for the first time since this ordeal began she began to think she could beat the cancer.

William T. Connoly, who had coached John's prep school track team, nearly fell out of his overstuffed recliner. Back when he was still working he would never have stayed up this late, but now that he was fat and retired there was as little reason to go to bed at night as to rise from it in the morning. He got up from his recliner at the sight of young Johnny boy, though. From the storage area beneath the stairs he pulled out an old, scuffed footlocker, blew some dust off the brass latches, and opened it. Sure enough, there among his coaching memorabilia he found a photo of John Ashe and his teammates, all of them with crew cuts as per the school dress code. Looking at the photograph, you would never know that all that hippie stuff, all that free love and pot-smoking stuff, had been starting up in the rest of the country. Little Johnny probably had the tight rules at Poindexter Prep to thank for his continued youthfulness! Wholesome living, that's what did it! Connoly was only twelve years older than Ashe, but since his retirement he had always guessed that the next time the local paper mentioned *his* name would be to announce his death in their potter's field of an obituary page. But after seeing young Johnny up there, he resolved to spend his time more wisely. He felt like volunteering for something, resuming his life. . . .

John's unlikely athletic achievement had the strongest impact on his old fraternity brothers, who mostly remembered him as a mediocre intramural athlete and champion drunk, the guy who used to wish you luck as you went off to class and then greet you on the stoop, beer in hand, when you returned around one or two. The old phone chain began to rattle, and for a little while these men forgot the problems of benign (so far) prostate enlargement, failing eyes, rebellious kids, doctors' orders, bran cereal, and the shrinking future in general. How did Time get its hand so far up my ass? When did I become its puppet? Of the nineteen men in his pledge class, spread across ten states, sixteen went jogging the next day, and one of these, Jim Jadwin, experienced the chest pains which would lead to a triple bypass, probably extending his life by decades. In their various places of employment (and Jim at the hospital) all nineteen told college anecdotes about the new marathon record holder. The time he did this, the time he did that.

Bill Walters, whose wife had left him recently after their son had died of complications from multiple sclerosis, was about to end it all when Letterman introduced "the man who ages backward." The gun was loaded, it was in his hand, and then John Ashe walked across the stage with the same easy gait that used to carry him across the fraternity lawn. Holy . . . they had shared a room in the house sophomore year! God, the guy looked great! When the segment was over, Bill stared at the gun and began the mental transformation that would someday lead him to wonder what the hell he had been thinking. His phone rang. He had to put down the gun to answer it. "Hey, snaky boy!" It was Ted Gramm, who had supported himself one summer selling leather crafts at Dead shows. Now he was a corporate lawyer in Boston. "You see *Letterman* tonight?" They were pretty sure John lived in Groveton. "You oughta just call information and get his number."

Not exactly an original idea. On Tuesday morning Elizabeth called the phone company to have her number changed; she was tired of explaining to all these people that she and John were no longer married and, oh no, don't be sorry for asking, it's fine . . .

In the love nest, John yanked his phone cord out of the wall. Didn't want to hear any more congratulations from friends he hadn't seen in years, didn't want to talk to any more reporters. Standing there with the limp phone cord in his hand, he felt as though he had taken his first positive action since coming home after the marathon and finding that Elena had replaced herself with a brief note to the effect that she was leaving for a few days and it was better that he not know her destination, which he therefore assumed to be L.A., home to a guy named Jake.

Walking out on him like that after all he'd done for her? Who needed her, anyway?

But what if she tried to call from wherever she was, wanting to apologize or needing help or something? Anything! He plugged the phone cord back in.

*   *   *

L.A. WAS GREAT. She didn't care what any of its detractors back home said—the weather, the sprawl, the rattish, even garish beauty, she loved it all. Here people surfed along above the muck. In New York people slogged through it. Seeing L.A. for the first time, and being so impressed by it, she was finally able to grasp how a small-town Midwesterner might feel at his first overwhelming glimpse of Manhattan.

Even though Jake Coates had already appeared in one released movie, filmed another, and would start filming yet another in a couple of weeks, he still lived in a tiny two-room apartment a block from the beach in Santa Monica, drove a Geo Metro, and seemed to have trouble coming up with his monthly gym fee. "I'm still working for union scale," he explained. "Things are expensive here." The unfinished pinewood futon on which she slept was clearly something he had bought for the occasion of her visit, to sort of say, I don't necessarily expect you to sleep with me, but which also said, What a sacrifice it was for me to buy a futon for you, what a trustworthy fellow I am, don't you want to sleep with me? The cheap sheets, pre-threadbare, were still creased in a checkerboard pattern from their factory packaging. Across the arms of Jake's only chair was a portable CD player beneath which were piled twenty or thirty discs, some of which she recognized from his room at Magnate. While he was out jogging, she walked into what for the duration of her visit would be "his" room, smaller than hers, and with an older but otherwise identical pinewood futon. Both rooms were essentially bare, and she took that as a metaphor for Jake's unwillingness to go quietly along the easy path laid out for him by his father, the St. Louis beer magnate. On the floor beside his bed she found a well-thumbed copy of Baltazar Brantley's *Unto the Seventh Generation*.

Jake came back from his run, shirt off, hairless chest tan and muscular. "They're shooting *Baywatch* out by the pier, if you want to go have a look." He winked at her. "They'll probably hire you."

She watched him do abdominals on the floor. He was so much more muscular than John, though the comparison really wasn't fair, she told herself. Not only was John fifty-one, his sport was not conducive to the development of upper-body strength. Jake was twenty-three, still on the upswing. She found herself wondering if he had improved as a lover as she had.

He took a shower, then walked back through to his bedroom with a small towel wrapped almost all the way around his waist. Amid all that muscular expanse of tight, tan flesh she saw a profile flash of his baby-white bottom.

"You're quite an exhibitionist," she said.

"Then I'm in the right business," he said, and smiled.

Together they walked out on the Santa Monica pier at sunset, Jake still trying to sell her the myth of Los Angeles. She felt no need to confess that she had already bought it. As the wind blew his hair back and rustled his baggy clothing, he compared L.A. to New York. "Don't get me wrong. I love Manhattan . . . but I can't do that life. Run around getting drunk every night, work your ass off, get fat, feel smug 'cause you're doing all this in New York, therefore you're real tough and with it. And then when you finally make it? I don't mean make it like moving to Fifth or Park. But say you just barely make it. You're a success. What does that mean? It means a house in Groveton and a train ride every morning and night." The photo-sensitive pier lights buzzed and crackled and began to brighten. The sun was bisected now by the orange horizon and the earth was flat, and Elena felt as though she stood on the very edge of the last piece of land, at the most advanced point in time.

"What you said about Groveton, did you know that's where John lived?"

"Oh, hey, no. Sorry. I wasn't making fun of the guy, and I sure as hell wasn't trying to remind you of him." Standing behind her, he put his hands on the pier railing and his square, cleft chin on the back of her head. She turned, pressed her forehead against the muscle of his chest. "We can't do this, Jake."

"Fine." He let go of the pier railing. "But you want to."

"I didn't say I didn't."

They walked farther out onto the pier, Jake continuing his pitch. "This town is so much more democratic than New York. It's not like connections don't matter, but on the other hand, if you're not born with them it's easier to make them. Your dad's last name goes further back East, see what I'm saying?"

"Fewer brand-name folks out here?"

"That's right. No Mabel Maytags."

On the way back down the pier, he said, "I'm surprised old Boltman let you come out here and stay with me. Even though we weren't doing anything."

"He doesn't know." But does he suspect?

"Ah." Jake tilted his head toward a bank of pay phones. "Well, you want to call him? If you're scared of losing him, maybe you could say you're staying with a girlfriend or something, you just needed to get away. You could concoct an emergency—"

She shook her head. "I'm not worried about losing him. Maybe . . . in a way I want to. Maybe I want my own life . . ."

"The old Elena Conifer resurfaces. I knew she would eventually."

Over espressos in a café they discussed Baltazar Brantley's work, particularly *Unto the Seventh Generation,* which both agreed was important for its treatment of generational issues and time. "I've always found Brantley to be especially adept at describing the *private* condition," she said.

"You're right, you're right." He shook his head, smiling. "I can't tell you what a pleasure it is to actually have a literary discussion. That's one thing I do miss about the East."

Before leaving New York she had withdrawn four hundred dollars from the checking account, and for the next three days she made sure Jake at least ate well. The food was so much better here and so much cheaper than any to be found in New York. One of her favorite culinary discoveries was a grilled chicken sandwich on focaccia bread with a big pile of fresh steamed vegetables on the side, all for about seven dollars. Jake took her everywhere she wanted to go and introduced her to three of his minor-celebrity friends, one of whom asked her out while Jake was in the bathroom. She and Jake sat on a bench at UCLA and watched harried law students rush to and from their classes. One woman descended the steps slowly, clutching a sheaf of papers. Suddenly she burst into tears.

"You really want to go to law school?" Jake asked.

"Desperately."

They drove up Sunset Boulevard in his Geo Metro. "I can tell you're hooked. Just think how it could turn out. You come out here, get a law degree. I become a successful actor and start my own production company, and I need a partner, someone with legal knowledge, someone I can trust, someone I know inside and out—"

"Shut up, Jake."

"Someone I know intimately."

Before leaving for the trip she had honestly wondered what the result would be. Would she realize that she still loved John and just had to work to maintain the relationship, even if it meant choosing a law school based on altitude and convenient access to running routes? Or would she realize that she had given him too much of her youth already? Having stayed with him until he won the marathon, having arranged that little treat with Sophie Peters to give him the extra speed he needed, and it had worked, her obligation was finished. And yes, it was going to hurt him, and yes, it would be unpleasant, but that was no reason to stay with him. She felt a little silly about the whole thing now, having escaped the wing of her father for the wing of one of his law school buddies. Now she was ready to leave them both *and* the whole East Coast. She wanted the sense of youth and promise of Los Angeles. She also wanted Jake.

But she did not sleep with him, would not this trip. The most she allowed was a kiss that took on a life of its own before she finally pulled away. "We can't."

"You want to."

"True."

"When you move out here," he said, "you can live with me until you find a place."

"I suspect I'll take you up on it." How pleased her father would be to hear that she was shacking up with someone her own age! Bill Conifer, perhaps foreseeing the end of her dalliance with John, had offered to support her for the summer before classes began just so she could familiarize herself with the town of her law school—Boston, he hoped. She knew his generosity was in part self-serving, to get her away from John, but to his credit the separation was not an overt condition of the offer, just its intended result.

Jake ran his thumb from the corner of her eye down the side of her cheek. She touched the cleft of his chin.

"You better get back," he said. "The old man must be getting real anxious." Jake could wait a while longer. He'd waited a long time, after all.

SHE LANDED IN La Guardia on Friday.

John had been frantic with worry and jealousy all week, even as endorsement-contract offers flowed in through his replugged phone line. To handle it all he had retained the famed sports agent Bud Framer. There were television appearances, dinner invitations from various prominent New Yorkers, and of course the matter of the Bolt! renewal. Bud kicked their big corporate ass for a one-year contract at one million dollars. Signing his name on the dotted line, all John could think about was the fact that he had no one with whom to celebrate. He declined all those dinner invitations. By Wednesday he had simply stopped acknowledging them at all. He searched out cheap bars on side streets that did no visible business yet somehow manage to stay open. Often he was the only patron. He'd find himself stumbling home at two a.m., thinking what a fool he had been to imagine that someone like Elena could still love him. Loved him at all. The age problem really was insurmountable, it seemed. At home he would find his answering-machine tape completely full. He would hit the playback button and fall asleep to Bud Framer's ingenious solicitations.

THURSDAY HE CAME home drunk at two a.m. and found Elena eating Chinese food at the kitchen table and working on one of her law school essays. She stood, moved toward him tentatively. "I've decided to go to UCLA, John . . ."

He hugged her in answer. "I missed you, I—"

"You're very drunk, John."

He held her by the shoulders at arm's length. In her narrowed eyes there was no evidence that she had missed him, but instead an alarming glint, as if she were calculating how old he would be at various important points in her own life. Suckle the baby, change the old man's diaper. He knew he was being compared to someone younger. When he had thought ahead to this moment of reunion, he had imagined the subtle manipulations he would employ to bring her into loving submission. Now that the scene was upon him, though, his subtleness, his wiles, failed him. He did have one thing over most other men—money. "I just got a million bucks from Bolt." An offering.

"That's great. I can feel less guilty about all the money we spent."

He plopped down on the couch. "What I *mean* is, there's really no reason for you to go to law school."

"Oh? John, are you going to buy me a career?"

"Careers are overrated, Elena. I had one, remember?" He patted the couch pillow next to him, but she remained standing with her arms folded "Well, at least you won't have to take out any loans," he said. "We can afford to pay cash. We'll find a great place to live. You'll be able to get a lot of work done if we stop going out so much at night. I could concentrate on my training—"

"I'm going to take out loans. I don't want you spending your money on me."

"Isn't it *our* money?"

"It's yours, from your accomplishments. I want to achieve things for myself, John, don't you *understand* that?"

"Dammit, Elena!" He swatted from the coffee table a vase of dead flowers. He longed to hear the shattering of porcelain, but the vase landed softly on the carpet without even spilling what small amount of pasty water remained at its base.

"I'm going to get you some water and aspirin," Elena said.

"Terrific."

While she was still in the kitchen, she heard him begin to snore, passed out on the couch. She left the aspirin and the water on the coffee table.

THE MARATHON, PARTICULARLY as fast as John had run it, was such a grueling race that most experts like Reynaldo Miller recommended a month of recovery time before resuming hard training. John and Rey would trot through the park together at what for them was a slow pace, John waving to strangers who recognized him. As the month progressed, he found that his training speed

wasn't improving as fast as he had hoped it would. In fact, it was
hard to keep up with Reynaldo, who had finished the New York
Marathon in sixth place.

"You loafing?" Rey would ask.

"No . . . I guess I'm thinking about Elena. She's dead set on
going to UCLA."

"Hey, I like her," Rey said, "but if she's screwing with your
head, then dump her." He had recently broken up with Carrington and considered it a smart move. He had no choice.

"It's not that simple."

IN THIS SLIGHTLY depressed training cycle he still ran well on days
after he and Elena had gone through the motions of intercourse.
On other mornings there was a slight pain in his Achilles' tendons. Fiske tried to tell him that maybe his age was just catching
up with him, finally.

John bounded off the table and grabbed the little bald guy by
his white lapels. "That sounds like the easy way out to me."

Hurvitz put his hands on the patient's shoulders and backed
him slowly against the wall. "Let me ask you, John, trouble at
home?" Fiske was coughing and rubbing his neck.

"Elena and I do argue more. We have sex less, and then she's
not all that into it. She's still living with me, and I want her to,
because I have no pride, because I *need* her. She's looking forward to moving out, though."

It wasn't just the Achilles' tendons that worried Fiske and
Hurvitz. The changes were so slight that someone not studying
John closely might have missed them. For one thing, the former
Boltman had gained two or three pounds across the middle, the
result apparently of accepting too many dinner invitations now
that Elena was back and could accompany him. His cholesterol
level, so recently unaffected by his poor diet, had begun to rise.
Lately he had been plucking gray hairs from his temples. His
lung capacity had decreased, commensurate with his maximum
pulse rate. When pressed on the subject, he admitted to irregular-
ity in his urine flow. "But there's no way you're sticking your
finger up my ass."

After he had left that afternoon, Fiske and Hurvitz sat down to a serious talk. "I've seen it before," Hurvitz said. "To have had one's youth for a second time and then to lose it is very hard to deal with. His arrogance will disappear, but probably not until after one last disastrous assertion of it. He will, I predict, be unpleasant for a while.

"But then he will perhaps be capable of nostalgia again. The facts that he remembers will fill out with their emotional meaning. He may grow more considerate, more mature. But less athletic. Remember, we are lucky if we can bring him back up to fifty-one without that surfboard hitting him and breaking his neck. Or a car hitting him, which would be an equivalent."

"You're saying he might die soon?"

"We all might die soon."

IN EARLY DECEMBER, Elena announced that she was going to spend Christmas with her parents in Connecticut. John was not invited. "I tried," she said. "But Dad wouldn't hear of it. You understand, don't you? But I do want to be with my family at Christmas."

During a training run later that week Rey invited John to spend the holiday with him and his extended family, many of whom, as luck would have it, were on parole that year. John begged off. "I really appreciate it, Rey. But Christmas is a family time. I wouldn't feel comfortable intruding."

A minute later he said, "I think I'm going to work something out, anyway. Bill Conifer couldn't turn down his daughter's fiancé, could he?"

"You gonna ask her?"

"I love her, Rey. I want to marry her."

"I didn't think things had been going that well lately."

"She's just nervous and upset about law school. It confuses her. She's young, you know? She needs some guidance . . ."

When he thought about it, he had to admit that the way he had treated Elena over the past few months was rather selfish. Sure, he *gave* her things. A place to live . . . a *great* place to live. Lots of dinners out with a minor celebrity, himself. But he hadn't given her anything he couldn't afford, and her L.A. trip notwithstanding, she had always been careful with—the family budget. But what had begun as an enormous, supervening lust, leading

to the worship of her youthful body, had degenerated into a simple medical procedure for which, though he once denied it, she
was the essential piece of equipment. He knew that he could
apologize for all that, and she would say that she forgave him,
but he feared that such a moment would also imply closure. She
would be able to go on about her plans, which, as much as he
tried to deny it, increasingly seemed to involve a separation from
him.

But a marriage proposal in this case was, he thought, the ultimate apology, and its acceptance would amount to a different
kind of forgiveness. It might even calm the swelling of his Achilles' tendons, help him get his speed back in time for the Boston
Marathon in April, though that was hardly the main reason for
asking.

Wearing a coat and tie, he picked out a ring at Tiffany's that set
him back twelve thousand dollars. It was so heavy, the diamond
so large, that John and the saleswoman had a serious discussion
about whether it would interfere with Elena's typing or using a
computer. *"Believe* me," said the saleswoman, "she'll get used to
it." He kept that velvet box in his sock drawer waiting for the
right moment.

ON THE MORNING of December 17 he made breakfast for Elena—
wanting to invoke the first morning they had awakened in the
same bed together. "Remember when I cooked breakfast for you
and Shannon and Kim?" He set a silver tray across her lap. Eggs
Benedict with a medley of fresh fruit around the plate. Fresh orange juice. Coffee, black.

"Oh, John, this looks wonderful. To what do I owe this?"

"To the fact that I love you."

"Well, it looks just great." She stuck her fork into one of the
poached eggs and let the yoke begin soaking into her English
muffin. "Mmm."

"I just . . . I realize I've been selfish lately, spending all these
days on myself. I got upset about that trip you took to L.A., but I
swear it wasn't jealousy, Elena. I just felt like setting the marathon record was a special moment in my life, and I wanted to
share it with you. I wish you'd been watching *Letterman.* You

would've seen me tell the whole world that I love you. I just got pissed off. I've been a jerk. Forgive me?"

Raising a bite of eggs Benedict, she said, "You're allowed to be a jerk if you wake me up like this every morning."

He tried to analyze that comment all day. Didn't it imply a certain permanence—*every morning*? Didn't it imply that she intended to wake up with him every morning so he could make breakfast for her every morning? Was it an invitation to follow her to law school? Wasn't she in effect saying she wanted to marry him? Her answer to tonight's question would be yes, he decided, which put him in a great mood for the rest of the day, even at noon when he had a tailor let a pair of pants out about two inches in the waist. No big deal. Once she agreed to marry him, he would be able to train well again and the fat would evaporate.

When he got home from the tailor's, he pulled the Tiffany's box from his sock drawer and shoved it into his pants pocket. With every step he felt it rubbing against his thigh.

They went to Roman's. He was recognized and given a table near the center of the room, which pleased him because more people would witness the drama of his proposal and Elena's acceptance. She looked so beautiful tonight. He ordered a bottle of Dom Perignon. Why not?

"You're spoiling me."

"Well, we're celebrating the end of me being a jerk, and we're celebrating our future."

She broke eye contact briefly. He said, "Sometimes the future is hard to talk about. I know that. Sometimes it's hard to face alone."

"I think you'll do all right, John."

Ignore that comment, he told himself. She was absorbed in the menu and no doubt unaware of the possible implication of what she had just said—that he would indeed be facing the future alone. The waiter took their orders and left. With her hands in her lap Elena tilted her body forward and spoke quietly. "I've been meaning to talk to you, John . . ."

"I've been meaning to talk to you, too. Wouldn't it be great if we both wanted to say the same thing?"

"It would be easier." Her eyes were clear and blue, her cheekbones wide, but the total expression said regret—this'll hurt me more than it hurts you. She had put her hair up tonight, and a few loose strands caught the candlelight around her face.

The waiter poured the champagne. John raised his glass. "Shall we have a toast?"

"Let's not, John, okay? What I want to say is that my father thinks I should move a little early to wherever I'm going to law school."

"Sure, that's a good idea. We'll get to know the place. Your father's a smart man—"

"He thinks I should go alone."

"What? Well, he'll come around. I know Bill Conifer, from law school, and I know he can be obstinate sometimes, but we just have to remember that he wants the same thing I do. He wants you to be happy."

"John." She placed her knife and fork down on her plate. *"I* think I should go alone. I *want* to go alone. Is this in any way what you wanted to say?"

He could feel the velvet box in his pocket against his thigh. He had known that in making the proposal he would be in effect begging her to stay with him. But he had no intention of *actually* begging her to stay. Not here in such a public place, anyway. "Sure," he said, smiling too brightly. "That's exactly what I wanted to say."

"Oh, John." She sighed. "I know you're upset. We'll keep in touch, we'll hook ourselves up on e-mail—"

"E-mail!" He finished off his champagne. "That's a great idea." He picked up the bottle, dripping ice water all over his chateaubriand as he poured himself another glass. The mannequin-like waiter rushed over with a cloth, spouting an apology that said I'm so sorry, I did not know you needed another glass, I would have poured it for you.

"Don't let it happen again, kid. I want another bottle of that stuff, too."

"John—"

"We're celebrating your independence. UCLA's a good school."

She leaned forward, whispering, "John, think about it. It's gone as far as it can. Think about it. We get married, I go to law school,

I get out and get a job. I make partner at thirty-three or so, assuming I work at a firm and don't get involved with, say, the entertainment industry."

"Bunch of crooks," John said. "You don't want to get involved in that."

She pressed on. "Suppose we have a baby when I'm thirty-three, you'll be sixty-one. Seventy-nine when our hypothetical child enters college. Eighty-three when he graduates." If you're even still alive then, she didn't add.

"Excuse me for a moment." In the bathroom he stared at himself in the mirror. His gray hair was coming back. For the past few days there had been circles under his eyes that no nap could smooth away. His skin had begun to sag around the jawline. He was still not a bad-looking fifty-one-year-old, he had to give himself that, but he didn't look thirty-five anymore, as when he crossed the finish line in record time. Looking like this, he perhaps had a few good years left for picking up women in their early thirties, women who wanted a baby *right now* from a man who could pay and pay. But for John Ashe there would be no more nubile mistresses because he was losing—had lost!—the one who had made it possible. He wasn't even going to spend Christmas with her, or his *own* family, for that matter. Not with anyone.

Back in the restaurant he saw the waiter talking to Elena. Closer, he realized that she was apologizing for her "companion's behavior." "He's had a hard few days, and I think he—" She stopped when she saw him approaching.

As John sat down, he asked the waiter how it was going.

"Fine, sir. The lady and I were just talking about law school. I'm in law school myself, so I thought I would give her some advice . . . but I guess that's what her father's for, right?"

"You think I'm her father?"

Elena said, "He holds the world record for the marathon."

"Really? How many years ago was that?"

"A long damn time ago," John said, not rising to the bait. "Can we have some more champagne?"

Though Elena was no farther from him than the length of a cozy tabletop, so close he could have reached out and touched her sternum without locking his elbow, he felt as though he were

eating alone, perhaps in front of a hologram. As difficult as things
had been at times, he had never, until now, lacked the motivation
to try to impress her. Why bother? Why comb his hair in the
morning, why brush his teeth, why even run anymore? This
abrupt and self-defeating change of mind manifested itself, at
least for the moment, in a strangely polite cheerfulness. Telling a
story about Bud Framer, he rolled his eyes and leaned forward
to invite commiseration, which Elena freely gave. He seemed to
have recovered completely, and she was more than willing to
stop for a drink on the way home. Even when he headed toward
a margarita bar, at which they would both be conspicuously
overdressed, the most she could say by way of objection was, "A
quick drink and then home, okay?"

But at the bar John ordered a double shot of tequila. "And
what are you drinking, Elena?"

"How about mineral water?"

John smiled. "How about lemon mineral water?" He raised a
finger as if saluting a great new idea. "On the rocks!"

Someone at the bar said, "Hey, you look like that guy . . .
you are that guy, aren't you?" He turned to a friend and said,
"Look, it's that guy. He doesn't look the same in person." To
John he said, "Lightning man, right?"

"Boltman," John corrected him.

More shooters appeared before him, and he was persuaded to
tell the story of his greatest triumph, last month's marathon. He
made several new best friends, none of whom seemed to mind
the slight spray coming from his mouth whenever he was overtaken by the excitement of having their attention. The story of the
Boltman incident in Atlanta was also a big hit. " 'Course, Elena
wasn't down in Atlanta." He looked around. "Where the hell'd
she go?"

"She took off," someone said.

"You wanna hear something funny? Tonight I was going to ask
her to marry me. Look at this." He took the black velvet box from
his pocket and held it up to the crowd with both hands. "Tiffany's." He opened it and a woman called out, "I'll marry you,
honey."

John said to the box, "Will you marry me, Elena?"

Using both hands, he opened and closed the box as if it were the mouth of a puppet. In a high-pitched voice he said, "No, John, I won't marry you. I've got law school, and you're too damn old!"

"Bummer," someone said.

He turned the box around and stared at the ring. It was so beautiful, so perfect, so . . . sterile, really. He recalled years ago having to scrimp and save for the slightly flawed, much smaller rock with which he had proposed to Elizabeth, and yet how happily, how unquestionably she had accepted it, so proud she spent the next few days on the phone jabbering about it with her friends.

He became aware now that his shoulders were shaking. He heard some sort of sob sound, realized it was coming from himself. One of the kids standing nearby slapped him on the back. "Forget about her, man. A woman like that, she'll break your heart."

Composing himself, he closed the box and planted his elbows firmly on the bar. He tried to summon his winning attitude— "Another shot of tequila!"—but there was no swagger to his voice. He proceeded to get stinking drunk. Several times he raised what he thought was his current shot glass, only to be undone by the feel of crushed velvet against his lips. At one a.m. he made his way back out to the street.

He smiled at several of the young women he passed on the sidewalk. None smiled back. Three altered their paths in order to stay out of his arm's reach. One young man, his protective instincts moistened by the sight of this leering older person in an overcoat, shoved him in the shoulder and said, "Can I help you? You need your ass kicked?"

"My ass is already kicked. Thanks very much, though."

Ah, well, the apartment was just up ahead. He found Elena at the kitchen table, tapping away at her Toshiba laptop. She had changed into sweatpants. Without looking up from her work she asked, "Did you have a good time?"

"Great time." He stood behind her and recognized on the screen several sentences from the middle of her UCLA essay.

"I'm just polishing this up." Suddenly she turned. "You smell flammable."

"You left."

"And how long did it take you to notice?" She stood, turned to face him. "I called my father. I asked him if I could come home tomorrow. He said yes."

John touched her chin with his forefinger. "I really, really want to make love to you right now. One last time. Come on, Elena, help me out here."

A look that was equal parts pity, contempt, and obligation came over her face. In the bedroom she stepped out of her sweatpants but didn't bother taking off her Magnate T-shirt. She lay on the bed with her head propped up and her legs spread, bent at the knees, while John fumbled with his shirt buttons.

"Maybe this isn't such a good idea," she said.

"I'm fine, I'm fine."

But there was a coldness in his groin. There had been incidents like this in the past, but with Elizabeth, which was understandable. Now he was on his knees between the parted thighs of one of the most beautiful women he or anyone else had ever seen. Her opening glistened about six inches from the tip of his penis, which was useless.

"You're just drunk," Elena assured him. "It's a well-known factor—"

"It wasn't a few weeks ago." He lay on his back beside her. "Stay with me for a bit."

"I've got to go work on that essay. They're never done, you know?" She was already pulling her sweatpants back on.

HE WOKE WITH a random jumble of body aches. The covers were like a dead man's shroud. He propped himself up on one elbow and saw Elena straightening the clothes he had left on the floor last night. The black velvet ring box fell out of his pants pocket. "What's this?" She opened it before he could think of some explanation that would salvage whatever pride was left.

"Oh, John, it's beautiful!"

"You like it?"

"Yes! But . . . I can't."

"I didn't ask you, goddammit."

"John—?"

"I just want it on record that I didn't ask my goddamn paralegal to marry me, and that she *therefore* could not have turned me down. Apparently all we did was rut for a little while."

She snapped the velvet box shut and tossed it onto the bed. "Fine."

When he woke up again, he found her father in the room, helping her box up all the clothes John had bought her during the past few months. Bill Conifer was in a great mood, humming to himself. He was surprised to find John looking at him. "Oh, good morning, Boltman. Or should I say good afternoon? You look like hell either way. You know you snore like a bandsaw?"

"Elena never complained. But she might not have noticed. She always sleeps so soundly after a good fuck."

Conifer was momentarily overtaken with his characteristic silencing fury. Then he smiled. "I can afford to ignore that comment."

Elena had covered John's nude body with a blanket. Now he needed to take a piss, but could not bring himself to stand up naked in front of Bill Conifer. His head hurt. He had the eerie sensation that he was dying in an old folks home, and these people were getting a head start on cleaning out his room for the next paying tenant.

CHAPTER 20

THE REAL ESTATE agent had shown Andy and Kristen several decent Midtown apartments, but so far none that were just right. Kristen's lease was expiring, Andy had never actually signed one, and their relationship was moving along so smoothly that they were now ready to "cohabitate," as Kristen clinically put it.

"Now is just not the best time to look," the agent kept saying. "The holidays? I don't think so. Renting apartments? People aren't thinking about it."

But the agent knew of one more possibility. A block or so away Kristen sized up the building from its ornate trim around the roof to the uniformed doorman twelve stories below. Andy was making quite a bit of money now; rent would be no problem. Her heels clopped substantially on the marble foyer, which was so polished that when she looked down she saw her reflection commemorated in stone. The clopping of her heels echoed off the ceiling and the walls as if to multiply her presence or suggest an entourage. This was it, the kind of place that connoted a sort of pre-Groveton prosperity. You could raise a kid here for the first two or three years before you needed a backyard, and then you'd move to Connecticut or Jersey, the wife would find local work, and Andy would begin his commuting years. As they followed the real estate agent toward the elevators, Kristen caught her fiancé's eye and gave a this-is-the-place nod.

The apartment itself was fairly plain. Three bedrooms, neutral paint. Throw a little art on the walls, install a sound system and some interesting lighting, and Andy would be able to hold salon for rockers and vee-jays and a few lucky cue-card holders. Kristen could have her out-of-town friends stay, no problem.

After they signed the lease, they went out to dinner. Excited by this new commitment, Andy rambled on about the future. "What I'd really like someday is a huge loft downtown. People say you can't raise kids there, that's bullshit. I don't ever want a house in Groveton."

"Really?"

"I'll never have a house in Groveton, I'll never be a commuter. I'm going to live in the city, and this is where my family will be. You saw what happened to Dad. It's not going to happen to me."

"That was caused by living in Groveton?"

"I think it was a factor."

She thought about it for a moment. "There are certain advantages to living in a place like Groveton, Andy."

"Not if you're living with me, there aren't."

"I didn't say I saw myself moving out of the city, necessarily."

"I'm saying I definitely won't, unless it's to L.A. for something career-related." He raised his glass. "Let's drink to it."

It was talk for a time capsule.

ABOUT 11:30 A.M. on the day before Christmas Eve, John answered the door with a beer in his hand. He found Andy and Kristen standing there, each holding a gift.

"Bit early, huh, Dad?"

John looked at the beer. "Sure, it's early, depending on when you got up, and I've been up since two in the morning." He crossed the living room and turned down the volume on his old movie. "I wish you had called. I would've tidied up or something." The place had a slightly funky smell now, or was that the soup he'd spilled on his bathrobe a couple of days ago? Hard to say. The condition of his apartment would provide conversation for the big gathering in Groveton tomorrow night. He swept several days' worth of *New York Times* from the couch. "Have a seat."

They sat on the very edge, as if to lean back would be to risk some sort of parasite.

"Can I get you something to drink?" he called from the kitchen. "Let's see, I have . . . just beer."

"No, thanks, Dad."

"No, thanks," Kristen said.

He slurped the foam off the tip of a new Anchor Steam and plopped down in the armchair.

"How's the running, Dad?"

"Well, you know they say it takes a little while to recover from a marathon, and so far my experience confirms it. I haven't been running in a while."

"Are you putting on a belly there?"

John raised his beer. "Too much of this stuff. Once I get back in training, it won't be a factor."

It was Kristen who brought up Elena. "What are you two doing for Christmas?"

"She's spending it with her family. She and I are . . . well, it seems we've broken up."

"Oh, I'm sorry to hear that," Andy said without a note of surprise or conviction in his voice. "Are you doing okay?"

"Oh, yeah, sure. It was mutual."

Kristen said, "What should we do with her present?" She held up the wrapped gift. "It's a nice hardcover set of Baltazar Brantley, everything from *Dare Not the Executioner* to *Unto the Seventh Generation*. We know she's a big fan."

"You can leave it with me. I'm sure she'll be by, and I'll pass it along."

Andy said, "I'll call Mom and Anne. Maybe you can spend Christmas with us."

"Oh, no, thanks. I've got plenty to do."

"Like what?"

"Plenty, *okay*?"

And they dropped it.

IN LATE FEBRUARY, Bud Framer disappointed officials at the Boston Marathon by confirming their suspicion that his client, who had made no public appearances since mid-December, had hung up his Bolt! shoes for good.

John slept late and spent his days feverishly reading Baltazar

Brantley's nine novels, from the set meant for Elena. How surprised he was to discover after so many years of dismissing the writer the subtle brilliance with which he wrote.

He began to remember things that his running success and his time with Elena had made him forget. Watching Andy on MTV, he would remember walking with the kid through the streets of Groveton, teaching the kid how to ride a bike and later how to drive. The pride he had felt, the inarticulate anguish and pride that had often risen up in his chest and throat at the sight of his growing son . . . would Andy have a happy life? How could he give the kid the best possible start? John remembered moments when he would have traded the rest of his life to secure his son's happiness.

Tweaked some by Baltazar Brantley, reinforced by the absence of Elena, the corpse of his memories was stirring; blood was flowing back into it. How much had he loved his family, how generously they had given it back to him! And what good times they had had . . . Elizabeth shortly after their wedding, svelte, bending naked over the back of the couch . . . God, he'd forgotten how she had given him a blow job when he was trying to talk business on the kitchen phone. A bit short of breath, he had to assure his callers that yes, *indeed*, he was all right. At one of the Newtons' parties in that old Victorian, she had, on pretense of showing him the upstairs, seduced him in Newty's spare room. Once she had demanded servicing in her proper tiny office at the Groveton Country Day School. They had been real lovers back then, not just a married couple with a sexual and monetary budget, and perhaps he carried at least part of the blame for the snuffing of her playful spirit. During the last few years—griping about the commuter train, resentful of Elizabeth's short ride to work—perhaps he had not been as attentive to her as, he now realized, he should have been. He realized that he could not remember when he had last told her she was beautiful or even attractive, or had said that he loved her and meant it. Usually it was just a perfunctory "love you" right before bed or before hanging up the phone if she called him at the office. And she really was very attractive for her age and for what he and she had been through together and for what she had been through alone while he was ignoring her. Elizabeth had deserved better than he had given her, and for that he would always bear, in some corner of his being, a shard of remorse.

OCCASIONALLY REYNALDO MILLER was able to talk him into coming out to walk around the park, or perhaps even eat lunch.

"Doc says I can't have these," John would say, munching on a bundle of french fries.

"Maybe you should listen to him."

"The only thing a doctor can do is help you die slowly. He can't help you live well, that's up to you." He flagged down the waiter and ordered another beer. "Rey, don't look at me like that. You know I'm never going to run well again."

"You're acting old and crotchety. You got to get out more, and I don't mean to buy beer. You're looking bad. Your clothes don't fit. Even if your running career is over, which I don't say it is, you don't have to roll over and die. You know, I got an aunt I want you to meet. Lot younger than you."

"How old?"

"She just moved here from Dallas."

"How old?"

"Makes her own tortillas and everything."

"How old?"

"Spring chicken, man. Forty-two."

"Shit, Rey."

"What do you expect?"

"I know, I know."

"You, uh, heard from Boltgirl yet?"

"Sent me a postcard. She loves L.A., she, of course, got into UCLA Law, she's living with some kid she knew in college. An actor. Surprise, surprise. And it's just my luck he's getting work."

BOLT! HAD FINANCED a paperback biography of the new marathon champ, timed to coincide with Boltman's anticipated victory in Boston in April. The book was produced so cheaply that the ink came off on one's fingers. *Although he worked as an attorney for twenty-five years, he never forgot his original dream of holding the world record for the 26.2-mile race known as the marathon.* Unfortunately, as part of his Bolt! contract he had to appear in various bookstores to promote the book, which sat mostly unbought in huge pyramids at either side of the signing table. John's appearance bore little resemblance to the Boltman shown in the photograph section of the book. He spent whole afternoons assuring those few customers who gave a damn that, yes, he was in fact the same John Ashe who held the world record for the marathon. Reluctantly, unsure if they were being tricked, they would let him sign.

THE ONLY PLACE where he continued to enjoy a measure of respect was in the sports stores, many of which still displayed the Boltman poster. But even at Hot Foot, Gil Stevenson's floor manager had long since stopped reaching for his Polaroid camera whenever the former Boltman walked through the front door wiggling a finger in his tinnitus ear. Still, the folks buying running shoes were impressed, even though they were under the impression that his running accomplishments were several years past.

Eventually they weren't so happy to see him. One day when it was particularly busy he sat unnoticed in the shoe section for thirty minutes, wishing like hell someone would speak to him. No one did.

At about this time Rey was becoming more exasperated with his friend. "You got to do something with your life! You can't just go around being the record holder, John. For one thing, someone'll beat your record. Look, for a long time after I graduated from high school, I kept going back there to hang out because I was like the shit, man. Everyone looked up to me. But the young kids kept getting older, and one day some little fucker whomped my ass in front of everybody."

"So what'd you do?"

"I got on with my life, and that's what you're going to have to do. I hate to say it, but you're never going to compete seriously again. It was already a miracle once. They don't happen in the first place, much less twice. It ain't going to happen again, John."

Two weeks later, Rey won the Boston Marathon but missed John's record by two minutes.

* * *

JOHN DID START going out more, to bars where as Boltman he would have been attracting feminine advances all night. Occasionally he was able to charm or bully his way into someone else's conversation, but more often he sat silently in the corner shadows where all the laughs seemed to gather.

On one of those nights he found himself staring at the ample, soft-looking ass of a thirtysomething woman. He had never, he thought, seen such a fine ass. Its owner tilted her head back in laughter and then leaned forward to whisper something into her female companion's ear. Her movements reawakened in John a desire that until that moment he had feared was purely historical. He was properly surprised when she turned around and he recognized her: Kelly Epstein. "John? John, is that you?" He waved. She approached. Her smile shrank just perceptibly when she saw he was drunk, or well on the way.

"Who are you with?" she asked.

"Nobody."

"What? Well, now you're with me." She grabbed his hand and dragged him out of the shadows.

The force of his hug caused her to spill her drink down his trouser leg. "Whoa, careful," she said. "It can't be that good to see me." With a pile of cocktail napkins she rubbed the stain on his thigh.

"How are things at Masterson, Grandissime, and Barradale?"

"Don't sound bitter. You heard about Haley, right?"

"What about him?"

"He's the latest portrait in our gallery."

"Really?" John felt a chill.

"He was up in Nantucket," Kelly said, "on his way to play tennis. He steps out in the middle of the street right in front of a garbage truck that's backing up and doesn't have one of those warning beepers because *that* would be so unseemly and might wake people up, might remind them that people on Nantucket produce garbage just like everyone else. According to eyewitnesses he was swatting at the back of the truck with his tennis racquet while the wheels went over his chest like a speed bump. The driver hears something. He stops with the tires on Haley's chest and gets out to see what's going on. Next stop, Portrait City."

"I'm really sorry." After an appropriate interval he asked, "Are people still sore at me about Maxine Estep?"

"A bit. But you figure you cost fifty partners twenty grand each. On the other hand, I think they each would've paid twenty grand to see you win the marathon at your age."

Kelly introduced him to various women friends, all of whom were at about the same stage of their careers in various respectable law firms throughout the city. But it was Kelly who paid him the most attention. "I'm surprised to find him alone, actually," she said to her friends as she patted his cheek. "He's quite the playboy. Whatever happened to that sweet young paralegal you had for a while?"

"I don't know. I think she mostly wanted a reference for law school." He immediately regretted the remark.

Later, when he and Kelly were at the bar together, he told her he didn't really regret the end of his marriage. "Funny, though, her turning lesbian. I'd never have guessed, although looking back I guess I saw signs . . ."

"You're not fooling me about how you feel being ditched, I gather, by Miss Gorgeous. If I may say so, your problem is your self-image is too tied up with the looks of the woman you're fucking."

"Maybe so." He'd heard it before. "And maybe that's why right now I feel like a zero. It's been months." And a moment later he said, "Did you ever get *your* little extra oomph?"

"Haley Wilson."

"No. I'm sorry—"

"Just a few times, when we were both working late. Obviously his death has left me with an empty feeling." She took John by the elbow. "Let's go see what we can do about it."

IN THE MORNING he looked over at Kelly's sleeping face and let the previous evening float back to him in a kind of hangover collage—himself revealing intimate details of his divorce to whole groups of strange women, who seemed interested in almost everything he said. They seemed, it occurred to him, pleased that

Elizabeth had gotten a good deal and was now happy. He remembered flirting with Kelly . . .

He shuffled into her kitchen now and drank three tall glasses of water. Found the aspirin in the medicine cabinet beside an assortment of contraceptives.

She had never been married, he recalled, which seemed strange for an attractive, relatively young woman with such a great job. But he had to admit that if she had asked for maternity leave before making partner, he and the other old boys wouldn't have taken her as seriously when she did finally return to work, and she would have had less chance for promotion. Your family life was supposed to be a series of snapshots as opposed to the movie of your career.

"How you feeling?" Kelly stood behind him, reaching around and rubbing a hand over his chest. "You know, you passed out on me last night before earning your keep." Her hand slid under the elastic waistband of his shorts and cupped his balls. "Nice and heavy," she said.

Erections had been rare lately, and so weak. John was surprised now to feel in his groin a stirring so strong and deep. Kelly said, "It's a great cure for a hangover, fucking in the morning." He felt her bare breasts against his back. When she pulled down his shorts, he felt against his bare ass the springiness of her pubic hair.

"I AM MEETING John Ashe at the Burger and Barrel, May one," Jeff Sutton said into his microcassette recorder. "He is late."

He took a sip of beer and glanced at the entrance. "This seems to support certain rumors I have heard about the breakdown of what we all thought was his remarkable life. Bolt! has wriggled out of its million-dollar contract by invoking not one but two escape clauses. First of all, Ashe supposedly weighs one-ninety now, and the contract stipulated that he had to stay in competition shape. Second, Ashe defaulted on some of his simplest contractual obligations and fulfilled several more of them grudgingly. At bookstore appearances he was morose and introverted at best, hostile at worst, and the book he was promoting was meant to be inspirational. I also know for a fact that John Ashe has ceased his visits to Ph.D. candidate and medical researcher Steven Fiske, in turn placing the young man's career in jeopardy or at least on hold. Fiske's mentor, Dr. Jeremy Hurvitz, has ceased his visits to New York, apparently resigned to the fact that John Ashe refuses to be studied."

Again Sutton looked at the entrance. An older man with short gray hair stood there wiggling a finger in his ear. Sutton went back to his recorder. "I have even heard that it is hard to recognize him these days." The man was approaching. "Can I help you?"

"How's it going, Jeff?"

"Oh, my God."

John Ashe looked twenty years older than he had only a few months earlier breaking the tape in record time at the New York Marathon. Sutton's obvious failure to recognize his interview subject left him scrambling for tactful ground. "Oh, the light from the bar, it was in my eyes." He looked around and realized that there was no light here even bright enough to read by. "I mean, it's so dark, and that combined with suddenly looking up, one of these dim lights sort of flashed right in my eye . . ."

John sat down. "It's okay, don't worry about it." Despite the former Boltman's weight gain his presence was somehow smaller. "I look a lot different, don't I?"

"Yeah, yeah, you do."

John ordered a lemon mineral water on the rocks. "Dr. Fiske says I've gotta be careful."

"I thought you weren't going to see him anymore."

"I'm not. I just know what he would say."

Sutton considered proceeding with the interview but then decided to hold off for a moment. He had been moved by Fiske's melancholy lament over having lost the sole subject of his research project, and now he put in a good word for the young man. "I mean, he's got a wife and a kid, John. He was counting on you. I really think the only decent thing would be for you to go back and let him finish his examinations."

John said, "A lot of people made the mistake of counting on me, I guess."

Throughout the interview the former Boltman seemed so much more subdued than at any time since Sutton had first met him.

He seemed to be acting his age. Gone was the hormonal young
man's swagger, the macho talk of prodigious semen load and the
pounding of brewskies. Gone too was the hope for an unlimited
future. "I loved it, Jeff. I loved running fast. But there are some
other things about me during that time that I'm not so proud of."

"Do you regret leaving your wife?"

"Believe it or not, no. I regret that I was never really able to
appreciate her in those last few years. But she's happier without
me, and I'm glad she's happy."

Two beautiful women sat down at the bar. The former John
Ashe would have come on to them. The real John Ashe glanced
over at them briefly, then stared into his lemon mineral water.

"Are you sure you're all right, John?"

"I'm fine. Older but fine."

THE NEXT DAY Sutton's literary agent called. "Bad news. I don't
think we can sell your John Ashe book. They're already
remaindering that Bolt book. They're turning them into fire-
starter logs."

"But his story's just now getting interesting! I saw him last
night, I didn't even recognize him! All that brashness I told you
about, it's gone. Look, there's a story here that's going to mean a
lot to a lot of people. Especially men but also women. It's not just
about John Ashe, one man, it's about what happened to him as a
metaphor. A cautionary tale."

The agent said, "I know that and you know that. But the fasci-
nation is gone. No one wants to read a book the whole point of
which is the guy's washed up! Can you give it a happy ending?"

"It's not really bad what's happened to him. It may save his
life."

JOHN TOOK SUTTON'S admonishment to heart and went to see Dr.
Fiske. The young man was impressed with his subject's physical
deterioration. It was just as Hurvitz had predicted. The former
Boltman's aggressive spirit was gone. He was so agreeable now!
Back in December he had been furious at the suggestion that his
physical problems were a function of age. Now he accepted this

proposition as a matter of fact. Although the patient's resumption of ordinary sexual relations with Kelly Epstein had improved his attitude, it had not increased his speed. "That's right," Hurvitz said when consulted by phone. "With my surfer, same thing."

"Maybe only one woman works for each man," Fiske said, "and the chances of finding her are one in a million."

Hurvitz said, "And maybe one is better off without her . . . Well, keep me posted. If anything major develops, I'll fly back out there."

CHAPTER 21

HE WAS ALMOST afraid to stop and look at the portraits in the Hallway of Death. What if someone had died since Haley? But no, the two most recent additions were still Haley Wilson and Lee Thomas, old but unwrinkled, each with the same red tie and gold clip.

In Nathan Barradale's reception room he chatted with the paralegal, some new girl he didn't recognize. He sat in an armchair in front of her while she continued typing. He was nervous at the prospect of seeing his old colleague, hat in hand, so to speak.

The door opened and Nathan stood there with his hand extended. "John! You old son of a gun!"

Crossing the floor with his own hand extended, John limped noticeably.

"What's this?" Nathan asked. "Temporary injury?"

"It's sort of permanent, I'm afraid."

Nathan pulled him into the office and shut the door. "What about your spirits, my friend? You seem down."

"Well, I've lost it, Nathan. I don't know what's happening to me. Even on my best training run I do about an eight-minute pace. Running in the morning is out of the question because of my heels. So I have all this free time now."

"I thought the heel thing was all cured." Barradale sat down behind his desk. "You know, you look a little older than when you left the firm. I had been under the impression from news reports and whatnot that you were . . . aging backward? You were the subject of a study?"

"Not anymore." John considered how best to make his request, finally deciding just to come right out with it. "As I was saying, I have a lot of free time on my hands. I might as well be making some money. I've sort of spent a lot of my own." Out with it: "Nathan, I'd like my old job back."

Barradale sucked air through his teeth. "That's going to be a tough one, John."

"I'm willing to work out an arrangement to pay back the Maxine settlement. It won't take that long. At least I'll have something to do besides bother Kelly all the time."

Nathan's grin was friendly now, and curious. "I'd heard that you two were involved. How is she? Haley always told me she was a little tiger."

Among the partners there was a sort of unwritten Freedom of Information Act regarding matters pertaining to side affairs. "We're having a pretty good time together," John said quietly. "Look, Nathan, I need something to do with myself. I need to get back into my life. Dr. Hurvitz—he's this guy I've been working with—seems to think that it would be a good idea to come back to the firm and reassume the responsibilities that go with my chronological age and experience."

"You want a drink?"

John declined. Barradale made one for himself and sat on the edge of the desk, staring thoughtfully into the amber liquor. "I'll see what I can do. The partners are of two minds about you. Either they're sore you saddled us with the Maxine lawsuit, or they're impressed by what you did on the marathon course. Some even talk about how your achievement helped improve their own attitude and was worth whatever the firm had to pay Maxine. Your accomplishment seems to have made them feel better about where they are in their lives. I still haven't figured that one out yet, but there it is."

"Well, I'm pleased by that. I just hope they don't feel too let down now."

Three days later, word came from Barradale that the partners would vote on John's proposal at the general meeting the next month.

ELIZABETH WAS WEEDING, humming to herself. She stacked the weeds in a neat pile beside her foot.

"Can I interrupt you for a minute?" Anne had brought her a glass of lemon mineral water on the rocks.

"Sure." Standing, she accepted the drink. "Oh, thank you."

"I really want to go into the city one of these weekends," Anne said. "You could probably live there for years, not just visit, and still never see John Ashe, and would it really matter if you did? Aren't you happy with me? You're not embarrassed to be seen with me, are you?"

"That last doesn't deserve an answer. If we weren't outside, I'd give you a kiss."

In truth, Elizabeth was very happy with her current arrangement. She felt as though her life had begun over again, without John around to stare at other women and make her feel obsolete, irrelevant. Amazing how she had gotten used to his wayward eye. In later years she no longer noticed it and would have been offended had anyone else so misinterpreted his thoughtful expressions. He wasn't staring at that girl's ass, he was contemplating some difficult legal problem. Now, of course, she knew better, and the most charitable spin she could put on it was that John's reaction to a beautiful young woman was nothing much more than a Pavlovian reflex.

She too thought it would be fun to spend a day or two in the city, where she and her lover could actually hold hands in public without having someone carping about "the complexion of the neighborhood." But on the other hand, she had begun to feel sorry for John as reports drifted back to her—via small news articles and the occasional piece of social gossip—that he was deteriorating. Some even suggested that his impossible running success was due to some sort of bizarre malady that gave the body unusual strength and then, as a sort of payback when time ran out, took even its normal strength away.

He surely could do her no harm, could take nothing away. And in fact she had hit him pretty hard with the divorce settlement—his behavior had been so "egregiously inexcusable," in the words of her lawyer. John hadn't bothered putting up a fight, knowing it would have been costly and futile. Now that she had beaten him so thoroughly, she felt this annoying sympathy, and with it a sense of responsibility. Was he stretching properly before he ran? Cutting down on his drinking? Eating his bran? Getting enough rest?

Damn it, she found that she still cared about the bastard.

THE POSSIBILITY OF getting his old job back was enough to get John out of bed in the morning. He got into the habit of limping down to the bagel shop for a toasted one with jelly, no butter, and a decaf coffee. He would sit at one of the small wooden tables and read Baltazar Brantley or the *New York Times* while people on their way to work rushed in and out of the shop. As in pre-Elena days, he always began with the obituaries. Legendary financiers, corrupt but rehabilitated ex-politicians, and the stars of bad fifties sitcoms were giving up their places in the world with regularity.

One morning in early June he was shocked to read:

Kurt Vermiel
Physicist, Nobel Prize Winner

The old guy had died "of an apparent heart attack while playing croquet in his yard." The article summarized the man's remarkable life. Ph.D. at twenty-three. Rose to prominence in the research community of Weimar Germany. Did his most brilliant work before forty. Became alarmed at the deteriorating political climate and worked against the Nazi party. One night the S.S. showed up at his house to take him prisoner, but even as their rifle butts splintered the front door he and his wife, Isabel, were on a ferry crossing the English Channel, sitting on a trunk full of the research notes that were eventually the basis of a Nobel prize. The Vermiels' first dinner in the United States was with the Roosevelts in the White House.

Rereading the obituary, John went back to the cash register.

"Another decaf?" asked the counter girl.

"No, I think I'm going to live dangerously now. I'll take the regular."

As the girl poured it, he stared at the article and said, "You know who Kurt Vermiel was?"

"No, Kurt Cobain I know, but not Kurt whoever-you-said."

"He was this old guy who used to live on my running route.

He played croquet in his front yard. He used to always wave to me and say, 'Good day for it!' It's what people sometimes say when you're running."

Briefly she feigned interest as she handed over his coffee, then turned her attention to the next customer, who stepped up to take John's place.

Outside with his coffee and the obituary page, he tried to imagine that time in the future when he, too, would join the gallery in the Hallway of Death and the young women would rush by without noticing him. If they did stop to look at him, though what on earth for, he would seem sort of comical in his stern, dignified irrelevance, a lifetime of action and thought reduced to a skillful configuration of oil paints. The artist would probably give him that same damn red tie and gold clip, too.

He was overcome with a desire to go running, though now, merely walking along the hard sidewalks, his heels protested the impact. Well, maybe his Achilles' tendons would loosen up after a couple of miles. He imagined a collage of faces—Fiske, Hurvitz, Barradale, Elizabeth, Kelly . . . Elena—all telling him to *forget* it, go put your feet up and have a glass of lemon mineral water. But it was Kurt Vermiel who had his ear right now—Kurt Vermiel who had never quit, who had persisted and prevailed, and whose heart did, inevitably, finally stop. The point wasn't to see how long you could live, but how well you could do while you lived. For Kurt Vermiel, for Lee Thomas, for the guy John hoped he himself might become, this charter member of the now defunct Silver Milers would, damn it, run again.

He threw the newspaper onto his bed and opened the closet door. Even now he still had several boxes of new Bolt! shoes. He squatted—oh, his heels!—and picked out the Featherbolt!, a light shoe that he had once preferred for quick, short training runs. Much to his embarrassment the Bolt! tank tops he had worn just the last summer were too tight now, revealing a pale tube of flesh that ringed his body above the elastic waistband of his Bolt! shorts, also too snug for comfort. He found a baggy Magnate T-shirt that Elena used to wear to bed. It hung down below his shorts, a sort of skirt effect. As he walked to the kitchen for a glass of water he was sure that the old familiar aching in his heels was dissipating. Attitude, attitude, he told himself. Don't *expect* your heels to hurt, since then they surely will. Expect not even to notice them.

He took the elevator down. It stopped on the floor below his, and a white-haired lady got on, cradling her little kick dog, as Andy would have called the poodle. At first she tried not to look at him, but then curiosity won out and she stared at his pale legs and bulgy belly. To demonstrate that he was in fact wearing shorts, he lifted the hem of his shirt and pretended to scratch his nose with it. The kick dog commenced growling. "Shhh, shhh," she said. "Don't bark at the gentleman." She turned away.

Downstairs, the doorman raised his eyebrows. "Good day for it," he said.

"You won't mention this to Kelly, will you? Technically speaking, I promised her I wouldn't go running."

"Technically speaking, I'm supposed to call her if you do."

"Is that right? She's got some sort of arrangement with you?"

The doorman lifted his cell phone. "I got her pager number and everything. She says your heels are in bad shape."

John rolled his eyes. "Nah. If Kelly had her way, I'd rest my heels on a silk pillow until the day I finally have my heart attack. I'd rather die outside on a beautiful day like today. Don't call her. Okay?"

"Okay."

John started walking toward the park, throwing his elbows back and forth and squinting up at the sky. It was a humid day for late August. At the spot where months earlier Andy had attacked him, he felt, inside the baggy T-shirt, a rivulet of sweat running from his armpit down to his waistband. This was the beginning of a comeback perhaps, a comeback so remarkable that even Reynaldo would start visiting again. Fair-weather friend, Reynaldo. Said he couldn't stand being around so much whining, was afraid it would rub off on him just as he reached his own peak condition at the relatively late age of thirty-two.

As he jogged along, pounding his painful heels, he considered how drastically his life had changed over the past few months. It wasn't just the loss of a girlfriend and the gain of a more mature, stable lover. His memory was once again fully functional, and perhaps even more acute than before. Lately he had even felt a desire to ride the commuter train at rush hour again just for the familiar human bustle. He wondered if he really had forgotten so much of the love he had given and received over the years, or if he had simply been so preoccupied with himself as Boltman that there was no room for remembering, really remembering, the best of his experiences. This was the theory he leaned toward because it allowed him a pang of guilt and the possibility if not of redemption—it was too late for that—then at least of preventing another such lapse in the future.

His heels hurt. Young kids, late twenties, were plodding by him with ease, earning their extra beers. One guy who looked about sixty passed him. A group of chubby secretaries on lunch break wafted by in a cloud of conflicting perfumes. And then, approaching rapidly from behind, the unmistakable footfalls of the Marathon King himself.

Whoosh! Rey was already leaping over the next rise in the terrain, his feet landing at nine-foot intervals, his grim facial expression frightening small children and scaring away whole flocks of pigeons. You could almost hear his legs whistling. And he was gone, apparently without recognizing the former Boltman.

John decided to pick up the pace, maybe catch up to Rey. With the extra effort his pain, if not his speed, increased by multiples. And suddenly he was alarmed to see careening toward him an incompetent rollerblader with dark sunglasses and a loud Walkman. The kid's arms started to windmill. Walter Payton in his prime might have successfully executed the evasive dive John was forced to attempt. But John?

Kapow! A cherry bomb in his left heel! His calf muscle rolled up against the bone. His foot was useless, loose. He collapsed onto an almost gravelike grassy mound and stared after the oblivious rollerblader.

John's heart was sending throbs of blood down to the severed Achilles of his left leg. Just like Al Gore, he could almost hear Elizabeth saying. Thank God she wasn't here; there was at least consolation in that. She would not see him crawl up the front lawn, would not get to take him to the emergency room, with accompanying *I told you so*'s, in looks if not in so many words.

"You all right, man?" A couple of kids in Johns Hopkins lacrosse T-shirts stood on the sidewalk near where he had jumped off.

John gritted his teeth and dragged himself forward by the elbows. "I'm just resting."

"You sure?"

"Oh, yeah, sure. It's such a nice day."

The young men walked on. Blocking out the pain for a moment, he sat up on the grassy mound to survey his position. He was about equidistant from either side of the park. He had a better chance of getting a cab on the east, near the Met. Gritting his teeth against the pain, he began to crawl.

ANNE AND ELIZABETH had come into the city that morning by train, both of them pondering the Vermiel obituary. During a breakfast in a café just off Fifth Avenue they debated whether to begin the day at the Met or at MOMA, finally deciding on the Met. The Velásquez exhibit there was drawing huge crowds, and it would be good to get there early, before the tour busses.

As they approached the Met, Elizabeth pointed to some man crawling toward the edge of the park, refusing the help of several concerned passersby. "Look at that poor man, he looks hurt." The man kept waving away the would-be Samaritans. "He's too proud to take their help—" and then she realized . . . "Oh, my God."

HE HAD THOUGHT New Yorkers were supposed to mind their own business. "I'm fine," he said, wincing, dragging himself toward the street. From the corner of his eye he saw two more rescuers running toward him. Stout middle-aged women with butch cuts. He tried to pretend he was looking for a contact lens.

But then his head snapped toward the two women again. "God, please, no," he whispered.

Elizabeth stood before him with her hands on her hips.

"Didn't I tell you this would happen, John? You're so damn stubborn." She looked at Anne. "So much for the Met."

"So much for MOMA and for shopping."

"Don't let me inconvenience you," John said.

"That's right," Anne said. "He sure as hell didn't let you inconvenience him."

For a moment he was worried that they would actually leave him there. Instead they picked him up. With his arms stretched across the broad shoulders of his ex-wife and her lover, he hobbled out toward a taxi whose observant driver had spotted the fare from several blocks away.

IN THE HOSPITAL room Kelly pressed her hand against John's forehead, as if the tendon rupture were perhaps a flu symptom. "You're a nut," she said.

"How so?"

"You knew you were going to rupture your Achilles and you went running anyway."

"Go easy on the doorman, by the way. I told him not to call you . . . and I *didn't* know I was going to rupture it." He tried to sit up in bed; she pressed him back.

"Just relax."

"There's nothing worse than the sight of an old man in a hospital bed, huh?"

"Don't even start on that, I won't indulge you."

"I'm just so depressed about it, Kelly."

Leaning over to kiss his forehead, she also startled him by cupping his genitals through the hospital frock. "Good, you've still got balls. For a second there I wasn't sure."

The surgery to reattach the Achilles had gone well, but now John would have to endure months of frustrating physical therapy to regain a reasonable range of motion. For a long time now it would be impossible to walk without a cane, and he had almost certainly run his last run.

The injury did put him back in the news again for a while. They ran clips of him crossing the finish line at the New York Marathon. He began receiving get-well cards from expert runners who were relieved now at the knowledge that something specific was wrong with him. Even better, it was age-related, proving that his accomplishments really had been impossible.

Reynaldo came by and apologized for being an absentee friend lately. John considered telling him that he had passed him just before the tendon rupture, but decided to save that story for a time when their renewed relationship would be further along.

Bud Framer sent a card. Frank Shorter called, as did Nathan Barradale—who said that the tendon rupture had inspired the partners to rise in sympathy for the former Boltman, and the vote on reinstatement looked good. Steven Fiske said that Dr. Hurvitz was flying back out to meet with the patient. Andy and Kristen came by with some Godiva chocolates and met Kelly for the first time, the three of them leaving John in bed while they went out to lunch. Most surprising to John was how aggressively Elizabeth stayed involved in his hospital treatment, especially for the first week or so. She asked the various doctors where they had trained and what were their reasons for recommending this or that drug or treatment.

The only person who didn't call while he was in the hospital was Elena. Didn't they show the news in California? Didn't she know he was laid up? The phone rang and rang, and every time he answered it he spoke with forced cheerfulness, just in case.

He left the hospital within the week and soon was wheeling himself about Kelly's apartment, making sandwiches and grabbing an occasional beer from the refrigerator. By the time Hurvitz flew in from California the former Boltman had worked his way up to a cane, and an entire wall of Kelly's living room was covered with get-well-soon cards from all over the country.

IN THE SAME room where they had run all the tests showing how young his fifty-one-year-old body was, John asked, "What the hell happened to me?"

"You got hit in the head with a surfboard." Hurvitz handed John a copy of his original 1961 case study. "I told you they moved to Australia. I lied. Timmerman died in calm surf. I suppose if you'd snapped your Achilles while swimming in the Pacific, you'd be dead, too. You're lucky yours was a dry-land sport.

Fiske took blood samples and, with calipers, measured John's body-fat percentage. "A bit higher than we like to see in a fifty-one-year-old man," he said, "but not all that unusual. When you won the marathon, you were at four percent body fat." His blood pressure was high enough to require drug treatment. His cholesterol was up. Fiske recommended that he start eating a good bran cereal for breakfast.

John asked Hurvitz, "What happens next, Doc?"

"I don't really know. I've never followed a case this far. I'm handing it over to young Fiske here. Is that okay with you?"

John looked at Fiske and nodded. "I'm all yours."

Hurvitz said, "Fiske should take over. I'm ancient, I should get out of his way."

BARRADALE WAS INSTRUMENTAL in the reinstatement debate, allowing his stentorian voice to quaver as he spoke of Lee Thomas' heart attack and the detrimental but understandable effect that witnessing it had had on John's state of mind. "I'm telling you that this man is hungry for purpose. He's way too young to just lie around. Even when he walked out on us, he wasn't just lying around, was he? Hell, no. He just did a different kind of work." In the end the partners voted to reinstate John under terms that allowed him to repay them the Maxine settlement over several years.

Even Barradale was surprised at the new vigor John brought to his work. With a new legal secretary, a stout, dependable woman slightly his senior, he worked as he recently had run, as if his life depended on it. What did it matter that part of the reason he left work so late was to keep the other partners from seeing him hobble out and use his cane to hail a cab? The same residue of vanity was also the reason he had his lunch delivered, to avoid making a spectacle of himself limping through the Hallway of Death.

He no longer thought of the apartment as the "love nest," though Kelly spent the night there three or four times a week, and to an increasing degree he was growing attached to her. She had been a godsend, helping him through his physical therapy, but she was also there for him on a less tangible if more fundamental level. Her companionship had a healing quality. They would sometimes spend two or three hours at a time simply preparing dinner. They went to see plays and art films. They went to a video rental store, where they would argue about what movies to get, and she would surprise him with an occasional urge for something pornographic. She would watch the blue movies with a smirk on her face, making fun of the actors, and then suddenly the smirk was gone and she was all over him.

It was for Kelly that he kept the Porsche around. He couldn't depress the clutch pedal without hurting his Achilles' tendon, but that summer on the weekends she would captain them down Route 1 through New Jersey or maybe up to the Hamptons, where friends of hers lived. John sat in the passenger seat with his cane between his knees and the wind in his short gray hair. If the top was down and they were going at least sixty, his tinnitus ear did not ring.

He was happy with Kelly. And yet every time he entered the former love nest he would look over at the answering machine, and if the message light was blinking, he would cross the room immediately to press the button. It would be Rey, Nathan, Andy, sometimes even Elizabeth . . . it was never Elena.

ON THE MORNING of his fifty-second birthday she appeared at his door with Jake Coates, whom John had until then seen only in Elena's college photographs. She hugged John, kissed his cheek. "It's been so long," she said.

"It has, come on in." He propped his cane behind the door and walked across the living room, hiding his limp.

The young man had golden-brown hair, blue eyes, and a square jaw above a terrific body. He held a wrapped gift, obviously a tie box.

"So how's show biz?" John asked.

"Small parts so far, but getting bigger."

"He's going to be famous," Elena said, beaming at him. "Can't you tell?"

"Actually, yes, I really can."

Walking through the love nest, Elena said, "God, it seems like so long ago, but I guess it's only been, what, a few months. Almost a year, I guess."

She and Jake were full of stories about L.A. For someone about to become a star, the kid seemed a bit starstruck himself, dropping names, telling anecdotes about famous people. "Oh, I almost forgot," Elena said. "We just had pictures developed." From her purse she pulled a stack of photos showing herself and Jake at various places of interest with various people of note. Flipping through the photographs of gorgeous, technicolor L.A., recognizing occasionally faces he had seen on both large screen and small, John stopped on one because it looked particularly familiar. It showed Jake Coates holding a baby wrapped in a pink blanket. "Isn't she adorable?" Elena asked. "Some friends of ours from Magnate got married, and they just had this beautiful baby, Jenelle. Jake absolutely adored her. He didn't want to let her go."

"It's true," Jake said. "I'm smitten."

"Real nice," John said. He was trying not to show how edgy he felt. What the hell was this surprise visit all about? Some kind of closure on John and Elena?

Elena had decided to do entertainment law, she said. "From there I can go into any number of fields within the movie business."

"She could end up being a producer or a studio head," Jake said.

"Or I could be an agent."

She was so tan, obviously happy, and still, of course, beautiful; he felt like her uncle or some older male relative granted an obligatory visit. His role was to shake hands with the boyfriend, nod politely through the conversation, and wish them well as they walked out the door into the golden glow of their future.

"I guess you heard about my Achilles' tendon," he said.

"Yes, but by the time I heard about it you were out of the hospital and the number here has been changed. I guess I could've called Elizabeth." A grin appeared. "But I guess it's good that I didn't, right?"

"You could have, actually. We keep in touch."

There was a brief silence, broken finally by Jake. "Say, uh, I see your son's show on MTV every now and then."

"Yeah, he and his girlfriend, Kristen, are getting married in the spring."

"Pam Newton's sister," Elena said to Jake.

"Really? Well, I'm sure Kristen is more reasonable. Anyway, I was wondering if you could put in a good word for me with Andy. Maybe he could interview me on the show or something."

John smiled. "Sure, Jake." So this was the real reason for the visit. He was, for God's sake, a *connection*.

"Give John his gift, Jake."

Jake handed over the tie box. As John slowly unwrapped it,

Elena said, "I seem to remember this was sort of the fashion around Masterson, Barradale, and Grandissime."

He unboxed the Hallway of Death red tie and gold clip. Jesus, did she understand what this meant to him? "You're right," he said. "More and more of my friends are getting red ties and gold clips."

She said, "Didn't Nathan wear a tie like this?"

"Not yet."

The gift, he decided, was not an intentional insult. In her memory of the firm Elena had simply lumped the living partners with the dead ones, there not being in her young mind much of a difference between the two. To her credit, he had to concede to himself that next to Jake he felt somewhat two-dimensional, a portrait.

He thanked them for the gift and wished them well as they walked out the door. With the tie draped over his neck like a boa, he stood at the window and watched her chat with the doorman for a moment before walking down the street hand in hand with Jake. They seemed, he had to admit, a good match.

WALKING BACK TO the former love nest in the evenings, he would periodically tip his hat at an old woman or jauntily twirl his cane after passing a young one. He sometimes found himself amazed at how well things had turned out. When he was asked, as he often was, what it had felt like to win the marathon, he would admit that it had been wonderful, but he would also protest that he was glad the whole Boltman episode was over. "There's a certain pleasure in experiencing one's age," he would say, tapping his cane on the sidewalk. "I actually find myself enjoying it." He and Kelly would sit up in bed and talk about how much he had learned, how much more mature he was now at nearly fifty-three than he had been at barely fifty. "You look really good with gray hair," she often said. She liked its law-firm shortness, too, like ruffling it the wrong way with the fingers of both hands. "So distinguished." And at night she liked the way his soft, slightly convex belly fit perfectly against the small of her back, and the way he sometimes squeezed her in his sleep. She was getting her little extra oomph now, and something better and more which she hesitated to call love.

"Sometimes I just can't believe you're really happy," she said to him one night. "You know how it's hard to trust a rehabilitated drug user, you keep expecting the relapse?"

"*She* wasn't the drug, Kelly. It was my attitude—"

"That's not what Dr. Hurvitz—"

"Hurvitz is out of it."

He lay awake for a long time that night, watching her sleep, commanding himself never to hurt her.

KELLY'S MUCH LESS frequent declarations that she considered this a casual relationship were belied by her reaction to a beautiful young temp who, through some administrative oversight or perhaps as one of Barradale's practical jokes, was assigned to assist John's matronly paralegal. Inga Larsen had been a former cross-country runner in college. Her mother had been a model in Sweden, her father a German banker. She was just shy of six feet. Between her Bolt! running shoes and the lofty hems of her skirts her legs were almost cinematic in their muscular perfection. Only the occasional red line of a razor nick proved that she was human, she bled; it also suggested the lathery complications of shaving. A foot on the edge of the tub. A pink razor in a sleek hand, sculpting a perfect leg out of cream.

She had been working with John's paralegal for three days when Kelly first saw her squatting before the lowest drawer of a file cabinet. Her long blond hair swept the tops of the files, and she kept flipping it back over her shoulder. The hem of her skirt barely reached the carpet. Finally she stood up, and up, and up—seven inches taller than Kelly.

John came out of his office just then and handled the introductions.

"I'm just temping, but I like it here," Inga said. "John's a great boss."

"Isn't he?" Kelly said. "He's such a fun guy."

That night she managed to hold her tongue until she and John were both in bed reading. "That new girl in your office—"

"I just put in a request for a temp. I didn't even pick her personally."

"You obviously want to sleep with her."

"What?"

"If your hair starts turning dark . . ."

THE NEXT MORNING he found Kelly staring at the sitting room couch, one hand on her hip and the other flat against the side of her face. "I think this would go better over toward the south-facing window," she said. "It'll get more sunlight."

"Okay." John propped his cane against the wall and moved toward the couch, limping slightly.

"I didn't mean for you to move it," she said. "I'll ask the maintenance people for help, what's that young guy's name?"

"It's not that heavy."

"I really don't think you should."

"The day I can't move a couch is the day we'll go bedpan shopping, okay?" He squatted before one end of it and hooked his fingers beneath the frame.

"I don't think you should."

He lifted. His manly grunt became a moan of pain. He dropped the couch and staggered away from it, clutching his lower back with one hand and reaching with the other toward the kitchen table.

DURING THE NEXT few days as he lay in bed, Kelly helped keep him abreast of his legal work by bringing home documents and correspondence. "And this," she said, handing over a bedpan.

"What the hell for?"

"The doctor said you're supposed to stay in bed."

"No offense, Kelly, and I'm sure you spent a lot of time picking out this nice blue one, but . . ." He handed it back. "I piss standing up."

"Fine, don't listen to doctors."

Flat on his back he would dictate memos and correspondence to his paralegal back at the firm. The system worked well enough

that most of his clients never guessed he was not behind his mahogany desk as usual.

But on the third day, with his paralegal out sick and Kelly in
court, and with developments occurring rapidly in a case on
which he was working, he had no choice but to ask Inga Larsen
to deliver the day's documents to his apartment. He supposed he
could've asked her to read them over the phone, but on the other
hand he was considering her for a permanent position on his staff
and he needed to get to know her a little better. He knew that
some would laugh at him for hiring Inga, but he would rather
endure their snickering than his own private guilt over denying
her an opportunity because of her looks and thoughts of Elena.
That would be unfair.

Lying in bed, he told Inga where in his desk she would find the
key to his apartment. She said she would be right over. Thirty
minutes later, he heard the front door open.

"In here," he called. "In the bedroom."

Embarrassed at his condition, he made an attempt to prop himself up on his elbows. The pain was so intense that he had to
stifle a moan.

"Oh, don't," Inga said, hurrying forward. She placed a hand
on his shoulder as if to prevent him from trying again. He noticed on the chair behind her—damn—the blue bedpan. Unused,
unnecessary, but Inga would not know that. He wished he had
asked her to read the documents over the phone. He lay back
down, miserable, willing her not to notice the bedpan.

When she sat on the bed, he moaned again.

"I'm sorry," she said. "How stupid of me."

"Just don't move, just don't move."

"Okay."

He stared at the ceiling while she read. Occasionally he asked
her to reread something or stop and take down some notes. Or
she would ask a question about a legal term or procedure and he
would explain it to her. An hour later, they were done.

"Thank you for coming over," he said.

"My pleasure. I really like working with you, John."

He smiled. "Even when I'm virtually crippled like this?"

"It brings out the mother in me. I have this weird impulse to
kiss your forehead."

He thought about that for a moment. He was committed to Kelly, loved her . . . so there would be no harm in letting Inga kiss his forehead.

She interpreted silence for consent, bent over, and pecked him briefly, her hair brushing against his cheeks. The spot was cool as the kiss evaporated. "You know, I kept the Boltman poster on the wall of my dorm room. I wanted to tell you for a while now. I was afraid you'd think I was foolish, immature or something."

"Hardly. I was the guy in the cape."

They laughed. "You're an interesting man," she said seriously. She had allowed her hand to rest on his T-shirt, and now she bent over to kiss his forehead again. She maintained the kiss for a few seconds, sending life to his groin and raising his consciousness several notches above legal briefs and back pain. She stood. "I hope you get back to the office soon, but if you don't I could keep bringing you stuff."

"Thank you."

She smiled, gathered up her notes and documents, and left. Thank God she had not noticed the bedpan. Thank God she was gone. Thank God he couldn't have embraced her, or more. He hated himself for even thinking about it. He told himself that this incident served to clarify and strengthen his commitment to Kelly.

He stared at the bathroom. A long way off, but he had to go. Wincing in preparation for pain, he sat up. Stood up.

No pain.

He walked to the bathroom, took a leak. Stared at himself in the mirror and did a couple of side bends and leaned forward and backward. No pain. His smile at this discovery gave way to a look of fear. It wasn't attitude. Face it—Inga had healed him. Kelly loved him.

Back in bed, he pulled the covers to his chin, shaking his head, unsure if he had, God help him, chosen, or was merely resting between what was good for him and what he wanted. And unsure, finally, which was which.

YOU have seen what John Adler's done to

coming face-to-face with his wildlife creatures.

Will he or won't he decide to accept? With his

next younger then younger... discussed

what he enjoyed with Oliver.

In 200 words or less, tell us briefly what you think John Adler

would do next time. Your [...] entries by August 31. [...] the

results [...] be announced September 30, [...] 1975. Address your

material to:

YOUNGER MAN SPRINGTIME CONTEST

[...] Madison Street

New York, N.Y. 10019

1st prize $5,000

2nd prize $500

See page [...] worth of the Penguin books of your choice